### "Do you think Daisy looks like Lissa?"

Jane's stomach lurched. Had Kyle guessed? Or did he somehow know? *I should have stayed in Denver. Should never have risked this.*

"I, uh, suppose so." Jane licked her lips, and saw him catalog the gesture. And the anxiety that triggered it.

"There's not much Everson in Daisy's features, is there?" Kyle said.

Jane's heart clenched. Okay, so she didn't like the guy. But he was the victim of a deception and she'd played a part in that, and while she wasn't about to rise to the bait in his questions…

Wait a minute. Something didn't quite add up, she realized. This conversation wasn't following the line she'd have expected if he had any real idea.

Jane replayed his previous question in her head. *There's not much Everson in Daisy's features, is there?*

Realization hit, her assumptions shaken up by a kaleidoscope, to settle on a completely different picture.

"You think Daisy's n~~ot~~ ~~~~

Dear Reader,

Nature, or nurture? Which has the bigger role to play in determining our character? It's a question that people far more qualified than I have failed to answer. I keep changing my mind on this one—depending on how well my kids are behaving at any given moment!

What makes a child your child? Is it DNA, or the fact that you raised them, or both? And the things you like—or hate—about yourself...do you have any say about whether you pass those on to your kids?

In *Jane's Gift,* Kyle thinks he knows exactly what constitutes a "good" family and parent...and there's no way Jane, who grew up on the wrong side of the tracks and later deceived Kyle, qualifies. Jane's moved on from the past but wants nothing to do with the present, especially when it includes someone as judgmental as Kyle.

But there's a little girl involved, too...and Kyle and Jane have reckoned without one important rule: love changes everything.

To share your thoughts about *Jane's Gift,* or any of my books, please email me at abby@abbygaines.com. To read an After-the-End scene, visit the For Readers page at www.abbygaines.com.

Sincerely,

Abby Gaines

# Jane's Gift

## ABBY GAINES

**HARLEQUIN**® SUPER ROMANCE®

Recycling programs
for this product may
not exist in your area.

ISBN-13: 978-0-373-71850-4

JANE'S GIFT

Copyright © 2013 by Abby Gaines

Printed in U.S.A.

# ABOUT THE AUTHOR

Abby Gaines writes contemporary romances for Harlequin Superromance, and Regency romances for Love Inspired Historical. Those might sound like two completely different genres, but Abby likes to say she writes "stories that leave you smiling"—wherever and whenever they are set. Her Harlequin Superromance novel *The Groom Came Back* won the 2010 Readers Crown Award, and her novella *One in a Million* won the 2011 Readers Crown. *Jane's Gift* is Abby Gaines's twenty-first book for Harlequin.

Abby loves cooking, reading, skiing and traveling...though not all at once! She lives with her husband and children—and a labradoodle and a cat—in a house with enough stairs to keep her semifit and a sun-filled office with a sea view that provides inspiration for her writing. Visit her at www.abbygaines.com.

## Books by Abby Gaines

### HARLEQUIN SUPERROMANCE

### HARLEQUIN NASCAR

### LOVE INSPIRED HISTORICAL

Other titles by this author available in ebook format.

With love to my friend Margaret Lewis,
who is smart, strong, kind and loving.
You go, girl!

# CHAPTER ONE

L<small>ATE FOR A FUNERAL</small>.

So much for Jane Slater's plan to be invisible among the crowd of mourners at Pinyon Ridge Community Church. An overturned semitrailer on I-70 had delayed her out of Denver, and now she was prowling the foyer of the stupidly hexagonal church, trying to find a way in. To the funeral of the woman who'd once been her best—and only—friend.

A surge of pain, grief mixed with anger, swamped Jane. She stopped still, her hand pressed to her heart. Melissa was gone. Having beaten cancer in her early twenties, she was dead at thirty-one years of age, courtesy of a date who'd driven home after a few drinks too many.

*If you were here right now, Lissa, I'd slap you silly for getting into that car.* Jane wobbled on her high heels, which she'd chosen to project authority and confidence. She took a deep, steadying breath. She was the last person who should judge someone for their bad decisions. Besides, right now, she needed to focus on finding a way into this damn place.

The church was a new addition to the outskirts of town, seemingly built to accommodate hordes of the faithful. Each side of the enormous hexagon had a set of double doors from the outside, and a matching set of double doors into the sanctuary from the foyer that ran around the entire building. Jane had dashed in from the crowded parking lot, through the entry nearest her car. With all those inner doors closed, it was impossible to tell which were at the back of the church. So far, she'd tried two of them, both locked.

Inside, the muffled rendition of "Amazing Grace" had been

going on for some time. Once the singing stopped, her tardy
arrival would be far more conspicuous. *What else would you
expect from a Slater?*

Jane headed for the next set of doors. *Please, let these ones
open.* She pushed on the right-hand door…it gave an inch or
two. *Thank you.* The volume of the singing rose and words
came clearly through the opening: "…tha-an when we-ee first
begun." Yikes. If she wasn't mistaken, those were the closing words of the hymn.

Jane pushed the door wide and stepped through.

And found herself at the *front* of the church, eyeballing a
polished wooden casket and what must be about five hundred
people. Five hundred pairs of eyes focused on her.

A ripple of interest ran through the congregation, still
standing from the hymn, as people craned to see the intruder.
The ripple swelled as some of them identified her.

Drawing on the skill she'd honed in her teens, Jane blanked
them from her mind. But she couldn't ignore the glare of Kyle
Everson standing in the front row. Hostility radiated from
those eyes that she knew to be a dark, bitter brown. Next to
him…Jane's gaze shied away from the fair-haired little girl
whose hand he held.

*Move, Jane, before you make even more of a scene.* She'd
blown her discreet entry, but if she could just slip to the back
and find anonymity in the crowd… It had been so long since
she'd spent any time in Pinyon Ridge, surely half these people had no idea who she was.

"Jane Slater, is that you?" said a voice to her left, loud
and clear.

From the pulpit.

*Oh, hell.*

The minister stepped out from behind his Plexiglas lectern. "Folks, why don't you all sit down, while I welcome
back an old friend."

Unlikely as it seemed, he did look familiar.

"Gabe? Gabe *Everson?*" she whispered.

He grinned. Yep, she'd know that smile, a blend of angelic and impish, anywhere. As he pulled her into a friendly hug, she just had time to register the name badge that said Pastor Gabe.

"Welcome home," he murmured.

Gabe, younger brother of the glaring Kyle, had taken her to senior prom about a thousand years ago. *Not* because he was interested in her intellect. And now he was a minister?

In the front row, Kyle's taut stance transmitted impatience. She knew what he was thinking. *Jane Slater, last in a long line of Slater screwups.*

He couldn't be more wrong.

But she wasn't here to correct Kyle's perception of her, even if that were possible. Or anyone else's, for that matter. She'd learned long ago that she wouldn't find acceptance in Pinyon Ridge. She was here for Lissa.

She pulled out of Gabe's purely platonic embrace. "I'm late," she whispered, and the mic on his lapel conveyed that news flash to the entire audience. *Duh.*

She heard a couple of snickers.

"Not to worry." Gabe patted her shoulder. "Having seen Melissa walk into church late every Sunday for the past six months, I'm certain she wouldn't judge. Go sit next to Kyle." He pointed, unnecessarily. "That's where Lissa's best friend should be. Alongside Lissa's husband and daughter."

*Ex*-husband, Jane mentally corrected. Was Kyle Everson, mayor of Pinyon Ridge and pillar of society, technically a widower, even though the divorce had been final for, what, three years? Whatever his status, he was the last person she wanted to sit with—proximity to him always made her feel as if guilt were seeping through her pores. Kyle was too smart not to pick up on her discomfort, which was one of the reasons Jane and Lissa had grown apart.

But she wasn't about to argue in the middle of Lissa's

funeral. Even if Kyle's wary expression said he wouldn't be
surprised if she did exactly that.

He nodded a stiff greeting. Jane perched next to him on the
gray vinyl-upholstered seat, avoiding his eyes, *trying* to avoid
the curious gaze of the little girl. Daisy. Melissa's daughter.

Why weren't Lissa's parents seated here at the front?

"It's fashionable to talk of funerals as a celebration of life."
Gabe began to speak, his voice clear and warm. "But let us
not forget that we are mourning today, too. Mourning the
loss of a mother, daughter, friend, who left us far too soon."

Jane's embarrassment and resentment fell away as she
turned her thoughts to the friend who'd been such a large
part of her life. Mostly a good part. And though in a way
she'd lost Lissa years ago, and "best friend" was very much
a historical term, tears sprang to her eyes.

Jane fumbled in her purse for a tissue, aware of Kyle's
skeptical, sidelong glance. *Jerk.* He'd never thought she was
good enough to be Lissa's friend, always thought she must
have some sleazy hidden agenda. He hadn't changed a bit.
As she blew her nose, she sensed Daisy's continued stare.
The girl was leaning forward slightly, the better to see Jane.

Feeling besieged by the past, Jane pressed back into her
seat and drew in a deep, calming breath. The scent of lilies
wafted over her. She forced her focus onto Gabe's words,
something about Lissa's happy childhood.

This service would last, what, an hour? She could pay her
respects and be back in Denver by two, since she'd be going
against the Friday exodus from the city.

*The minute this ends, I'm out of here.*


BEING THE EX-HUSBAND of the deceased made a funeral about
as awkward as it could be. Standing outside the church next
to the hearse, as the mourners filed past to pay their respects,
Kyle accepted another "I'm so sorry for your loss," paired
with a gaze that didn't quite meet his eyes.

"Daisy and I appreciate your sympathy," he said firmly, and the latest well-wisher looked reassured.

No matter that he and Lissa had divorced, they'd been a family, to some degree or other, for eight years. Honoring that was the last thing he would do for her.

Daisy's fingers were clammy in his. He'd instructed her to stay with him, to greet people. It was the right thing, but he was aware of his mother-in-law's scrutiny. Barb Peters, Lissa's mom, stood a little away from the crowd—her husband, Hal, had been in a wheelchair since his stroke a few months ago and didn't like being front and center. Barb was multitasking: in addition to monitoring her granddaughter's state of mind, she was accepting condolences, talking at a rapid clip so people wouldn't try addressing Hal, whose words slurred too badly for him to be understood.

Kyle's brother, Gabe, stood next to Barb. He murmured something close to her ear as he gave her shoulders a comforting squeeze. Barb visibly relaxed, and smiled for the first time today. What had Gabe said? Kyle still couldn't understand how he'd morphed almost overnight from self-centered kid brother to irritatingly wise pastor.

The last few people were coming out of the church now. Kyle scanned their faces. No sign of her. *Jane Slater.* Hopefully, she'd slipped out through a side door and was on her way back to Denver.

"Kyle, Kyle, Kyle, this is a sad day." Roger Hurst, Lissa's lawyer, stepped up to shake his hand.

"Daisy and I appreciate your sympathy," Kyle said.

Hurst looked gratified, as if he had no idea he was the latest in a long line to hear that response. He was as far from a shark as a lawyer could get; Kyle himself had been the one to make sure Lissa received her fair share in their divorce settlement.

The attorney rubbed one side of his nose. "How are you coping with being a full-time dad?"

Kyle felt heat in his face, though there'd been no accusation in the words. "Daisy's been with her grandmother since…" His daughter's refusal to be parted from Barb this past week had shocked him. He reminded himself again that Daisy knew her grandmother better than she knew him, so it was natural for her to cling to Barb. But they couldn't go on that way. "She'll come home with me tonight."

"Of course," Roger said, sympathetic. "Kyle, are you aware of the contents of Melissa's will?"

Something in the man's tone made Kyle pause. *Are you still trying to manipulate me, Lissa?* "Under Colorado law I automatically have full custody of Daisy," he said. He'd checked that already. Guardianship of their daughter was surely the only aspect of Lissa's will that could be relevant to him.

"True." But Hurst looked uncertain. "Where did Jane Slater get to?" he asked, surveying the crowd.

"I haven't seen her in a while." It wouldn't surprise Kyle if Lissa had left something to Jane. Her pearls, maybe. The ones Kyle had bought for their first anniversary. He'd have liked Daisy to have them, but he wouldn't quibble. "You could write Jane a letter," Kyle suggested. "Barb will have her address in Denver."

"I'd rather find her now." The lawyer dived into the throng with surprising speed. Kyle turned to the next mourner, old Betty Gray, who wore an Everson for Mayor button. Ugh. No doubt Betty meant to be supportive, but the last thing Kyle wanted to think about right now was his faltering reelection campaign.

Five minutes later, Roger Hurst returned. "I caught Jane getting into her car," he said, triumphant. "She'll meet us at my office in fifteen minutes. Along with Barb. Hal's a bit drained, so Barb will take him home first."

Kyle wished Jane had been faster in her escape. Today was hard enough without having to worry about what she was up to. He didn't trust the woman, plain and simple.

He crouched down to Daisy. "I need to go to a meeting. You can hang out with Grandpa for a while, okay?"

She didn't complain; she never did.

*Grandpa* was Kyle's father, Charles Everson. Recently retired chief of police, elder of the church—the Episcopalians, not "this modern crowd," as he called Gabe's congregation— and the kind of dad every kid should have.

Kyle found his father in the crowd and handed Daisy over with a promise to join the mourners for refreshments at his dad's house as soon as he could.

Just as soon as he could get through the reading of Lissa's will and deal with whatever curveball she'd thrown him.

Roger Hurst's office was in the heart of Pinyon Ridge's historic center, tucked between one of the many outdoor stores lining the main street that catered to hikers in summer and skiers in winter, and the Eating Post café on the corner. Micki Barton, the café's owner, waved through the window as Kyle passed. She'd been a couple of years ahead of him in high school, and they were good friends, just as their parents had been. Micki had attended Lissa's funeral, then hurried back to the café so Margaret, her employee, could attend the wake.

In the lawyer's office at the back of the narrow building, Barb was already seated on a maroon leather couch. Her brave smile reminded Kyle of Lissa when he'd first met her, near the end of her chemo. He'd fallen in love with that smile.

Though he hadn't loved Lissa in years, they'd remained on good terms, committed to maintaining a positive relationship as Daisy's parents. He would miss her. *Why didn't you refuse to get in that car, Lissa?*

The air in the office felt stale, too hot. Kyle loosened the knot of his tie and unbuttoned his collar. He was about to sit down when Jane came in.

"Jane, dear, I didn't get to talk to you at the church." Barb stood and hugged her.

Almost immediately, Jane pulled away. "I'm sorry I made

such a public entrance." Though she sounded apologetic, there
was also an edge of confidence in her voice he hadn't heard
before. But then, he hadn't seen her in, what, five years? He
wasn't sure when Lissa had last seen her—maybe that trip to
Denver with Daisy. Daisy would have been two.

Jane looked entirely respectable in her black jacket, cream-
colored blouse and slim skirt ending just above the knee.
Kyle's gaze dropped lower, down shapely calves to her high-
heeled shoes with a peep of scarlet-tipped toes. He jerked
his eyes up.

"No problem, dear," Barb said. "I'm just glad you could
get here. We're having a private burial for Melissa later—
you'll stay, won't you?"

"Where's Hal?" Jane asked. "I didn't see either of you at
the church."

"Oh, dear." Barbara blinked, hard. "I assumed Lissa would
have…" Her voice quavered.

"Hal had a stroke, a few months ago," Kyle said. "Surely
Lissa told you?"

"We haven't been in touch for a while."

Really? He'd assumed they'd at least continued emailing—
Kyle had more than once been tempted to sneak a peek at
those emails Lissa used to delete immediately upon reply-
ing. "Why not?" he asked. "What happened?" Which, come
to think of it, was the same question he'd asked last time
they spoke.

He wasn't about to get an answer this time, either, it
seemed.

"I'm so sorry about Hal," Jane said to Barb. "How's he
doing?"

"Not great," Barb admitted. "We sat at the back of the
church—it's the best place for his wheelchair. He's very self-
conscious, poor dear."

Roger Hurst cleared his throat. "Folks, I have Melissa's

will here." The single sheet of white paper he held immediately caught their attention; they settled into their seats.

Hurst began to read aloud. "'I, Melissa Eve Everson...'"

Kyle let the standard jargon wash over him. It took less than a minute for Roger to reach the meat of the will. Besides leaving her pearls to her mother—not to Jane, then—Melissa had bequeathed all of her money and material possessions to Daisy, with Kyle to serve as trustee until Daisy turned twenty-one. No problem there, though Kyle felt twenty-five would be a better age for Daisy to come into her inheritance.

Roger paused. "The next section pertains to guardianship of Daisy," he said.

Barb sat straight. Jane glanced at her watch.

"'If Kyle Everson should predecease me,'" the lawyer read, "'I appoint Jane Slater as guardian of my daughter, Daisy Patricia Everson.'"

Jane's head jerked back, her eyes wide. Barb made a sound that indicated her surprise.

Foreboding held Kyle very still. "Since I didn't predecease Melissa, the clause isn't relevant," he pointed out.

"Correct," Roger said. "Let me read on. 'If Kyle Everson does not predecease me, he will have automatic full custody of Daisy. However, it is my deepest wish that Jane Slater establish a meaningful relationship with Daisy, with a view to providing a positive female influence on her life.'"

"No!" Kyle said. The word seemed to echo oddly—then he realized Jane had said it a scant second after him. Quite possibly the first time they'd agreed on something.

"You're under no legal compulsion to consider Melissa's wishes, either of you," Roger Hurst said, flustered. "But morally..."

"I live in Denver," Jane said. "There's no way I can get involved in Daisy's life." She looked horrified.

Which seemed like an overreaction to Kyle, even though she was the *last* person he wanted having a say in Daisy's upbringing. Not because she was a Slater—though people like his father would see that as an insurmountable problem—but because she'd been instrumental in the breakdown of his marriage.

He didn't know how, but he was certain she had played a part.

"I can't come back here, which is what I'd need to do to have a *meaningful* influence," Jane said. "I have a job, an apartment."

Kyle noticed she didn't mention a boyfriend, friends, or any other personal tie to the city. She must be thirty-one, the same age as Lissa; strange that she should have so few connections. *Not my problem.*

"Thanks for sharing Melissa's wishes," he told Roger. "We'll certainly take those into consideration as we make our plans." *As in, we'll consider them, then ignore them.* Lissa must have made that will back when she and Jane were close. The woman was a stranger to Daisy.

Barb cleared her throat. "What rights do Hal and I have as grandparents, Roger?"

"You don't need rights," Kyle said, startled into speaking too loudly. "You're Daisy's Nana and Pop. You'll always be able to see her."

"That's not what I'm worried about." Barb straightened her spine. "It seems to me you and Daisy don't get along."

Kyle darted a glance at Jane. She was inspecting her fingernails, but he sensed her alertness. She could stay out of this, thank you very much.

"Daisy and I get along," he said. "I mean, sure, she's reserved by nature...."

"Not when she's with me." Barb looked exactly what she was—a small-town librarian, soft-spoken and plump with life's comforts. But she had a core of steel, one that Melissa had inherited. "Kyle, I can't give her the attention she needs right now and you're a busy man—I think it's a great idea for Jane to get involved."

"That won't be necessary," Kyle said, his voice clipped. If he could run this town—which, despite his rival's claims, he'd done successfully for the past four years—he could manage one five-year-old girl. "Besides, Jane's virtually a stranger to Daisy."

According to Lissa, Jane had never gotten over not being invited to be Daisy's godmother. She never even showed up to the christening. Not the behavior of a true friend. And with Jane's past, he couldn't imagine why Lissa thought she'd be a positive influence for their daughter.

"Sometimes grandparents share custody, is that right?" Barb asked the lawyer.

What the hell?

"Uh…" Roger ran a finger around his collar. "Usually only if a parent is considered unfit."

"Hmm," Barb said. "That's not exactly… I'm not saying you're a *bad* father, Kyle. The one day a week that you have Daisy, you do okay."

Ouch. Talk about being damned with faint praise.

"But you don't *know* her," Barb finished.

Kyle unclenched his fingers. "Of course I know her. And I often have her for two days."

Okay, so weekends with his daughter were occasionally whittled down to one day. Maybe more than occasionally. Did that make him the world's worst dad? *I'm a good father, dammit.*

Not only did the criticism sting, but the last thing he needed going into his reelection campaign was a custody battle with the town's extremely popular librarian. This election needed to be about what kind of community Pinyon Ridge should be in the long-term, not the mayor's private life.

"Like a lot of fathers, I've let Daisy's mom do most of the

work," he admitted in an attempt to be conciliatory. "I plan to be more hands-on from now on."

Barb nodded encouragement, but concern creased her forehead. Jane checked her watch. All those tears in church, and now it seemed she couldn't wait to get away. She annoyed the hell out of him.

*Jane Slater is irrelevant.* What mattered was doing his job as a dad and as mayor.

"I intend to do this right," he told Barb. Then he corrected himself. "I *will* do this right."

JANE STIFLED A SNORT, out of respect for Barb, not Kyle. She might not have much personal experience of how functional families operated, but she did know that Kyle should be saying he loved Daisy and would do anything for her happiness. Instead, his tone said, *I'll do the right thing if it kills me.*

She remembered Lissa, pregnant with Daisy, tearfully confessing that Kyle hadn't wanted to try for a baby again. They'd undergone three rounds of IVF already, using eggs harvested and frozen before Melissa's chemotherapy. Jane had assumed Kyle would outgrow his lack of enthusiasm once his daughter was born. But maybe that was another thing that hadn't changed, along with his self-righteous arrogance.

*It's none of my business how he and Daisy get along. If asking me to get involved was an attempt to make amends, Lissa, you couldn't have chosen a worse way to go about it.*

"Barb, this talk of custody, it's not wise," Roger volunteered. "You have your hands full with Hal. No judge will deem you capable of looking after a five-year-old." He capped and uncapped his pen. "I'm sure Kyle will put in whatever time Daisy needs, even if Jane isn't willing to comply with Melissa's wishes." He gave Jane a pointed look, which said that although she might dress nicely and have a decent life in Denver, here in Pinyon Ridge she was still a Slater and she wasn't fooling anyone.

He seemed to conveniently overlook the fact that Kyle was equally reluctant to comply with Lissa's wishes. But Kyle was an Everson. Pinyon Ridge royalty, just like Lissa and her family.

It wasn't as if Jane had expected anything different.

"But if Kyle can't cope," Barb began.

"I can cope," Kyle snapped.

For Lissa's sake, maybe Jane should… *No. I'm out of here.* Lissa had no right to her continued loyalty. But old habits were hard to break.

"Whatever you decide," the lawyer pointed out, "we should all be careful not to say things we'll regret later. Very, very, very careful."

Good advice, even without the triplicate. There was no need to panic, Jane told herself. Kyle must surely love his daughter. There might be teething problems, but as he spent more time with Daisy, they'd grow closer.

Barb looked as if she was about to argue, so Jane spoke up. "Kyle, it sounds like you're committed to giving Daisy the time and attention she needs."

Instead of looking appreciative, his dark eyes narrowed. *We're on the same side, for once, jerk.* "I need to get back to Denver, but let's keep in touch." Just mentioning the city made her hunger to be back where no one thought *Slater* was a dirty word. In Denver, people accepted her for who she was today.

At last, Kyle caught on that she was helping him out. "That'd be great. Thanks for coming," he said insincerely.

Jane gave him an equally fake smile, and picked up her purse from the floor.

"Stop!" Barb barked the word, causing Jane to freeze half out of her chair. "Do you really plan to ignore my daughter's wishes, Jane?"

*The way your daughter ignored me the past few years?* Jane tamped down the long-stifled hurt. "I'm thinking I'll give Kyle and Daisy some time to adjust. I'll check in with them in a couple of weeks." By phone.

"Sounds good," Kyle said.

Barb's steely gaze held Jane's.

Damn. "I'll come back for a visit in a month or so," Jane conceded grudgingly.

"I'm surprised at you, Jane," Barb said.

She didn't say, "After all I did for you." Jane filled in that blank herself. If Jane owed anyone in this town anything, it was Barbara Peters, who'd accepted Lissa's friendship with a girl from the wrong side of the tracks. More than that, she'd welcomed Jane into her home, allowing her to see what family life should be and encouraging her to aim for a different kind of life for herself.

She swallowed. "You can't expect me to stay, Barb. My clients need me." She'd recently hired an associate into First Impressions—the business she'd founded to help women who wanted to change their lives—but Jane was still the driving force.

"I'm not asking you to stay forever." Barb's mutinous look reminded her of Lissa. "Just long enough to help Daisy adapt to a new routine with her father. Exactly what I'd do, if I wasn't occupied with Hal."

"Daisy and I don't need her help," Kyle said.

"Daisy doesn't know me," Jane protested. "Before today, I hadn't seen her since she was two." Since Lissa had decided their friendship was too risky.

Barb leaned forward, hands clasped. "Stay, Jane. Please."

"It really isn't necessary," Kyle said.

"*You* can have some respect for Lissa's wishes, too," Barb snapped.

Kyle folded his arms across his chest, lips clamped as if he were biting down on further comment. But the glower in his dark eyes sent Jane a clear message: *leave.*

She was fed up with being made to feel she had no right to

be here. *I should get out and not come back*. And yet...even without Barb's entreaty, the fact was, Jane had never been able to refuse Lissa. Isn't that what had gotten their friendship into trouble in the first place? Now, the ingrained urge to help her friend overrode the voice of reason reminding her nothing good could come from a return to Pinyon Ridge.

"I'd need to go back to the city first," she said to Barb. Kyle's hiss of annoyance gave her surprising satisfaction. "I'll have to make arrangements to work with my clients remotely."

"Of course, dear," Barb said, gracious in victory, once again the cuddly small-town librarian. "Do whatever you need to. I'll expect you back here in, shall we say, a week? And you'll stay a couple of weeks?"

"I guess." A flood of reservations kicked in. *Too late*.

Jane met Kyle's glare head-on. *I don't care if you don't want me here,* she tried to transmit. *It was never about you, always about Lissa.*

Okay, so two hours in Pinyon Ridge had morphed into two weeks, and she suspected they might feel more like two months. Not a problem, not really. And though Lissa's will might require her to stay in touch with Daisy—rather ironic after the past few years—that didn't mean she had to be here in Pinyon Ridge or deal with Kyle any longer than necessary.

When this stint was done, she would leave, and this time she wouldn't come back. *Two weeks. I can handle it. No need to panic.*

# CHAPTER TWO

IF ANYONE HAD TOLD KYLE he'd be desperate for a break after just seven days of full-time parenting, he'd have laughed them out of town.

He'd been a dad for nearly six years—he knew what it was about.

But here he was, holding open the door of the Eating Post café for Daisy early Saturday afternoon, hoping like heck his dad would take her off his hands for a few hours. He felt like a jerk, but that didn't stop him pointing out his father to Daisy. "Look, there's Grandpa."

Daisy nodded. She'd barely said a word to him since he'd taken her home to the house she'd shared with Melissa. The house where they'd once lived as a family.

No matter that he understood she was sad and probably disoriented, he still found her silence hard to handle.

Kyle followed her across the café, crowded with tourists and locals. Spring and fall were supposed to be quieter times in Pinyon Ridge, but the unseasonal warmth had brought a much-needed influx of visitors.

As they approached his dad's regular booth, next to the window overlooking Clark Street, Kyle realized his brother was there ahead of him. He hesitated. Gabe was altogether too intuitive these days; the last thing Kyle wanted was his brother figuring out what a crap job he was doing as a father. Growing up, Kyle had always been the responsible son, the high achiever. Gabe hadn't exactly been bad, but he'd given their parents one or two scares. Kyle didn't like the current role reversal.

Daisy had reached the booth, and Gabe was greeting her, so Kyle had no choice but to carry on.

His brother had a latte in front of him. Charles was finishing a meal—his favorite, the All-Day Lumberjack Breakfast, Kyle guessed.

"Got room for a couple more?" Kyle greeted them.

The two men shifted so that Kyle and Daisy could fit. Daisy planted a dutiful, if grave, kiss on her grandfather's cheek, then folded her hands in her lap, her knees pressed together. As if she were trying not to take up too much space.

"Do I get one of those?" Gabe pointed to his own cheek.

Daisy smiled—Gabe seemed to have a knack with her that Kyle and his dad lacked. "You're too far away," she said.

"Okay, but I'm taking a rain check," Gabe warned.

Micki Barton, standing behind the counter, caught Kyle's eye. "The usual?" she called.

"Thanks, Micki. And a hot chocolate for Daisy."

"Nice girl, that one," his father said about Micki, as he always did. Charles should know—he'd been a frequent visitor to the café throughout his career as a police officer, and he'd found the habit hard to break in the months since he retired. He came in for breakfast most days and ate a late lunch here on Saturdays. "You ought to ask Micki out," he told Kyle. For the hundredth time.

"I'm not looking for a girlfriend—how about Gabe asks her out instead?"

"Micki's an Episcopalian," Charles said. "Why would she marry into a church where they don't know any good hymns?" He turned to Gabe. "But after the election—" Gabe was Kyle's campaign manager "—you *should* get yourself a nice girlfriend. One who'll make a good pastor's wife. I can't understand why that church hired a single man."

Gabe shrugged. "Me, neither. Single pastors mostly get associate roles. I figure the local-boy-made-good thing swung me the senior pastor gig."

Charles snorted, but his smile was affectionate. "You boys should both be out there looking for a wife. A man doesn't get what I had with your mother by sitting on his butt."

"Don't you think my life is a little complicated right now?" Kyle asked.

His father conceded the point with a grimace. "You'll get through this. This time next year, you'll be a second-term mayor, Daisy will be settled and you might even have met a nice lady."

"Sure, Dad." Kyle was starting to wish he hadn't come in. His father's prediction was more than just a fond hope. Not exactly an order, but an expectation, one Kyle was on track to fall short of.

Not that his dad was asking anything of Kyle that he hadn't lived up to himself. Charles Everson was one of the good guys—not just in the cop sense. He'd always ranked family number one in his life. He'd been a devoted husband to Patti, Kyle's mom, until her death from cancer five years ago, and the kind of firm-but-fair dad who coached Little League, came along on Cub Scout camps and taught his sons how to treat a lady.

Now that he was retired, he spent much of his free time helping out in the community. He was arguably the most respected man in town.

If Kyle could be half the father, half the man, Charles was, he'd have achieved something.

Too bad his marriage had fallen apart, he was staring at an electoral defeat that would allow Pinyon Ridge to end up a tacky, low-rent tourist mecca and now Lissa's death had shone a light on the damn poor job he was doing as a dad.

He waited for an opportune moment to ask Charles to babysit, listening with half an ear as his father and Gabe debated the likely outcome of tonight's baseball game—the Rockies were playing the Dodgers in Denver. Thinking of Denver reminded him of Jane Slater, another hassle he didn't need.

Micki arrived with their coffees, with a side of extra marshmallows for Daisy. "On the house," she told Daisy.

Charles gave Kyle a significant look, as if to say, "See, she likes you."

Which Kyle knew wasn't true—at least, not in that way. Micki was showing kindness to a little girl who'd lost her mother.

Daisy set two of the marshmallows on a paper napkin. "I'll save these for Mommy."

The adults at the table froze.

"Uh, Daisy," Kyle said.

"When's Mommy coming home?" Daisy asked.

Kyle swallowed. Surely even the best father in the world would struggle right now?

"Your mommy won't be coming home, Daisy," Gabe said. He reached across the table and took Daisy's hand. "Remember at the church last week, what we talked about?"

"You said we'll get to see Mommy in heaven."

"That's right." Gabe squeezed her hand. "But here, it's just you and Daddy now, so you need to look after each other."

"Would you like my marshmallow, Daddy?" Daisy asked.

"Sure. Thanks." Kyle almost choked on the words, and then again on the powdered sugar dusting the marshmallow as he popped it in his mouth.

"I wish Mommy was here," Daisy said on a sigh.

Kyle closed his eyes.

"Daisy, how about a cupcake?" Charles said with heavy-handed heartiness. "Micki has some on the counter—go choose one with the nicest frosting."

"You okay, bro?" Gabe asked, his eyes keen with concern, after Daisy had trotted off to the cupcakes.

Kyle blinked, also aware of his dad's worried scrutiny. "I'm fine."

"That's what Superman said right before the kryptonite kicked in," Gabe said, lightening the moment at the same time as he made his point.

"Don't you have a sermon to write or some pastoral visiting to do?" Kyle asked.

"Sermon's done," Gabe said smugly. "And I'm pastoral visiting with you and Dad right now. Wanna pray?"

"I liked you better when you were a sinner," Kyle muttered.

"Still a sinner, bro, just forgiven." Gabe faked such a saintly expression, Kyle couldn't help laughing.

Charles shook his head, but he was smiling, too.

"Seriously, Kyle," Gabe said, "if you need anything…"

"There'll be some major adjusting over the next couple of weeks," Kyle said. "But I'm on it."

"When does Jane arrive?" Gabe asked.

Charles's lips pursed.

Kyle shrugged one shoulder. "Who knows? Sometime, never?" He hoped.

Daisy arrived back with her cupcake. "I chose pink," she informed her grandfather. Back in her seat, she blew on her drink, then took a sip.

"I can't understand why Melissa thought Jane Slater should have anything to do with Daisy," Charles said. Daisy's head came up.

Kyle frowned a warning to his dad. "Remember how good Jane was to Lissa when she was sick?"

Lissa had dropped out of college after she was diagnosed with cancer. She'd come home to Pinyon Ridge, traveling to Denver for oncologist appointments and chemotherapy. The way Kyle had heard it, Jane had taken unpaid leave from her job to accompany Lissa and Barb to chemo, then taken turns with Barb at keeping Lissa's spirits up through nights of nausea.

"That's true," Charles said fairly. "Jane did a good thing. Wasn't her fault her dad stole the church bake sale takings."

The bake sale had been one of many events held to raise money for the copayments for Lissa's treatment. Kyle cringed to think how Jane must have felt at her father's sleazy behavior.

Kyle hadn't been around through any of it. He'd met Lissa later, toward the end of her treatment, when he arrived home from studying landscape architecture at Berkeley. She'd been so frail of body, but so determined to get past the disease, he'd fallen in love with her gutsiness. Through Lissa, he'd met Jane, but he already knew her family by reputation. He'd lost count of the number of times his dad would come home from a shift shaking his head and saying, "Those Slaters."

Kyle's instinct had been to protect Lissa from Jane, but at that stage their friendship was rock-solid.

"Speak of the—oh, yeah, I'm not supposed to say that anymore." Gabe grinned as he pointed out the window.

A white Toyota Corolla had pulled into a parking space on Clark Street next to Kyle's truck. At this time of day, Clark was the shadier side of the building—the sun streamed in through the windows that fronted onto Main Street. Locals, people in the know who didn't want broiled car seats, parked on Clark.

The driver door on the Corolla opened; Jane got out.

Gabe sighed appreciatively. "She's quite a babe."

"You're not supposed to say that kind of thing anymore, either." Jane Slater, a babe? Kyle tried to see what his brother saw, rather than just the woman he was certain had kept secrets from him. Hair a rich walnut-brown fell below her shoulders. Her crimson cotton-knit top molded shapely curves above black skinny pants. She looked confident, self-assured. And, yeah, pretty.

"I'm a pastor, not blind," Gabe said.

"Gabe, I don't think Jane Slater is the kind of woman you want to date," Charles said carefully.

"Hey, she and I have history." Gabe ran a hand through

his hair, fluffing it up as if he might actually be trying to impress Jane. "I took her to senior prom."

Kyle hadn't known that; he'd been away at college by then.

"I only invited her because I thought she'd sleep with me," Gabe admitted. Kyle froze, his coffee halfway to his mouth. "I was wrong," Gabe finished with a grin.

Charles looked as relieved as Kyle felt.

"And now your womanizing is behind you," Kyle reminded him drily.

"You bet." Gabe did that holy look again.

Jane caught them watching her; her chin tilted up as she headed around the corner.

"I figured she wouldn't get here until Monday," Kyle said. Behind him, the café door opened.

"Hello, Janelle," his father said when she reached their booth.

Kyle had forgotten her full name was Janelle. According to Lissa, she'd shortened it to the more neutral Jane as part of creating a new image for herself.

"I understand you're rejoining us for a couple of weeks," Charles continued, his tone a mix of condescension and I'm-watching-you warning.

"Hello, Charles," Jane said coolly.

At the look on his father's face, Kyle stifled a snort. Most people in town still called Charles Everson "Chief," out of respect. Jane's use of his first name had been a deliberate withholding of that respect. Fond though he was of his father, Dad deserved it.

Her tawny brown eyes met Kyle's. He saw a little flare of surprise as she registered his amusement. His father wasn't the only one capable of stereotyping—Kyle suspected Jane had pegged him as an uptight jerk years ago and hadn't moved on from that.

Where she would say "uptight jerk," he would say "guy

trying to do the right thing." So excuse him if he didn't have much sense of humor about threats to his family's stability.

"Barb said I'd find you here," she said. "I assume you have a key to Lissa's house?"

Daisy piped up, which was unusual. "You sat with us in the church." There was a question in the words.

"Um, yeah. Hi, I'm Jane." The cool control of a moment ago vanished. Her gaze sat somewhere above Daisy's head, on the back of the booth, as she said awkwardly, "You and I have met before, but it's been a long time."

Kyle realized she hadn't yet looked directly at Daisy.

This was never going to work. With her family background, Jane surely had no clue how to relate to Daisy the way Lissa might have intended.

Unless Jane's awkwardness was because she knew... Kyle quashed the old suspicion. Years of second- and third-guessing had proved only that speculation was a waste of time.

"Uncle Gabe said you're a baby," Daisy said to Jane.

"Er...excuse me?"

"The word was *babe*," Gabe corrected Daisy, with a disarming grin.

That drew a soft snort from Jane. It was an oddly warm sound, one that suggested she was a good sport.

"Have a seat," Gabe invited. "It's good to see you again."

What, was he making a play for her? Kyle frowned at his brother, who countered with his usual sunny smile.

Jane hesitated, then, with an air of resignation, squeezed into the booth next to Daisy.

"Why do you need a key to Lissa's house?" Charles demanded.

Great. His father sounded as if he thought Jane planned to clear the place out and sell Lissa's stuff on eBay.

"Barb said I should stay there, *Charles*," she said. The

lips beneath her straight nose were rather full, Kyle noticed. "Since I no longer have a home in Pinyon Ridge."

Her parents had rented an old dump of a house on the edge of town. Jane's mother, who'd died a year ago, had been its last inhabitant, the last remaining Slater in Pinyon Ridge. The rest were in jail, dead or missing/presumed engaged in criminal activity.

Except Jane.

"Daisy and I are staying in the house just now," Kyle informed her. "To give Daisy some continuity." Barb was overstepping the mark, thinking he needed such close supervision.

"Oh." She bit that full lower lip. "Barb didn't mention that. Any chance you can stay in your own place?"

"I've been living with Dad." Which sounded more pathetic than it was. Kyle had moved in with his father after the split with Lissa, who'd stayed in the family home with Daisy. Charles appreciated the company and the arrangement worked fine—though better when his dad had been working. "I'm finishing off a new house on Sawmill Road, but that won't be ready for another month or so." That's what he planned to work on this afternoon. "Daisy has stayed at Dad's in the past, but it's not home to her. I want her to feel settled."

Besides, he suspected his dad's well-meaning suggestions sometimes hurt Daisy's feelings, though she would never say as much.

"Fine, I'll find somewhere else." Jane hesitated. "I don't think staying with Barb would work."

"No," Kyle agreed. Hal didn't like having other people around, now that he was a shadow of his former self. Besides, Barb was busy looking after him—Kyle doubted she could handle even an undemanding guest.

"Maybe a bed-and-breakfast," Jane suggested. "If there's one that's not too expensive."

Pinyon Ridge wasn't a cheap destination.

"The town's pretty full," Kyle said. He should know, he

was meeting with the accommodation providers this week to talk about how to manage the increasing demand for rooms, the first sign they were coming out of the recession. "It's unlikely anyone will have a room for the whole two weeks." She might have to go back to Denver. What a shame.

"Do you know of anyone who'd put Janelle up, Gabe?" his father asked, unexpectedly helpful.

"Sorry, no. I'd offer to have you stay with me," Gabe said, "but a single male pastor can't get away with hosting female guests under sixty-five. Especially not babes."

Jane smiled, her mouth suddenly generous. Gabe's returning smile was appreciative; Kyle found himself stiffening. Huh, who'd have thought he'd feel protective toward his kid brother at this advanced age?

"Dad, you have plenty of room," Gabe said. "I'm sure you wouldn't mind having Jane stay with you." That mischief in his grin was downright unholy.

Hard to say who looked more horrified at the suggestion, Charles or Jane.

"Thanks for the offer, Charles," Jane drawled, "but I don't fancy being frisked for any missing family silver every time I walk out the door."

"You Slaters were always good at holding a grudge," Charles said. "Might I remind you, the last time I saw you was when I was one of the few people to attend your mother's funeral."

A flash of pain crossed Jane's face so fast, Kyle almost missed it. Then she was back to her usual distant expression as she said calmly, "I figured you wanted to make sure she was really dead."

His father chuffed with annoyance.

"You could stay with us," Daisy told Jane.

Kyle realized Daisy had been paying close attention. Like him, the rest of his family weren't used to having her around all the time; they needed to censor themselves. His daughter's surreptitious look in his direction said there was more to her invitation than a child's instinctive kindness. It was as if she liked the thought of someone else being in the house. As if she were reluctant for it to be just the two of them.

Surely he wasn't *that* bad a dad? And if that's how Daisy felt, how were they supposed to get through the next dozen or so years?

At last, Jane met Daisy's eyes, though with apparent reluctance. "That's sweet of you, Daisy, but—"

"We have a guest room," Daisy said. "It's next to mine."

"That won't work, Daisy," Kyle said. "Jane needs…somewhere else."

"Daisy's right," Gabe countered. "It makes sense for Jane to stay with you guys."

Daisy beamed at him. That was one thing that hadn't changed since Kyle's brother turned righteous. Females of all ages and stages still adored him, only now he kept his responses G-rated. Kyle wondered if his brother missed that casual, sensual connection. Missed sex. Kyle sure as hell did.

Jane clasped her hands behind her head and flexed her shoulders, as if they were stiff from the long drive. The movement lifted her breasts in that clinging sweater.

"—any more than I do, but I guess it's logical," she finished.

Oops, she'd been saying something. And now everyone was looking expectantly at Kyle.

"Excuse me?" He shook his head. "My mind was on, uh, tonight's council meeting."

Gabe's smirk suggested he'd noticed the direction of Kyle's gaze. "We were saying it makes sense for Jane to stay with you and Daisy for a couple of weeks, since the whole reason she's here is to make sure you two are set up okay."

Kyle could think of several reasons why it made no sense at all. *She undermined my marriage. Whatever she and Lissa got up to that week in Denver, things were never the same again.* When Lissa had started shutting him out, while she was pregnant with Daisy, he'd phoned Jane—which he'd hated doing—to ask if there was anything he should know.

He'd promised he wouldn't tell Lissa about their conversation, he just needed to understand if anything had happened, and what he could do to fix his marriage. Hell, he'd practically begged. Jane had paused just long enough for him to conclude his suspicions were well-founded, then she'd told him he had nothing to worry about. Her voice had risen a shade higher. His dad always said that was a good clue a suspect was lying.

"More coffee, Charles?" Micki appeared alongside their table, coffeepot in hand. His father was the only one having a simple filter coffee, but Micki's warm smile encompassed all of them. Kyle could sense his dad giving him a significant look—*ask her on a date*—and his head started to pound.

He needed to get out of here, get some work done on the new house, then prepare for tonight's council meeting. Most of all, he needed not to be worrying about how he might be messing up where Daisy was concerned.

Micki focused in on Jane. "Hi, have we met?"

"Jane Slater. I grew up here." She imparted the information as if it were a challenge.

"Welcome back, Jane. I think I knew your brother—Darren?"

Jane nodded, her expression wary. Kyle remembered Darren as a total lowlife, and it seemed Micki suddenly came to the same recollection. She cleared her throat as she held up the coffeepot. "Coffee?"

"No, thanks," Jane said.

Kyle pulled his keys from his pocket and twisted the house key off the ring. "Jane, this is for you."

She looked at the key as if she'd never seen one before.

"Gabe's right, you might as well stay with us." He shoved out of the booth. "I have some work to do, so how about you and Daisy spend the afternoon getting to know each other."

Jane eyes widened in alarm. "I'm not sure I'm ready...."

She stopped. Maybe she'd seen, as Kyle had, the flash of hurt across Daisy's face.

"Sure," she said, "that'll be nice." Stilted, but not a bad effort.

Kyle thawed infinitesimally toward her.

"Are you okay to hang out with Jane?" he asked Daisy.

She nodded.

"Dad, can you lend Jane the booster seat you have in your truck?" He didn't wait for a reply before he turned to Jane. "I'll be at the new house, then at a council meeting. Call my cell if you need anything—the number's on the wall next to the phone at Lissa's place."

"But—" Her tawny eyes, more expressive than he remembered, held an appeal for...what, mercy?

He squelched the impulse to let her off the hook. She was the one who'd come back when she wasn't wanted, and spending time with Daisy was what her visit was all about. He couldn't imagine why she would suddenly develop cold feet, but he didn't care. He felt guilty enough already about his marriage, his daughter...Jane Slater didn't get to add to that.

"See you tonight," he said, and left.

# CHAPTER THREE

WHO KNEW A well-behaved five-year-old could be so exhausting?

After Kyle had dumped her in the deep end, Jane had taken Daisy back to Lissa's Victorian house—*Kyle* and Lissa's Victorian house—with the eggshell-blue siding and white shutters. The effect was pretty and welcoming. Much more welcoming than the host, who would clearly be delighted never to see her again.

Jane had settled into the guest room and unpacked her wheelie bag, hanging sundresses, skirts and blouses in the closet, folding shorts and T-shirts into drawers. She'd changed out of the clothes she'd driven in, having overheated in the effort to keep her cool in that encounter with the ex-police chief. Now, she wore a cream-colored T-shirt and a pair of khaki shorts.

Downstairs in the kitchen, she eyeballed the meager contents of the fridge and waited for an answer to her question: What would you like for dinner?

"Anything's okay. I don't mind," Daisy said.

Daisy's compliance was what made her so tiring. She refused to voice an opinion on anything, leaving Jane, who knew less than nothing about five-year-olds, to second-guess her. And herself.

Okay, maybe there was more to Jane's sense of exhaustion. Maybe the baggage she'd carried for the past six years had become too heavy, as she was finally face-to-face with Lissa's daughter.

"There's not much food here." Jane tried to keep her mind

in the here and now as she inspected the shelves of the refrigerator. "Do you know what your Dad had planned?"

"He planned for Grandpa to give me dinner."

Jane turned at the longer-than-usual response. "Does Grandpa cook nice food?"

A shrug indicated the standard fell somewhere short of "nice." "He says my table manners need work."

Jane pffed. That sounded like Charles. "He always used to tell me to behave better, too," she said. "I ignored him."

The little girl's eyes widened at such reckless disregard for authority.

"I mean, I'm sure he's trying to help," Jane said belatedly. It wasn't her place to interfere in Daisy's relationship with her grandfather, she reminded herself. Even if Charles's disapproval gave them something in common.

She pulled a pack of pepperoni from the refrigerator—the meat was two weeks past its expiration date. Did that matter? Not to Jane, but what if Daisy got food poisoning? She shoved the pepperoni back in the fridge. Damn Kyle, leaving them alone this long.

He probably hoped she'd be so out of her depth, she'd turn tail and run back to Denver, another Slater letting everyone down.

Not going to happen.

Jane might be a reluctant returner to Pinyon Ridge, but now she was here, she would do her best for Lissa.

"We'll have toasted cheese sandwiches," Jane announced.

Before leaving Denver, she'd questioned a counselor, a woman who worked with some of Jane's clients, about how to handle a five-year-old. The woman had supplied five rules that she assured Jane would stand her in good stead.

1. Be decisive—kids like to know who's in charge.

2. Be predictable—consistency and routine make kids feel secure.

3. Get down to the kid's level without condescending.

4. Don't promise what you can't deliver, or you'll break trust.

5. Don't get too attached.

It seemed the perfect protocol, not just for working with Daisy, but for Jane's entire stay in Pinyon Ridge. If she could stick with the protocol, maybe she could accomplish what she'd come here to do and get out again unscathed.

Her culinary decisiveness elicited no response.

She prepared the food, and they ate at the pine table in silence. What would Lissa make of this scene? Would she be anxious, possessive? Or would she realize Jane had no intention of, and no interest in, muscling in on Lissa's family?

*I wish I knew what you were thinking when you made that will.*

After they ate, Jane put on a SpongeBob SquarePants DVD for Daisy and retreated to the kitchen. Cleanup from their meal didn't take long. Then she plugged in her laptop and started work on some notes about next week's clients for Amy, her associate. She couldn't send them without knowing Lissa's Wi-Fi password—she'd need to ask Kyle. She set her laptop to hibernate and glanced at her watch. Eight o'clock already.

Jane hurried to the living room and found Daisy had turned off the TV and was reading a picture book.

"Sorry," Jane said. "I got caught up."

Daisy turned a page.

"What time do you usually go to bed?" She couldn't enforce a routine, as per protocol number two, without knowing what it was.

"Um, now, I think." Daisy closed her book and slipped off the couch.

Jane waited a few minutes before following her upstairs. When she reached Daisy's room, the little girl was already in her pj's and under the covers. She looked tiny, taking up hardly any space in the bed. A smudge of toothpaste marked the corner of her mouth. Jane had the unexpected urge to wipe it away with her finger.

"All set?" she asked instead.

Daisy nodded.

Jane felt as if there was something else she should be doing, but she had no idea what. She hesitated, the switch of the Little Mermaid bedside lamp gripped between her thumb and forefinger, aware of Daisy's expectant gaze. Feeling the weight of Lissa's anxiety.

At a sound from the doorway, she turned.

"Hi," Kyle said. He advanced into the room. "What's going on? Daisy, you should be asleep."

His tone was accusing—of Jane.

"I didn't know her bedtime," Jane said. *You didn't tell me.* She stepped back so he could take the prime position at Daisy's bedside.

"Lights out now." He bent to kiss his daughter's forehead. As he straightened, Daisy's eyes met Jane's. Was it her imagination, or was there a question in them?

At a loss, Jane waggled her fingers. "Good night, Daisy."

"Can you tell me a story?" Daisy asked.

Jane froze midwave. Kyle seemed similarly arrested. As if, like Jane, he'd never heard Daisy actually ask for anything before.

"It's late," Kyle reminded his daughter with a dismissive glance at Jane.

A glance that said, "This is my territory, keep out."

This whole damn town was Kyle's territory.

The you're-not-welcome message was one she'd heard, in varying degrees of subtlety, all through her youth. It had driven her out of town, and that had been a positive step. But these days, she wasn't a Slater kid trapped in a dysfunctional family. She no longer chose to respond to that rejection. At least, not in the way people like Kyle wanted.

"What kind of story?" she asked Daisy.

Kyle opened his mouth to object.

"One about Mommy," Daisy said.

Kyle closed his mouth with a snap.

"A funny one," Daisy added. She looked amazed at her own temerity. Why was she so reluctant to say what she wanted, whether it be her choice of dinner or a request for a story? Lissa had been devoted to her, and while Kyle might be a bit rigid, Jane doubted he was mean.

"Uh…" Jane racked her brain. Funny wasn't the first thing to come to mind. Then she hit on something. "I'll tell you about a time your Mommy came to stay with me in Denver."

"Did I come, too?" Daisy asked.

It was the nearest they'd come to a conversation all day.

"This was before you were born." Was it Jane's imagination, or did Kyle tense? "Your mom wanted to go dancing, so we got dressed in our best clothes—"

"Were they sparkly?" Daisy sounded wistful.

"I'm afraid not," Jane confessed. "But your mom wore a bright pink dress."

Daisy nodded, her lips pressed together in a slight upward curve.

Jane felt absurdly pleased she'd been able to give that satisfaction. "We went to a, uh, dancing place," she continued. It didn't feel right talking about a nightclub to a five-year-old.

"Like a ball?" Daisy asked. "Like in *Cinderella?*"

"Kind of. But with no princes." *No fairy tales here, folks*.

Daisy's disappointment was evident. Jane turned to exchange a rueful smile with Kyle…and found him scowling, his eyebrows drawn together in a dark slash.

"This is a funny story," she reminded him.

His scowl deepened.

Kyle Everson would find a way to disapprove if she helped an old lady across the street. Jane turned back to Daisy. "The, uh, dancing place was so full, they wouldn't let us in."

"Oh, no," Daisy whispered.

"Your mom was very upset, almost crying," Jane said, not just for dramatic effect. Lissa had always had a strong objection to not getting her way. "She really loved to dance."

Daisy nodded. "What did you do?"

"We went around the back and found an open window. Your mom figured it was the window of the lady's bathroom. We decided to climb in." Jane smiled at the memory—her friendship with Lissa had never been dull. "I lifted your mom up so she could reach the window." Lissa had been only five foot two as opposed to Jane's five-five. "She scrambled inside, quick as a flash."

Daisy's eyes were bright. "Then what?"

"She was supposed to lean back out the window so I could jump up and grab her hands, and she could pull me high enough to grab hold of the window," Jane said. She'd realized back then that part of the plan was flawed—it was hard to pull someone up—but Lissa had been confident. "But instead...your mommy disappeared," she said with a theatrical flourish.

Daisy gasped. "Was it magic?"

"Of course it wasn't," Kyle snapped.

His daughter's face dimmed.

What was his problem? He was glaring at Jane, his stance rigid, arms folded across his chest.

Jane allowed herself a second's glare back at him before she addressed Daisy. "I thought it must be magic, too. And maybe it was, because next minute, your mom appeared right behind me."

Daisy's little mouth hung open. "How come?"

"Turned out that open window was for the *men's* bathroom," Jane admitted. "When your mom climbed in, she landed right on top of the man who wouldn't let us in the front door. He'd gone on a potty break."

Daisy giggled. Actually giggled. It was the sweetest sound, like a wind chime in the hint of a summer breeze.

Jane sensed rather than saw Kyle's amazement. She smoothed the covers over Daisy's knees, then pulled her hand away. "He got a fright when your mom popped through that window—he was really mad." She chuckled, remembering the bouncer's bluster, made worse by his embarrassment at being caught with his pants down. "He dragged her back outside and yelled at both of us. Luckily, some nice guys— *people*—heard, and came to rescue us. And we all went out for ice cream—"

"That's it." Kyle's harsh interjection startled her. "Daisy, story's over. This light's going out now."

In the second before he snapped off the lamp, Jane glimpsed Daisy's hurt expression. "Kyle, there's no need to—"

"Downstairs," he ordered.

She should have refused. But his anger was palpable and she'd grown up with a father prone to anger. For Daisy's sake, she walked stiffly out of the room.

JANE WAITED FOR KYLE in the kitchen, her fist pressed to her chest to still her agitation. *Don't get involved, it can only lead to trouble.*

She'd known from Barb that Kyle and Daisy didn't get along, but she'd assumed that was just lack of familiarity. A matter of time.

In which case, it had made sense that she might serve as a buffer, a smoother of the waters, for a couple of weeks while they figured out a routine that involved some give-and-take.

But his reaction now had been totally unreasonable.

She let out a long, slow breath and scanned the room, focusing on the details. When Kyle and Lissa had bought the house, this room had looked and felt like what it was, a space tacked on to the back of the original cottage. They'd renovated, and widened the opening to the dining area, letting in more light. The kitchen sported rustic-style white cabinets with pine accents.

Jane ran herself a glass of water at the double sink and gulped it down.

"You have some nerve." Kyle spoke behind her, startling her.

Jane choked. She dumped the rest of the glass into the sink and turned to face him, still spluttering.

He closed the double doors that separated the dining area from the living room, presumably so Daisy wouldn't hear, before he strode across the polished floorboards.

"I ought to run you out of town right now," he growled, looming over her, as if he might make that threat a reality.

She found her voice. "Cut it out, Kyle. If you have an anger management problem, go punch a wall. Don't take it out on me, and *don't* take it out on Daisy."

"Anger management?" he said, incredulous. But not, now she thought about it, angry. "I'm not arguing with you, Jane, I'm ordering you. Don't share the sordid details of what you and Lissa got up to with my daughter."

It was a slap in the face, turning a harmless girls' night out into something *sordid,* just because of who she was. "You think that by telling Daisy that her mom climbed a window, I'm setting your daughter up for a career in breaking and entering?" she demanded. "For your information, the window was open, we weren't trying to avoid paying an entry charge—women were allowed in for free. We were jumping the line, that's all."

He blinked, as if he had no idea what she was talking about.

"I was telling your daughter a funny story," she said, "just like she asked. *You—*" she jabbed a finger at his chest "—need an attitude adjustment."

He grabbed her hand, his strong fingers wrapped around

hers. "Talking about that week is off-limits with my daughter. I know damn well Lissa lied to me, and you did, too."

She froze. He thought she'd been talking about *that* week?

"That night, the one I just mentioned to Daisy, was when Lissa was in college," Jane said slowly, to counter the rapid beating of her heart. "Before she got sick. She caught the bus from Fort Collins to Denver and stayed the weekend."

"Oh." He let go of her and ran his hand through his hair, disconcerted. "Are you sure?"

She nodded.

His gaze raked her face. Then he pinched the bridge of his nose. "In that case, I'm sorry. I was out of line."

An Everson apologizing to a Slater? Until this moment, she'd have said it would never happen.

"No problem." Jane realized he was still standing very close to her. For all that she'd accused him of an anger management problem, she hadn't for one second felt threatened. Still, she sidestepped around him, away from the counter. Suddenly drained, she pulled one of the rush-bottomed dining chairs out from the table and sat.

"How about we start over?" He opened the fridge and pulled out a Coors. "Want one?"

"No, thanks." Then, in case he thought she was rejecting a peace offering, she added, "I'm not a beer drinker."

He twisted the cap off his bottle. "There's no wine, sorry."

"I don't need anything. Thanks." She relaxed against the back of her chair.

Kyle pulled out a chair, turned it around and straddled it.

"So tell me, Jane," he said, his tone conversational, "what did happen that week?"

Jane's heart skipped a beat. "Excuse me?"

His mouth set in a grim line—so much for the peace offering. "The week Lissa came to stay with you while I was at that conference in San Diego." As if they didn't both know exactly which week he meant.

She played for time. "It was a conference on eco-friendly tourism developments, wasn't it? Did you ever get to use that stuff?" Her hope that she would get through this visit without giving him the opportunity to ask that question—again—now seemed stupidly naive.

"What happened?" he repeated.

The first time he'd asked that question had been six years ago, a few months after that week she'd had with Lissa in Denver. Kyle had phoned Jane out of the blue. He'd said Lissa wasn't herself—she was secretive, moody—and he thought there was more to it than pregnancy hormones.

Jane had been a better liar back then. She'd pretended she had no idea what was wrong, insisted nothing had happened. Her loyalty had been to Lissa. Not to Kyle, who'd made his contempt for her plain from the moment they'd met.

Now, she wanted to say "Nothing," but the word wouldn't come out. She sat there, opening and closing her mouth like a stunned goldfish. What few Slater deception skills she'd possessed had apparently rusted over.

"Silence—that's progress," Kyle said grimly. "How about we put an end to this charade and you tell me what really went on?"

She might struggle to lie, but she didn't consider telling him the truth, not even for half a second.

"Lissa and I spent a lot of time talking that week," she said. "We went out to dinner. No nightclubbing, no parties."

His brown eyes searched her face. "You're lying," he said, disgusted. Yes, she was lying, if only by omission.

"Let's try another question." He set his beer bottle down on the table so calmly, she knew she should be worried. "Do you think Daisy looks like Lissa?"

Her stomach lurched. Had he guessed? Or did he some-how *know? I should have stayed in Denver. Should never have risked this.*

"I, uh, suppose so." Jane licked her lips, and saw him

catalogue the gesture. And the anxiety that triggered it. She wouldn't last five minutes under his scrutiny if she acted like a nervous wreck. "She has Lissa's hair coloring," she said more firmly.

"Going by her kindergarten class, most kids have fair hair at this age," he said.

"If you say so." Jane's childhood had never brimmed with Kodak moments, but in the one school photo she recalled, from around third grade, she'd had fair hair herself. She didn't remember when it had darkened to its current brown. Maybe around the time she became friends with Lissa.

"There's not much Everson in Daisy's features, is there?" Kyle said.

"Lots of people don't look like their family," she said, feeling her way. "Take my sister, Cat—she's a redhead, the rest of us are brunette."

"Isn't Cat the one who—" He stopped.

Jane felt heat in her cheeks. He must have heard, doubtless from his dad, how Jane's mother used to sleep with men for cash. There'd been gossip, over the years, suggesting maybe Cat wasn't a Slater, but Jane had never believed it. Her mom's…activities hadn't been a regular thing, only when money was particularly tight. Her discreet liaisons would never have come to anyone's attention, least of all Police Chief Charles Everson's, if Jane's father hadn't decided to boost the earning potential of those trysts by blackmailing a couple of the guys involved.

"Isn't Cat the one who *what?*" Jane forced herself to ask coldly. Maybe, if she pushed, Kyle would back off the conversation altogether.

He didn't react. More out of preoccupation than courtesy, it seemed. He sat, deep in thought, his expression not so much suspicious as…bleak. Jane's heart clenched. Okay, so she didn't like the guy. But he was the victim of a deception in which she'd played a part.

She wondered again how much he knew, and how much was a clever guess by that razor-sharp mind of his. She replayed his previous question in her head. *There's not much Everson in Daisy's features, is there?*

Realization hit, her assumptions shaken up by a kaleidoscope, to settle in a completely different picture.

"You think Daisy's not your daughter," she blurted.

## CHAPTER FOUR

KYLE'S FACE WAS A STUDY in conflict. In denial and longing. "Am I right?" he asked.

"No!" Jane's heart thumped so loudly, she wondered how he couldn't hear it.

He ran a hand around the back of his neck. "Are you saying you know for sure that Daisy is my daughter?"

The question sat stark between them.

"Yes, I am. Kyle…" She would need to tread carefully if she didn't want to lie to him any more than she had already. It would be even harder face-to-face than it had been on the phone. "Lissa was faithful to you."

He pushed himself off his chair, paced toward the oven. "How do you know?"

"I can't know for sure," Jane admitted. "But she never gave any indication she'd even thought about cheating. And, Kyle, Lissa wasn't perfect, but I don't believe she'd have done that." During that long-ago phone call she'd guessed he suspected Lissa of an affair—but it had never occurred to her he might also consider Daisy's paternity to be in doubt. Had he harbored that suspicion since way back then?

"I went to the clinic with her, she had the IVF treatment," Jane said. "I have to assume those were your sperm the lab pulled out of the freezer." Kyle and Lissa had used fresh sperm on earlier attempts, but they'd also frozen some on Lissa's insistence, in case something happened to impair Kyle's fertility.

"So why did she have a round of treatment without telling me?" he demanded. "When we signed the papers giving each other total control of our frozen 'assets,' it was in case one of us died or was incapacitated. Not so one of us could go ahead without the other knowing."

He would undoubtedly hate that Jane had heard the wealth of hurt behind his words. Jane thought back to how she'd found him earlier today, in the café, with his father and brother and Daisy. Sure, Charles was a narrow-minded old goat and Gabe was a bit of a mystery. But there was no denying those guys had a powerful bond. Family was a huge deal for them. Unlike for her.

What Jane knew would change everything for Kyle.

"Maybe…" She hesitated, aware her next words were crucial. "Maybe Lissa didn't tell you because you'd said you didn't want to try again." Lissa hadn't told Jane until afterward that Kyle didn't know about her plan. She'd said they'd had the appointment booked for weeks, then Kyle had been called away on business. Lissa didn't want to miss the appointment, since she'd been taking the drugs to prepare her uterus for the implanting of the embryos….

Jane closed her eyes briefly. Daisy's conception was only the start of a long list of wrongs on Lissa's part. "Kyle, what's done is done. How about you focus on the fact that Daisy was the result, and she *is* your daughter."

He searched her face as he drummed his fingers on the table. Then, with some effort, he said, "Maybe you're right."

"Can I have that in writing?" she asked lightly, steering away from the potential quagmire where further questioning might lead. "I don't think anyone in this town has spoken those words to me before."

He rolled his eyes, but not in a hostile way, and she had the distinct sense of having dodged a bullet. She reached across for Kyle's beer and took a swig.

"I thought you don't drink beer." But his protest was mild, as if, like her, relief had the upper hand.

When she set the bottle down, Kyle took a drink himself. He nursed the bottle in his hands, staring at the label.

"The thing is," he said slowly, "there was always a chance that Lissa's ability to conceive naturally would come back. The negative effects that chemo have on fertility can wear off."

Ugh, she'd hoped they were done with this. "I didn't know that."

"Lissa wasn't willing to wait a few years to see if that happened," he said. "And since IVF with frozen eggs was a long shot back then, she wanted us to start sooner rather than later." He raked a hand through his dark hair, leaving it spikier than Jane would have thought hair that short could be. "If Lissa had slept with someone else before that week…maybe she was already pregnant with someone else's baby, so she faked going for fertility treatment to pass Daisy off as mine."

Which begged the question as to why the baby couldn't have been his if it had been conceived earlier…but Jane wasn't about to inquire into the state of his and Lissa's sex life. "I took Lissa to the fertility clinic myself," she reminded him.

Her adamancy shut him up, but she suspected a man as smart as he was would soon start thinking in other directions. She needed to close down this discussion. *Now.*

She mustered every ounce of hard-won credibility. "Kyle, I swear, unless someone made a labeling error on a test tube, Daisy is your daughter."

He held her gaze with those dark eyes. Somehow, she managed not to look away. Behind him, through the window, the silhouette of one of the pinyon trees that gave the town its name was barely visible in the moments before dusk turned to darkness.

Just when she thought she couldn't last another second, Kyle nodded. He tipped the beer up and drained the last of the bottle.

"Thank you, Jane," he said, sounding almost formal. "You

put my mind at rest, and I appreciate it. Maybe we can bury
the hatchet for the next couple of weeks—get this right for
Daisy." Unexpectedly, one side of his mouth quirked. He
sounded as if the overture were genuine. He sounded...hope-
ful.

Jane made an indistinct sound that may or may not have
been a commitment to hatchet-burying. If Kyle knew the
truth, he'd be back to despising her in a nanosecond.

Better to keep her distance, where no one's hatchet could
cause any trouble. It was better for Kyle, better for Daisy,
better for everyone, that Jane's secret should remain a secret.

THE NEXT DAY, SUNDAY, Kyle took advantage of Jane's presence to head over to the new house and get some work done
while Jane looked after Daisy.

He skipped church, which his father called to query in the
afternoon. "There's an election coming up, you know, and
folk like to see the mayor in church."

As if Kyle wasn't aware he was facing a serious challenge
at the ballot box. He probably should have gone to church,
on several counts, but the house was so close to being finished, a solid twelve-hour stint would make a big difference.

A local construction firm had built the place, but he'd chosen to do the finishing himself. Partly for cost reasons—like
most building projects, it had blown its budget long ago, and
Kyle earned a lot less as mayor than he had in his landscape
architecture practice. The other reason was that his dad often
reminisced about the satisfaction he'd derived from doing the
finishing on their family home. Kyle had thought it would be
a nice memory to share with Daisy in years to come. Not that
she showed much interest in the place right now.

Today, the work gave him more pleasure than usual. Maybe
due to the lightness in his heart that he hadn't realized had
been lacking. Everything felt easier, simpler.

He had Jane to thank for that.

He'd never trusted her before, but when she'd told him last night that Daisy was his daughter, he'd known at his very core that she was telling the truth.

He could have ordered a DNA test at any time these last few years to attain that surety, but he'd decided long ago not to go down that route. Though the suspicion of infidelity had continued to niggle, he'd thought he was handling it. He hadn't realized what a burden the doubt had been until Jane took it away.

Not that everything was crystal clear. He trusted his instincts enough to know there was something fishy about Lissa's "vacation" in Denver with Jane. But the big question of whether he was Daisy's father had been answered. He could let the rest go.

Including his longtime suspicion of Jane. He would make a fresh start with her, for Daisy's sake. He stopped to buy a bottle of wine at the grocery store on his way home at nearly nine that night with the thought they would chat over a drink.

But when he arrived at the cottage, Daisy was sound asleep, as expected, and Jane was in her room, with the door closed. Not as expected. He paused outside her door, eyeing the strip of light seeping beneath it. He probably shouldn't disturb her—he, of all people, knew how tiring a day of Daisy's near-silence could be.

They could have their fresh start tomorrow.

BUT ON MONDAY MORNING, they didn't get a chance to talk before Daisy woke up and the scramble to get ready for kindergarten started. Jane seemed pensive as she helped Daisy assemble cereal and milk, then ate toast with peanut butter at the kitchen counter for her own breakfast.

At quarter to eight, Kyle drove them all to Pinyon Ridge Elementary School. Mornings were busy on the roads, as the tourists got started on their hiking and sightseeing. It took a good three minutes to drive down Main Street. Three silent minutes—Jane was still munching on the last of her toast, and Daisy was her usual quiet self.

When they reached the school, Daisy had her door open almost before Kyle stopped the car. Did that mean she was desperate to get away from him, or merely that she wanted to resume a normal routine, having been off kindergarten all last week? He held off on scolding his daughter over the premature door opening.

"I'll introduce you to the teacher," he told Jane. "That way you'll have no trouble picking Daisy up at the end of the day."

They walked inside, Daisy between him and Jane. Jane drew several glances. At first, Kyle assumed it was the usual small-town curiosity. Then he noticed the dads were looking a lot harder than the moms. He checked Jane out with a sidelong glance. She looked bright and fresh in her cherry-pink sundress with a white sweater slung over her shoulders. Definitely worth a second glance. Maybe even a third.

Kyle restricted himself to just the one.

He led the way to the first of the two kindergarten classrooms. Mrs. Mason, Daisy's teacher, put down the stapler she was using to attach a poster to the noticeboard and came to greet them.

"Daisy, dear, welcome back. Hello, Kyle."

Daisy threw her arms around the teacher, clinging to her as if no one else had offered her a hug all week. Mrs. Mason hugged her back, then looked at Jane over the top of her spectacles. "Now, who have we here?"

"I'm Jane Slater, Mrs. Mason." Of course, the older woman would have been on staff when Jane was at school.

"Ja-*nelle?*" Mrs. Mason asked.

"It's Jane now."

"Janelle Slater." No mistaking the disapproval in the usually warm Mrs. Mason's face. "When did you get back into town? Is Darren with you?"

"I arrived Saturday. I don't know where my brother is."

Kyle couldn't conceive of not knowing where his family was.

"That boy was the worst student I ever had—he could disrupt a class like nobody else." Mrs. Mason tutted. "You weren't much better, young lady."

Ouch. Kyle winced on Jane's behalf. She squared her shoulders and said nothing, her gaze somewhere over the teacher's shoulder. Her withdrawal was almost tangible. It reminded him of something….

"Did you ever make anything of yourself?" Mrs. Mason asked. "You had a brain under all that attitude, you know."

Was that meant to be a compliment?

"I have my own business in Denver," Jane said.

Her company had something to do with helping women, Kyle recalled.

The teacher harrumphed. "That's not so bad…assuming it's legitimate."

"You're too kind." Jane pressed her lips together as if she regretted the sarcasm, regretted rising to Mrs. Mason's bait.

Jane's achievement was more than "not so bad," Kyle thought, especially if this had been the attitude of the people who were supposed to guide her. She couldn't have been *that* disruptive in school—he knew from Lissa they'd scored identically on their SATs.

Mrs. Mason hadn't missed the sarcasm. "Watch your step, young lady," she said. "Because you can bet I'll be watching, too, and so will plenty of others. This town doesn't need any more trouble from your family."

"Jane's a visitor to our town and a guest in my house," Kyle said sharply. "She's been away a long time, so I hope you'll extend her the kind of welcome we pride ourselves on in Pinyon Ridge."

The kind of welcome he hadn't given her himself, either at Lissa's funeral or when she arrived on Saturday. He'd been a jerk.

Jane had gone quiet—a combination of hurt at the teacher's remarks and gratitude for his intervention, he guessed.

Mrs. Mason, who'd traipsed the streets of Pinyon Ridge door-knocking to support Kyle's first mayoral campaign, huffed and bristled like an outraged hedgehog.

"Let's go," he told Jane. "Have a nice day, Mrs. Mason." He suspected he'd lost her vote. He couldn't afford to throw away votes...but he couldn't let that kind of behavior slide.

Back in the car, he drove to the Eating Post.

"I thought we could have coffee," he said to Jane. "We can go somewhere else if you prefer, but I have a standing order here on school mornings."

Inside, Micki noted their arrival—she jerked her chin at a cup, already lidded, on the circular end of the counter next to the supplies of cream and sugar.

Kyle picked it up, raised it to her in thanks. "What will you have?" he asked Jane. "We can sit down."

"I don't want coffee," she said. "You got out of the car so fast, I didn't get a chance to say so."

Huh? She sounded ticked off.

"We need to talk about what this period of shared care of Daisy will entail," he pointed out. "You're supposed to be helping 'settle' Daisy, but what does that mean?" He pulled one of the laminated menus from the holder on the counter. "Do you want something to eat?"

"No. Thank you," she said. "How about I figure out a plan for the next couple of weeks, then run it by you?" She glanced toward the door, as if she were anxious to be out of here.

Suddenly, he figured out the reason for her discomfort. "Look, I'm sorry Mrs. Mason was so rude," he said. "Just ignore her."

"Not your fault. I'm used to it." She tugged her sweater tighter around her shoulders. "Can we go? I have some things I need to do."

In Pinyon Ridge? Really?

He tried again. "If you're worried Micki or anyone else here will speak to you that way, I'll make sure they don't."

Her chin shot up, and she stared as if she couldn't believe he would do that for her.

He gave her a nod, intended to convey reassurance. Because, contrary to her belief, he was a nice guy who knew what was right and did it.

"Butt out, Kyle," she ordered.

"Hey!" What happened to gratitude?

"I'm happy to do what Lissa wanted as far as Daisy's concerned," she said. "And if you and I can work peaceably together the next couple of weeks, so much the better. But we're not friends, and you're not responsible for me. So let's keep out of each other's space."

"I'm trying to be *nice*," he said. "I know I wasn't much more welcoming than Mrs. Mason when you showed up last week, but I'm trying for a fresh start here."

Micki directed a curious gaze at them. Kyle took a sip of his coffee through the hole in the lid.

"A fresh start like the one you said you wanted on Saturday night, right before you accused me of lying?" Jane asked.

Damn. "Okay, I'm sorry about that. Look, Jane, you're right, we're not friends. But Lissa's death reminded me life's too short to hang on to old resentments. I thought for Daisy's sake we could at least be friend*ly*. But if you don't want that, no problem."

He stuck the menu back in its holder and left.

JANE OBSERVED THE STIFFNESS in Kyle's shoulders as he walked out the door of the café. She let out a long breath, relaxed her own stance. It had been a long time since she'd put herself in a situation where someone could reject her, so accepting his overture had never been an option. But it had been harder than expected to turn him down. Much harder.

When he'd defended her from *Meanie Mason,* as Jane and

her sister Cat used to call the teacher, she'd felt a strange mushiness inside. She wasn't used to anyone taking her side, not since Lissa.

But the secret he didn't know existed meant she couldn't commit to any kind of...of *friendship*. Because it would be gone in sixty seconds if he knew the truth.

Besides, she'd grown used to relying only on herself.

"Coffee?" Micki called.

Jane supposed she couldn't stand there without buying anything. "A cappuccino, thanks." At least by the time Micki made the drink, Kyle would be long gone.

While she waited at the pick-up area, she surveyed the café.

The place wasn't that busy, but it gave the impression of a recent rush. A middle-aged woman was busing tables, and a half-empty dishwasher tray of clean cups sat on a shelf behind the bar. Micki must have been too busy to put them away— she had a couple of coffees on the go at the big Italian machine on the counter as she chatted to a customer.

Jane moved to the magazine rack and pulled out the latest issue of an outdoor adventure title. She flipped through glossy pages with photos of kayakers in foamy white waters and climbers hanging off cliff faces.

Micki spoke right next to her. "Where do you want this?"

"Oh." Jane eyed the speckle-glazed brown cup and saucer she was holding. "I forgot to say I wanted it to go."

"I could make you another one," Micki said, "but why don't you take a load off at that table nearest the counter, and I'll join you for a chat."

The offer was unexpected. And after offending Kyle, it seemed a chance to make amends, however indirect. Jane sat at the table Micki suggested. Micki issued a couple of instructions to her staffer, then took the seat opposite.

"This is my favorite time of day," she said. "The breathing space after the morning rush."

"Sounds like business is good," Jane said.

"It is, so long as I work like a dog." Micki stretched her arms and clasped them behind her head. She gave a little groan. "The old shoulder muscles tend to knot when I hunch over that coffee machine."

They talked for a couple of minutes about the café business. When the door from the street opened, Jane glanced over and saw Kyle's father. Ugh, this town was full of people she'd rather not see.

"Morning, Charles," Micki called. "The usual?"

"Good morning, Micki." The ex-police chief didn't look thrilled to see the woman who would cook his breakfast in cahoots with a Slater. It took him a moment to mutter, "Hello, Jane."

At least he'd got her name right. "Good morning, Charles," Jane said, equally frostily.

Micki snickered.

He paused next to their table. "How's my granddaughter?" An unmistakable whiff of territorialism.

"She's doing fine." An exaggeration. Daisy might have let slip that one, precious giggle on Saturday night, but she'd since reverted to her somber self.

"Don't forget to tell her she needs to speak up when people talk to her," Charles ordered. "Folk will think she's rude."

Typical of the old coot. Indignation surged within Jane on Daisy's behalf. "Folk would be wrong," she said.

He frowned. "Right or wrong, a negative perception is hard to shake. You should know that."

Jane stiffened. "Anyone with a grain of sensitivity would understand that Daisy's a little girl who just lost her mother."

He harrumphed.

"Sit down, Charles, I'll get your breakfast started," Micki said.

With a warm smile at Micki, he headed for the booth where he'd been sitting when Jane arrived in town on Saturday.

"One of my best customers," Micki said, following Jane's gaze following Charles.

"Shame about the stick up his backside," Jane muttered.

To her surprise, Micki hooted a laugh. "All the Eversons are a bit uptight," she said. "Comes with the genes. Even Gabe has the habit, though he controls it better now that he's practicing Christian tolerance. Thing is, they're such good guys, they get away with it." She flipped a sugar sachet between her fingers and said casually, "They're probably Pinyon Ridge's most eligible bachelors, if you're interested."

"I'm not interested." Jane eyed that sugar sachet, rotating much faster than Micki had spoken. "But you clearly are."

The sachet landed on the table. "I…no…what do you mean?" Micki demanded.

"Sorry, it's none of my business. My professional instincts kicked in."

"*What* professional instincts?" Micki said, aghast.

Jane held up both hands in a gesture of peace. "Reading the subtext behind people's words and facial expressions is my job." Or rather, it was the first part of what she did for her clients—assessing the messages they didn't even know they were giving out. The second part was helping them rewrite those messages. "Don't worry, I won't tell anyone."

Micki leaned across the table. "But you can tell me what I did, right? How did I give it away?"

"It was just an impression. Your tone and words were casual, but your gesture was nervous." Jane picked up the sugar sachet and flipped it to illustrate.

Micki eyed it with dislike. "Do you think anyone else might have noticed? I mean generally, not just now."

"Hard to say," Jane said. "Not if this is the biggest clue you've given."

Micki puffed out a relieved breath.

"Not consciously, anyway," Jane added honestly. Because people often made judgments on subconscious observations.

Micki groaned.

"The Everson men aren't sensitive enough to pick up on something like that," Jane assured her. Except maybe Gabe. Micki had brought up Gabe's name just now, but Kyle had suggested he was in here most mornings for his coffee—was that maybe more than just a coffee run? "Is it Kyle or Gabe you like?" she asked.

"So how *is* Daisy doing?" Micki asked, a blatant change of subject. "She's such a quiet little thing, it's hard to know what she's thinking." Of course, it might not really be a change of subject if Micki had ambitions to be Daisy's stepmother.

And why not? Kyle and Lissa had been divorced for years. Someone like Micki might loosen Kyle up. A stepmother could be good for Daisy.

"She doesn't say much," Jane said, "but when she does talk it's usually about her mom. I don't know if she grasps the fact that Lissa's not coming back."

"She and Lissa were inseparable," Micki said soberly. "I mean, sure, Daisy went to school, and Lissa went out with friends or on dates—though only ever after Daisy was asleep. She was protective, I guess."

"Were you and Lissa friends?" Jane asked, aware of a twinge of jealousy. *Stupid.*

Micki shrugged as she stood up. "Since you'll probably read my subtext, I'll be honest and say no. Lissa liked to control the people she was in relationships with. Not in a bad way. At least, not mostly. I like my independence."

"Me, too," Jane murmured. She'd never thought of Lissa as controlling. But it made sense. Jane had promised to keep their secret, but maybe Lissa had felt she didn't have enough control over Jane to be able to trust her. And so she'd pulled back from their friendship.

"It's great Daisy spent so much time with Lissa," Jane said, trying to be positive. "Daisy must have felt very loved."

"I think Daisy adored her even more than most kids adore

their mom." Micki splayed her fingers—ringless, with her unpainted nails cut sensibly short—on the table. "But maybe in a way that wasn't quite healthy."

"What do you mean?"

"There always seemed to be, I don't know, an *edge* to their closeness," Micki said. "As if Lissa had something to prove. Don't get me wrong, Lissa loved Daisy. But, maybe because of the divorce, I don't know, her devotion seemed more about possessiveness than closeness."

Something flared deep inside Jane, some kind of protective instinct. She pressed a hand to her middle, willed the sensation to subside. *No way, I'm not going there.* Lissa was dead, and if there had been any problem in her relationship with Daisy—and who's to say Micki was right about that?—the problem was dead, too. Jane's job was to help Daisy and her dad into a new routine, then to get out of town.

Rule number five of her looking-after-Daisy protocol just happened to be rule number one in Jane's life: don't get too attached.

Developing feelings for Lissa's daughter was not an option.

## CHAPTER FIVE

JANE ATTRIBUTED THE EASE with which the rest of her two weeks passed to her strict adherence to her protocol.

She was decisive and predictable—rules one and two—having established a routine after that first Monday, the day she'd turned down Kyle's offer of a fresh start. Each morning, she helped Daisy get ready, drove her to kindergarten, then had coffee at Micki's. Charles Everson's arrival was her cue to leave the café each day, after which she spent an hour or two with Hal while Barb ran errands, then checked in with her clients by phone or email. By the time she'd done all that, it was time to pick up Daisy from school. The rest of the day passed in preparing dinner for the two of them, then getting Daisy to bed. On time.

Being used to reading people and assessing their personal styles, Jane felt she'd had no trouble getting down to Daisy's level without condescension—number three in the protocol—and she certainly hadn't promised anything she couldn't deliver. She hadn't promised anything at all.

Lastly, although there were times she was tempted to stray into things that weren't her concern—to ask questions or share things about herself that might coax Daisy to talk—she managed to pull back. She stuck with a "friendly babysitter" manner that didn't encourage Daisy to get too close to someone who didn't plan to stick around. Definitely no attachment.

If she assessed "Project Daisy" objectively, Jane thought, as she pulled into the cottage driveway after school on Friday, with Daisy in the backseat, she'd rate it a success.

With one fairly major exception.

The routine she'd cultivated didn't include Kyle. Tonight, her last night in Pinyon Ridge, she knew he planned to arrive home early. Charles was hosting a farewell barbecue for Jane at his place—Micki had suggested it to Kyle when he'd called into the Eating Post for his coffee a couple of days ago. She'd badgered him until he'd given in, then she'd promptly added herself to the guest list. Jane had to admire her determination.

So, yes, Kyle would be home early this evening. But every other night he'd walked in the door at five to eight, just in time to say good-night to his daughter, having gone to work on the new house after putting in a full day at city hall. Then he'd microwave himself a meal, or reheat some of what Jane had cooked. At which point Jane would retire to her bedroom to read or do some work.

Jane was perfectly happy to see so little of Kyle. But though she had little experience of normal family life, she suspected it was a problem that Daisy seemed equally content.

Jane couldn't help thinking the way she and Kyle had made things work—largely due to her desire to avoid proximity to him—wasn't what Lissa would have had in mind. Lissa had been an only child, like Daisy, and she'd been devoted to both her parents. As they were to her.

"Maybe we should call in to your dad's office to remind him about tonight's barbecue," she suggested as she followed Daisy inside. It would mean going out again, and no doubt Kyle would consider it odd. But once they got to Charles's house, he would be in demand from his dad, his brother and Micki—Daisy wouldn't get a look in.

Daisy wasn't the kind of kid to say an outright no to the suggestion, but she made a negative noise.

Jane dithered. Should she force the issue? Was it too late to engineer a token conversation at this stage? It wasn't as if Kyle was a bad father. He was working to get a new home ready for his daughter—that was a good thing. And when the house was done, in a few weeks' time—and after next month's election—he'd have a lot more time for Daisy.

She would let it go, she decided. But before she left town tomorrow morning she'd tell Kyle he needed to get home earlier *every* night, even if it meant the house took a little longer to finish.

She set out cookies and milk while Daisy took her backpack upstairs, then called the girl down for her snack. It took a couple of minutes for Daisy to arrive, and when she entered the kitchen, she was carrying a red spiral-bound notebook.

"This is Mommy's book," she said accusingly.

Jane put the cookie jar back in the pantry and closed the door. "That's right, it is. Did you go into my room, Daisy?"

Daisy looked sheepish. "I saw it on your bed when I went past."

Jane decided to let the invasion of privacy slide. "It's your mom's diary. I found it when I was tidying her things." Barb had asked Jane to start sorting through Lissa's effects—she was too upset to do it herself and she didn't think it was right for Lissa's ex-husband to go through her belongings. "I'm going to give it to your nana to look after until you're old enough to read it."

Daisy bit her lip. She set the book on the table next to her glass of milk while she climbed onto a chair. "I opened it."

"You opened the diary?" Jane pulled out a chair opposite and sat. "That's okay this time, Daisy, but people's diaries are private and in the future you shouldn't peek."

Daisy stared down at her cookie, her cheeks flushed.

"Did you read it?" Jane asked, alarmed. "Did something upset you?" Daisy couldn't read, could she? Jane hadn't read the diary at all herself, beyond opening the notebook to verify what it was.

"I found a picture," Daisy mumbled.

*Oh, heck.* Jane tried to imagine what kind of image might

have disturbed her so badly. "Maybe you should show it to me."

The speed with which Daisy flipped open the book and pulled out a photo suggested she'd been hoping for the invitation.

Jane took the snapshot from her.

"It's you, with your mommy and daddy, when you were a baby," she said, relieved. "It's lovely." Lissa was holding the newborn Daisy, wrapped in white, with a white woolen hat on her tiny head, two wrinkled fists tucked beneath her chin. Lissa and Kyle were beaming down at her, entranced.

Jane cleared her throat to ease a sudden scratchiness.

"I think…" Daisy murmured, so quietly Jane had to strain to hear.

"What do you think?" she asked, when nothing else was forthcoming.

"Mommy loves me," Daisy whispered.

Jane's jaw sagged; she snapped her mouth shut. "Of course she loves you, Daisy. Always." The use of the present tense felt awkward, but anything else was too hard.

Daisy nodded, head down, her eyes focused on the edge of the table.

"Look at me, Daisy," Jane ordered.

Daisy's natural obedience had her complying.

"Your mommy loves you a lot. I'm sure she told you that." *Please let Lissa have told you that.*

Daisy nodded.

Phew.

"Sometimes," Daisy said, "she comes into my bedroom at night when I'm pretending to be asleep, and she cries."

Jane froze. Was she saying Lissa was *haunting* her?

Damn Kyle, why was he never around? How was Jane supposed to handle a haunted five-year-old? Her throat was dry, her palms sweaty. "You know, sweetie, your mom's not really here in this house now."

"I know," Daisy said. "She's deaded."

"I—uh, yes." Jane grabbed Daisy's glass and took a swig of milk before she remembered she hated the stuff. She swallowed a gag. "So when you say your mom comes into your bedroom…"

"Before," Daisy said. "Before the car crash. She can't come now."

"N-no, that's right." Jane felt as if she were groping through fog. "Maybe you were only dreaming about her coming—" She broke off at the uncharacteristically mutinous set of Daisy's mouth. "Okay." She let out a slow breath. Beneath the table, she rubbed her damp palms against her jeans. "Okay, so your mom was crying. That…that's because mommies worry about their children growing up and, uh, leaving their mommies. They think about how much they're going to miss them and it makes them cry." She was fairly sure her own mom had never had that kind of thought. *Please, let her believe me.*

Slowly, Daisy nodded.

*Thank you.*

"My daddy doesn't love me," Daisy said.

The downturn of her sweet little mouth grabbed Jane by the heart and squeezed. Hard. She resisted as long as she could—a pathetic few seconds. Then she undid two weeks of avoiding physical contact by reaching, reluctantly, across the table for Daisy's hand. It was so small, half the size of her own.

"He does love you, Daisy. I promise." To her horror, not only did her voice shake, but the words also lacked conviction. Kyle was determined to provide a home for his daughter, no doubt about that. But had his doubts that he was Daisy's father compromised his ability to love her?

Daisy shook her head. "You don't love me, either."

"I, uh…" Danger signals flashed red lights and rang bells in Jane's head. *Runaway train, get out of the way.*

She couldn't do it. Though her fingers were slippery; she held tighter to Daisy's. "You and I don't know each other that well, but we're, uh, friends." It was like trying to stop that runaway train by waving a handkerchief at it. Useless.

"Mrs. Mason said you're going away." Daisy pulled her hand out of Jane's and reclaimed her milk glass.

"You knew that. We're going to Grandpa's house tonight because it's my last night, remember?" Hadn't she explained the reason for the barbecue clearly? "When I got here, I told you I was here for two weeks, and last Monday I reminded you I'd be leaving on Saturday. Tomorrow morning."

Daisy's blank look told Jane, too late, that days and dates meant nothing to a five-year-old. "I need to go home to Denver," she explained. "But you can come visit me." Chances were, once Jane left, Daisy would forget all about her.

The thought didn't bring the relief she'd expected.

"Doesn't matter." Daisy's voice turned distant, her demeanor so completely closed it was disturbing.

And familiar.

Jane recognized the expression she had cultivated herself as a girl. The aloof stare that said, "I'm not here, not listening to your hurtful words."

All of a sudden, Daisy's introverted nature made perfect sense. Jane couldn't believe she—a supposed expert in reading people—hadn't figured it out before.

Daisy withdrew to protect herself from rejection by the parents whose love she doubted. From rejection by Charles Everson, who worried her quietness might be regarded as bad manners, among goodness knows what other subtle criticisms. By Jane, who was about to leave.

Jane wanted to haul Daisy into her arms and squeeze her tight. Assure her she was loved, as every child should be.

But...

Lissa was gone, her love only a memory. Jane had little faith in Charles's ability to love Daisy the way she deserved. And Kyle...Kyle was going about fatherhood the wrong way, and Jane had been so intent on protecting herself and her secret, she hadn't confronted him about it.

And now she was about to abandon Daisy to this life—this *half life*—of protecting herself from hurt. Jane pulled her thoughts up. *My life's not a half life.* Okay, wrong term. But Daisy shouldn't have to grow up that way—no kid should.

"Get in the car, Daisy." Jane's voice was tight.

Daisy blinked. "I'm eating my cookie."

"You're going to visit with Nana for an hour."

Daisy's face lit up at the thought of Barb—the only person whose love was beyond question. Though even Barb had been forced to pull back from Daisy, due to Hal's condition.

"But where are you going?" Daisy asked anxiously, as if Jane might already be on her way to Denver.

"To see your dad."

Daisy's eyes widened, more at Jane's gritted teeth than the actual words, Jane suspected.

"Um…" Daisy said uncertainly.

"Nothing to worry about," Jane assured her. "It's just, your daddy loves you, Daisy, and I'm not leaving here until you know it."

*Ding-ding-ding.* The alarm bells again. This time sounding a warning that rule number four of her protocol might be about to be shattered. *Don't promise what you can't deliver.*

THE MEETING OF THE COUNCIL'S economic development and planning committee had started late. Five minutes in, it went south, when two of the councilors shared objections from "a concerned citizen" about the proposal Kyle was developing for the future of Pinyon Ridge.

"Would this concerned citizen happen to be Wayne Tully?" Kyle asked.

He didn't need an answer; the councilors' truculent expressions gave it away. Tully had served three terms as mayor before Kyle took the gold chain off him, and now he was running again. His campaign involved playing on the boom time Pinyon Ridge had enjoyed before Kyle took over, and blaming the entire global financial crisis on Kyle's term in office. Which would be laughable if a whole bunch of people whose wallets were hurting didn't respond to that kind of propaganda.

They seemed to have forgotten that under Tully, the town's budget had been spent acquiring products and services from businesses run by Tully's friends, rather than on long-term plans that would build a sustainable future.

For a town that sold itself to visitors on the strength of its natural beauty and pure environment, committing to a carefully planned development program that allowed growth while retaining history and protecting and enhancing the landscape should be a no-brainer.

Instead, certain councilors thought the town should aim to fill the coffers with tourist dollars as fast as possible, without worrying too much about how the place might look with a bunch of tacky high-rises obscuring the view. Said highrises would doubtless be built by contractors who were good friends of Wayne Tully, using cheap, temporary labor from out of town. Kyle's vision was for a slower pace of development, employing local workers—craftspeople—and attracting new families to the area to fill any gaps in the workforce.

Whose dumb idea had it been to appoint a cross section of political views to the economic development and planning committee, rather than stacking it with people who agreed with the mayor? *Oh, yeah, that would have been mine.* Kyle had taken office determined to be different from Tully and his rampant cronyism. Now, the thought of easy committee meetings with a bunch of yes-men made a hell of a lot of sense.

When his secretary interrupted, his first reaction was relief. "Kyle, Jane Slater is here. Apparently, it's about Daisy, and it's urgent." She said *Jane Slater* with obvious disapproval.

Whatever the reason for Jane's visit, it couldn't be life or death, or even serious injury—the police or fire department would have contacted him directly. Still, the thought of escaping this deadlocked meeting had him getting to his feet.

"You guys finish the discussion of Tully's letter without me," he told the committee. "I'll summarize when I get back."

"How can you summarize if you're not here?" his deputy asked.

"I'll just repeat the waffle Wayne Tully's been spouting since he lost the last election." Kyle strode from the room.

He switched his mind into dad mode as he entered his office. The change in gears hadn't got any easier over the past couple of weeks.

With Jane leaving, he'd need to pick up his game.

She was inspecting the photo on the wall behind his desk, taken by the *Pinyon Ridge Gazette* the day he was sworn in as mayor. Him, Gabe and their dad, all smiling.

She wore denim cutoffs, which showed off her slim legs. Kyle sighed. No matter how few words they exchanged, no matter how much she irritated him, he couldn't stop noticing her…physical details. A three-year stint of celibacy probably didn't help on that score.

"What's the problem with Daisy?" he asked abruptly.

Instead of answering, she pointed to the photo. "The town triumvirate—mayor, police chief and pastor. You must be so proud."

That was definitely not admiration in her voice.

Over the past two weeks, he'd kept his distance from her, in every sense—except for those pesky physical observations. The distance thing had been her call, and it had annoyed him when she'd made it, but she'd been right. He didn't need an argument now when she was about to leave town.

"Daisy?" he prompted.

She came around from behind his desk. Her white T-shirt,

with a splodge of what might have been orange juice on the front, suggested this was an unplanned visit.

"There's no easy way to say this," she began.

Great, he might as well have stayed in with the committee. "How about you just spit it out? I have meetings out the wazoo today."

Her eyes flashed. "That's a surprise."

"You know I'm busy," he said. "That's why Barb wanted you to stay."

"Barb wanted me to make sure you and Daisy could get along."

"That's not exactly what she said." Though perhaps the gist was correct.

"Instead, I've done nothing," she said, "except let you off the hook of being a dad to Daisy."

He had no idea what she was talking about, but he was fairly certain he didn't like it. "If you're trying to say you wish you'd done things differently, don't beat yourself up. I think you've done a great job."

She gave that platitude the withering look it deserved. "Daisy thinks Lissa didn't love her."

Kyle recoiled. "That's ridiculous. Lissa was devoted to her. They were inseparable, they—"

Jane spoke over the top of him. "She also thinks you don't love her. And since Lissa's not here, this is *your* problem, Kyle."

She'd spent two weeks here, and she waited until now to deliver her judgment. Was it her idea of a parting shot?

"If you've come to tell me I'm a terrible father, that's old news," he said. "Just ask Barb. But for the record, you're wrong. I love Daisy, and I know Lissa did, too. What I don't know is why you're starting this conversation now, when you're about to leave town. Other than to make trouble. I guess you're playing to the Slater strength."

Her hiss confirmed that was a low blow. "Daisy started the

conversation *now,*" she said. "And thank goodness she did, since I've been too blind—*willfully* blind—to see the problem. And too busy avoiding you."

"That was your choice."

"All I said was, we're not friends," she corrected. "I didn't say you had to spend every waking moment away from Daisy."

Kyle pinched the bridge of his nose. "I admit I took advantage of having you here to make some progress on the new house so I can *give Daisy a proper home.* Clearly, that makes me evil."

Jane rolled her eyes. "The home she needs is one filled with love." She leaned her butt against Kyle's desk, as if she were settling in for a long discussion. "I'm not necessarily saying you don't love Daisy."

"Thanks a lot."

She ignored him. "I'm saying she doesn't *know* you love her."

"A fine distinction," he observed. "Some would say it's no distinction at all."

"Come on, Kyle. For years, you've been hung up on the idea Daisy might not be your daughter—don't you think there's a chance that might have colored your responses to her?"

"No," he growled. What kind of jerk would do that to an innocent kid?

"Do you ever tell Daisy you love her?" she demanded.

"Of course I do." Probably. Maybe not in those exact words…

"Do you ever *show* her?"

"Damn straight I do," he said. "I work hard to support her, I'm building a new home for her—"

"Both those things mean you leave her with other people, mostly your dad, a lot."

"Dad adores Daisy," Kyle said.

"Maybe. But he can't help trying to 'improve' her, and for a girl who's already insecure, that makes her feel she's not good enough."

He'd had that thought himself…which meant he didn't need Jane telling him. "Dad's not perfect, but he's a good grand-father," he said.

She smacked her forehead. "Why am I bothering, when you won't listen to a word I say?"

"I have no idea," he said. "Maybe you should stop now."

Her eyes narrowed. "I should have said this a week ago. It's as much my fault as yours that nothing will change when I'm gone."

"But as you said, it's my problem. I suggest you go back to Denver and put us out of your mind."

She folded her arms beneath her breasts. "Daisy told me Lissa used to come into her bedroom at nights and cry."

The news jolted Kyle. Raised all kinds of suspicions, old and new. Would he never be free of them? "Do you have any idea why?"

Jane shook her head. "I think you need some professional help."

"Take Daisy to a shrink?" Word would be all over town in five minutes—he could just imagine what his dad would say to that.

"Actually," she said, "I meant *you* should see a shrink."

He barked a laugh.

Her face didn't flicker. "I know a dysfunctional family when I see one," she said. "And I know all about feeling as if no one wants you."

She made him sound like a monster, when he was just a regular guy—a *good* guy—doing his imperfect best. Her criticism pierced him, slid deep to the bone.

Kyle tried to summon examples he could fling at Jane—good times he'd had with Daisy, things he'd said, moments when his daughter had acknowledged the bond between them...

Nothing. Crap.

This barrage of accusations had befuddled him, that's all. He didn't need her criticism, he needed some time with his daughter—Jane was right about that much. They would fix this the way his family always fixed things, by pulling together. Without Jane.

He strode to the door and opened it. "Thanks for stopping by. You can go now."

"No." She spoke so quietly, he almost missed it.

He opened the door wider. "In fact, you can go all the way back to Denver. Forget staying until tomorrow, you're no longer welcome here."

"As if I ever was," she muttered. "I'm not going, Kyle." She uncrossed her ankles and planted her feet squarely on the floor. "Not without being sure things will change around here. *You'll* change."

"Dammit, Jane, I love my daughter. Now get out."

In the hallway, a clerk turned at the sound of his raised voice, forcing Kyle to close the door again.

"One of the first rules of dealing with kids is not to promise what you can't deliver," Jane said. "I told Daisy I won't leave until I've proved you love her." She curled her hands over the edge of his desk, as if she thought he might physically remove her. He was tempted.

"How do you expect to prove that?" he demanded. "Love isn't something you prove with a...a birthday present or by saying 'I love you.' It's a lifetime thing."

Her lips parted, and he hated that his gaze was drawn to her mouth.

"You're right." She sounded amazed. "It's not going to be that straightforward. I guess I'll know it when I see it. And so will Daisy."

"This is nuts," he said.

"I make a living out of helping women change the way other people see them. If they can project confidence and competence, even when they don't feel those things, other people believe they possess those qualities. Over time, the confidence and competence become natural."

"Is this credentials pitch going somewhere?" he demanded.

"Showing Daisy you love her in a way that she understands doesn't come naturally to you. So I'll coach you."

"You will not," he said grimly.

"You need to make a new impression on your daughter," she said. "I'm going to help you. I won't leave until you do it, so it's in your interest to work with me."

"You have some nerve, thinking *you* can tell me how to be a parent," he said, aggravated beyond measure. "Lissa told me you were jealous of her having a husband and a baby— I'm starting to think that's true."

As tactics went, it was brutal. A part of him felt like a jerk. Yet, from the moment Jane had walked into the wrong end of the church during Lissa's funeral, he'd had a sense of her strength. That any battle between them would be between equals.

It was oddly freeing. With Lissa, he'd been hamstrung in their fights by her extreme reactions to any argument. As if in disagreeing, he was attacking her very core.

Jane's face had paled at his sally, but she didn't back down, not one inch. "Lissa would never say that."

She had to know it was exactly the kind of thing Lissa would say, if only for dramatic effect.

"My family's not perfect, but it's solid, strong," he said, "and that's something you've never had. So you've decided— maybe subconsciously," he conceded, "that a few hiccups between me and Daisy are a sign of a fundamental flaw."

"There *is* a fundamental flaw if your daughter feels unloved." Her voice shook.

"Daisy's in a rough patch, but deep down she knows I love her. Or she did, until you started planting doubts."

"I didn't!"

"How did she end up telling you about Lissa crying at nights if you weren't digging into this stuff?" Kyle didn't wait for an answer. "Leave, Jane. Leave tonight. What's best for Daisy is that she and I have some time together, just the two of us."

Momentarily, she looked torn—he suspected that in some ways the last thing she wanted was to stay on in Pinyon Ridge. He pushed home his point. "I'll go home with you now, and I'll take Daisy to Dad's while you pack your bags. It's better for everyone if you don't spend any more time with her."

Damn, he'd overplayed that. Two red spots in her cheeks suggested gathering fury.

"You can email Daisy if you want to keep in touch," he said quickly. "Send your emails to me, and I'll read them to her."

Jane dipped her head. Her walnut hair slid forward, a silken screen that hid her face.

Hell, was she crying? Had he totally misread her?

"Jane?" He reached out, touched her shoulder.

She shot out of the chair, startling him. Her eyes blazed. But when she spoke, she was very, very calm. "My first night here, I told you that you're Daisy's father, remember?"

The balance of power shifted between them in an instant. Something cold ran down Kyle's spine; his mouth seemed suddenly paralyzed. "I remember," he managed to respond.

Was she about to say that was a lie?

"It's true," she said.

Before he could sag in relief, or wonder why she'd brought the subject up, she continued, "It's true, inasmuch as it was your sperm that the clinic used. Even if emotionally you're not much of a dad."

Ah, she wanted to land one more punch before she left.

Kyle didn't bother to fight back; he didn't care about her assessment of him *emotionally*.

"But, Kyle…" Her voice turned so serious, he found his gaze riveted on her. "Daisy wasn't conceived using one of Lissa's eggs—the egg was mine."

# CHAPTER SIX

The rushing in Kyle's ears drowned out Jane's next words. Her lips moved, but he had no idea what she said.

"*Your* egg?" he barked, way too loud.

"Lissa told me that frozen eggs had a very low success rate, like you said, and she was worried this might be her last chance." Jane spoke slowly and clearly, as if she were repeating herself. Which she probably was.

Lissa's real worry had been that, with her marriage going downhill fast and Kyle having put any more fertility treatments on hold, this might be her last chance for a pregnancy.

"I'd been taking drugs to induce excess ovulation for a few weeks before Lissa came to town," Jane said. "I donated an egg—several eggs."

"*Your* egg," he said again.

Jane eyed him with what looked like concern. "They harvested the eggs a few days before Lissa arrived. They created three embryos using your sperm and implanted the two most viable into Lissa."

Kyle headed for the meeting table in the corner of his office. "Can we sit down?"

Too abrupt for courtesy, but she didn't object. She pushed away from his desk and joined him at the table, sitting sedately, as if she hadn't just dropped a two-ton bombshell.

Kyle sank into the other chair. "Is this true?" he demanded.

She didn't answer, but her gaze didn't waver.

Her story explained a lot. Everything. Lissa's secretiveness, her guilt, the way she'd withdrawn from Kyle as the pregnancy progressed. Their already rocky marriage had stood no chance after that.

Anger at Lissa surged, bitter in his throat. Then it spread to encompass Jane, who was still alive, still here.

"I called you," he accused her. "You told me I had nothing to worry about. You *lied*."

"You think I owed *you* the truth?" She gripped the edge of the table, and her knuckles whitened. "You made it plain I wasn't good enough to be Lissa's friend, you did everything you could to discourage her contact with me—"

"That's not true." And even if there were a thread of truth, *he* had the moral high ground here.

"What about the blues festival?" she demanded.

Lissa had planned a weekend in Denver, he remembered, to attend the festival with Jane. Until Kyle had surprised her with tickets to New York and a Broadway show. "That wasn't deliberate," he retorted. But he was uncomfortably aware that he'd known about the date clash and yet had gone ahead with his surprise. "You think a grudge about a music festival gave you the right to get involved in this *sham?*" He scrambled back onto that moral high ground.

"Lissa was my friend," she said, her cheeks pink. "My loyalty was to her."

"That lie broke up our marriage," he snapped. "If I'd known the truth—"

"You'd have forgiven her?"

Okay, it would have been hard to get past the deception. Maybe impossible. "I would have worked on it," he muttered.

Something like sympathy crossed her face. "If it makes you feel better," she said, "I lost my only friend."

He snorted. "I happen to know you stayed friends for years after that." Besides, compared to the loss of his marriage…

"At first Lissa was grateful," Jane admitted. "She kept in touch constantly while she was pregnant, and I felt like a part of her life in a way I hadn't been since you came along."

There was a poignancy in the words that Kyle refused to acknowledge.

"But after Daisy was born," Jane said, "she was…afraid."

"Of what?" he said impatiently.

"I know you didn't want me at the christening, but even so, she—"

"Lissa said you wouldn't come because she hadn't asked you to be godmother," he interrupted.

Jane drew in a breath. "She told me you refused to have me as godmother."

Kyle winced. "And you believed her."

She laced her fingers on the tabletop. "Why wouldn't I? You'd made it plain you disapproved of me, of my family."

"Like everybody else," he pointed out.

"Except Lissa's family," she countered. She huffed out a breath. "Let's not get bogged down with the details. Whatever really happened about the christening…"

"I'm telling the truth."

To his irritation, she lifted one shoulder, as if the jury were out on his honesty. "Lissa said she thought it was best if I didn't come at all, because I was bound to act guilty around you. She was afraid you'd guess the truth."

"No one would guess something that outlandish," he said.

"I think…" Jane bit her lip. "I'd been asking her lots of questions about Daisy, about how she was doing. Purely as a friend, but I suspect Lissa worried I might think of Daisy as mine."

*Hers?* Every instinct screamed against the idea.

Then Kyle realized what this all meant.

He slammed back in his chair.

"That's right," Jane said. "I'm Daisy's biological mother."

Hell. How had that not occurred to him already? "You are *not* my daughter's mother." He would defend that position to the ends of the earth.

"I know. I've never, not once, thought that." She sounded

remote. "But the more Lissa thought about it, the more she worried, and the more distance she put between us."

For a moment, he felt sorry for Jane—sorry, after all, for the loss of her friendship. But then the implications of her confession hit home.

Lissa had indeed lied to him all these years.

Jane Slater was Daisy's biological mother.

Daisy was a Slater.

He cursed.

Jane's chin jutted. "I'm sorry you have to suffer the horror of having my DNA present in your daughter."

She'd read his thoughts, dammit. "You didn't expect me to be *pleased,* did you?" he demanded.

"More pleased than discovering some random stranger had donated an egg, yeah."

*Uh, no.* Wasn't it common for prospective parents to specify that donors shouldn't have a criminal record? Or, in her case, be from a criminal family? "Is there anything else?" he demanded. "Any more lies?"

She gave him a look of disdain. "Not that I know of. But I haven't been Lissa's confidante in years."

Kyle knuckled his temples, where a headache was building. In the space of fifteen minutes, Jane had taken away what he knew to be his family. The life he'd constructed with Lissa, imperfect as it had been, had at least been real. Him and Lissa and their daughter, Daisy.

Or so he'd thought.

Now, his family would be forever distorted by the intrusion of Jane.

No matter that the egg donation had been Lissa's idea— and he believed that—Jane had inserted herself into his life in the most intimate of ways.

"This doesn't have to change anything," he said, mainly to himself. More out of hope than belief.

"Excuse me?"

"You're about to leave town," he said, thinking out loud. "No one else needs to know about this. You'll be gone. Daisy and I will get on with our lives."

"Have you forgotten where we started this conversation?" she asked.

Kyle racked his brain. The distance they'd traveled in the past few minutes felt like a lifetime.

"I told you I'm not leaving town," she reminded him.

Oh, yeah, that. The threat seemed trifling in the context of his newer, bigger worries. "And I told you, Daisy's *my* daughter, and you can't stay."

"She's mine, too. Biologically."

He didn't miss the pause in what should have been one sentence. Revulsion slammed in his gut. Jane Slater—a liar and the product of the most deadbeat family he knew—was his daughter's biological mother, and just now she'd been in no hurry to add the *biological*.

"She is not your daughter and she never will be." He cudgeled his brain for the argument that would convince Jane to leave. "Do you need money? Running your own business is tough in the current economy." He tried to sound sympathetic, but landed somewhere around smarmy. Still, money talked with the Slaters.

Maybe not this Slater. She stood so suddenly, her chair almost toppled over. With her hands planted on her hips, her expression ferocious, she looked like a warrior, ready to run him through with a sword.

"Since it seems your memory is faulty, I'll tell you again," she said. "I'm staying until you've learned to show Daisy you love her. Money won't speed up the process. Letting me coach you will."

He stood, too. "If you think what you just told me makes me more likely to take you up on your offer, you're dead wrong. More than ever, I'm going to protect Daisy—and that means from you."

JANE HAD TO RESPECT HIS single-mindedness. She'd delivered a sucker punch with her revelation, but he was still standing, still fighting to "protect" his daughter.

As if Lissa's daughter needed protecting from her. Jane's decision to donate her eggs had been all about their friendship—in all its glory and its flaws. She would do anything for Lissa, and by extension, for Daisy.

She didn't believe production of the egg in any way conferred motherhood. Lissa was Daisy's mother.

But the egg was Jane's best bargaining chip. Her only bargaining chip.

"If you refuse to accept my help," she said, "I'll tell the whole town the truth about Daisy's conception."

She saw the moment it dawned on him what she was saying. Shock, disgust…fear.

"You wouldn't," he snapped.

She licked her lips. A sign of weakness. To compensate, she made sure her voice came out hard, the way she'd heard her father talk. "Starting with Barb and Hal."

"Barb would be devastated," he said tightly. "I know you care too much for her to hurt her."

"You wish." Jane forced a sneer into her voice. "You'll only have yourself to blame when I tell her Daisy has no Peters blood in her veins. It'll be quite a blow, so soon after Lissa's death." She felt nauseous even saying the words.

"You're sick," he said.

Two weeks ago, he'd suggested they could start afresh, be friendly toward each other, if not friends. She'd been right to refuse, but now, for a nanosecond, she regretted that she'd never experienced that slate wiped clean.

Now she never would.

She forced herself to continue.

"After Barb and Hal, I'll tell your father to enlist his help to persuade you to cooperate."

"My father hates blackmailers. He won't—" Kyle stopped.

His eyes narrowed. "No way would you give my father the satisfaction of being proved right about another Slater. You're bluffing."

She flinched inwardly. "Letting Charles be right about me is a small sacrifice. He won't want the shine taken off the Everson reputation—which is what'll happen when all of Pinyon Ridge knows the sordid truth. That his granddaughter is a Slater."

"You'd really sink that low?" he asked. "You'd do that to a little girl? To Lissa, your best friend?"

"You may not like my methods, but I'm doing this to *help* Daisy." Jane heard the quaver in her own voice, but she didn't think Kyle had. He was too busy wrestling with the consequences of her threat to think straight. Which was how blackmail worked. No wonder her father had found it so efficacious.

She felt sick to her stomach that she was in any way like Mike Slater. The fact that she truly had no intention of telling Charles, or Barb or anyone else the truth made no difference.

"It won't help Daisy, having the whole town gossiping about her."

"You might have to move," she agreed. "Just like I did. But that's no bad thing, I assure you."

He let out a hiss. "You won't do it," he said again.

"Try me." Luckily that came out just the way she'd hoped. Jane eyeballed Kyle, challenging him to call her bluff. Beneath the table, she clutched her knees, afraid they would knock in fear.

He eyeballed her right back, but just when she thought he might tell her to do her worst and be damned, he said, "I can't afford to take that risk."

Adrenaline drained out of Jane, leaving her with the backbone of a wet noodle. She sank back into her chair. It was a struggle to speak in a normal tone. "So you'll cooperate," she said.

"What exactly do you want?" Kyle didn't sit, and his words were glacial, but they were a surrender, and she'd take it.

"I'll stay on at your place. But this time, you don't get to avoid me—and I don't get to avoid you," she added. "I'll monitor your interactions with Daisy and coach you through some techniques that will communicate your feelings to her." Talking the way she would to any client helped lift the shame of what she was doing. "Our goal—" his snort said there was no *our* here "—is for Daisy to know she's loved, to feel secure."

"Hard to feel secure when someone's threatening to ruin your life," he said.

She blocked out the words. "I'll drive back to the city tomorrow to collect some more clothes and catch up with a couple of clients. I'll be back Sunday night. We'll start then."

"How long will this take?" he demanded. "Not more than a week, surely."

"I usually work with clients over a couple of months." She smiled grimly at the horror on his face. "Since we're in a live-in situation, we should progress faster. But there's a lot to be done."

"One month," he said.

"Excuse me?"

He shoved his hands in his pockets. "You have one month to work your magic." His tone said he didn't believe in magic. "Four weeks. Not a second longer. During that time you won't drop so much as a hint of what you've told me today, not to anyone."

"Of course not," she said, happy to clear away the taint of that toxic threat.

He snorted. "What, you don't want to breach the blackmailer's code of honor?"

She deserved that. "But you need to keep your end of the bargain. There has to be real change."

"I'll do whatever it takes to get rid of you," he promised.

"Fine." It was beyond stupid to feel hurt at that dig. "Four weeks it is."

"At the end of that time," he said inexorably, "you'll leave Pinyon Ridge."

"There's nothing I'd like more." She was pretty sure Kyle could make this work within a month, motivated by the prospect of getting rid of her. Daisy would be happy, knowing her dad loved her, and Jane would have fulfilled Lissa's final wish.

She could foresee that moment as one of closure to their friendship. One of healing. *Maybe Lissa did know what she was doing when she made that will, after all.*

She realized Kyle was watching her closely. If she wasn't careful, he'd figure out she was about as tough as a feather pillow. "Anything else?" she asked, before she remembered she was supposed to be calling the shots.

"After you leave," Kyle said, "you'll never contact my daughter again."

Her chest constricted so tightly, she gasped for breath.

He folded his arms, implacable. "You hate this town. It's no big deal for you to not come back."

What he was asking—no, demanding—felt like a huge deal, no matter that she'd always said she didn't want to come back to Pinyon Ridge. She was being banished.

But in his view, he was protecting his daughter from the woman who'd threatened to destroy what little security she had left.

"I accept that you don't want me here," Jane said, with difficulty. "But there's no reason Daisy can't visit me in Denver."

"There's every reason," he growled. "It's not like you've had any contact with her before. Nothing's changed."

Everything had changed, and he knew it. But Jane didn't want to play the biological mother card again.

She settled for stating, "What's changed is that Lissa's will said she wants me around as a positive female influence on Daisy's life."

"Blackmail doesn't qualify as positive. You said yourself, Lissa was worried you'd give away her secret inadvertently. You just threatened to do it deliberately."

Jane's mouth dried. "Because I'm trying to help Daisy."

Kyle's lip curled, but he didn't argue. "I'm giving you free rein to be a positive influence on Daisy, and me, for the next month," he said. "I'll do whatever you say. But then you need to go away and not come back. Without that, there's no deal."

"I—I'd need reports," she said, her clogged throat a sign she was horribly close to tears. "When I'm gone. From you, or from Barb. What if you go back to your old ways the moment I leave?"

"If you're any good at your job, I won't want to," he said. "Don't you have faith in your abilities?"

"Of course I do." It was hard-won faith; nothing about it had come naturally or easily. So, yes, she knew she could achieve the goal.

"Then we're agreed," he said. "After you go, you won't contact Daisy directly again."

"Daisy was upset enough that I was leaving tomorrow," Jane blurted. "She wants me to stay. To completely ban any contact…"

Ugh, where had that come from? She knew how absurd she sounded—because if Daisy understood that Jane had threatened to undermine the most important truth she knew, there was no way she'd want anything to do with Jane…ever.

Kyle's face darkened. "Don't even think about using this time to get close to Daisy."

"It's about getting *you* close to her," she said. "Which was my idea, remember?"

He scanned her face, unable to contest that. "Just don't hurt my daughter."

With that blend of determination, anger and worry in his

voice, there was no doubting his love for Daisy. All he needed to do was show it.

Kyle glanced at the clock on the wall behind his desk—according to the plaque it was a gift from a sister town in Japan. "I'll wrap up my meeting here and see you at home. The sooner we start this coaching, the sooner we're done."

"We're going to your father's house tonight," she reminded him. "The barbecue." Her *farewell* barbecue.

He cursed. "I'll cancel."

"We're due there in half an hour—it'll cause speculation if you pull out. And Daisy's looking forward to seeing Gabe." Not to mention, Jane didn't think she could handle an evening of just her and Kyle after what they'd just put each other through. "It'll be a good chance to explain to everyone that I'm staying."

He rubbed his temples. "Fine, we'll go. We'll start the coaching tomorrow."

"I'm going to Denver tomorrow," she reminded him. "We'll start Sunday night." By then she'd have marshaled the thick skin she would need.

He cursed under his breath. "Sunday night," he said reluctantly. "We work together for four weeks, and then you leave and never come back. Never contact Daisy again."

The sheer isolation of what he was proposing whistled through her like a winter wind through a mountain pass.

Which it shouldn't, she scolded herself. In reality, nothing would change from the way things had been the past few years.

"Agreed?" he demanded.

It was a deal with the devil, and didn't legend suggest people always regretted those?

But if this was the only way to secure Daisy's happiness…

Jane lifted her chin. "Agreed."

## CHAPTER SEVEN

CHARLES EVERSON WIPED the stainless-steel grill with a paper towel soaked in vegetable oil, held in a pair of tongs. He'd scoured the hot plate after the last time he used it, and it looked immaculate, but he wasn't about to risk giving his guests food poisoning. Not even Jane Slater—wouldn't want to delay her departure from Pinyon Ridge.

Mentally, he scolded himself for the uncharitable thought, unbecoming of an elder of the church.

But he'd been a cop far longer than he'd been an elder, longer even than he'd been a dad, and he had a nose for trouble.

His nose told him—and his gut, that other essential policing tool, agreed—that regardless of the fact that Jane Slater spoke with a more educated accent and according to Barb had a good job down in Denver, she was Trouble with a capital T.

He'd seen a glint in Gabe's eye and something altogether more complicated in Kyle's when they talked to Jane, and he didn't like it.

But at the same time, Micki liked the woman, and Charles trusted Micki's judgment. So maybe he shouldn't have been so cool toward Jane whenever he'd encountered her in the café these past couple of weeks. She'd been just as cool, of course, but someone had to be the better person. Obviously, that duty fell to him.

Tonight would be an opportunity to make sure they parted on amicable, if not good, terms. He would be a gracious host.

Satisfied that a person could eat dinner directly off the grill with no ill effects, Charles closed the lid and turned up the heat. By the time his guests arrived it'd be good and hot.

Gabe, the fancy cook in the family, planned to grill shrimp; Charles would do the steaks. Micki had offered to bring a salad. There was ice cream for dessert, with chocolate syrup for Daisy. Good, simple food.

The chime of the doorbell interrupted his planning. Neither of his sons would ring the bell, and over the past couple of weeks Jane Slater had taken evident satisfaction from walking into his house in Daisy's wake without knocking. This must be Micki.

He went to open the door.

"Micki, come on in—let me take that." As he wrested the salad bowl from her—the colorful contents looked amazing, and glistened with some kind of herbed dressing—he realized she was wearing a dress instead of her usual jeans and T-shirt.

Was she out to impress one of his sons? Charles gave her a quick once-over as he stepped aside, gesturing for her to precede him through the house. "You look very nice," he said. "Delightful."

He was being kind. The dress was blue with red swirls, polyester and shapeless, even though she'd put a wide belt around the waist. It was too big.

Of course, he hoped he'd raised his sons to look beyond the surface. He wondered which one of his boys she liked. Either of them would be lucky to have her, but Kyle's need was probably greater.

She wrinkled her nose, as if she knew he didn't really like the dress. "Are we out in the garden?"

"You bet." Charles followed her out to the deck. "It's been a while since you were last here."

She grinned over her shoulder. "Yeah, you've redecorated."

Not in years, but she'd probably been a teenager when she last hung out here. He and Patti had redecorated at least once since then, but the layout hadn't changed.

They stepped out onto the deck, bathed in late-afternoon

sunlight. He loved this space. Micki tilted her face to the sun with a hum of pleasure.

He set her salad down on the table. "I have some wine in the cooler."

"I'd rather have a beer, thanks." Micki slung her purse over the back of a chair.

"Sure." He grabbed two bottles from the cooler, opening one before he passed it to her.

When they'd both taken a drink, silence fell.

"Am I early?" Micki asked. "Gabe told me five-thirty."

"Unlike my sons, you're right on time," Charles said. "I do like punctuality."

"I've noticed," Micki said. "You turn up at the café at eight-thirty sharp every morning."

"I guess I'm a creature of habit." He checked the temperature gauge on the hood of the grill. Heating up nicely. "Nothing wrong with that, so long as the habit is a good one. And your breakfasts definitely qualify."

She raised her bottle to him in a toast. "Here's to one of my best customers."

He clinked his bottle against hers, and they drank again. Charles found himself with nothing to say after that, and Micki seemed to be in the same boat. Which was odd, since they could talk for hours at the Eating Post. She shifted her weight from one foot to the other, then back again. Maybe she was nervous about impressing Gabe.

"Nice evening," Charles said, at the same time as Micki said, "I'll miss Jane when she goes tomorrow."

"Really?" He knew she liked Jane, but surely a Slater could be no great loss.

"She's so observant, and she has a lot of style and confidence," Micki said. "I could learn a lot from her about setting a direction for my life."

"You don't need to learn anything from a Slater," Charles said, alarmed. He meant it as a compliment to Micki but obvi-

ously it came out more like an insult to Jane. Micki looked...
disappointed in him.

Charles felt heat around the back of his neck. "I mean, you
have a great business and you run it like a pro. And you're
a good girl—your parents raised you right." Roger and Sue
Barton had died ten years ago, when the light aircraft Roger
was flying suffered engine failure. They were a lovely couple, good friends to him and Patti. He bet they'd love to see
their daughter dating one of Charles's sons.

"Mom taught me to cook and Dad taught me to run a
business—I couldn't be where I am today without them,"
she agreed. "But it's too easy to get into a rut in a place like
Pinyon Ridge. If you don't know what you really want from
life, you could miss an opportunity for change. I would've
liked to talk to Jane some more about that."

"You could always talk to me," he said.

She looked horrified. It dawned on him the "opportunity
for change" she'd mentioned probably had to do with her soft
spot for one of his sons.

"Maybe not," he muttered. "If Jane Slater has been good
company for you, well, I'm glad."

Still, the thought of Micki discussing her hopes with Jane
left him oddly unsettled. Not that she wasn't free to talk to
whomever she liked, but with Lissa dying and Kyle on edge
about the election and about Daisy, Charles just wanted things
back to normal. Jane's departure would be a step in the right
direction.

To his relief, he heard his younger son yell a greeting from
the house.

"Out here," Charles called.

Micki seemed relieved, too, going up on the balls of her
feet—she wore pretty sandals instead of sneakers—and keeping her gaze on the French doors frmo which Gabe emerged
a moment later.

"Gabe, great to see you," Charles said too heartily.

Gabe gave him a curious look. "Hey, Micki." He kissed her cheek then slung an arm around her shoulder in a way that may or may not have been platonic. Micki grinned up at him.

Charles felt a flash of annoyance toward his charming son. Micki wasn't the kind of girl a young man should toy with. Gabe might be a pastor, but he didn't know everything. Maybe it was time for another one of those father-son talks that hadn't gone down too well when Gabe was eighteen.

KYLE BROKE THE NEWS about Jane's extended stay the moment they arrived at his dad's house—he told them Daisy hadn't wanted Jane to go, so she'd decided to stay another month. Which was true—Kyle had just happened to omit a ton of complications in between those two points. Gabe and Micki seemed genuinely pleased Jane wasn't leaving. Charles responded with an almost plausible, "If it makes Daisy happy, then that's great."

One thing about his dad, he wouldn't lie. Wouldn't say he personally was pleased Jane was sticking around for the sake of politeness. Kyle knew that as a cop, many of the criminals Charles had arrested had respected the store he set by the truth, even if they hated his guts.

If Charles knew how Lissa had lied and how Jane had abetted her, he'd frog-march her out of town.

Not only because of the lie, but also because of the implications of that lie. Kyle could admit his father wasn't the most open-minded of men. Charles was a believer in "bad blood," in the apple never falling far from the tree and other axioms that suggested if you were born into a bad family there wasn't much hope for you.

The way Charles would see it, bad Slater blood was coursing through his granddaughter's veins.

Much as Kyle loved his dad, he knew Charles's standards could be hard to live up to. Jane was right—he hated even thinking that—about Daisy not needing Charles's criticism.

How much more all over Daisy's slightest error or supposed flaw Charles would be if he knew she was part-Slater.

There'd been no mistaking Daisy's satisfaction when Kyle had told her on the way here that Jane wasn't leaving. Jane had explained she would put a calendar on the fridge, and they would cross off the days until she left. Presumably so Daisy wouldn't be upset when the next departure date came up.

Couldn't come soon enough for Kyle. He'd follow to the letter whatever cockamamie—to borrow a word from his dad—instructions Jane issued if it would get them through this time faster, and get her away from his daughter.

Who was also, biologically, *her* daughter.

He watched Daisy, delivering monosyllabic answers to Micki's questions about her day. Then he switched his gaze to Jane, talking to Gabe and his dad. She seemed subdued, not baiting Charles at all.

Briefly, her gaze collided with Kyle's, then she turned her head so he was out of her range of vision. Fine by him. He had no intention of talking to her—he didn't trust himself not to get mad, and he didn't want his father guessing there was a problem.

He focused again on Daisy. Sensing his interest, she looked up at him. Like Jane, she looked away again.

Daisy had brown eyes like Kyle's, but lighter. A lot lighter. Lissa's eyes had been blue, but everyone knew from high school biology that brown was dominant.

Now, he realized Daisy's eyes were more...tawny.

Had she inherited her eye color from Jane? Come to think of it, Daisy's eyes were wide-spaced, like Jane's. And now that he looked at both of them in quick succession, he could see they had the same chin.

*Hell.* All of a sudden it seemed to Kyle the similarities between Jane and Daisy shone like a beacon no one could ignore. If anyone—his dad, Gabe, Micki—really looked, they would see instantly that his daughter and his ex-wife's best friend shared a big chunk of DNA.

Suddenly hot, Kyle swiped a hand over his brow.

"You okay?" Gabe materialized beside him. Following the direction of Kyle's gaze, he looked at Jane.

Kyle kept his gaze away from Daisy, so Gabe wouldn't look at his daughter and see the wide-spaced eyes and matching chin. "I'm fine, just standing too close to the grill." He took a long swig of his beer, finishing the bottle. The cooler was empty, he knew. "I'll get another cold one from the kitchen. How about you?"

Gabe, not teetotal, but newly abstemious as a drinker, shook his head. Relieved to get away, Kyle headed to the kitchen.

"The shrimp is ready, and I'll be in with the steaks in two minutes," Charles called after him. "Can you get the garlic butter out of the fridge?"

Kyle waved an acknowledgment. Inside, he found the garlic butter and set it on the island. As he reached into the fridge for the beer, he heard a light, feminine footstep behind him. Jane, come to issue another ultimatum? He spun around. "Don't start—"

He stopped. It was Micki. She raised her eyebrows at his tone.

"Sorry," he said anyway. "Did you need something? Another beer?"

"In a minute. Right now, I need something else." Micki, always briskly confident in her domain at the Eating Post, sounded nervous.

Kyle closed the fridge. "What's that?"

"Do you remember in high school—your sophomore year—when you asked Jenny Swain on a date?" She fidgeted with the ring she wore on her middle finger, as if she were still in high school herself.

"Not the kind of humiliation a guy forgets," he joked. He'd

had a massive crush on Jenny, who at fifteen had been two inches taller than he was and ten years more sophisticated. When he'd asked her on a date, she'd laughed at him then told all of her friends. Who'd also laughed.

Kyle had been unsure what was worse, the broken heart or the embarrassment. Micki had found him behind the gymnasium, kicking at the dirt, cursing girls in general and Jenny in particular.

"I helped you out then, right?" she said.

"Uh, yeah. Yeah, you did." He hadn't thought about that day in years. Micki had listened to his woes with a sympathetic ear…but that wasn't all. When Kyle had finished railing against the fairer sex, accidentally admitting that he'd never kissed a girl and had planned to rectify that with Jenny, Micki had said casually, "You can kiss *me* if you want."

He'd been speechless. Micki was a senior, dating one of the guys on the football team. She was generally regarded as at least mildly hot, though their families had known each other too long for Kyle to think of her that way.

"K-kiss you," he'd answered at last, stupidly.

"Sure, why not? You know, for practice. Confidence." She moved closer, and he caught a hint of flowery perfume. She chuckled. "You're looking doubtful, Kyle, which is almost as insulting as what Jenny did to you."

"No." His voice cracked in a way it hadn't done in months. "I mean, yes, I'd like to. I'd love to. Please."

"Mmm, much better. Girls like a polite boy." Micki leaned in and down and kissed him. After a few moments, Kyle got the hang of things—she told him to go easy when he tried to put too much Hollywood into it—and the kiss became a thoroughly enjoyable event. For him, at least, and Micki had seemed happy enough. He'd gone back to class with a swagger that disconcerted Jenny and soon got him a new girlfriend. He and Micki had never tried anything like that again.

Now she said, "I want you to help me out the same way."

"What?" His voice cracked, just as it had when he was fifteen.

She glanced over her shoulder, checking they were alone. "You owe me."

"For a make-out session twenty years ago?" He scrubbed the back of his head with his fist. "Micki, I'm not looking for a relationship right now."

She rolled her eyes. "I want a kiss, Kyle, in return for the one I gave you. That's all. And I want it now."

"This isn't a good time." It was bad enough that he had to be here with a woman he despised, who happened to be the spitting image of his daughter. No way did he want to complicate the evening by kissing Micki.

Micki moved around the island. It took all of the good manners his father had taught him not to retreat.

"Now," she said firmly. "No one will see."

"Can I ask why?" He held his beer bottle in front of him, as if it was some kind of antivamp talisman. "After all, *you* knew why I wanted you to kiss me."

She rolled her eyes. "Let's just say, it's time."

"Have you considered internet dating?" he asked. Maybe the bachelor pool in Pinyon Ridge wasn't huge, but in the wider county...

"One kiss, Kyle," she said, impatient. "Is that too much to ask?"

Her no-nonsense tone reassured him that, whatever this was about, it wasn't a sudden attraction to him.

"Of course not," he said.

"Then could you hurry up?"

She was right, he owed her. Kyle always paid his debts. He put his hands to her hips.

Micki closed her eyes and squared her shoulders, as if bracing herself. Which wasn't exactly inspiring. Kyle half shook his head, then gave in and got on with the job. His mouth met hers.

Micki wrapped her arms around his neck and responded with more skill than enthusiasm. No sparks for him, and he was pretty sure not for her, either. This kiss must be about her worrying that she was going rusty…poor Micki, he had no idea her love life was so dire.

Since Kyle liked to do a good job of anything he set his mind to, he didn't stint, just as she hadn't twenty years ago. His head wasn't in it—his mind wandered to the dimensions of the office in his new house and whether it was big enough—and his heart certainly wasn't engaged, but his lips gave good service. Presumably, she would end it when she was done.

Before they got to that point, a loud cough had them springing apart. Kyle shoved his hands in his pockets as he leaned back against the counter, but it was too late to pretend nothing had happened. His father, brother and Jane all stared at them from the doorway. He knew a moment of immense gratitude when he realized that Daisy wasn't with them.

Another cough came from his dad, then another and another until he was red in the face.

"I'll get you some water, Charles," Jane said. Everyone else stayed frozen as she took a glass that was draining on the counter and filled it with cold water from the faucet. She handed it to Charles, still sputtering.

"I, uh…" Kyle felt the need to explain. He glanced at Micki, who shrugged, clearly not planning to be any help. Belatedly, it occurred to him she might have been trying to get Gabe's attention. If so, she'd succeeded. Gabe, carrying a plate laden with the freshly grilled steaks, was glancing between her and Kyle with puzzlement.

It would be churlish for Kyle to announce he'd been doing her a favor.

His gaze slid to Jane, who was now thumping his dad between the shoulder blades. Maybe harder than she needed to, but it seemed to be helping. She met his eyes, hers filled with disdain.

He knew exactly what she was thinking. That he couldn't be too cut up about Lissa's betrayal if he could make out with another woman five minutes later. That yet again, Daisy wasn't his number one priority.

Wrong. And he'd tell her so, given half a chance.

For now, he offered, "Gabe, are those steaks ready?"

"Here's how this will work," Jane said on Sunday night. She was sitting at the dining table in the cottage; Kyle was making coffee and Daisy was in bed. "I have a list of observations about your interactions with Daisy." She patted the sheet of paper in front of her, on top of a manila folder of notes and other materials. "For each one, we'll discuss how you can counter the negative impressions you're giving her."

Spending the weekend back in Denver had enabled Jane to literally take a step back from the mess she'd left in Pinyon Ridge. Even better, meetings with a couple of her clients had sparked invaluable insights into Kyle's situation with Daisy that she hadn't clued into while she was here.

In Denver, she'd realized she needed to treat this like a job, with Kyle as a client, just like any other, and get on with it. She needed to forget she was blackmailing him and that he hated her guts. Forget she didn't like his dad, who happened to be Daisy's grandfather. Forget she had a connection to this family that ran deeper than any of them wanted.

Forget the things Kyle had told her Lissa had said about her. Hurtful things. She couldn't afford to be fragile.

Kyle carried the two coffees he'd just poured to the table and set one in front of Jane. "Okay."

"Really?" She'd expected an immediate declaration that she knew nothing about him and didn't have anything to teach him about dealing with his daughter. She'd mentally rehearsed staying calm through his attacks on her credibility.

He offered her the carton of milk. When she'd added some to her coffee, he spiked his own, then added a spoon of sugar. "We have a job to do," he said. "Let's get on and do it."

She blinked. He'd just summarized her two days of deliberations in Denver. "Uh, great," she said. "My sentiments exactly."

Did his pragmatic approach mean he wasn't still furious with her? Or merely that he could lock the emotion away when it wasn't serving any purpose?

She glanced down at her sheet of paper, momentarily unable to remember her next step. "How did things go with Daisy this weekend?" she asked as she skimmed her bullet points.

"Fine." He cleared his throat. "Actually, I had a couple of events to attend as mayor on Saturday morning, and after that I took the opportunity to get some work done on the house. Daisy spent most of the weekend with my dad."

She set down her paper. "You're kidding."

"Being the mayor is my job, and the house is important," he said defensively. "It's going to be her home. Besides, I figured you'll have me spending a lot of time with her this week."

"So you might as well ignore her while you can?"

His lips thinned. "Is this your usual approach with clients? Guilt them into change?"

She counted to five in her head. "Sorry," she said. "You're right. We're both professionals. We can work better than this."

It was worth the climb-down to see the surprise on his face.

"I probably shouldn't have left her with Dad," he admitted.

Now she was the one who was surprised.

"But I had a lot on my mind and not much sleep, and I didn't want to get grouchy with Daisy and make things worse than they already are."

Jane guessed the reason for his lack of sleep was the news she'd given him about her egg donation.

He did look tired, she realized. His hands were wrapped around his coffee mug as if he could draw energy through the china, and lines of exhaustion etched from his nose to the corners of his mouth. Oddly, that hint of vulnerability, the first she'd seen in him, made him even more handsome.

"I get that you didn't want to risk upsetting Daisy by being grouchy," she said. "But she'd be happier knowing you want her with you, even when you're tired. Kids are very forgiving." At his skeptical look, she added, "I forgave my mom any amount of neglect in exchange for occasional shows of affection."

"Which is why you stayed so close to her as an adult," he said. No mistaking the sarcasm.

"In my case," she said calmly, "I realized things would never change—my mom would always put my father and his sleazy schemes ahead of her kids. But Daisy has a father who'll do anything to protect her. Who loves her. She's lucky."

Jane rubbed her eyes, suddenly drained herself. When she opened them again, Kyle was eyeing her speculatively.

"What?" she asked.

"What you just said. That didn't sound like a woman who plans to destroy my daughter's life if I don't cooperate. You were bluffing with that threat, weren't you?"

"No," she said quickly.

When he looked as if he might argue, she said, "Smiling."

He blinked. "What about it?"

"That's the first thing you need to fix. It's hard for Daisy to feel loved when your natural expression is a frown." She slid her fingers beneath the top cover of her manila folder.

"It's not," Kyle said.

She whipped a small mirror from the folder and held it up to him.

He glared. "Of course I'm frowning right now. You're accusing me of something that's not true."

"Let's not use words like *accusing*," she said. "Not when

we're off to such a good start. All I'm doing is identifying the need to display a more positive facial expression."

He scowled, and she flashed the mirror at him again.

"Quit doing that," he ordered. But he replaced the scowl with a neutral expression.

"Better," she said. "But not good enough. You need to put a smile on your face and in your voice when you talk to Daisy."

"If I frown, it's not at her," Kyle said. "I have a lot on my mind."

"Kids don't think about what else you might have to worry about. If you're scowling at her, she takes it personally. And before you accuse me of not knowing what I'm talking about, I have that direct from a counselor who works with kids."

"Let's not use words like *accuse,*" he said.

She snickered, and the moment lightened. "So, you think you can smile more?"

"No problem," he said. Straight-faced.

"Any chance I could see an example?"

"Now? You want me to smile at you?"

He made it sound as if she'd asked him to cure cancer.

"Humor me," she said.

For a long moment, he stared at her, as if he could think of a hundred reasons why humoring her shouldn't be on the agenda. Then he stretched his lips in a caricature of a grin, baring teeth that were white against his tan.

"Good." She ignored that he looked more like a wolf wanting to devour Red Riding Hood than a loving dad. The smile would surely come more easily with his daughter than with Jane, the woman who'd exploded the myth of his wife and family. "The next step is to put the smile in your voice."

Kyle had already resumed his scowl.

"Try this exercise," she said. "Repeat after me, 'It's going to rain today.'"

"It's going to rain today," he growled.

Jane couldn't help laughing.

His eyebrows drew together. "What's the point of this?"

"Now smile—go on, fake it, the way you did before." She waited while he curved his lips into that parody again. "Now say it again, while you're smiling. 'It's going to rain today.'"

"It's going to rain—" He stopped.

"You heard it, didn't you?" Jane said smugly. "Putting a smile in your voice, even a fake one, lightens your tone and makes you sound friendlier."

"I'll bet it looks stupid." He grabbed the mirror and watched himself as he repeated the sentence. "Yep, I look like a half-wit. I'm more likely to spook Daisy than make her feel loved."

"I tried this technique with a client who was about to lose her job because she was too aggressive with customers. It made a big difference for her."

He set the mirror down. "It feels dishonest. Fake."

"You're a politician," Jane said. "Are you telling me you never once faked a smile at those events you attended on Saturday?"

"I smiled out of courtesy once or twice," he admitted. "But lately there hasn't been a lot to laugh about."

Jane drank some of her coffee. "Beats me how you got elected in the first place. I always thought charm was supposed to be important in politics."

His lips twitched…but didn't make it any further. "Last election, smiling was easy," he said. "Four years ago, Lissa and I were still together, Daisy was a cute, smiling toddler and people had woken up to the fact that Wayne Tully might not have Pinyon Ridge's interests at heart."

"Surely you don't expect to lose to Tully. The guy's a two-bit has-been. Not to mention an idiot." She recalled him from when she'd lived here—he must be about ten years older than Kyle, and his claim to fame was a brief stint in the NFL, starting around Jane's senior year, which he'd never let anyone forget.

"I like the way you think." Kyle's lips twitched a bit further. "But Tully's the football coach at Pinyon Ridge High now and the team's currently number one in the district. He also has plenty of inherited wealth that he flashes about town."

"So what'll make people vote for him?"

"The promise of fast money in a town that's been hit by the recession like everywhere else," Kyle said. "I've been working on a plan for sustainable development that will allow Pinyon Ridge to grow without losing the best things about it."

"There are some *best things?*" she asked.

"Absolutely." Before she could point out that she had no interest, he'd launched into details of a development program that, she had to admit, was well thought out. He was so passionate, she almost got caught up in the picture he painted. Almost.

"If you explain it like that to people, you should pick up a few votes," she said in an offhand manner when he finished.

"The money from my preferred development will come in a few years after Tully's. Not to mention, Tully is married."

Jane snorted. "You think people will hold your divorce against you?"

"I know they will," Kyle said. "People don't trust a divorced mayor."

"You just reinforced everything I ever thought about the small-minded folk around here."

He rolled his eyes. "There's a reason why senators and presidential candidates aren't usually divorced. Small-mindedness—or respect for family values, as some people would call it—is everywhere. People think if a guy can't get run his family, how can he run a city, or a state or a country?"

"Is that why you kissed Micki?" she blurted. At his stunned expression, she added, "It may be none of my business—"

"It's definitely none of your business."

"—but Micki deserves a guy who's serious about her."

"You think I would date someone just to impress the voters?" he asked, incredulous.

She drained her coffee cup. "Let's get back to your ability to smile. Which, by the way, is not in evidence at the moment."

"You accused me of dating Micki to fool the voters."

"Let's not use words like *accuse*. It was a query, a preposterous one."

"A damn fool one."

Unexpectedly, she laughed. His bemused gaze seemed to get hung up on her mouth. Probably because they were talking about smiling.

"It doesn't have to be exaggerated," she said.

"Huh?"

"A small smile is enough."

"Right." He contorted his mouth again.

"Less Big Bad Wolf," she advised, "and more Happy the Dwarf."

He recoiled. "I am *not* trying to look like a happy dwarf."

"I didn't say—" She sighed. "Never mind. I'll let you figure it out."

There was a pause.

"What's next?" he asked.

"Excuse me?"

"I believe we've only covered the first point on that list of yours." He nodded at the sheet of paper she'd long since forgotten.

Jane ran a finger down the page. *Don't get distracted by worries unrelated to Daisy. Don't overcomplicate simple decisions. Don't read cell phone messages while talking to Daisy.* And so on and so on. Thirteen points in all. An exhausting prospect. The clock on the microwave showed only nine o'clock, but after the drive out from the city, she was ready for bed.

"Let's not push our luck," she said. "I'm still not convinced of your ability to smile."

He gave her that forced grin again.

"Exactly." She put a hand over her mouth to cover a yawn.

"Smiling might come more naturally," he mused, "if I did something fun with Daisy."

"That's a great idea."

He looked at her expectantly.

"What?" she asked.

"So what should I do with her?"

Jane tsked. "Anything you like. Anything *she* likes." She'd never had to entertain a kid—she didn't know where to start.

He raked a hand through his hair. "I just need something that sounds like fun." Again, that expectant look.

"I have no idea," Jane said. "In my family, fun was getting through an evening without Dad hitting anyone." Yikes, did she really just say that? "Kidding," she added quickly.

His carefully bland expression said he didn't believe her.

"Surely *you* have plenty of happy memories to draw on," she said.

"We had lots of fun when I was a kid," he agreed. "But it's been a while. I guess life got in the way, and now I don't know where to start."

He drummed his fingers on the table as they eyed each other.

"Loser," Jane said.

One side of his mouth quirked. "Right back at ya."

She grimaced. "Poor Daisy, having you and me in charge of her fun."

"Totally sucks."

And then it happened.

He smiled. Not Big Bad Wolf, not Happy the Dwarf. A warm, unmistakably real smile that turned him from handsome to devastating, hit her in the chest and spread, like one of those bullets that expand on impact.

It left her reeling.

*No way, I do not reel when Kyle Everson smiles.*

"It's late," she muttered. "I'd better go to…" The *bed* dropped off, suddenly seeming an unsuitable word. Too suggestive. *This is nuts—what am I, fifteen?*

She reached for her coffee cup, just as Kyle did the same, presumably planning to clear it away. Instead, his fingers wrapped over hers.

The unexpected touch startled her. She tried to pull away, but her thumb was through the cup handle, and instead, she got tangled up with Kyle.

Jane didn't touch people often, not beyond a handshake. She felt hot, flustered, panicky.

"Sorry," she said, breathless, still trying to wrestle the mug out of his grasp.

"Hang on," Kyle said. He moved his hand to hold the cup at the top. "Okay, I've got it."

Jane freed her thumb, then rubbed her tingling fingers down her skirt.

"Are you okay?" he asked.

"Fine." *I have tingles up my arm from a casual touch, but that's not a problem.* "I think I'll turn in." Why couldn't she have thought of *turn in* a minute ago?

*Calm down,* she told herself, as she pushed her chair back from the table, then picked up her folder. *So you felt a second's fleeting attraction to Kyle. Big deal.*

She needed to lift her game. She'd started tonight determined to act like a professional, and ended it blabbing about the misery of her childhood and overreacting to a meaningless touch.

*Tomorrow,* she would act like a professional.

## CHAPTER EIGHT

"SO WHAT'S THE REAL DEAL about you staying on in Pinyon Ridge? Neither you nor Kyle looked too happy about it Friday night." Micki set Jane's coffee in front of her and sat down. She gave a little groan of pleasure at taking the weight off her feet. Only eight-thirty, only Monday, and already she was tired.

"I realized I wasn't done yet," Jane said vaguely.

Micki rolled her eyes; Jane was queen of the mind-your-own-business evasion. There was no such thing as minding your own business in Pinyon Ridge, which was both a blessing and a curse. "You mean, not done with Daisy? Or not done with Kyle?"

She'd said it to be provocative, but Jane's spoon rattled against her cup as she stirred in her sugar. "With Daisy, of course." She clattered the spoon into the saucer.

Hmm, interesting.

"It's just...Kyle was looking at you oddly all evening." Micki knew Kyle pretty well, but his face had been unreadable when he looked at Jane. Which he did a lot.

Jane looked flustered. "We'd argued earlier about whether I should stay. He doesn't think Daisy needs more help. But I talked him into it."

"So there's nothing going on between you?" Jane deserved to find a nice guy, but maybe Kyle wasn't the one. Micki glanced at the door. Charles would arrive any moment.

"It would be strange if there was, given the clinch I caught you two in." Jane had recovered her usual poise.

Micki deflected that with a backhanded wave. "That was for old times' sake."

"Right," Jane said. "It had nothing to do with the fact that you like one of the Everson men. Which I presume is Kyle, given *you were kissing him.*"

"Actually, *he* kissed *me,*" Micki said.

"You *moaned,*" Jane said.

Micki grinned. "Did it sound convincing?" The kiss had done nothing for her—it had taken all the acting skills that had landed her the part of lead angel in the church Christmas pageant last year, and then some.

Jane pinched the bridge of her nose, which also happened to be a habit of Kyle's. Again, interesting.

"It convinced your audience you're crazy about Kyle, if that's what you mean."

"I didn't want to look crazy about him!" Micki checked the door again. "I wanted to look like I'm incredibly hot."

Ugh, had she just said that? There was something about Jane that made her easy to confide in. Micki sensed she'd had enough trouble in her own life not to be fazed by other people's insecurities.

"Are you saying Kyle *isn't* the one you like?"

Micki made a lip-zipping motion. One more word and she might give herself away completely.

Jane drummed her fingers on the table. "So you kissed Kyle, hoping Gabe would catch you in the act. How did you guess Gabe would come in at that moment—or were you planning to hang in there all night?"

Micki laughed. "I think that minute or so stretched Kyle's patience to the limit. All night was never an option."

"Which means you *knew* Gabe would come inside right then..." Jane frowned. "Kyle was giving me the evil eye over our argument about Daisy—" in Micki's judgment, it hadn't exactly been the *evil* eye "—then Gabe came to talk to him."

"No need to rehash," Micki said quickly, her face heating. "I was right there."

"Then Kyle announced he was going inside for more beer," Jane continued. "And Gabe said…" She paused. "No, *Charles* said, I'm about to bring these steaks in, can you get the garlic butter."

"Do you remember every conversation word for word?" Micki demanded.

"It's my job to observe people." Jane's forehead wrinkled in puzzlement. "How did you know Gabe would—" She stopped.

Micki's cheeks were so hot, she could be standing over a pan of frying bacon during the morning rush.

Jane gasped. "No way."

*Uh-oh.*

"You don't like Gabe, you like *Charles*."

"Are you nuts?" Micki attempted a laugh; it sounded shrill.

"You have a *crush* on Charles Everson?" Jane obviously realized she'd spoken too loudly, despite the buzz of breakfast conversation around them, and lowered her voice. "You… and *Charles?*"

"Shut up!" Micki hissed, leaning forward. "What are you, some psychic freak of nature?" A horrible thought occurred to her. "Please tell me the entire Everson family didn't come to the same conclusion on Friday night."

"I only just reached it myself," Jane said. "I don't imagine that scenario would occur to those guys, not even Gabe, who has some intuition—it's too far-fetched."

"Hey!" Micki said.

"Sorry, I didn't mean…" Jane stirred her coffee again. *"Charles?"*

"Why not? He's a great guy." Micki tried to sound casual, but like all her thoughts about Charles, it came out intense. "I love talking to him. He's honest and caring. I have huge respect for him."

"And also the hots," Jane suggested, looking appalled.

"Well, yeah," Micki said helplessly. "He reminds me of Sean Connery. Twenty years ago."

"I guess there is a resemblance," Jane conceded. "A faint one."

"He has a sexy voice," Micki said. "Different from Sean Connery's, but just as sexy. And he's kept in shape—he never did that fat cop thing."

"He's lean," Jane agreed. "But...how old is he?"

"Fifty-nine," Micki admitted. "And I'm thirty-seven. Twenty-two years," she added, before Jane could complete the math. "It's not unheard of. In fact, it's more common than you think. I read an article in *Cosmo*."

"Bound to be true," Jane deadpanned. "So, judging by your bizarre decision to kiss Kyle on Friday—"

"*He* kissed *me*," Micki inserted automatically.

"—Charles doesn't know you're interested?"

Micki propped her chin on her hands. "I've talked to him over breakfast every weekday morning for four years—he started coming in for more than just a coffee about a year after Patti died. For the past year, it's been Saturdays, too. We laugh, we debate, we connect in an unbelievable way... but no, I don't think he's ever thought of me as more than a friend." She sighed. "Which is a step up from my being *Kyle's* friend, which is how he used to think of me."

Jane nodded. "So that kiss..."

"Was intended to make him realize I'm a desirable, grown-up woman, not just a coffee buddy."

"You don't think making out with his son might have reminded him you're a generation younger?"

Micki groaned. "I know, I know. It's just, for a minute there, before you all arrived, I felt like he was seeing me in a different light, and I wanted to push that. And Kyle owed me a kiss from high school." She told Jane how she'd been target practice for Kyle's kissing skills back in high school.

"Impressive debt collecting," Jane said. "Remind me never to borrow a buck from you."

Micki snorted. "Thanks."

"I'm surprised Kyle agreed to do it," Jane said. "It seems a bit out there for him."

"Kyle's very responsible," Micki said. "He pays his debts." She snickered, then grew serious again. "But like you said, Charles probably just thinks I'm a slut. A *young* slut."

"That's not what I said." But Jane's face betrayed that was near enough to what she'd meant. "Have you tried dating anyone your own age lately? For real?"

"A couple of guys, once or twice. Didn't work out." Micki pressed her finger into some grains of sugar on the table and picked them up. "I haven't met anyone recently that I find as attractive as Charles, so I haven't bothered."

"How likely is it that Charles returns your feelings?"

"I don't suppose he's ever considered me as a romantic prospect," Micki said. "But if I could make him think about it, maybe he'd realize…" She broached the thought that had been germinating in her head over the past week. "It might be possible, if you helped me."

JANE WAS STILL WRESTLING with the idea of Micki having a crush on Charles; the other woman's bright, eager expression caught her by surprise. "Help you?"

"You just pointed out how my behavior on Friday night may have given Charles the wrong impression. That's what your work's all about, right? Coaching women to get the right message across?"

"Ye-es." Jane took a cautious sip of coffee. "To employers and potential landlords and the like."

Micki pressed both palms into the table and leaned forward. "You could coach me to present myself to Charles in the best possible light."

"I don't advise people on their love lives."

"I can pay you."

"Don't be dumb. It's not about money." A part of her was flattered. Micki's attitude couldn't be more different than Kyle's—he was only accepting her help because she'd blackmailed him into it, and she suspected he didn't believe her advice would make any difference. But she wasn't much more experienced with male-female relationships than she was with parenting. "I don't want to let you down. Getting Charles Everson to date one of his son's friends…that's beyond anything I've done before."

"You don't think it's possible." Micki's perky face sagged.

"Anything's possible." Truthfully, she doubted Charles would relax his iron discipline long enough to fall for Micki. Jane wanted to help—she'd taken an instant liking to the other woman, which didn't often happen—but if she tried, and failed, how would that affect their budding friendship?

Before she could say more, the door opened and Charles himself came in.

"Hi, Charles," Micki called in her usual friendly manner.

"Hey, Micki." Charles's glance didn't quite meet hers, Jane noticed. "Hello, Jane."

Wow, her very own greeting, complete with eye contact. Something was definitely off. Jane wasn't about to be outdone in the courtesy stakes, not by him. "Thanks for dinner on Friday, Charles," she said. "I had a lovely time."

"You're welcome." Charles's politeness turned dogged. He looked to Micki. "Breakfast?" he said hopefully.

"Coming right up."

The same words Micki had uttered to Jane when she'd asked for her usual cappuccino. And every other customer Jane had heard her speak to. How could Charles know she was more to him than just a customer, so that he might start thinking about the possibilities?

Though his expression was jovial, it seemed to Jane he still wasn't quite looking directly at Micki.

Jane waded in to test the waters. "I was just teasing Micki about her intimate encounter with Kyle the other night."

Charles froze, the joviality fading, as if he'd surprised a burglar and found himself staring down the barrel of a gun. "Her what?"

"You mean, you didn't notice her and Kyle locking lips in your kitchen?" Jane said innocently.

Cue a strangled sound from Micki.

"I, uh, of course I did." Was it the light in here, or was Charles's face a little red? "Are you and Kyle, uh, dating, Micki?"

Jane had never seen Police Chief Everson discomfited. She jumped in before Micki could answer. "It was a bet. You know how uptight Kyle is—he bugs the heck out of me."

"No, I don't know," Charles said frostily.

"I bet Micki he wouldn't kiss her back." She shrugged. "I lost twenty bucks." She was taking a risk that Charles wouldn't repeat this to Kyle, but it had to be done.

"Only you would come up with something like that," he said, annoyed.

Jane wondered if she detected a hint of relief in there, too.

Micki looked worried, as if she wanted to intervene to save Jane's reputation. Which was way too far gone with Charles Everson for her to worry about.

"Sorry, Micki, I'm a bad influence," Jane said. "Aren't I, Charles?"

She might have overdone it; he darted her a suspicious look. "Breakfast, Micki?" he asked.

"Of course. You go sit down."

*He's adorable,* Micki mouthed, as Charles headed for his booth.

*No accounting for taste,* Jane mouthed back. Which, fortunately, was too hard to interpret.

Micki grabbed Jane's arm. "This means you're helping me, right?" she said in a low voice. "Because I have no idea where to go from where you just left me. I'm no longer a slut, which is great, but now I kiss for bets?"

"I guess you do need my help," Jane said with an odd sense of exhilaration. "So, okay."

"That's all right, then." Micki headed back to the counter. "I have complete faith in you."

Trouble was, Jane couldn't imagine Charles asking Micki on a date. But it was nice to have someone who knew her as one of *those Slaters* actually trusting her. In fact, Micki was the closest she'd had to a real friend, one who knew the bad as well as the good, since Lissa.

*Micki's lovely, she deserves every chance at this.* Jane was certain a romance between her and Charles would never happen of its own accord, but if Jane could advise her...

Of course, a successful outcome would bring a suite of complications. If Charles asked Micki on a date, Kyle would—Jane's mind boggled. She had no idea what he would do, but she knew he wouldn't like it.

But that was his narrow-minded problem, not hers.

KYLE'S CELL PHONE alarm went off at ten to six on Tuesday. He hit the button to mute the buzzer, pushed the covers aside and got out of bed. He pulled on underwear, jeans and a T-shirt—he would shower later—and headed quietly downstairs.

He was pouring milk over a bowl of granola when Jane spoke from the doorway. "Good morning," she said.

Milk slopped over the side of his bowl. "Now look what you made me do."

She crossed to the sink and tossed him a sponge. "Didn't we agree yesterday you would stick around in the mornings?" Her coaching plan required him to spend time with Daisy mornings and evenings. Yesterday, he'd gone out early, planning to spend an hour at the new house. An hour had turned into two, and he'd ended up rushing home to change after she and Daisy had left for school.

"We didn't exactly agree—what are you wearing?"

Jane glanced down. "These would be my pajamas."

"With rubber duckies on them." Bright yellow duckies swam on a pale blue cotton background, grinning madly. Who wouldn't grin, atop those very feminine curves? The totally inappropriate thought hit Kyle's mind front and center before he could censor it. "They're very short," he said, possibly trying to justify his lapse in judgment.

"They're *shortie* pajamas. I didn't bring a robe with me." She tugged the bottom of the shorts, but failed to cover even another inch of bare, slim thigh. Kyle remembered how awkward she'd been Sunday night, when their fingers had gotten tangled. He'd thought nothing of it at the time, but later, in bed, he'd remembered her flustered state and been intrigued.

Then last night, she'd been coolly professional throughout their coaching session, leaving him wondering if he'd imagined her reaction.

"Stop changing the subject," she said. "It's not acceptable for you to be gone before Daisy wakes up in the morning—" he opened his mouth "—and don't tell me you'll be back in time to see her because you won't."

He closed his mouth again.

"Why don't you hire someone to do the work on the house for you?" she asked. "Or with you? So you can have more time at home."

He finished wiping the spilled milk and threw the sponge into the sink. "Pretty much every laborer in town is working on the ski-lift upgrade project over summer—it's a total overhaul, with new restaurants going in, too. I get help when someone's available, but that's not often enough."

The first button of her pj top was undone. He caught a glimpse of creamy skin—skin that hadn't seen the sun much.

"You have my sympathy, but you still don't get to leave here in the morning."

"I'm up now," he coaxed her. "What else am I going to do with the time?"

She planted her hands on her hips, bringing a couple of strategically placed duckies into prominence. "We'll do the next lesson. Which is a bit harder than not checking your cell phone messages while you're talking to Daisy." One of last night's homilies. "Today's lesson is keep your promises."

"Not a problem," he said.

"You told Daisy last night you'd see her this morning."

He had, too. Rats. "Point taken."

"I just said, it's not that easy," she reminded him. "Yesterday morning, you told her you'd make her some raisin toast to have after her cereal."

"Then the deputy mayor called, and by the time I got off the phone…" He could see that didn't cut any ice with Jane, so he stopped. "Daisy's old enough to make her own toast," he suggested.

Her mouth curved. "Really? That's the best you can do?"

He scowled. Which, perversely, made her smile more widely. He liked her smile—wide or cute, it was always pretty.

"I've discovered," she said, "that Daisy takes little things like a willingness to make toast for her as a sign of love."

His skepticism must have showed, because she said, "It's true. I've had to encourage her to do more for herself, to make sure she doesn't get attached to me. But you *do* want her to get attached. Not making her toast was a double whammy— you broke your promise and you didn't perform that little act of love."

"One little piece of uncooked toast is that big an issue, huh?"

"Occasionally promises have to be broken," she said. "But it's better not to make even casual offers if you can't live up to them."

He couldn't help smiling at her earnest expression, so at odds with those ridiculous yellow ducks.

"What?" she said, suspicious.

"Thanks for being on Daisy's side," he said, surprising himself.

He'd obviously surprised her, too. Her hand went to her throat, then moved down to play with that top button. "It's what I'm here for."

The more he thought about it, the less he believed Jane would have carried through on her threat to leak the truth about Daisy's conception.

She clearly had Daisy's best interests at heart all of the time. She went out of her way to make sure Daisy didn't get too attached…he wondered what that effort cost her. And she'd put a lot of thought into this coaching.

*I could pull out, now that I know Jane's no threat.* And yet…Daisy had smiled at him last night, in response to one of those awkward smiles he was working on improving, and he'd felt like the effort was all worthwhile.

So he would hang in with Jane and her coaching.

Right now, with her legs on display and those oddly sensuous duckies beckoning his attention, that was no hardship at all.

OVER THE NEXT WEEK, Jane and Kyle worked out a compromise that allowed Kyle to continue working on the new house, but also gave him more time and responsibility for Daisy. Around five o'clock each evening, Jane took Daisy up to the house, arriving the same time as Kyle. Father and daughter hung out together in a low-pressure situation for a couple of hours, before Jane returned to take Daisy home for bed.

At seven on Wednesday night, Jane texted Kyle, as she usually did, to say she was waiting in the driveway of his new house, but Daisy didn't come out. Nor was she in the front yard on the trampoline, which Jane had suggested Kyle buy, and where she loved to spend much of the time, bouncing or just lying on her tummy reading a book.

Jane sent another text, and waited a couple more minutes. No sign of Daisy, so she would have to go inside.

She hadn't done that before.

While she'd been putting as much time as she deemed necessary into her coaching sessions with Kyle, and monitoring the results, Jane had also been keeping her distance when she didn't have a reason to be near him.

It made sense to be careful, now that she'd noticed how attractive his smile was, and especially since said smile had been making more frequent appearances these past few days.

She climbed out of her car and headed up the walk. The house hugged the contour of the land, a mix of glass and concrete and wood, highly contemporary, yet somehow also a part of its environment.

The extra-tall cedar front door looked heavy, but was mounted on quality fittings that meant Jane had no trouble pushing it open.

"Hello?" she called.

No reply.

A double doorway to her left seemed to indicate a living room, so she walked that way. And stopped.

The room was magnificent, soaring ceilings above polished floorboards—recycled, going by the scars and flaws that lent character to their golden warmth. Floor-to-ceiling windows on the west side gave a view of the mountains that would be even more spectacular at sunset.

The place looked crafted, but natural. Sophisticated, but homey.

It was nothing like what she'd have envisaged Kyle building for himself. She'd pictured something far more conservative.

"Jane?" Kyle said from behind.

Jane realized her mouth was still open. She closed it as she turned around. "This place is amazing, Kyle. Stunning."

He smiled. "Thanks. It's been way too long in the finishing."

"It's worth the wait," she assured him. Their gazes caught, held. "Um, is Daisy ready?"

He hooked his thumbs in his jeans, his biceps flexing in his gray T-shirt. "I guess she's in her room. Sorry, you probably texted—I don't know where I left my cell."

He was standing closer than she was comfortable with. Jane turned back to the view. "You'll never get tired of looking out this window."

"I hope not." He moved so he was too close again. "Do you miss the mountains?"

"I can see the mountains from Denver."

"Not up close."

"Distance is good," she said pointedly.

He obviously didn't get it. "You really hate this town, huh?"

"I don't hate it." She didn't like to expend that much negative energy on something that no longer mattered. "I just don't want to be here."

"So you have a grudge against it, like my dad said."

"The town has a grudge against me." She took a step away from him. "I managed to acquire a bad reputation without doing anything seriously wrong. That's why I left Pinyon Ridge—figured I'd have more chance of getting a job where no one knew my family."

Kyle remembered how well she'd done in school. "Did you consider college?"

She blinked, as if the question surprised her. "I didn't have good enough grades for a full ride and there was no way I could pay fees myself. I didn't want to get a loan I might not be able to repay."

"Barb and Hal might have helped out. They've always been comfortably off."

"Barb had already done more than enough for me—she

was the one who encouraged me to get out of Pinyon Ridge to make a fresh start," Jane said. "Turned out it wasn't any easier getting a job in Denver, thanks to an attitude problem I didn't know I had. In the end, Barb talked to a friend of hers who ran a fancy boutique in Cherry Creek." One of Denver's most expensive neighborhoods. "She hired me to fetch and carry, mostly as a favor to Barb."

"How did you get from that to running your own business?" He noticed an uneven patch in the polyurethane around the bifold doors, and walked over to check it. Nope, just a trick of the light.

"I wanted a sales role, which would earn more money, but my boss said I wasn't suitable," Jane said. "She didn't know my background, so it had to be something I was doing. Or not doing. When I started paying attention, I realized the way I acted was different from the way my boss and her customers did. I tried some of the things they did, like making eye contact in a way that was friendly but not challenging. Not getting defensive at any question I didn't know the answer to. Choosing to say please and thank-you out of courtesy, rather than seeing those words as kowtowing to people who thought they were better than I was."

Kyle was impressed that she'd made those observations and decided to change, rather than blaming others for not responding to her the way she was.

"I'd been watching the Peters family in action for years," Jane said, "without ever thinking I could be like that. But once I started, although I didn't nail it right away, it took surprisingly little time to get my act together. My boss gave me more responsibility, the customers engaged with me. I could actually sell them nice clothes because they trusted my recommendations, when a few weeks earlier they'd have assumed I knew nothing."

Kyle found himself intrigued by her story. By her. He was getting the uncomfortable feeling he might have misjudged

Jane on several fronts. Even though she might have encouraged that misjudgment, he felt bad about it. "And somehow you ended up running your own business," he prompted.

"Not for a while," Jane said, "After I'd been there a couple of years a woman walked in off the street looking for a job. She obviously had a background that disadvantaged her—I could see she would never get a job in a place like that, if anywhere. When my boss sent her on her way, I chased after her, offered to give her a few pointers."

She wandered down to the window to look out at the view. Kyle wondered if she registered she'd moved closer to him. That wasn't her motivation, he was certain.

"A few weeks later she got a job," Jane said. "Nothing fancy, flipping burgers, but she was thrilled. The halfway house where she was staying asked me to help another woman, and then another, and it went from there. All on a volunteer basis, in my spare time. But when the state released some funding, the director of the halfway house suggested I apply for a grant to turn it into a business. They didn't give me much, but it was enough to get started."

"So you work mostly with women from halfway houses?"

"And women coming out of prison, or in battered women shelters."

"Sounds like you make quite a difference in their lives."

She slanted him a suspicious look. "A lot of the women I work with are in serious therapy for their issues—what I do in no way solves their underlying problems."

"Except," he said, "I imagine finding a job does solve a bunch of issues."

"It helps them feed their kids and shows those kids a different side to their mom," she agreed. "Even my private clients, middle-class women whose husbands have left them, and now they feel worthless, even they can benefit from a stint of fake-it-till-you-make-it."

Which was what she'd done. He had a glimpse of how dif-

ficult it must have been to reinvent herself. To put on an unfamiliar mantle of confident respectability, day in, day out,
until people stopped treating her like a second-class citizen.

"You're not faking it now, right?" he asked. "When you
do that stuff long enough, it becomes part of you. Like you
said about that smiling you have me doing."

She shrugged. "To some extent. But we're all faking ele-
ments of ourselves—we hide our insecurities."

*I admire her.* The thought took Kyle by surprise. But the
way she'd overcome her past to accept herself and to move
on was nothing short of impressive.

He couldn't help not only admiring her, but liking her for
it. Probably not a good idea, considering the context. The
context where she was blackmailing him and he'd made her
promise to leave town and never come back. Adding anything
else to the mix would be way too complicated.

"Let's go find Daisy," he said abruptly. He ushered her
out the door. "Her room's the third on the left." Walking behind her, he noticed the subtle sway of Jane's hips down the
hallway.

"Jane!" Daisy smiled to see her. "Did you come to see my
new bedroom?"

"Sure did." Jane sounded much more natural with Daisy
now than she had when she'd first arrived, though she hadn't
entirely put aside her reserve.

Daisy's room had the same mountain view as the living
area. It was large, light and warm, with a closet that would
hold Daisy's undoubtedly growing number of possessions
right through her teenage years.

"It's beautiful," Jane said.

"Where will you sleep?" Daisy asked. "You could have
the room next to mine, couldn't she, Daddy?"

Jane's eyes met Kyle's. He had a sudden shocking thought
as to where she could sleep and it wasn't the next room.

Whoa. To go from admiring her to thinking about sleeping with her in the space of five minutes was way too fast.

"Daisy, you know Jane's going back to Denver," he said.

"But when she comes to visit," Daisy persisted.

Kyle had made her promise never to come back. How was he supposed to answer that?

Jane let him off the hook. "What color walls do you want, Daisy?"

"I've chosen a neutral palette for the whole place," Kyle told her. "Colors that fit with the stone and wood."

"Can I have pink?" Daisy asked, and Kyle realized *neutral palette* meant nothing to a little girl.

"Sounds lovely," Jane said, before he could explain. "Doesn't it, Kyle?" Maybe she hadn't let him off the hook, after all.

"We'll see," he said. It was good that Daisy had asked for something, and he didn't want to discourage her, but he wasn't having pink.

"What color was your room when you were a girl?" Daisy asked Jane.

"I shared a room with my sister and brothers," Jane said. "So it wasn't really mine. It was white, I think. We need to go, Daisy."

"I'll see you at home before bedtime," Kyle promised. He reached out and ruffled Daisy's hair before he even realized what he was doing.

Daisy gave him a curious look, but she didn't pull away. He should make physical contact with her more often. He always kissed her good-night, but that was rote behavior. Prescribed touches. He needed to be more spontaneous. Aw, what the heck. "Love you, sweetie," he said.

Jane's jaw dropped. Daisy darted a glance at him through lowered lashes.

Had he done it right? Was that what Jane had meant when she asked if he ever told Daisy he loved her?

When she mouthed *Thank you* over Daisy's head, he figured he must have done okay.

He followed Jane and Daisy down the hallway, intending to resume work in the kitchen. Again, he noticed Jane's distinctive walk. Would Daisy walk like that one day?

Which would prevail in his daughter? Nature, or nurture? Slater DNA, or Everson upbringing?

## *CHAPTER NINE*

JANE HAD ARRANGED TO MEET Micki in her apartment above the Eating Post, after the café closed at three on Saturday. Entering Micki's private domain seemed a strangely personal step.

"Come on in," Micki said as she showed Jane into her small, cheerfully decorated living room.

She directed Jane to the window seat, where the sun streamed in. Jane settled at one end, Micki took the other.

"So, tell me what I need to do to get my man," Micki said. "I'm putty in your hands."

"You sound like the dream client." Though in fact it was Kyle who'd featured in Jane's daydreams, at least in recent days. He was working so hard to follow her advice, she couldn't help but be moved by his commitment. It was paying off, too, in Daisy's increased confidence around her dad.

Jane pulled her notebook from her purse and flipped past the pages of notes she'd made on Kyle. She wrote Micki's name and the date at the top of a new page. "Okay, let's talk about what you're trying to achieve."

"I want Charles to want me," Micki said.

Jane set down her pen. "That's easy. Lock him in the café and take your clothes off. I guarantee that'll do it."

Micki gaped. "Are you nuts?"

Jane rolled her eyes. "Think harder. What do you really want? A quick fling? Something more serious? You'll act differently depending on the goal."

"Something more serious," Micki said. Then, firmly she added, "Something very serious."

Wow. Jane sat back against the cushions. "Are you…in love with Charles?"

Micki bit her lip, uncharacteristically hesitant. "I think I might be. But it seems dumb to say that without ever having dated him, so I reserve the right not to be."

"Fair enough." Jane picked up her pen again. "So let's talk about the obstacles to your goal. You've already said Charles thinks of you as a friend and nothing more. Is he averse to dating?"

"I don't think so. He's dated a few times since Patti died, but in a small town like Pinyon Ridge you have to decide early on if it's going to work out. Breaking up can get messy."

"I can imagine." Jane made a couple of notes. "So reluctance to date isn't an obstacle."

"In general, no. But I'm pretty sure he'll think I'm too young for him."

Jane was inclined to agree. But she didn't say so, just wrote "too young" on her page.

"He doesn't think of me sexually," Micki said. "I can tell."

Jane tilted her head to one side. "He just about choked to death when you kissed Kyle."

Micki's eyes widened. "You think that was because he's interested? He's always telling Kyle and Gabe to ask me out."

"He tells them that because you have qualities he admires, the kind he'd like to have in the family," Jane pointed out.

"I never thought of it like that." A slow smile spread over Micki's face.

"Since we know he has a high opinion of you just as you are, we don't need a radical transformation. How often do you see him outside of the café?"

"I hadn't been to his house in years, before that barbecue. I see him in church on Sundays, but we mix in different circles there."

Jane tapped her pen against her lip. "So we need to encourage him to see you fitting into his life in a wider context than just cooking him breakfast. Though cooking him breakfast has a certain, uh, wifely charm."

Micki laughed, blushing. "I don't know what kind of wider context is available. Charles isn't a big drinker. He doesn't go to bars on Saturday nights." She wrinkled her nose. "I'm not a big drinker myself."

"Sounds like you have plenty in common," Jane said.

"I could invite him to dinner with some friends...."

"That's just encouraging him to see you as a cook," Jane said. "Sure, he'd be upstairs rather than downstairs, but you're playing the same role. We need to broaden his horizons."

"You're smart," Micki said admiringly.

It wasn't a serious comment, but it warmed Jane. Sure, she was used to the appreciation of her clients in the city, but they knew nothing about her past. To have Micki respect her despite knowing her background felt like something special.

Just as she'd felt special when Kyle had made it plain he respected her work when they'd talked at his new house the other day.

"I'm planning a birthday party for Daisy—she turns six next week," Jane said. "How about you come along? Have Charles see how well you fit into a family event...one where you don't make out with one of his sons."

Micki blushed. "Can we move on from that?"

Jane grinned. "When I'm good and ready." She doodled on her pad as she thought. "How would you feel about letting someone else cook Charles's breakfast at the café?"

Micki's eyes widened. "Really?"

"It'll shake things up, let him know he can't take your presence in his life for granted, not even at the café. Even if at this stage he's only concerned about losing your friendship, he needs to realize even that relationship requires more of an effort from him than merely ordering breakfast."

Micki looked terrified. "What if he doesn't care who cooks

his breakfast? What if he asks Margaret to sit and talk with him instead?"

"Then your friendship's not as strong as you thought, and you have a different problem," Jane said baldly.

"Ouch." Micki looked sick. "I usually do all of the cooking myself—Margaret does the support stuff. But she's a good cook—she fills in when I can't work."

"So she'll cook for Charles," Jane said. "I tell all my clients it's important to look as if you have options. Never look desperate. Charles will see that cooking for him is just one of the ways you might choose to spend your morning."

Micki ran her hands through her short hair. "Can I still sit and talk with him while he eats?"

"Sometimes," Jane said. "But again, options. You're a busy woman with demands on your time. I'll come in for breakfast if you like, and you can choose to talk to me."

Micki started to agree, then stopped. "Uh-uh. If there's even a remote chance of this working, I don't want Charles to dislike you because you're getting in the way of our romance. I want him to *like* my friends."

Jane got a lump in her throat. "Thanks," she said gruffly, "but he already dislikes me. I'll try not to make that worse." She cleared her throat. "Next thing on the list. I'd like you to make occasional physical contact with him. A casual touch on his arm or hand as you talk."

"You don't think that's a bit forward?" Micki asked. "Charles is old-school. He's not touchy-feely."

"He has to want to be touchy-feely with you," Jane pointed out. "This is just a foretaste, the merest hint. Nothing he can get awkward about, and nothing that puts you out there as a love stalker."

Micki snickered.

"He can either ignore it," Jane said, "or he can start paying attention and realizing that you don't touch every friend that way."

Micki nodded, though she looked unconvinced. "What about my clothes? I sometimes wonder if part of the problem is I still dress the way I have since I knew him as teenager—jeans and T-shirts every day. Though I wouldn't say he looked any more interested when I wore a dress to that barbecue...."

Jane winced. "That wasn't a great dress."

"A moment's madness," Micki admitted. "It was one of my mom's. I have no idea how old it was, and Mom was somewhat rounder than I am."

"No more of Mom's dresses," Jane advised. "Is there a store in town that has clothes you like?"

"Rich Rags," Micki said. "I buy the occasional accessory there. But Theresa will think it odd if I show up wanting a dress. She knows I'm not a dress kind of gal."

"Does it matter what she thinks?"

"In Pinyon Ridge?" Micki gave her a look of disbelief.

"Yeah, right." Jane laughed. "How about a couple of blouses, then, to wear with your jeans?"

Micki considered. "I could do that."

"And maybe *one* dress—you could say it's for Daisy's party and I'm making you dress up. Or you could even shop online."

Micki nodded. "It's worth a try." She beamed. "This is so exciting."

"Just remember," Jane warned her, "you can change your look, change your behavior, be as fabulous as it's possible for you to be. But, as I tell my clients when they go to a job interview, there's still a chemistry factor. A client can get rid of the obstacles that might blind the other person to their strengths, but if they don't click in the interview..."

"You're saying Charles might just plain not be interested," Micki said.

Jane nodded. "Through no fault of yours. Plus, even if there is chemistry, a man like Charles Everson might take some persuading that it's okay for him to date a woman so much younger."

"He likes to do the right thing," Micki agreed.

Jane's interpretation had been, *he's narrow-minded.* But maybe there was something to what Micki said. Kyle was fixated on getting it right, too. He wanted to do the right thing for Daisy, for his family, for the town.

"The question is," she said slowly, "is he doing the right thing with his head or with his heart?

"Are you talking about Charles?" Micki asked, confused.

"Uh, of course."

"Because for a moment there you seemed a long way away. As if you were thinking of someone else altogether. Such as Kyle."

"Not at all," Jane lied.

"You're not the only one who can observe others. Running this place, I get to see my regulars a lot, and I notice changes. Kyle's been different lately. More relaxed."

"If that's true," Jane said, "it's because he's working on being more relaxed with Daisy. I wouldn't be surprised if it started to spill over into other aspects of his life."

"I think he likes you," Micki said. "A lot."

The surge of hope that swamped Jane took her by surprise. She *wanted* Kyle to like her. Which was beyond stupid.

"You're wrong," she said. "Kyle and I have had some serious disagreements." *I deceived him about Daisy's conception, and I blackmailed him into letting me stay.* "Plus, I told him he needs therapy, for Pete's sake."

Micki hooted a laugh. "I'll bet that went down well. By the way, in the interest of keeping the peace, I suggest you don't mention therapy in front of Charles. He's not exactly a New Age guy about that sort of thing."

"And yet you're crazy about him?" Jane grabbed the change of subject.

"I never said he's perfect," Micki said. "Just like I'm not. Neither is Kyle, by the way." Subject returned.

"I know that," Jane said.

"But he's a good man, and he needs a good woman."

Jane's cell phone rang, and she grabbed the reprieve. Unfortunately, the display read *Kyle*.

She pressed to answer.

"I just had a great idea," he said. "A way we can give Daisy some fun."

He wasn't just a good man, he was a good father.

"What's your idea?" Jane said.

"We can take her to the funfair in Frisco tonight. Get it? *Fun*fair. Even you and I could find some fun there."

He was kind, thoughtful, funny.

"Uh…" Jane said, tempted when she shouldn't be. Micki eyed her speculatively. "I'm kind of tied up with Micki…"

"No, she's not," Micki called. "She's free to go."

Jane glared at her.

"Sounds like Micki's done," Kyle said.

"The funfair is something you and Daisy should do, just the two of you," Jane said.

"If you come, there's much more chance I'll stick to those lessons you taught me."

"You need to get used to me not being there," she countered.

"Not tonight," he said. "Daisy and I aren't ready to let you go just yet."

It could have meant a million things. *Not going to analyze it.*

"Come on, Jane," he said, "I'm not sure I can be fun enough on my own."

She couldn't help laughing. "I'm no more fun than you are. Probably less."

"Which of us has rubber duckies on their pajamas?" he asked.

Her mind went back to that morning in the kitchen early last week, him looking at her legs with blatant appreciation.

"I've never *seen* your pajamas," she pointed out.

Micki's eyes widened. Jane felt heat in her cheeks.

"They're navy blue with pinstripes," he said.

"Ouch, that's sad."

"Told you," he said smugly. "Though I should add, I often don't wear them."

"No, you *shouldn't* add that."

He chuckled. "We'll leave for Frisco in half an hour. Are you okay to get home by then?"

"I really don't think…"

"You want Daisy to have some fun, don't you?" he asked.

There was only one answer to that.


KYLE CLOSED HIS CAR DOOR and hit the remote lock. "Let's go have some fun." He gestured to the archway of bright lights ahead.

Daisy was bouncing on the balls of her feet in excitement, a state he'd never seen her in. Her whole face had lit up at the word *funfair;* just the concept was magic, it seemed—not to mention the perfect solution to Kyle and Jane's mutual lack of fun-ness. His daughter had even chattered during the half-hour drive to Frisco.

As they crossed the parking lot, Daisy skipped to keep up with him and Jane. As Kyle paid their admission, she was openmouthed with excitement, turning in all directions to see the lights, the rides, the food stalls.

Electronic sounds—music from the carousel and other rides, prize buzzers, the shouts of hawkers selling hot dogs and cotton candy—made a cacophony drowned only by the shrieks of people on roller coasters.

Kyle leaned into Jane. "Not the most impressive funfair I've seen, but Daisy seems to like it."

Up close, he caught the scent of Jane's perfume—vanilla

and jasmine. She eased away. "Look, a haunted railway." She pointed. "Can we go on that? Or will it be too scary for Daisy? How scary are these things?"

"You've never been on one?"

She shrugged, her attention caught by a spinning wheel of fortune. Going by the excited shrieks, a customer had just been promised a major lottery win.

"You look like Daisy with your mouth hanging open," Kyle teased. Daisy laughed, but there was an awkward moment between him and Jane while they both processed what "You look like Daisy" could mean.

"Probably because I've never been to a funfair before," she said quickly.

"What, never?"

"There wasn't one in Pinyon Ridge," Jane reminded him. "Barb did offer to bring me with them down here to Frisco one year, but Mom wasn't well, so I pulled out." Her voice was carefully neutral.

"Sounds like there's more to the story than that," he said.

"It's not a day I like to remember," she admitted.

He stopped walking, waited for more, keeping an eye on Daisy as she darted to check out a shooting gallery offering the ugliest range of pastel teddy bear prizes.

After a moment, Jane said, "I rushed home from school to get ready for the funfair, and found Mom nursing a broken nose. Blood everywhere."

He winced. "What happened?"

"It was one of those times when money was scarce. Mom had turned to the only way she knew of earning cash to pay the power bill and groceries fast. The guy—I have no idea who it was—had gotten upset about his lack of exclusivity with her and punched her."

"Did you call the cops?" Namely, Kyle's dad.

Her mouth turned down. "We didn't have a phone. I left a note for Barb to say I couldn't make it, then walked Mom to the other end of town to see Dr. Graham—he didn't charge folk who couldn't pay."

"I'm sorry," he said. "Sorry you had to go through that."

Her smile was rueful. "The worst part of it is, the whole time, when I should have been worried about Mom, I was seething with disappointment and anger at missing the funfair." She shoved her hands in the pockets of her jeans, her shoulders hunched forward. "Not one of my proudest moments."

Kyle wanted to haul her into his arms and tell her she *should* be proud of herself, making it through times like that and eventually getting away so she could make something of herself. And while he had her in his arms, he might as well kiss those luscious lips....

Daisy returned from the shooting gallery. "Can we go on a ride? Which ride can we do?"

"Definitely the Haunted Railway," Kyle said. "Think you can handle it, Daisy? For Jane's sake?"

"Definitely," she echoed, and Kyle laughed.

They lined up for the ride and within minutes were being ushered into a little car. Daisy sat between Kyle and Jane, and the attendant lowered the safety bar.

"Keep your hands in the car," he instructed.

Daisy wrapped her hands around the bar, her eyes wide.

The ride jerked into operation.

They rattled through a series of supposedly scary encounters over the course of about a minute. Daisy shrieked at every single one, and Jane joined her, out of empathy rather than fear, Kyle figured.

"We need a sugar fix after that," Jane said as they got out of the car at the other end.

"Cotton candy?" Kyle guessed.

Daisy was immediately utterly absorbed in the pink cloud of spun sugar that he bought her. After she'd walked into three people, not looking where she was going, Jane made her stop and sit on a bench while she finished eating. She and Kyle stood alongside. He'd bought Jane her own stick of the stuff, too, which they shared.

"This was a good idea, coming to the fair," Jane said, nodding at Daisy's rapt expression.

"Hello, Kyle," someone called.

He looked around and saw Susan Tully, Wayne's daughter.

"Hi, Susan, you having a good time?" She was holding hands with her two kids, who bore traces of cotton candy on their sweatshirts.

"You bet." Susan was noting Jane's presence with interest. But everyone knew Jane was back in town to help Kyle, so that could hardly lead to gossip.

"Enjoy your night," he said, and she correctly took it as dismissal and left.

When Daisy finished eating, they rode the Ferris wheel.

"Time for something more sedate," Jane said after they dismounted. "I feel dizzy."

"What's *sedate*?" Daisy asked. Ever since they got here, she'd been asking questions. Short ones, but more proactive conversation than Kyle had heard from her before. It had to be a good sign.

"*Sedate* means slow and maybe a little bit dull," Jane admitted.

Daisy looked dismayed.

"Like me," Kyle said, and she giggled. "How about the carousel?"

"Ooh, yes, please." Daisy clearly didn't connect that ride with the word *sedate*.

Jane and Kyle ended up on adult-size carousel horses. Hers was cream with a golden mane, while Kyle's black steed had an incongruous blue mane. Daisy was just ahead of them, on a smaller horse, white with a black mane.

The fake organ music started, and the carousel began to

turn. Jane's horse rose up as Kyle's went down, and vice versa, but that didn't restrict their ability to converse.

"Against all odds, given the company she's in, she's having fun." Kyle nodded at Daisy, who was gazing around, enthralled.

"Amazing." Jane patted her horse's neck. "Whoa, Nelly."

"I've been thinking," he said, as his horse went down and hers rose up. "You and I haven't always seen eye-to-eye...."

"Understatement of the year," she said.

"But Daisy likes you. She likes having you around."

"Thanks." Jane sounded surprised.

"I'm getting used to you myself," he added lightly.

Her smile was puzzled.

"Here's the thing..." He paused, because once he said this there was no taking it back. "I think you have a part to play in Daisy's life. Maybe, you even have a *right* to play that part."

She gaped, took a moment to find her voice. "I signed a waiver at the clinic," she began.

"I'm not talking about legal rights," he said. Jane was right—she had no legal rights where Daisy was concerned. The first thing he'd done after she broke the news to him was call a lawyer in Denver, who had confirmed that Jane had no recourse, no claim under the law.

"I've realized there's a certain moral right involved," he said.

When she'd first told him the truth, he'd have said no way did she have a moral claim, plain and simple. But now, he saw how she cared for Daisy, even if she held herself aloof. She'd gone to extreme lengths to make sure he let her stay, even committing to walking away at the end of this month.

Jane realized she was holding her horse's mane in a death grip. She loosened her fingers. "Why are you saying this now, Kyle? I haven't asked—I've told you, I don't think of Daisy as..."

"But she is," he said.

They were both skirting around the big words. *Mother. Daughter. Family.*

"I can't believe you're comfortable with what you just offered." Her left heel thudded against her stirrup, an agitated beat. His offer was oh so tempting....

"I'm not," he said, honest—or blunt—as ever. "Not entirely. But I want to do the right thing." He paused. "I'm revoking the condition of our deal, the one requiring you to leave town and never come back. I shouldn't have said it in the first place, and I'm sorry."

She should just grab it, like she should grab the carousel pole in front of her, and enjoy the ride. As long as it lasted. But...

"I appreciate what you're trying to do, Kyle, but you're not facing reality."

He frowned. "I know you care for Daisy."

Jane swallowed. She didn't like to think about how much she cared for the little girl. "Who wouldn't be fond of her?"

"It's more than that," he said. "I thought you'd welcome the chance to stay a part of her life."

"For how long?" she asked.

"For...as long as you want, I guess."

"Right now, things are going well with Daisy and you're giving me some credit for that. But what if she were to, say, get involved in drugs or petty crime. What are the odds you'd blame her Slater blood?"

"What are you talking about?"

"Or what if one day a biological mother gets in the way of your family? Say, you marry again, and your wife doesn't want me connected to you." The thought was painful on more than one level.

"Nothing stays the same forever," he said. "I guess we'll deal with each challenge as it comes along."

"What if your way of dealing with it is to remind me I

don't have any rights, and I'm no longer part of this cozy setup you're suggesting?"

"I don't think I would do that." At least he was honest enough not to be categorical.

"I don't want to be exposed again to that kind of hurt," she said. The kind of hurt Lissa's rejection had inflicted. "You and I might see eye-to-eye for a few months, maybe even years, for Daisy's sake, but we're too different. And when something happens to end this…this relationship you're talking about, which it will, you'll still have your daughter and your tight-knit family and your hometown harmony, and I'll have…"

He waited.

"Not *nothing*," she said. "Because I have my work and my apartment. But I won't have what you've got."

"That might never happen," he said. "Why would it?"

"Because I'm a Slater. Eversons and Slaters don't mix."

"It's not like my family's perfect," he said. "You know damn well I have my share of faults, and Gabe got into some trouble when he was younger."

She snorted. "But he ended up a pastor."

"You're living proof that a dodgy family doesn't make you a bad person," he said. "Can't you trust me not to hold your family against you in future? If I'm willing to put the past behind us, I don't see why you can't."

"Because it's not just down to you and me," she said.

"I know people like my dad can seem a bit closed-minded, but he's not a bad guy," Kyle said. "In fact, he's a great guy and he's trying hard to move on. You could try cutting him some slack."

"Your father never once cut *me* an inch of slack, and I was a decent enough kid—mainly thanks to Barb," Jane admitted. "Your dad figured there was no such thing as a good Slater, and he harassed the heck out of me."

She could see him fighting the instinct to automatically assume his dad had been in the right.

"What do you mean 'harassed'?" he asked.

"When Lissa and I were fifteen," she said, "Lissa wanted to shoplift some nail polish—you know, just to see if she could. I said no, I had this thing that I didn't want to let Barb down. But Lissa talked me into it. We got caught—your dad hauled us to the station."

He waited.

"Lissa told him the shoplifting was her idea, that she'd had to practically force me into it," Jane said.

"That was good of her."

That was the Lissa he'd fallen in love with, Jane knew. The gutsy young woman who faced trouble head-on.

"Very good," Jane agreed. "Unfortunately, your dad didn't believe her. Purely on the basis of our parentage, he drove her home to Barb, and stuck me in a cell for the night."

Kyle winced.

"So excuse me if my views are a little jaundiced." She drew a breath. "But hey, let's not talk about your father. Let's talk about mine."

"O-kay," he said warily. He was right to be wary.

"Did I ever tell you where he lives?" Jane asked.

"I thought you didn't know."

Her smile was grim. "Oh, I know. My dad lives in Bentwood."

Kyle froze.

Bentwood might be marked as a town on the map, but everyone around here knew that 90 percent of its residents lived in one building—guests of the Colorado Department of Corrections at the Bentwood Correctional Facility.

## CHAPTER TEN

"YOUR DAD'S IN JAIL?" KYLE demanded.

"Yep." Jane checked on Daisy, and found her still happily riding her horse. "Not for the first time, either." She saw Kyle's struggle not to overreact.

"What did he do?"

"Armed robbery," Jane said. "Though he said he was only driving the getaway car." She believed it—her dad was not exactly a criminal mastermind.

"It's not…" He raked a hand through his hair. "It's not your fault he did whatever he did. And ended up in jail."

"He's Daisy's biological grandfather," she said.

She'd done it, used one of the big words.

And Kyle didn't like it, not one bit. He sat upright, rigid on his horse with that silly blue mane, his brows drawn together. Jane didn't blame him.

"My father was horrible to my mom," she said, "and not much better to us kids. I lost touch with him when I left Pinyon Ridge—I no longer see him. In fact, I don't see any of my family."

He nodded jerkily.

"I don't know where Darren is, but I wouldn't be surprised if he's in jail, too," she said, pushing him harder. "Cat, my sister…we text occasionally, and she visits me once in a blue moon." She grimaced. "When she wants money. Johnno, the youngest—he's the one who got the fire chief's daughter pregnant."

"If I remember rightly, that was a consensual sexual act,"

Kyle said. "The gossip was all over town, and everyone was clear that she was crazy about your brother."

"Who agreed to marry her, then snuck out of town in the middle of the night...with the proceeds of the fireman's ball," she reminded him.

He turned, and held her gaze. "Why are you doing this?" he demanded. "Saying these things?"

"Because they're the truth. This is Daisy's DNA, even if no one other than you or I ever knows it. Whatever trust or respect or liking you have for me will always be vulnerable to the reality of my family."

The carousel began to slow.

"I don't know what to say," Kyle said.

A part of her appreciated that he didn't rush in with platitudes that would ultimately prove meaningless. Another part of her was hurt that he didn't immediately assure her—and mean it—that her family's antics made no difference at all.

"Don't say anything," Jane said. "I don't want to talk about it."

AFTER THEY GOT OFF the carousel, Daisy skipped ahead to the junior bumper cars, and got the last one. She waved to Jane—not Kyle—as the attendant checked her harness. When the green light came on, she sat still while the other cars took off.

"They'll smash her." Kyle tensed, ready to jump the picket fence and drag his daughter out of her car.

"Look, she's moving." Jane touched his arm. Instead of looking at Daisy, he looked down at her hand. He couldn't believe how badly that conversation had gone, couldn't believe... Not now. He corralled his thoughts and focused on his daughter.

As Jane had said, Daisy was moving through the traffic. Tentatively, but definitely not a sitting duck for a case of juvenile road rage. Kyle winced as a kid in a red car bumped her. Daisy circled the perimeter, slowly. A girl in a yellow car bounced off her right wing, then Daisy bumped hard into the girl.

"You go, Daisy," Kyle called.

"Get her, Daisy," Jane said at the same time.

They traded glances. Kyle imagined his was as sheepish as hers.

"I had a lousy upbringing," she said. "What's your excuse?"

He chuckled…then it died away as he caught sight of Daisy. "What the hell?"

The other girl, the one in the yellow car she'd just bumped, had ended up at the side of the track. Daisy had followed—or chased?—and now rammed hard into the side of the girl's car. Instead of driving away, Daisy backed up and rammed hard again.

"Oh, dear," Jane said in total understatement.

"Daisy," Kyle yelled. Even if there hadn't been the noise of the cars and the music, she wouldn't have heard him.

Her mouth was wide-open. She was yelling, or screaming, he couldn't tell which.

Jane ran around the side of the bumper car rink. Good idea—Kyle followed.

By the time they got there, the other kid's mom was there, too, leaning over the fence, trying to reach her daughter, whose face was contorted with tears. The operator finally noticed what was going on, and cut the power.

At which time, Daisy's screaming could be heard by everyone.

Kyle jumped the fence and went to grab her. Daisy's hands were clenched around her steering wheel; he had to pry them free.

"Control your kid, mister," the girl's mother spat. "She's a psycho."

"Watch your mouth," Jane ordered.

Busy unclipping the harness, Kyle appreciated her defense

of Daisy. But the fact was, Daisy's behavior had been inexcusable.

He glanced up and found Susan Tully watching him with undisguised fascination. Great. It would be all over Pinyon Ridge tomorrow that his daughter had lost the plot. He knew how the comments would play.... "The man can't run his own family, how can he run our town?" Plenty of people would think that. Heck, even *he* thought it.

Then at last Daisy was free and he pulled her from the car. "What was that?" he asked.

She was as silent now as she'd been loud a minute ago.

"Dammit, Daisy—"

Jane touched his arm again, shutting him up. Oddly, her presence soothed him, even though she'd just been doing her level best to show him how poorly she fit into his life. He stretched his mouth into one of those fake grins she was so keen on and said, "You better make that therapy appointment."

Once again, he was screwing up as a dad. It had to stop, for Daisy's sake. But also because if he wanted to win the election, he had to be the kind of guy who could care for his daughter right. At this moment, neither of those things seemed possible.

"I DON'T OFTEN SEE YOU at this time of day." Micki set Charles's coffee in front of him. It was four o'clock on Tuesday. She was about to close. Ordinarily, she'd stay open for him. But Jane was due any second for another coaching session.

"I didn't get to talk to you this morning," Charles said. No, he *grumbled*.

Her heart leaped. Two days running, she'd had Margaret cook his breakfast. His disappointment had been obvious, but she suspected it had more to do with her ability to perfectly poach an egg than any attraction to her. Today, she'd gone a step further and told Charles she couldn't sit down with him at breakfast, as she was late with her pantry staples order. Had he missed their conversation so much, he'd had to come back?

"We can talk now for a couple minutes before I close up." She slid in the other side of the booth, and he smiled. It almost gave her the confidence to follow Jane's next piece of advice.

Touch him.

Just the thought made her palms perspire. Wouldn't that make for a pleasant touch?

"I wanted to ask you what you think of the plan to hold Sunday school after church instead of before," Charles said. "Reverend Thackeray is concerned about so many of the younger people moving to Gabe's church. Obviously I have divided loyalties," he said ruefully. "I figured you could give an objective view."

So she had clammy palms for nothing. Micki rubbed them against her jeans. Charles was here as an elder of her church, wanting to sound out one of the members about a new policy. Nothing more. "I'm in favor," she said. "But my reasons aren't particularly holy. I have early starts every other day of the week. Sunday is my only morning to sleep in."

There was a pause. In her dreams, the pause was Charles thinking about her sleeping. In bed. In reality, it was him sipping his coffee.

He set his cup down again. "You work hard, you deserve that sleep-in." His eyes lingered on her cherry-colored blouse with the top two buttons undone. Not revealing anything at all, but possibly *hinting.* He didn't look away.

His hand rested on the table, curled in a loose fist. She could reach out and touch it. . . .

"Maybe you work *too* hard," Charles blurted. "Cooking and serving from the crack of dawn, and then you have all that admin on top. Like that order you were doing this morning."

He was still hung up on the fact she hadn't had time to talk to him this morning. *Interesting.* Micki reached across the table and placed her hand over his. His eyes jolted from her blouse down to her hand, then up to her face, wide with surprise.

"Thanks for your concern, Charles, but I'm fine." She struggled to speak through the breath-shortening physical contact. She'd seen him pretty much every day for the past four years, and she'd wanted him for the past year. But she'd never touched him before, not with deliberate, personal intent. Now, the rugged strength of his hand beneath hers, the contour of knuckle and flesh, fascinated her. She couldn't resist the impulse to squeeze, just a little. A *friendly* squeeze. "You're very thoughtful, a good friend. I appreciate it." Yikes, she was babbling.

Charles's hand jerked away. "I, uh, need to go—I forgot to tell Kyle…something. Something important." He slid out of the booth and stood. "Thanks for the coffee."

He charged out of the café without looking back, leaving behind his almost untouched coffee. Leaving Micki with her hand sitting on the table, bereft.

She'd reached out to Charles, literally and figuratively, and he couldn't get away fast enough.

BACK IN HIS OWN KITCHEN, Charles put the kettle on the stove. His coffee was nowhere near as good as Micki's but it would have to do. He needed the edge taken off his dissatisfaction. He needed…something. Something to settle the churning in his gut.

Probably he should brew up some decaf, but Micki despised the stuff, so he'd let her talk him out of keeping it in the house.

He didn't want to think about her. But he didn't know what he *did* want to think about.

Blast it. The past couple of weeks, he'd had this nagging feeling of something missing, and it had intensified the past couple of days. Since he wasn't a guy who analyzed his own feelings much, he didn't know what to make of it. He could tell you when he was happy, or mad or mildly ticked off. He could say when he felt proud of his sons or worried about them. But this feeling…

Whatever it was, it was producing strange longings. Charles took a mug from the cupboard and set it on the counter with a thud. Micki had touched him, and he'd had the wildest urge to flip his hand over and capture her fingers. Sweet little Micki—he'd known her since she was knee-high!

"I'm a pervert," he muttered.

"Did you just say what I thought you said?" Gabe asked from behind him.

Charles wheeled around. "Dammit, Gabe, why are you sneaking up on me?" What the heck? Now he was cursing and yelling at his son? *Dear God, am I ill?* He'd heard brain tumors could change people's behavior.…

"I'm not sneaking, I told you I'd call in and update you about Kyle's campaign," Gabe said mildly. He pulled another mug from the cupboard. "I'll have one of those, thanks."

Charles added another scoop of coffee to the French press.

He stood in silence until the kettle boiled, then he poured the water into the press. "Are Kyle and Micki dating?" he asked.

Gabe reached into the pantry for the sugar. "Not that I know of. That stunt they pulled last week was… I don't know what it was, but I don't think it meant anything."

"Good," Charles said.

"I thought you wanted Kyle to ask Micki out?" Gabe reminded him. "Or would you rather I did?"

Charles gave the coffee a vigorous stir, then pushed the plunger down. "I'm starting to think she's too busy with that café to have time for a relationship. Kyle needs someone who can put some focus on him and Daisy."

"I guess. Maybe she just needs to find the right guy who can distract her from her work."

Charles pushed the plunger too hard the last inch, and coffee spurted out the spout. He only just managed not to curse again. He wasn't a cursing man, never had been, not even when he was dealing with lowlifes like Mike Slater, Jane's father. *Maybe I have Tourette's. Can that come on suddenly?*

"Why this concern about Micki?" Gabe asked with the perspicacity he seemed to have developed since he'd become a pastor. Was it a divine gift? It was annoying, that was for sure.

"My concern is for Kyle," Charles corrected him sharply. "Do you think he's interested in Jane Slater?"

"If he was, why would he have kissed Micki?" Gabe asked with an obliqueness Charles didn't like.

"He can't seem to keep his eyes off her. That Slater girl seems nice enough now, but she has bad blood," Charles said.

"Dad." No mistaking the reprimand in Gabe's voice.

Charles felt himself flushing. That hadn't come out right, but everything was topsy-turvy these days. "I'm just saying, background matters. What does she know about raising a decent family? If she and Kyle got together and had a baby…"

"Whoa, Dad, they're not even dating." Gabe grabbed a cloth and wiped the spilled coffee. "And even if they were, anyone can put their past behind them. With God's help," he added.

"Don't you preach to me."

"I don't need to," Gabe said. "*You* told me that when I had those couple of years messing around. I don't imagine you've forgotten the lesson yourself."

Had he really said that? Charles supposed he had—the theory sounded great, and when it came to his own son, the evidence stood right in front of him. But those Slaters…

Gabe kept on looking at him with patience and more understanding than he should have at his age.

Charles shook his head. "Whippersnapper. There's a fine line between righteous and obnoxious, you know."

"Oh, I know." Gabe grinned. "I'm far too obnoxious for the Episcopalians."

Charles chuckled. "You need to find yourself a wife—it's

easy to see things in black and white when you only have yourself to think about. Once you have a wife and kids, things get complicated."

"Think I'll stick with the simple life for now," Gabe said. "You ready to talk about Kyle's campaign?"

"You bet." Charles realized it must be his concern for Kyle that was unsettling him. He didn't like to see his older son worried. He was relieved his angst was nothing more serious. *Kids.*


DR. BRENDAN FRANKS, family therapist, had his practice on the second floor of a two-story block at the far end of Frisco. The walls were covered in murals, and mobiles hung from the ceiling.

Jane went with Kyle to the appointment at his request. Although he'd conceded they needed professional help, he didn't necessarily want Daisy talking to a shrink. He'd told Jane he didn't care if that made him old-school. At the very least, Kyle thought he should talk to the doctor himself first.

She wanted to be here, too.

Since the disastrous—in more ways than one—evening at the funfair, he'd said nothing further about her remaining in some way involved with Daisy. Possibly, either Daisy's outburst or the unvarnished truth about Jane's family—or both—had deterred him. Which, really, would be for the best. Because she'd meant it when she said she wouldn't let herself get hurt again.

And yet…she didn't think he'd abandoned the idea. He'd put it in the too-hard basket, maybe, but he wasn't hostile, or even cold toward her. On the contrary, their conversations seemed underpinned by a cautious warmth. One that fit her own mood perfectly.

Now, on Thursday afternoon, they sat side by side on the couch in Dr. Franks's office, a good two feet of space between them, with Kyle relating the background to their visit, from Daisy's conception right through to how Jane had been advising Kyle on showing his feelings for Daisy. He ended with the bumper car incident. A few times, he asked Jane to comment; once or twice, she chipped in uninvited. Dr. Franks had the most mobile eyebrows Jane had ever encountered. During the story, which admittedly had its more outlandish points, they roved all over the place. A couple of times, it seemed they might leave his head altogether.

Shouldn't a psychologist be a little more inscrutable?

"That's quite a tale." Dr. Franks steepled his fingers at the end of Kyle's explanation. "I'm sensing a fair amount of tension between you two."

Well, duh.

"Nothing we can't handle," Jane said.

"It's Daisy we're worried about," Kyle agreed.

"Hmm." The therapist's eyebrows rose again. "How would you describe Daisy's nature before her mother's death?"

Kyle clasped his hands loosely between his knees and leaned forward. "I didn't see as much of her as I should have. So she's always been shy with me."

"That's not entirely Kyle's fault," Jane inserted. "Daisy is slow to warm up, and having her for only a day or two a week would have made it hard to build rapport."

"Daisy's grandmother, Barb, finds her quite lively," Kyle said.

"What was her mother—" the man glanced at his notes "—Lissa, like?"

"Charming, fun, willful," Kyle said. "She was devoted to Daisy. Lissa was an extrovert, and most people loved her."

*Kyle* had loved her, enough to marry her, enough to go through the emotional and physical strain of IVF. Enough to swallow his pride and ask Jane for help when Lissa had shut him out during the pregnancy. Jane felt a pang of envy, swiftly followed by shame that she hadn't done more. Maybe if she'd pressed Lissa harder to tell Kyle the truth…maybe they could have had an honest conversation, and their marriage would have survived.

"Daisy told me she wasn't sure if her mom loved her," Jane blurted. She felt mean even saying it, but it was important.

"Any idea why?" Dr. Franks asked.

"Lissa's behavior was sometimes over-the-top," Kyle said slowly. "A bit possessive. I thought it was because of the divorce—we shared custody—but maybe she was staking a stronger claim. I also at times wondered if I wasn't really Daisy's father," he explained, recounting that old doubt to the psychologist. "Maybe I inadvertently made Lissa feel like the only parent, so she had to overcompensate."

"Or maybe she caused herself to overcompensate," Jane added. "Lissa lied about Daisy, but she was generally honest and wouldn't have lived with her deception easily. She would have likely continued to feel guilty."

Kyle gave her a sideways look, with a warmth in it that made her feel oddly shy.

Dr. Franks didn't look impressed with their amateur attempts at doing his job.

"How do you feel about Daisy, Jane?"

She froze; for some reason she hadn't expected any questions about herself. "I, uh, am fond of her. Anyone would be. She's very sweet."

"When you say anyone would be fond of her, you imply your feelings toward her are no different from anyone else's," he said.

Her throat dried. "I, uh…"

"You're her biological mother," Dr. Franks said. "Doesn't that mean something to you?"

"It means I gave an egg," Jane said.

"You have no maternal feelings toward her?"

"No!" Her heart thudded. "Daisy is Lissa's daughter." She couldn't forget that. *Mustn't* forget that.

"I believe you do feel a maternal connection toward her,"

the psychologist said. "I believe you feel possessive toward her, responsible toward her. Do you think that might confuse Daisy?"

"That's not true."

"Jane has never acted in a way that could hurt Daisy," Kyle said. "She's displayed total integrity throughout this process."

Not entirely true—he was overlooking the blackmail. Jane sent him a grateful smile.

"I'd like you both to try something," Dr. Franks said. "Kyle, could you extend your left hand, palm up, please."

Kyle did as he asked.

"Now, Jane, could you place your right hand on top of Kyle's, palm down."

Jane hesitated. "I don't get it. Why?"

"No big deal," the man said pleasantly. "Could you do it, please."

He was right, it was no big deal. Jane's reluctance risked making it bigger than it was. She put her hand on Kyle's.

It was like touching a lodestone, baked by the sun. The warmth of his palm was a magnet to hers as they pressed flesh to flesh. His strong, lean fingers supported hers.

Jane's heart stuttered in the most pathetically teenage fashion. Did his do the same?

"Can we stop now?" he asked.

Dr. Franks's eyebrows rose at his sharp tone. "In a moment. First, I'd like you both to spread your fingers wide, then curl them together."

Neither of them moved.

"You mean," Jane said, "hold hands?"

"Exactly."

"What's the point of—oh."

Kyle had complied, and now their fingers were interlocked.

"Here's how I see it," the psychologist said. "Daisy's mother died a month ago—of course she's off-kilter. She has a crappy relationship with her dad, like thousands of other children of divorce. It sucks, but that's normal and it can get better. Daisy needs time and love, and a bit of thought put into making her feel secure, and that's exactly what you're giving her." The doctor spread his hands. "So what if she has the occasional meltdown while driving bumper cars? Some kids do that every time they go to the supermarket."

"You're saying there's nothing to worry about?" Jane asked.

"I'm saying, keep doing what you're doing and let time get on with the healing. And ten out of ten for effort to both of you."

Jane felt the warmth of Kyle's grin, the squeeze of his fingers around hers.

"That's such a relief," she said.

"Thanks, Doctor," Kyle said.

Dr. Franks cracked his knuckles. "Actually, you two misunderstood where the issue lay." He shrugged. "Don't feel bad about it—figuring out the problem is my job."

"What do you mean?" Kyle asked.

"The only threats to Daisy's stability are how you're going to manage telling her the truth about her conception—if you do—and that's not an immediate concern. The second stability factor is your relationships, Kyle, and right now that means what's going on between you and Jane."

Kyle let go of Jane's hand. "There's nothing going on."

"You walk in here, sit as far apart as possible on my couch, freak out when I suggest you touch hands. Yet during my questions, you each tried to exonerate the other of any blame for Daisy's state of mind."

"That's garbage," Kyle said.

"You're confused, and that's understandable," Dr. Franks told him. "This woman, Jane, whom you've never particularly liked, contributed her DNA to the daughter you love."

"*I'm* not confused." But Kyle's brow furrowed; Jane sensed his thoughts moving in a direction she couldn't discern.

"While you—" the psychologist turned to Jane "—feel safer without any relationships. But Lissa's death has forced you into close confines not only with a child who's arguably yours, but also with that child's father."

"She's not my child," Jane said tensely.

"How would you describe your relationship with Kyle?" Dr. Franks asked.

"It's…outside normal definition," she admitted. "But nothing's going on."

"We're cocarers of Daisy." Kyle came back into the conversation. "We're friends."

"I'd say you're sex waiting to happen," the psychologist said bluntly.

"What the hell does that mean?" Kyle barked.

Dr. Franks looked amused. "You want me to draw a picture?"

"We're not going to have sex," Jane said. Her insides quivered with tension, like a bow drawn tight. "I like Kyle as a friend, that's all."

"You *like* like him," the psychologist said.

"We're not in high school, Dr. Franks," Kyle snapped.

"The possibility of anything more than friendship has never crossed my mind, not for a nanosecond," Jane said. Her cheeks felt hot just saying it. "Heck, even friendship is a stretch with our history." She looked at Kyle expectantly.

"Never crossed my mind, either," he said.

Was it her imagination, or had his denial come a shade too late and a shade too emphatically?

Jane stilled. Kyle *had* thought about sleeping with her?

Before she could process that possibility, Kyle stood. "We're done here."

Dr. Franks's eyebrows settled in a straight*ish* line. "You're right, time's up." He rose from his chair. "I think we're agreed, Daisy needs time, love and stability. The stability is down to the two of you, who need to sort out your feelings for each other." He came around the desk to open the door for them. "I don't give a damn if you two go at it like rabbits or don't touch each other with a ten-foot pole. But for Daisy's sake, pick one and be honest about it."

THEY SAID NOTHING as they got in the car. Nothing as Kyle turned onto Highway 9 out of Frisco, toward Pinyon Ridge. But as they passed the sign marking the city limit, Kyle said, "Total waste of two hundred bucks."

"Total," Jane agreed. "You'd have got better value if you'd ripped up the money and burned it for heat."

"Yeah," he agreed. He flipped his turn signal and passed a semitrailer. "Still, I hope he's right that all Daisy needs is time and a continued effort by us."

"We haven't done too badly," she said.

"We're on the right track," he agreed. "Thanks to your coaching."

"You're the one who put it into action," she said. "You've put a lot of work into changing the way you deal with Daisy."

She realized they were doing what the therapist had said—giving each other credit—and clammed up.

"Just because he was right about some things, doesn't mean he was right about the rest of it." It seemed Kyle had come to the same realization. "Even quacks must get lucky sometimes."

"Absolutely." Jane pulled her sunglasses, perched on her head, down over her eyes. "I did notice—I did wonder…"

"What?"

"When I said I hadn't thought about sex…for us…you kind of hesitated before you agreed."

Another hesitation. Uh-oh.

"I'm a guy," he said. "Guys think about sex all the time."

"Does that mean you've thought about it with me?"

"Why do you want to know?" he hedged.

Deep inside her, everything tightened.

"Because if Dr. Franks is right, and we're causing confusion, maybe we need to fix that."

"You could stop walking around in those pajamas," he said.

"My rubber ducky pj's?" she said.

"They make your legs look—" one hand left the steering wheel in an expressive gesture "—incredible." He passed an RV hugging the center line. "Look, Jane, I'm a guy. You're an attractive woman who swans around my house in her teeny tiny pajamas. Naturally, sex has crossed my mind."

She pffed. "I don't *swan*."

They drove maybe another half mile before he said, "Are you telling me you've never thought of it?"

"That's exactly what I'm telling you." She blew out a breath. "Maybe, since Dr. Franks thinks Daisy's on the right track, I should pack up and leave. It might make things simpler."

The car hit the shoulder at speed, gravel flying out from the wheels. Jane squawked.

Kyle pulled into a picnic area she hadn't noticed—trees screened it from this end, meaning it would only be visible coming from the other direction. He braked, turned the engine off.

"What are you *doing?*" she demanded.

He twisted to face her. "Three weeks ago, I'd have grabbed your offer to leave with both hands. But we've come a long way since then—*Daisy's* come a long way. Don't you dare walk out on her now."

"This is somewhat ironic," she said. "You're now forbidding me to leave, when a few weeks ago you offered to pay me to go."

"So I've seen sense. Whatever." He lifted her sunglasses from her nose so he could look into her eyes. "Are you staying?"

His dark eyes were intense, but no longer bitter. Jane swallowed. "I'll stay if Daisy needs me."

He set her glasses up on her head. "Good," he said gruffly.

"But I can see Dr. Franks might be right about potential confusion for her. You need to stop thinking about sleeping with me."

He rolled his eyes. "Two things. First, it's not like I'm thinking about it all the time—it's just something that pops up when you're in those pj's. Second, technically, it's not *sleeping* that's on my mind."

Liquid heat pooled deep inside her. "Stop that," she said.

"Third…"

"You said two things. Can we get back to driving now, please."

"I've been honest with you, I'd like you to do the same. In the spirit of therapy."

She snorted. "You don't believe in therapy."

"But you do. Are you saying you've never felt even a spark of physical attraction for me?"

"Kyle!"

"Well?" he demanded.

"Maybe a *spark*," she conceded. His eyes lit in triumph. "But that's mainly because of this weird situation we're in," she added quickly. "There's a forced connection between us, through Daisy, so it's natural to think about what other, uh, aspects might come into that. Neither of us would be attracted to the other if the circumstances were different. I mean, were you ever attracted to me before?"

She was out of her depth. The air in the truck had grown heavy.

"No," Kyle said. "I wasn't."

"Exactly."

"But the fact that it didn't happen then doesn't make it less real now," he said.

Jane opened her door, and even the blast of heat that flooded in was less oppressive than the air in the cab. "I need to stretch my legs."

She got out of the truck. Much better. She took a few steps away. Then turned around as a door slammed.

Kyle was out, too. "You can't run away when the conversation gets difficult," he said as he approached. "Okay, let's move on from the alleged attraction between us. There's one more thing I need to say."

He stopped in front of her, too close for comfort, but she planted her feet in the scrabbly dirt. Because she didn't run away. "Say it," she told him.

One side of his mouth quirked. Then he sobered. "When Dr. Franks was talking…what did he say? Something like, that you, a woman I've never particularly liked, contributed your DNA to the daughter I love."

"I wasn't offended," she assured him. "I know you never liked me, and the feeling was mutual."

"Shut up," he said, and she was so surprised, she obeyed. "I can't believe I never thought about this before." He raked a hand through his hair. "Jane, if it wasn't for you, Daisy wouldn't exist."

She opened her mouth to say…what? Nothing came to her.

"I've been so mad at Lissa for lying to me," he continued, "so mad at *you,* I've ignored the—the magnitude of what you did."

"It was…"

"Don't you dare say it was nothing." He grasped her arms, sending a tingle right through her. "My daughter—my amazing, wonderful, quiet, frustrating, adorable bumper-car road hog…"

Jane gave a watery chortle. It was either that or dissolve into sappy tears.

"She's a gift," he said, his voice deep with emotion. "From you. Jane, you gave me my daughter."

Perspiration trickled down her spine; her knees felt suddenly weak. Maybe he sensed it, because he pulled her to him, his arms going around her waist, loosely, but in a way that made her feel…*safe.* But not *entirely* safe. The length of his body was hard enough to remind her that this was unfamiliar territory, and the heat kindling in his eyes had potential to sear.

She pressed her palms flat against his chest, intending to push, to create some distance. Instead, she seemed superglued to him. "I didn't do it for you," she felt compelled to remind him.

His chuckle, his smile, held a tenderness she'd never seen in him. "I know. But thank you anyway." He tucked a strand of hair behind her ear. His thumb rested on her cheek, his fingers in her hair. "Thank you, Jane."

It was the most natural thing in the world for his lips to meet hers.

Their touch was firm, yet gentle. Coaxing. She couldn't help but respond, moving against him, her eyes closed against the warmth of the sun. For what seemed a long time, the kiss stayed almost chaste. Gratitude given and received. Hurts healed.

Then Kyle's fingers moved deeper into her hair, a slow massage of her scalp. When Jane made a noise of pleasure, his tongue slipped between her parted lips.

Everything changed.

His mouth firmed, grew demanding, and Jane eagerly opened up for his exploration. He tasted of coffee and warmth and lingering mint. His taste, his scent, his fingers in her hair and the caress of his other hand, which had somehow found its way to the curve of her bottom, combined in a sensual assault she couldn't resist.

Her arms twined around his neck and she pressed herself closer, fused herself to him. His groan acknowledged both of their needs, found an echo deep inside her.

The crazy blaring of a car horn ended the kiss.

Jane and Kyle sprang apart to see a Chevy truck shoot

by, heading toward Frisco, the driver's fist pumping out the window.

"Anyone you know?" Jane tried to sound casual, as if that hadn't been the best kiss of her life. She tucked her blouse back in her jeans, firmly, so her hands wouldn't shake from unfulfilled desire.

"Just a spectator, I guess." Kyle was watching her movements, making her feel self-conscious. But he didn't seem inclined to look away. "Jane..." He paused, forcing her to look up at him. "That was amazing."

Too amazing. Too good to be true.

"It's been a weird day," she said. "An emotional one. I don't think we should read too much into one kiss."

"We could do it again," he said. "See if maybe it wasn't a one-off."

She wanted to with a hunger that scared her. She took a step backward. "I don't think so." She glanced at her watch. "Hey, look, we'd better get back. Daisy will be finishing school soon."

The wry twist of his mouth said he wasn't buying her lack of interest. But he strode back to the truck, held her door open for her.

Jane kept her eyes firmly on the road for the remainder of the trip. She tried to ignore the way her lips burned for more of Kyle's mouth.

She should never have admitted to the existence of a *spark*.

As any Coloradan knew, a spark was how forest fires started.

## CHAPTER ELEVEN

DUE TO STOPPING for a make-out session at the side of the highway, they arrived back in Pinyon Ridge barely in time to collect Daisy from school.

"I'll get her." Jane had her door open almost before Kyle stopped the car. He didn't argue, since the parking lot was crowded and he needed to wait for a space.

Besides, he needed some space himself to process what had just happened.

Not even when he'd entertained thoughts about getting Jane out of those pajamas had it occurred to him that kissing her would be so damn hot. That unbelievable kiss had come out of nowhere.

He didn't know what the hell he should do about it. He knew what he *wanted* to do, he thought, as he watched Jane walking briskly through the stream of parents and children coming the other way.

He wanted to do it again, but this time on a bed, and see what happened next.

But that might not be the smartest idea. As Jane had said, they were in an unnatural situation. *She's Daisy's biological mother, she's living with me, she's wearing those pj's.* Any guy facing those complications could get the wrong idea about what he really wanted.

She'd asked him outright if he'd been attracted to her before, and he'd answered honestly. No. So if she'd still been just plain Jane Slater—not that there was anything plain about her—Lissa's friend with the sleazy family, but no other connection, would he be attracted to her now?

He would have liked to answer a glib *no,* but he couldn't be sure.

Besides, all those complications *did* exist. And they weren't going anywhere.

CHARLES REVELED IN the familiarity of his granddaughter's birthday party on Friday afternoon. The whole occasion was a balm to his increasingly, inexplicably tormented soul. The Happy Birthday banner Patti had painted when the boys were young, which still came out every year to be hung between the dining area and living room of Kyle's cottage. The smell of frosting and candles. The shrieks of kids who'd likely be throwing up before the night was out. Kyle and Gabe ribbing each other over who was better at pin the tail on the donkey. Most of all, it was lovely to see Daisy with that big smile on her face.

This was what Charles wanted. This was enough.

Not everything was like the good old days. Lissa was gone, and Jane Slater was directing the proceedings like she owned the place.

Someone had to do it, he conceded. And it was the kind of thing women seemed better at. He certainly wouldn't have known where to start, with five of Daisy's kindergarten friends invited, along with Charles and Gabe, and Barb and Hal.

The kids had arrived at three, right after kindergarten, and would be gone by five. After that, the family would have a sit-down dinner—Gabe had volunteered to cook, since Jane was busy with the kids.

Charles still couldn't figure out whether or not there was something between her and Kyle. There was a— Well, he wasn't the kind of man to say there was a *crackle* in the air. But there was something suspiciously like that when Kyle and Jane got within a couple of feet of each other. It was even more pronounced today than usual. Their eyes barely met, but he sensed that each knew where the other was at any given moment. That they were responding to cues no one else saw.

It was worrying…if it was true. He hoped it was just his imagination, attributable to whatever bugbear was eating at him. Kyle was too sensible to get involved with a woman like that, he hoped, but one thing he'd learned as his boys grew up was that it always paid to keep tabs on them.

If they'd let him. Truth to tell, Charles was starting to feel like a spare wheel around here.

Best just to enjoy this family occasion, a warm reminder of what really mattered in his life. So what if he'd felt dissatisfied lately? He was a father, a grandfather and a respected citizen of Pinyon Ridge. What more could a man want?

The kids had just finished a game of pass the parcel. Daisy seemed to be enjoying herself, which was something.

"What's next?" Charles asked Jane, since she was standing right next to him.

"The kids get a choice of face painting or cupcake decorating," she said.

"How are you going to run both those at once?" he asked. "Because I can tell you, Kyle won't be any use at either."

She laughed. Did her gaze soften as it landed on his older son? "I'm doing face painting. Micki's teaching cupcake class."

"Micki!" The name burst from his lips. "I mean, she's not here…is she?"

"She will be—" Jane glanced at her watch "—any second now. Just as soon as she can get away from the café."

Almost before she finished speaking, a knock sounded on the front door. Before anyone could open it or call a "Come in," Micki stepped inside.

Charles lost his breath.

She wore a skirt that sat just above the knee, giving him a look at her legs that he wasn't sure he'd had before. On second thought, he knew he hadn't. He would remember if he had—her legs were sensational.

She looked completely different from the girl who made his breakfast every morning. This Micki wore makeup that made her eyes look bigger and drew his attention to her lips, courtesy of some kind of glossy lipstick. Her skirt turned out to be a dress, a sleeveless burgundy-colored thing with a high, Chinese-style collar but a vee that went so deep he could see cleavage.

She looked amazing.

"Evening, all." She stopped in front of him. Smiled. "Hi, Charles."

"Hi." Did he whisper, or shout? He wasn't sure. "You look, uh, very nice." For whose benefit was all this—this *prettifying?* Gabe had suggested she wasn't involved with Kyle. Was that because she was with Gabe?

"Thank you." Her smile was downright mysterious.

Or was she seeing someone else? Did one of these kids have a single dad?

"Can I get you a drink?" Charles asked too abruptly.

She didn't seem to notice. "Is there anything that isn't bright pink and full of chemicals?"

He chuckled, and it felt like their old camaraderie. "There's tea in the refrigerator."

"Sounds good." She followed him to the kitchen. A kid ran past her, and as she dodged him, her breasts grazed Charles's arm.

He almost had a heart attack.

Instead, he sped up and raced to the refrigerator. By the time she got there he was ready to ward her off with a glass of tea.

"Thanks." She sipped it slowly, and Charles found himself watching.

"I missed you at the café this morning," he blurted. "I know you can't always cook, and you don't always have time to talk." Although she used to always do both those things. "But today I didn't even see you." He sounded like a fool. An *old* fool.

"I helped Jane decorate this place—I didn't get into the café until ten." Micki swept the room with her free hand. "She really wanted to get this party right."

It stuck in his craw to say anything decent about Jane Slater. Which he knew he should be ashamed of, but it was just the way it was. "That was good of her," Charles said.

"She's…" Whatever the rest of her sentence was, Charles didn't hear it. Micki had laid a hand on his arm and leaned in, as if she were confiding something for his ears only, and he couldn't think about anything but the sensation of her touch.

He should pull away, pull himself together…but he couldn't move. He cast a wild glance around the room, seeking something that might stake a greater claim on his attention than Micki.

There.

Barb and Hal, who had withdrawn from the action in the living room, sat quietly in a corner. Barb looked haggard; Hal looked like death warmed over. Charles felt a surge of shame. These two good people had lost their daughter far too soon, were dealing with a debilitating condition, and here Charles was obsessing about a young woman touching his arm in what was surely the most platonic manner.

*I want her.* He closed his eyes in frustration.

"Charles, are you okay?" Micki asked.

Hell's bells, did he say that out loud?

"You look like you've seen a ghost," she said.

Not out loud, then. "No, it's just I…uh…I— Excuse me," he said, "I must go talk to Barb and Hal."

So much for this family gathering being all he could want. He pressed a palm to his forehead as he crossed the room, as if a window might have opened up, letting everyone see into his mind, see what a crass fool he was.

"Barb, Hal," he more or less croaked. They both smiled a welcome, too tired to talk, it seemed.

He could tell already their company wasn't going to fill the void. *I need to find someone who can stop me thinking about Micki.*

*I need a girlfriend.*

THE PARTY WAS a roaring success, if the volume of the children's shrieks was anything to go by. Jane had loved decorating the house and preparing the food, and she'd enjoyed painting lions, zebras and cats on children's faces, while Micki helped them create frosting extravaganzas on the cupcakes she'd brought from the café. The kids had wolfed down a ton of junk food.

And beneath the excitement of the party, another excitement had hummed. The electric tension between her and Kyle had added another dimension to the occasion. Purely because they'd left things up in the air after that kiss—one quick, rational conversation would probably deflate the whole thing. But they hadn't had that conversation yet. Instead, they'd tried to carry on with the routine Jane had created…but there were subtle differences. While they were doing dishes, Kyle might brush past her. Their fingers would touch, linger, as they handed over coffee or a meal. They were exactly the kind of touches Jane had advised Micki to try on Charles. Touches that could be interpreted as *interest*.

They were both doing a good job of pretending the touches weren't happening. Which suggested Kyle was as unprepared as she was for that conversation they needed to have.

Even though the sensible part of her knew this wasn't going anywhere, the tension was undeniably thrilling.

Now, it was time for presents. Daisy started with the gifts her friends from kindergarten had brought. Then Micki gave her a frosting set for future cupcake occasions. "I'll teach you to use it," she promised.

Jane noticed how Charles hung on Micki's every word, and took a while to look away after she finished speaking. Micki did look great in that burgundy color.

Jane handed over her own gift, and was surprised how nervous she felt as Daisy neatly removed and folded the paper.

Maybe she should have chosen a toy.

Instead, she'd given one of her precious photos of her and Lissa, taken the weekend Lissa had dived headfirst through the men's washroom window at that nightclub. Jane had set the photo in a pink glass frame that matched Lissa's dress.

Daisy lifted her eyes to Jane and said, "Mommy."

For one incredible, amazing, daunting, terrifying, exhilarating second, Jane thought Daisy was talking to her. Was calling Jane *Mommy*.

Then she realized the shine in Daisy's eyes, the slow widening of her smile, was because the picture was of Lissa.

*Of course it is.*

So there was no reason for this unbearable, stabbing chill in her heart.

"That's right," Jane wheezed, aware of Kyle's gaze, intent on her. "It's your mommy."

To her shock, Daisy threw her arms around her and hugged her. Before Jane could remember to *not get attached,* her own arms went around Daisy and squeezed.

She had to force herself not to cling too tight. Because it turned out Dr. Franks had spoken the truth: in some deep part of her, she thought of herself as Daisy's mother.

As Daisy pulled away, Jane was left reeling. Emotionally, and almost physically. *It's just biology. Not an emotional attachment. I can get past it.*

Barb took the photo from Daisy's slackened grip. She stared down at Lissa's laughing image. "I don't think I've seen this one before."

"It was just after Lissa's twentieth birthday," Jane said.

Tears glistened in Barb's eyes. "Daisy, darling, you're going to look just like your mommy when you grow up."

Jane couldn't help an involuntary glance at Kyle...who was looking at her.

Barb drew a sharp, shuddery breath. She handed the photo back to Daisy, who clutched it to her chest.

"Are you okay?" Kyle asked in a low voice. He'd moved to stand next to Jane.

She turned her head, forced a smile. "I'm fine." *I'm not fine. Daisy should be mine.* Telling herself it was wrong to think that way didn't change a thing.

His hand touched her shoulder briefly, then he moved forward to help Daisy untie a knotted ribbon on her next gift.

It was just past eight o'clock when Charles and Gabe offered to help Hal into the car on their way out. They made a head start while Barb gathered her purse and a handkerchief she'd misplaced. The older woman had grown increasingly quiet as the evening went on, and now her silence seemed tense.

"I think Daisy had a nice time," Jane offered. The little girl had gone upstairs to get ready for bed; Kyle had gone with her.

"How nice could it be when her mother's dead?" Barb demanded.

Jane flinched.

Barb shook her head. She brushed away a tear. "I'm sorry, Jane, that was rude after all your hard work. But I miss Lissa so much. The thought that I have to face every day for the rest of my life with this—this *vacuum*..." Her voice cracked.

"I'm so sorry." Jane put her arms around Barb. "I can't imagine.... If there's anything I can do..."

"There is." Barb pulled away. "I wasn't going to say this, but you did ask... Jane, it looks to me like you're very settled here."

Jane tensed. "Kyle and I agreed I should stay on another month, but that'll be up soon."

"And will there be an excuse to stay another month and another?" Barb asked.

"I don't understand." But she was afraid she did.

"I get the impression you can't wait to step into Lissa's shoes."

Even though she'd almost expected it, Jane gasped. "I didn't— I'm not..."

"It's not surprising you should be drawn to the prospect of a ready-made family, given your own unhappy home life." Barb spoke with unbearable kindness. "But Jane, this is Lissa's family."

"*You* asked me to come here." Jane blinked back tears of humiliation. "To stay here."

"For two weeks, that's all," Barb reminded her. "From what I saw tonight, you have your feet under my daughter's table and you like it."

"I have no intention of taking Lissa's place." She forced the words out, suddenly unsure if they were true.

"Then perhaps you're not aware of how it looks, dear," Barb said. "The way you and Kyle look at each other, how close he stands to you."

"Did I hear my name?" Kyle appeared in the doorway.

*Don't say it,* Jane willed her.

But Barb wasn't one to hold back in her views, just as she hadn't the day of Lissa's funeral. "Whatever's going on between you and Jane," she told Kyle, "it needs to stop."

Kyle advanced into the room. "Excuse me?"

"It's not good for Daisy, seeing her dad interested in another woman when her mother's barely cold in her grave."

Kyle glanced at Jane. "Come off it, Barb. Lissa and I have been divorced as long as Daisy can remember, and Lissa dated plenty of men."

His perspective was a welcome blast of fresh air. A reminder that Barb was speaking nostalgically, from an era that hadn't existed in a while.

"Jane and I share some responsibility for Daisy," he continued. "We're spending a lot of time together and I hope we're getting along well, for Daisy's sake."

*And we share knowledge of the truth about Daisy's conception. And an incredible kiss.*

"Just so long as you remember," Barb told Jane, "Lissa is Daisy's mom, and she always will be."

Jane knew the older woman was speaking from her pain, her loss. And Barb had no idea of Jane's involvement in Daisy's conception. So Jane had no right to feel hurt. "I know," she said huskily.

"Good." Barb patted her arm. "Kyle, when you do find someone, and heaven knows I hope you do, just remember that the woman you choose will be the nearest thing to a mother Daisy has."

"I realize that." Kyle clearly had no idea where Barb was going, and nor did Jane.

Barb clicked her tongue. "I'm saying, choose wisely. Find someone who'll bring only positive associations to your home. To your daughter." Her cheeks were pink, her eyes fixed on Kyle, so there was no chance they could meet Jane's.

The other shoe dropped. "You mean, he should stay away from a Slater?" Jane demanded.

"Your family has baggage in this town," Barb said. "Daisy doesn't need that taint."

"That's enough," Kyle snapped. "Barb, you need to apologize."

"For you to say that now," Barb said, "when for years you thought Jane an unsuitable friend for Lissa, you're clearly more involved with her than you're admitting."

"Because I'm pointing out your rudeness?"

"Don't," Jane said. "Don't fight. Daisy will hear."

Both of them looked shamefaced.

"You need to go, Barb," Kyle said. Deliberately, he put an arm around Jane's shoulders and drew her to him. It was a kind gesture, but it didn't take away that feeling of being a complete outsider. "You're tired."

"What I am is *right*," Barb said implacably. "If you don't believe me, try dating Jane openly, and see how far you get in the election. Nothing good will come of a connection with a Slater in Pinyon Ridge, for you or for Daisy."

## CHAPTER TWELVE

MICKI HAD MISSED being the one to poach Charles's eggs exactly how he liked them. The way a wife would. When he walked in today, Saturday morning, the day after Daisy's party, and saw her behind the counter his face lit up in a way she considered more than platonic...maybe.

Result: she wasn't able to resist saying breezily, "The usual, Charles?"

His gratitude was heartwarming, and so was his obvious delight when she set the plate down in front of him. "Micki, you're the best cook I know."

Ugh, she was supposed to be making sure he didn't see her purely as a cook.

Deliberately, Micki took off her apron. Charles's gaze flickered over her pale yellow blouse as she sat down opposite him. She liked to think there was more than just customer-to-cook appreciation in his blue-gray eyes.

Micki called to Margaret for coffee, and leaned back against the booth.

"Tired?" Charles sounded concerned.

"I'm fine. Sometimes I wish I didn't have to start so early."

"You put in a big day yesterday with Daisy's party. But then," he said, almost bitterly, "you're young. You have tons of energy."

"And you don't, Chief?"

He gave her a brooding look. "Let's just say I'm feeling my age."

"You don't look it." She stretched her arms behind her

head, saw his eyes follow the movement. "You look good."
It was bold, far bolder than she'd been before.

Charles's mouth opened, then closed. "Do you think Kyle's
seeing Jane?" he asked.

Micki blinked. "Jane's never given any indication she's
interested," she hedged. Personally, she was still convinced
there was something going on. But Jane was very private.
Happy to interfere in Micki's life, and Micki believed Jane
felt the same bond of friendship that she did, but the younger
woman maintained a shield of reserve about her own relationships.

"Hmm." Charles digested that, along with a forkful of
poached egg. "And you're not interested in Kyle."

"Nope." Micki tried not to let her disappointment show.
He was still thinking of her as daughter-in-law material? "I'm
not interested in Gabe, either," she said for good measure.

Charles sighed.

"Your sons can look after themselves," she snapped. "You
should think about yourself for a change, about what *you*
want."

He didn't seem surprised by her outburst; he barely seemed
to notice. "What do you know about internet dating?" he
asked.

"I think your sons can find their own girlfriends," she
said crossly.

"Not for them. For me."

Micki's jaw dropped.

A dull red crept up Charles's face. Her irritation melted
away.

"I guess internet dating's a possibility," she said. "I mean,
if there's no one in Pinyon Ridge you're interested in. Maybe
you should take a good look around here first."

"I've looked," he said. "It's not like I haven't tried dating—
you know I went out with Ida Lane and Sally Beaufort a few
times each."

That had been before she'd realized what an amazing guy he was—she'd had no interest back then in whom he dated.

"Why didn't it work out with those two?" It was *so* none of her business, but, hey, he'd raised the subject.

"No, uh, connection," he said awkwardly. "I'd been feeling a little lonely, thought I should get out more. But dating those two, nice though they are, convinced me the loneliness doesn't get better unless you're with the right person. Not that I'm sitting at home crying into my beer," he assured her.

"I never imagined you were," she said.

He grinned, and there was a flash of their old ease, so familiar and warm that she wondered if it was worth risking the loss of it, if her romantic plans went south.

"So, the internet?" he prompted.

"Are you sure there's *no one else* in Pinyon Ridge?" she asked. "Maybe you need to look outside the square." Why didn't she just put up her hand and say, "Pick me, pick me"?

"There's no one," he said firmly.

Her hopes dissolved, leaving her empty. Lost.

She pulled his empty plate toward her with a brisk movement, then edged out of the booth. "I know a couple of people who've met their partners on SingleInColorado.com." As she picked up her cup, still three-quarters full, then his plate, she registered Charles's distaste for the modern term: *partner.* "Good luck."

"Don't go." Charles sounded so alarmed, for a moment she thought he'd suddenly realized the woman of his dreams was standing right in of him. "Not without telling me what you think of this. Please." He pulled a folded sheet of paper from the pocket of his plaid flannel shirt and spread it on the table in front of him. He cleared his throat. And stopped.

"You'll have to read it before I can tell you what I think." She perched on the edge of her seat again.

Charles bent his head over the page. "Man, fifty-nine, Summit County, seeks lady fifty-five to sixty for companionship, meals together, et cetera." He glanced up, not quite meeting Micki's eyes. "It's for the internet."

"Hmm." She drummed her fingers on the table.

"You don't like it," he guessed.

"It's kind of dull."

He reddened. "I'm not exactly a thrill a minute, Micki."

"Can I take a look?" She set down the cup and plate, and gestured to the paper. He handed it over. "Pen?" she asked.

He reached in his pocket and slid over the silver ballpoint Micki knew Patti had given him on some major anniversary.

Micki set to writing.

Charles noticed the way her lashes fanned above her cheeks, the catch of her teeth on her bottom lip as she concentrated. He lifted his gaze to the ceiling, letting it trace a knot in the pine beam directly above his booth.

"How's this?" Micki asked, drawing his gaze back to her pretty face. "Man, fifty-nine, intelligent and fit, enjoys good food, broad conversation and an active involvement in community and family. Seeking a lady of integrity with a passion for life."

It sounded as if he wanted sex. *Which I do.* His skin prickled. "You didn't mention her age," he said.

"You should be flexible. What if the right woman is younger than fifty-five to sixty?"

"You mean…fifty-four?"

She gave him a secret kind of smile that baffled him and made him feel old. "I'm just saying, don't close off any possibilities. When you specify age, you really mean maturity and how much you might have in common, right?"

"I guess." He hadn't been thinking much at all, just reacting to that sudden, pressing need that made him feel uncomfortable—a need he'd decided couldn't actually be for Micki, but was in fact for *some* form of female companionship. He'd ended up watching *Dr. Phil* on TV yesterday, and learned about transference. When you want something and subconsciously transfer that want to something—or someone—near to you.

"Maybe I shouldn't do this." He folded the paper and tucked it back inside his shirt pocket, against his chest. He might not place the ad, but he might keep those words, written in Micki's loopy handwriting, that described him as *intelligent and fit.*

"You mean you won't try internet dating?" Micki sounded disappointed.

"Yes—no—I don't know," he said. "Maybe." Where was Chief Everson, the cop who always knew what should happen next?

Her face lit up, her gray-green eyes twinkling, as if she'd just heard a good joke. "I think you should do it."

Was she laughing at him? Micki wouldn't do that.

"Seriously, Charles," she said. "Go for it."

"Maybe I will." Her approval left him oddly deflated. As if, instead of being inspired to strike out in a new direction, he'd lost a treasure he didn't know he had.

KYLE POPPED UP the toaster so Daisy's raisin toast wouldn't burn. Jane had been right: his daughter liked having him do things for her. It wasn't laziness on her part, as he'd once suspected. When he made her toast and buttered it while it was hot so the butter formed yellow pools over the raisins, she read that as "I love you."

So now he was making the toast, while Daisy watched a DVD in the other room.

Jane walked into the kitchen. Wearing those damn rubber ducky pajamas.

She stopped in the doorway, clearly surprised to see him— he'd been heading over to the new house early on the weekends, getting a few hours' work done before he put in his time with Daisy. He would have gone by now, if he hadn't gotten sidetracked by Daisy's toast.

"Coffee?" Kyle asked.

"Uh, thanks." Jane crossed the kitchen to the refrigerator. He tried not to notice the way that skimpy cotton hugged the rounded cheeks of her butt.

He poured her a mug from the press and set it on the island as she pulled the milk from the refrigerator. She'd gone very quiet after Barb's outburst at the party last night, and so had Kyle. He'd spent much of the night thinking about whether he wanted to take their fledgling connection further. If Barb was right, it could jeopardize the election.

At some unearthly hour of the morning he'd concluded Barb was probably wrong. And that Jane had done so much for him, given him Daisy, that he owed it to all of them— himself, her and Daisy—to see where this might go.

Besides, he couldn't stop thinking about her. Couldn't stop wanting her.

He would need to convince Jane that it was a good idea to move forward. He could tell from her stance, half turned away from him, that she didn't want him to broach the subject. Given half a chance, she'd do that withdrawal thing she was so good at.

Best not to give her half a chance, then.

"I've been thinking…." He waited while she stirred her coffee.

"What?" Those tawny eyes met his, guarded, but not so guarded he couldn't see the flicker of interest as she scanned him.

"About this." He slipped his arms around her waist.

"Kyle, this is a bad idea."

He noticed she wasn't pulling away.

"You shouldn't wear those pajamas if you don't want me to think like this." With his finger, he traced the vee of skin at the opening of the pj's, above the buttons.

"It was these or none at all," she said, then clapped a hand over her mouth.

"If I'd known those were the choices—" he flicked the top button undone, exposing a deeper vee "—I'd have opted for none."

"I meant, these are the only pj's I have with me." She was short of breath, which made her chest rise and fall. All in all, a very satisfactory state of affairs, given that his hand was now caressing that chest, albeit through the cotton of her pajamas.

"We shouldn't be doing this," she said on a sharp exhalation.

"We'll stop in a minute," he promised, and kissed her. This time, she parted her lips right away. He pulled back for a moment. "You brushed your teeth," he said, grinning. So much for her supposed reluctance to kiss him.

"So did you." She tasted him, with an aggressive flick of her tongue that turned him on unbelievably.

"I'm not the one saying we shouldn't be doing this." But who cared who said what? He abandoned the argument and got back to the kissing.

The thin cotton of the pajamas did little to mask the soft warmth of her curves pressed up against him. His hands cupped her bottom, pulling her closer.

When her hands slipped inside his T-shirt at the same moment as her tongue trailed a path down his neck, Kyle lost all grip on his surroundings. He knew only the heated path of her caress, the feverish haste with which he pulled off his T-shirt at her wordless insistence, and the incredible sensitivity his skin seemed to have developed in direct response to the exploration of her hands.

He didn't remember ever feeling this *wanted,* this wanting.

"Kyle," Jane murmured, and his name was sweet on her lips. He pulled away, enough to see she looked gorgeously disheveled, with another button having somehow come undone and a generous cleavage now on display.

Then he heard, "Daddy?"

He swore. Jane yelped and dived into the walk-in pantry.

Too late to pull his T-shirt on; Kyle spun around and began slathering butter on the raisin toast. Which was now almost cold, so the melted butter effect wouldn't happen.

"Here's your toast," he said to Daisy as she walked into the kitchen.

Jane emerged from the pantry, buttoned up, hair almost tidy, a cereal carton in her hand. "I thought I'd give this a try," she said brightly.

"You said Cap'n Crunch has too much sugar," Daisy said, puzzled.

Jane grimaced. "I don't think I should criticize it without trying it first." Resolute, she poured a heap of cereal into a bowl.

"My DVD finished," Daisy said.

"You were watching a DVD in the room next door?" Jane asked, her voice strangled. "Did your dad know?"

Daisy's dad tried to give her a warning look, but Daisy had no idea about such things. "Daddy put it on for me," she said. *"Sesame Street."*

"How nice," Jane said through gritted teeth. "Such a responsible father."

"Can I make you some toast?" Kyle offered, struggling not to laugh. He wasn't used to kidding around like this; he suspected Jane wasn't, either. He liked it.

She rolled her eyes. "No, thanks."

"Are you going to work on the house?" Daisy asked.

About to say yes, he changed his mind. "Nope. We're going to choose the paint for your new bedroom."

Her eyes widened, and he was instantly glad he'd come up with the idea.

"Cool," she said. "Will you come, Jane?"

"I'm kind of busy," Jane said. "I have some emails…."

"If you don't come, I'll force Daisy to have battleship-gray on her walls," Kyle told her.

Those lips he'd just been kissing curved. "Blackmail?"

"I've heard it's very effective."

"A slippery slope," she warned.

He leaned right into her. "So is making out in the kitchen."

She smacked his arm. "You were out of line."

"You can spank me later." Out of Daisy's view, he patted her bottom, a kind of demonstration. "First we need to buy paint."

"Can we go now?" Daisy asked. Little questions like that were such a leap forward from her silent acquiescence a few weeks ago.

"Sure," Kyle said. "Or shall we let Jane get dressed first?"

Daisy giggled; Jane shot out of the kitchen. Kyle folded his arms and enjoyed the view of her walking up the stairs.

THEY HEADED TO THE SUPERSTORE outside town, across the highway from Gabe's church. The paint section was in the back.

Jane tagged along behind Kyle and Daisy; this was really *their* expedition, father and daughter.

"We're looking for pink, right?" Kyle sounded resigned.

"Yes, please." Daisy's eyes were busy, scanning the color charts and paint chips on the walls.

"I suppose you're not even going to try to talk her out of it," he grumbled to Jane. "You do realize the house is meant to look like part of nature, right?"

"Pink occurs in nature," she said. "In the sunset." After that stunt he'd pulled, practically undressing her with Daisy only a few feet away, he deserved the pinkest pink that money could buy.

"I like this one." Daisy pointed to the most lurid shade on a chart of about a dozen shades of pink. Way more Pepto-Bismol than sunset.

Jane bit her lip, trying not to laugh. This was punishment on a karmic scale. She waited for Kyle to vent his disgust.

"So this is the one you want," he said stoically.

Huh? He would paint that beautiful room such a hideous

color, just to show his daughter he cared? Tenderness welled up inside Jane.

"Kyle, can I have a word?" She grabbed his arm, aware of the play of muscle through the sleeve of his cotton shirt, and pulled him aside. He seemed similarly focused on that physical connection, eyeing her hand as if he wanted to direct it to all kinds of places. Jane shook off the distraction and shook his arm for good measure to make sure he was listening.

"Giving Daisy everything she wants isn't necessary to show her you love her," she advised. "Quite the opposite. What matters is that you value her opinions."

"Maybe, but discussing sick-pink and then choosing beige doesn't seem right," he said.

"Of course not. But it's your house, too, so you have a right to a color you consider at least tolerable. Find one that she likes and you can live with."

Relief made his eyes crinkle. "Thanks, Jane." He was standing so close, if one of them moved just a few inches they could...*no*. She stamped on the mental brakes. *Not going there.*

"Have you thought about yellow?" she asked Daisy, and received identical looks of horror from both father and daughter.

"Fine, I'll stay out of it. How about you both hunt for your absolute favorite color, and show them to each other," Jane suggested.

Daisy loved that idea. "You, too, Jane," she insisted. "You pick your favorite, too."

Looking at paint samples beat standing around doing nothing, so she agreed. "We'll set a deadline—eleven o'clock."

"Then we'll get burgers for lunch," Kyle said.

For the better part of an hour, they flipped through trays of paint chips and pored over charts.

"Time's up," Jane said at eleven.

Daisy had her chosen paint chip covered inside her clasped hands. Jane did the same. "On the count of three, show your hand," she said. Kyle rolled his eyes, but obligingly concealed his choice.

"One...two...three." Jane opened her hand to reveal the pale pink just this side of orange that made her think of the sun setting over the Rockies in summer. "Let's see what you two—oh."

Kyle held a cotton-candy-pink that was better than the Pepto-Bismol, but not much. Daisy held a light turquoise.

Jane got a lump in her throat the size of Colorado. Father and daughter had gone all out to find something each thought the other would like.

"I thought you wanted pink?" Kyle said.

"Kind of," Daisy said. "That pink is real pretty." She ran a finger over Kyle's paint chip. "But I really like this one." She held up the turquoise.

"I like that one, too," Kyle admitted.

"What about mine?" Jane asked.

"Yours is nice too, Jane," Daisy said earnestly, obviously not wanting to offend.

"Yeah, yours is nice, too, Jane." Kyle, on the other hand, was deliberately mocking.

Jane pouted. "Hey, it looks like a sunset. It's *called* Tropical Sunset."

"What's tropical?" Daisy asked.

"Nowhere near here." Kyle grinned down at her. "But we won't tell Jane that."

Daisy looked beyond delighted to be part of a conspiracy with her dad. Joy welled up inside Jane so fierce she could scarcely contain it.

*I love Daisy.* The thought spilled out before she could censor it. Before she could tell herself her reaction was due to biology, not emotion.

Her heart was overflowing, and not with biology.

Too late to shut that floodgate now. She'd broken protocol number five, gotten unmistakably, irrevocably attached. And she'd picked a doozy of a moment to do it. She was finally ready to admit she had a mother's interest in Daisy, just as Kyle and Daisy reached a stage where they didn't need her.

What a mess.

Jane dragged her attention back to the moment. Kyle was trying to talk Daisy into the pink, but the little girl was adamant she wanted the turquoise.

"How about a bright pink duvet for your bed?" Jane suggested. "It'll make a nice contrast against the turquoise."

The suggestion made everyone happy. As they stood in line at the register waiting to pay, a vision floated into Jane's head. A family, herself as mommy, with a daughter like Daisy. And a husband like—

"Janelle Slater, what are you doing here?" the cashier asked. Her manner was openly hostile.

Jane had no idea who she was, but that was how it had always been around here. People knew her and her family, or thought they did, but she didn't necessarily know them. "Have we met?" she asked coolly, declining to answer the question, aware of Daisy's curious glance.

The woman snorted. "I'm Annie Talbot. You have a nerve showing your face in this town."

"I'm sorry, I don't remember…." Jane cloaked herself in the distance that divorced her from whatever disgrace her name was about to taint her with.

"My husband, Phil," the woman snapped. "Your low-life father blackmailed him." Which meant Phil had cheated on Annie with Jane's mother, but funnily enough she didn't mention that.

Kyle spoke up. "That's ancient history now, Annie. You must be talking twenty years ago."

"You're not with her, are you, Kyle?" Annie demanded. "Because if you think I'd vote for a mayor in cahoots with the Slaters, you're wrong."

Her words were an uncanny echo of Barb's after Daisy's birthday party.

"I'm babysitting Daisy," Jane said. "It's a temporary arrangement." She felt like a Judas, denying her own daughter. But there would always be people who thought like Annie, and there was no point in Kyle losing their votes over her.

"Jane, could you take Daisy to the car?" Kyle asked evenly. "While I settle up here?"

"I just want to know when she's leaving." The woman's words floated after Jane as she walked out to the parking lot.

"What's tempry?" Daisy asked, as Jane clipped her seat belt.

"What do you mean, sweetheart?"

Daisy looked confused at the endearment; Jane cursed her own lack of self-control. Just because she loved Daisy, she couldn't expect the girl to love her back. Not after she'd been so careful to create some distance.

"You said a tempry arrangement," Daisy said.

"Temporary," Jane amended. "It means not forever. You know I'm not staying with you forever, right?" All the more reason not to go showing Daisy how she felt.

Daisy nodded. "I guess."

Kyle joined them a couple of minutes later. He stowed the paint in the trunk.

"Are you okay?" he asked Jane, as he turned the key in the ignition. "Annie was out of line, and I told her so."

She'd expected some carefully hidden contempt about her family background; his genuine concern just made her feel worse. More of a misfit. She would never be a part of the kind of family she'd envisaged back in the store.

He pulled out of the parking space.

"Actually, I have a headache," she said. "Can you drop me at home, then you and Daisy can get burgers without me."

Daisy protested. "I want you to come, Jane. Please come."

Kyle, however, didn't argue. He flicked his turn signal and headed for the cottage.

She suspected he saw the sense of what she was doing.

Better to keep her distance now, than end up longing for something she could never have.

## CHAPTER THIRTEEN

ON MONDAY, AFTER JANE DROPPED Daisy at school, she headed for Bentwood. At nine-thirty she arrived at the prison, a concrete slab of a building set with narrow windows

This was probably a dumb idea. But having refused to go to lunch with Kyle and Daisy on Saturday, she'd spent all of Sunday wondering if she'd been too hasty.

Before she decided once and for all that she shouldn't take up Kyle on the offer he hadn't yet revoked—his offer for her to remain in Daisy's life—she wanted to be a hundred percent sure it couldn't work. And since her feelings of inadequacy on the family front were all tied up in her own, hopeless family, visiting her father had seemed essential.

She didn't hate her family, not at all. There'd been a few good times, and she had that blood-is-thicker-than-water bond with them. The exception was her dad. She'd come close to hating him.

Inside, she went through the routine she was familiar with from other prisons, from her childhood. Having her bag searched, walking through the metal detector. She followed the guard to the visiting room. The guard said, "Michael Slater," to the visiting officer, and once again Jane had to wait.

Her father had been in prison before for short stints. His current sentence was fifteen years and his record meant he wouldn't be paroled for good behavior, though he was appealing the initial sentence. He was two years into his term.

"Janelle, girl." Mike Slater's eyes assessed her, as he made his way over to the table and sat on the other side from her.

She knew he'd be trying to estimate the cost of her clothes, her purse. "It's been a while."

She hadn't seen her father in ten years, but he hadn't changed. The same lean build and narrow face, though maybe that crude tattoo of a bird on his right wrist, next to the equally crude anchor, was new.

"How are you doing?" She ignored the reproach, which she knew was intended to make her feel guilty, and thus more likely to hand over money when he asked for it.

"How do you think I'm doing, locked up like this?" he demanded. "How are *you* doing, out there in the land of the free?"

"If you're so interested in the land of the free, maybe you shouldn't rob banks," she snapped. She sounded as sanctimonious as an Everson. "I'm here because I wanted to see family," she said. "I—I miss Mom." It was part of the truth, and she was suddenly glad she'd come.

"Me, too." Her father sounded as if he meant it. Given he'd spent at least half his marriage fooling around or risking everything on a criminal venture, it didn't seem likely. But Jane had to take the words at face value.

"Have you seen much of the others?" she asked her father.

He shook his head. "Darren's locked up, like me."

Jane had to grit her teeth to refrain from scolding him for the offhand pride in his voice.

"Johnno's still in Australia, far as I know," her dad continued. "Young Cat…I've seen her. She's gone straight."

"Really?" Jane couldn't keep the skepticism out of her voice. Of course, her dad's definition of going straight was somewhat looser than Jane's. Her younger sister had had a line in charming old people out of their money for a while. Nothing illegal, but definitely immoral. "What's she doing now?"

"Ah, I don't know." Her father looked shifty, making her doubt the veracity of his report. "How much money you making these days?"

Jane stifled a sigh. She shouldn't have come. She'd had some misguided urge to see the only parent she still had, perhaps to capture the sense of family that Barb suggested she was desperate for.

"I need to go," Jane said. "I left some cigarette money at the office."

"You're a good girl," he said halfheartedly. "Got any more cash? There's a guy on the block looking to do me an injury—I got the better of him in a deal. Wouldn't mind being able to buy him off."

"I'll see what I can do," Jane said stiffly. She no longer knew which of her father's tales were true, and which were fables designed to extort cash.

By the time she left, she knew one thing for sure. Mike Slater was Daisy's biological grandfather...but Jane didn't want him anywhere near her daughter. Kyle's daughter, she corrected herself. Then: my *daughter, dammit, even if she never knows it. Even if no one does except me and Kyle.*

"MAN, AM I GLAD to see you." Micki grabbed Jane's arm and practically hauled her into the café.

"I'm here to wallow in self-pity and I want sympathy," Jane said. "You're looking annoyingly pleased with yourself."

Micki tried—and failed—to rearrange her expression into one of sympathy.

"Pathetic," Jane grumbled.

"Romance with Kyle gone sour?" Micki asked innocently.

"Pretty much," Jane said.

Mickie squawked. "You said there was no romance!"

"There was the potential for one," Jane said. "But it's not going to happen."

"Bummer." Micki flipped the sign on the door to Closed. "Does it have anything to do with that therapist visit? I forgot to ask how that went."

"That feels like a lifetime ago," Jane said with feeling. "It opened a can of worms that might have been best left…in the can." She frowned. "That metaphor is silly."

"I still can't believe Kyle agreed to see a therapist." Micki lifted a couple of chairs down from the table where they'd been stacked while she mopped the floor. "When Lissa wanted them to see a counselor after they separated, he flat-out refused."

Because he was afraid of what would come out during those sessions, Jane guessed. He'd likely been worried Lissa would reveal Daisy wasn't his daughter. She couldn't blame him for not wanting to face that possibility and its emotional consequences.

"I guess the timing was right," she said.

"Or the persuader was." Micki raised her eyebrows. "I've said it before, Kyle likes you."

*Like isn't enough, not with all that's gone on.*

"I'm not really in an opening-up mood," Jane apologized. "Let's talk about your good news instead."

"Great idea." Micki beamed. "I have a date with Charles!"

"He asked you out?" Jane gaped. "I hate to say it, but I owe you twenty bucks."

Micki snickered. "Your money's safe. He didn't ask me out, not knowingly. He put an ad on SingleInColorado.com, and I replied. He replied to my reply…and we have a date."

"Presumably you lied about your age."

"Well, duh." Micki poured two glasses of water from a carafe. "But the thing is, I didn't lie about anything else. All my answers to his questions, all my emails, were one hundred percent me. And he said I sound charming."

"So who does he think you are?"

"Charles is taking Michelle Barratt, age fifty-three, to dinner in Frisco on Saturday night."

"Makes sense to go to Frisco," Jane approved. Until now, the prospect of a relationship between Charles and Micki had seemed so unlikely, she hadn't considered the logistics. But any romance would need to be conducted out of the public eye. In a place like Pinyon Ridge, that would be a challenge. "Good luck."

"Not so fast, missy," Micki said. "There's every chance I'll walk into the restaurant and he'll walk right out."

"More likely he'll have a heart attack," Jane quipped. "Sorry," she said at Micki's horrified expression.

"My point is, I need more coaching." Micki gulped down some water. "I'm bringing Charles to a crunch point. It's my big chance to make him see the possibilities, and I don't want to blow it."

"Why would you blow it?"

"How would I know? I'm not prepared to take the risk. You need to help me."

Jane eyed her determined expression. "You're not going to let this guy get away, are you?"

Micki looked at her as if she were crazy. "I believe Charles and I could have something amazing. It makes no sense not to do everything I can to grasp it."

"I can't argue with that," Jane said. "Let's get to work."

As they talked about what might happen, and how Micki could shape the evening for success, the other woman's determination made Jane reevaluate her own attitude. She'd decided there was no future for her as part of Daisy's life. And by extension, of Kyle's. Kyle had offered her the opportunity and she'd backed away, justifying her decision on her own principles of self-defense, of not letting herself get hurt. *Because I'm afraid.*

"What if it doesn't work out with Charles?" she asked Micki. "You'll be heartbroken. Don't tell me you won't."

"Yeah," Micki said soberly. "Not to mention mortified, having to face him every day. But the reward outweighs the risk. Nothing is more important than love."

Micki was right, Jane realized. Cowards couldn't win. *Since when have I been a coward?*

"HEAR YOU HAD A LITTLE trouble in the hardware store the other day." Gabe closed the door behind him as he entered Kyle's office.

Kyle kicked back in his mayoral chair, more than ready to temporarily abandon his work on the town development proposal. "Isn't gossip a sin?"

"Not when it's pastoral care." Gabe sat down, one foot resting on the other knee. "And not when your campaign manager is trying to help you."

Kyle rolled his eyes. "Drop the pastoral care, and I'll talk campaign with you. Did Annie Talbot say something?"

"Just that you're hooking up with Janelle Slater, and there's no way this town needs a Slater behind the throne."

Kyle groaned. "Like being mayor of this town bears any resemblance to royalty."

"You're not denying you and Jane are an item?" Gabe asked. "You seemed pretty cozy at Daisy's party."

Kyle pinched the bridge of his nose. "It's complicated."

"Try me," Gabe said lightly. "People tell me I'm a good listener."

Not that Kyle could tell his brother the whole sorry story, but he was suddenly tempted to talk about Jane to someone who wouldn't have a knee-jerk bad reaction.

"I'm not sure what's going on, or what I want from her," Kyle said. "One minute we're burning up…"

Gabe pointed at his ears. "Holy ears, be careful."

Kyle grinned. "Next minute, she's backing off like I have double dose of leprosy—that's a biblical thing, right?"

"Not in the sense you're talking about."

"Jane thinks we're too different, and that in the long term we won't be able to get past those differences." The whole thing would make a lot more sense if he could tell Gabe the truth about the donor egg, but he didn't want to.

"She may be right," Gabe said. "And I don't say that lightly. People aren't as good at forgiving and forgetting as they should be. Mostly because it's not easy." He swung his feet up to rest on the other side of Kyle's desk. "How do you feel about her?"

A month ago, he'd have said he disliked her. Two weeks ago, he'd have suggested his liking for her was all wrapped up in that DNA she'd supplied. Now…there was more to it than DNA, he was pretty sure. "I think I like her."

Gabe looked disappointed in his lukewarm answer. He lowered his feet to the floor. "Do you *like* her enough to give up on this election?"

Kyle's jaw dropped. "You think it'll come to that?"

"People have strong views about the personal lives of those in power." Gabe's gaze searched Kyle. "I know you feel strongly about the direction Pinyon Ridge should take, and if you don't get elected that probably won't happen."

Kyle scowled at the thought of Wayne Tully's cheap and cheerless plans coming to fruition.

"You might need to decide between Jane and this town." Gabe paused. "I can't tell you what that choice should be."

"You're a preacher—shouldn't you be advocating love above all else?" Kyle asked.

"Absolutely. *Love* is above all else," Gabe said. "But liking, or mild interest, or lust, curiosity…those things may not compete with the future of Pinyon Ridge."

"Do I have to decide what I feel right now?" Kyle asked.

"Ordinarily I'd say take your time, don't rush it," Gabe said. "But if you're going to stand down, you might want to do it in time for someone else to have a run at the mayoralty."

Kyle wasn't sure who else would stand, but anyone would be better than Tully.

"And if you decide to stick with the mayoralty and it becomes clear a relationship with Jane will stop you winning, the sooner you let her down the better," Gabe said. "She's vulnerable beneath that smart-mouth Slater surface."

"I know that," Kyle said, annoyed. He didn't like the

thought of Gabe having insight into Jane. "It's not like there's anything formal to put an end to at this stage. We're not dating. There's no commitment." Someone knocked on the office door. "That'll be Trisha with the coffee. Come in," Kyle called.

It wasn't Trisha. Jane walked into his office, cute as anything in that cherry-red sundress he liked. "Hi, I wanted— oh, hi, Gabe."

"Hey, Jane." Gabe stood. "Didn't see you in church on Sunday."

"No? Maybe you're shortsighted." She widened those tawny eyes, and Kyle chuckled. Attagirl.

He felt Gabe's interested gaze on him.

"Is there a problem?" he asked. It was unusual for her to show up at his office. In fact, the last time had been when she'd broken the news about Daisy's DNA.

"Not at all," she assured him. "Actually, I just came to, uh—" her cheeks pinkened and she darted a look at Gabe "—ask if you want to go to dinner Friday night."

"You mean, like, out for a burger with Daisy?"

Her color deepened. "Not a burger. And not Daisy. Just you—" she drew a fortifying breath "—and me."

She was asking him on a date! Elation surged through Kyle…followed swiftly by the recollection of his brother's words. Gabe would say he shouldn't agree unless he'd made up his mind he wanted her more than the mayoralty. But Kyle knew how much it had cost her to ask him out. To put herself in a place where he could reject her. He couldn't say no.

"I'd love to," he said, and a big part of him meant it. "But I have a planning and development committee meeting Friday. Could we switch to Saturday? Assuming Dad's free to babysit."

"Dad's going into Frisco on Saturday," Gabe said. "Some guy he used to know is passing through the area."

"I didn't hear about that." Or was Gabe making that up to

let him off the hook? Which wasn't necessarily a bad idea. "Maybe another time," he told Jane.

"*I* can babysit Saturday, though," Gabe offered.

Huh? What was his brother up to?

"You have church Sunday morning." Kyle stated the obvious.

"So you'll need to be back by eleven," Gabe said.

"That's fine," Jane said quickly, as if she might lose her nerve if she didn't snap up his offer.

"Maybe we should go into Frisco for dinner," Kyle said. *Where voters like Annie Talbot won't see us.*

"No." Jane looked alarmed. "That won't be an early night for Gabe. Besides, I'm keen to try the French place here in town."

"The French place sounds good." Kyle surrendered. "I'll make a reservation."

"Great." She sounded more relieved than excited. But she looked kind of…hot and bothered, her cheeks pink, eyes bright.

He rather liked the thought of her hot and bothered. He found himself looking forward to their dinner. One date didn't count as a commitment, he told himself as Jane departed. He could still back out without anyone getting hurt.

He wrapped up the meeting with Gabe soon after, neither of them very satisfied with how it had gone.

After his brother left, Kyle sat thinking about Jane, about their upcoming date. It was all very well for Gabe to be simplistic—he would surely agree it was more complicated if he knew the whole story. If Jane wasn't Daisy's biological mother, and Kyle was forced to choose between her and the mayoralty, what would he do?

Probably, he'd pick the mayoralty. He didn't like himself for it, but the fact was, he loved this town; he and his family were invested in its future. Whereas with Jane, he wasn't sure what he felt and he wasn't sure she would ever be able to commit to a future that involved him. And vice versa.

CHARLES STEPPED INTO the Eating Post for the second time that Saturday, shutting the door behind him. He'd waited in his truck until he could see the place was near empty. A bunch of young moms, regulars who left the kids with their husbands for an hour on a Saturday afternoon, had just departed in a noisy gaggle, and through the window, Charles had seen Micki clearing their table.

Micki hadn't heard him come in over the clatter of dishes she was piling into the sink. He watched her for a moment, enjoying her brisk, economic movements, the slight sway of the womanly hips that her jeans hugged as she moved along the counter, wiping and tidying.

He shouldn't be here. This was foolishness, an old man's vanity, to think who he dated might matter to her. Yet he felt guilty, as if he were cheating on their friendship. The urge to obtain her blessing had grown irresistible.

Before he could make good on the impulse to turn tail, Micki turned. Her face lit up with the smile he...liked.

"Charles! Wow, you look great." She wiped her hands on a towel and came around the counter to inspect him.

Okay, maybe he was also here out of insecurity, needing some kind of reassurance before he went to meet Michelle Barratt. Because Micki's approval filled him with confidence.

"Ve-ry nice," Micki said, ending her thorough perusal.

She probably meant "for an old guy." Still, Charles was fairly sure his grin was goofy. He'd worked hard on his appearance. Got a haircut this morning, shined his boots. And he wore new tan chinos with a navy blue shirt.

"I wondered if I should leave the shirt hanging out," he said, "the way Kyle and Gabe do. But..."

"Not your style," she assured him.

"No," he agreed, relieved. He wasn't a young guy, and

he wasn't meeting a young woman. So the shirt was tucked into his pants, and Charles was proud to note he still had a pretty fine figure.

"You look great, too," he mumbled, suddenly shy. He realized it was true. She was…alight in a way he hadn't seen her before. He groaned inwardly—this was so not what he needed.

She chortled and rubbed at a mark on her T-shirt, just above her right breast. "Oh, yeah, bacon fat is a good look."

"You always look good to me, Micki," he said, bold now that he had a date with another woman, a *suitable* woman.

As if she'd read his mind, she said, "So, what's with the new clothes? Do you have a hot date?"

"No!" Which was kind of true. Michelle Barratt sounded charming in her letters, but she didn't sound *hot*. "I'm headed into Frisco. I have, uh, business there."

"You're going to Frisco? Now? Great, could you give me a ride?"

"No!" Charles said again, aghast.

She raised her eyebrows in hurt surprise, and Charles babbled, "It's just, I'm not sure when I'll be coming back. And I have a lot to think about on the way. I'll be bad company." All of those excuses sounded pathetic.

"I won't make a sound," Micki promised. "And it doesn't matter when you're coming back. I'm overnighting with a friend. I can get a ride up with the Sunday milk run tomorrow."

"But—" Charles couldn't think of a good reason to refuse. He could hardly explain that after half an hour cooped up in his truck with the gorgeous Micki, he'd be in no shape to look at Michelle Barratt with an open mind. "Can't you take your own car?"

She shook her head. "I got a flat this morning and Joe didn't have the right size in his workshop. He's ordered one up from Frisco, but I'd been thinking I'd have to cancel my evening."

"Why do you want to go to town tonight anyhow?" he asked, sounding churlish.

Micki didn't seem to notice. "A couple of ex-Pinyon Ridge girls are having a night out at the Lizard Lounge."

He couldn't reasonably refuse Micki's request. Charles knew the Lizard Lounge—it stood at the other end of Frisco from the restaurant where he'd arranged to meet Michelle. It wasn't the sort of place a fifty-three-year-old woman would hang out. And truth to tell, he couldn't resist the opportunity to spend the time with Micki.

*Just one last time thinking of her as more than a friend.*

"Okay," he said on a sigh. He liked the sound of Michelle Barratt but he wasn't holding out much hope she'd be *hot,* as Gabe would say. But he sure hoped she was at least warm.

## CHAPTER FOURTEEN

WHEN JANE HAD asked Kyle to dinner, the idea had been to give the vision of a romance and of a new family every possible chance to flourish.

She couldn't help thinking that 6:00 p.m. wasn't the most romantic of times. The candle at their table by the window in La Maison Jaune remained unlit, and they were the only people in the place. But the available tables had been either six or eight-thirty, and eight-thirty would have been too late for Gabe.

Jane had dressed in a red silk wrap dress that showed off her figure, with a hint of cleavage and a split that revealed her thighs as she moved. Gratifyingly, Kyle hadn't been able to take his eyes off her. She was having a similar problem. His dark shirt and pants, dressier than his usual jeans and T-shirt but more relaxed than his mayoral suits, made him look lean and dark and delicious.

"I haven't been to this place in years," Kyle said as he scanned the menu. "But they used to be famous for their *boeuf en croute*."

"Sounds good." Jane fiddled with the base of her empty wineglass. Kyle had ordered a bottle of cabernet, but it hadn't arrived yet.

In a moment of supreme bad timing—or maybe it was a family instinct she didn't understand—he turned his head to look out the window. "Hey, there's Dad."

He pointed to Charles's truck, passing the restaurant at snail's pace behind a slow-moving delivery truck. "Who's that with him?"

"Micki asked him for a ride into town," Jane said. She felt bad not telling him the whole truth; she would have liked to prepare him for the shock...but as Micki had said, if the "blind date" didn't work out, she didn't want the humiliation of Kyle knowing she'd chased after his dad.

Kyle craned his neck to follow Charles's progress. "Dad's been jumpy lately, have you noticed?"

"Maybe because a Slater is back in town," she joked.

He chuckled. "Either that, or retirement isn't keeping him busy. He should take his own advice and find a nice woman to date."

Jane considered that encouraging. "So you wouldn't mind him dating?"

"Not at all." He set down the menu and broke open his bread roll. "It's not like he's going to do anything stupid."

Uh-oh. "Stupid?"

He lifted one shoulder. "Date some twenty-year-old who's after his life savings."

"That would be bad," Jane said. Much worse than a thirty-seven-year-old with her own flourishing business.

"Dad's too sensible for that," Kyle assured her. "But maybe I should suggest he look around for someone."

"Because you so appreciate when he takes an interest in your own love life."

He chuckled. "It'd be sweet revenge. He never stops hounding me and Gabe to find someone. I don't think he's ever got over the fact that I'm divorced."

The waitress arrived, so Jane waited until they'd ordered—a mixed appetizer platter, then *boeuf en croute* for him, fish baked with mushrooms for her—before she followed that up.

"It sounds like you're taking the entire blame for the breakup with Lissa."

He shrugged one shoulder.

"No one likes a martyr, Kyle," she said.

He stared, then cracked a laugh. "Okay, it wasn't all my

fault by any stretch. But you can't change someone else. You can only change what you do."

"You tried," she said. "I know, because you called me all those years ago when things started to go wrong. That can't have been easy."

"Things had been going bad a while before that," he said. "Shouldn't have been so damn hard to call you, either. I really was a pompous jerk back then. I'm sorry."

She caught her breath. "Everyone makes mistakes. So, by the way, don't let your dad get to you, because he makes them, too."

"Dad doesn't get to me, he just has high hopes for me and Gabe."

"He and your mom must have been pleased when Gabe became a pastor," Jane said. "You said he had a couple of slightly wild years."

"Yeah, that was before he 'found God' five or six years ago. He enrolled in the seminary shortly before Mom died."

"I think Lissa said your mom died of cancer?" Jane queried. "But it was sudden?"

He nodded. "She'd had a bad back for years. By the time they found a tumor in her spine, she only had a few weeks left to live."

"I'm sorry," she said. "I really am."

He nodded his thanks. "Me, too. About your mom, I mean. Last year."

She wasn't prepared for the rush of tears to her eyes—she blinked them away, appalled. "You're the first person who hasn't spoken as if my mother's death must have been a relief to me," she said.

He shook his head. "She can't have been that old. Was she ill?"

"The doctor said her heart gave out for no real reason. Other than years of hard living, I guess. She was no saint and she was in some ways an awful mother. But I know she loved me in her own peculiar, negligent style and...I loved her, too. Even if I couldn't live with her."

"Whereas I had the perfect upbringing," he said wryly. "Mom stayed home with us kids, while dad won the respect of the whole town as a great cop. We went to church on Sundays, and it was more than lip service. Mom was on the PTA and the garden club committee. My parents loved each other, and they loved me and Gabe."

"That's quite a litany," she said uncertainly. Was he trying to make her feel bad?

"How much of the fact that my brother's a pastor and I'm the mayor is down to nature, and how much to nurture?" he asked.

"Oh." Surprise had her blinking again. "When you put it like that..." It seemed obvious that nurture was the main factor.

"Maybe you're wrong when you say I'd blame the Slater DNA for any problems that might occur in Daisy's life," he suggested.

She'd love to believe that. "Logic doesn't always apply to life. Even you've been guilty of making assumptions about me."

"I shouldn't have," he said. "Not when I also knew how good you'd been to Lissa."

"So did everyone else around here, if they thought about it. But in the eyes of some people I'll only ever be *not quite* as bad as the rest of the Slaters."

He nodded slowly.

"It's not like I care." Her laugh sounded brittle in her own ears. "I know the kind of person I am. It doesn't matter what other people think."

Kyle leaned forward, and his eyes were very dark. He placed his hand over hers, sending a trail of tingles up her arm.

"*I* think you're an honorable, honest woman," he said.

Her pulse thrummed. "I hid the truth about Daisy from you."

"You didn't owe me the truth," he said. "Lissa did."

And right now, she was hiding the fact that his dad was on a date with Micki. Did she owe him that truth?

QUARTER PAST SEVEN, and Charles's date hadn't arrived. Had Michelle Barratt stood him up, or was she fashionably late—whatever the heck that was?

Charles resisted the urge to check his watch yet again—the last time he looked at the time, the waitress had given him a pitying look. He didn't have a cell phone number for Michelle, so he couldn't check if she was on her way.

He realized he had a distinct preference for punctual women. He'd arrived at Sam's Steakhouse two minutes before seven, and that had been no mean feat. He'd dropped Micki and her overnight bag at the Lizard Lounge a half hour ago, then had a quick drink at a little bar down the road to calm his stomach, all knotted from the tension of having Micki in his car and the sight and scent of her, while he was on his way to date another woman. Micki had touched his hand on the steering wheel as she wished him a great night. It had felt as if any chance of *great*ness evaporated when she closed the door of his truck behind her.

Charles had stopped to buy a packet of mints, in case Michelle Barratt didn't like whiskey breath. He'd felt furtive, as if already he was trying to please a persnickety woman.

He frowned. He had to stop thinking of his date in negative terms before he'd even met the lady. He shouldn't assume that every woman he met would compare unfavorably to Micki. Michelle Barratt sounded lively and warm in her emails—she seemed to share a lot of his views. And while it was unlikely she'd be as pretty as Micki, there were plenty of women in their fifties who kept a trim figure. Not that that really mattered at his stage of life.

Heck, who was he kidding? Micki's curves haunted his dreams—he couldn't look at her these days without wondering how she would feel in his arms. Pathetic.

Charles had asked the maître d' for a corner booth, from where he could watch the door. He deliberately hadn't asked Michelle what she looked like or what she'd be wearing. He hadn't wanted to make her feel her appearance was more important than her personality. Now, he wondered if that had been a bad idea.

If she weighed three hundred pounds, it was best he knew beforehand, so he didn't look too surprised. And to be honest, he'd never really gone for big women. Not that he liked them skinny, either. A woman should have curves, like Micki.

The restaurant door opened; next moment, Charles choked on his iced water. *Hell's bells!* Micki had just walked in!

Despite the icy water, Charles broke out in a sweat. Why wasn't she at the Lizard Lounge? He hadn't told her he was going to Sam's and she hadn't asked.

Blast it, he'd told her he wasn't on a date. If Michelle arrived now, Micki would know he'd lied—something he never did. Worse, he felt as if he were cheating on her, which was plumb crazy. She'd laugh that big, generous laugh of hers to hear that.

He couldn't let her see him. Charles looked around discreetly. The men's room was on the other side of the restaurant; she'd be bound to notice if he tried to make a dash for it. Micki's gaze roved the room. Charles put his napkin up to his face and scooted around the other side of the semicircular booth's padded seat, so he was now side-on to Micki. Then he got a better idea—he traded the napkin for the leather-bound menu, which he held open in front of his nose.

The words merged in a fuzzy mess that was already giving him a headache. He felt like Mr. Magoo.

"Hello, Charles." It was a familiar, feminine voice.

So much for hiding. Charles lowered the menu. He cleared

his throat. "Micki! Hi! Fancy seeing you here." Then he added, "Wow!"

The word just slipped out. He'd been so panicked at the sight of her entering the restaurant, he hadn't noticed what she wore. When he dropped her at the Lizard Lounge, she'd worn jeans and a denim jacket. Now he saw a black dress in some sort of clingy fabric that wrapped across her breasts, leaving a tantalizing vee. Three-quarter sleeves emphasized her strong but slim wrists. Lower down, the skirt was slit at the side to reveal a glimpse of shapely leg.

There was something different about her face, too. Makeup, that was it. Charles liked the scrubbed clean look she normally presented, but with color in her cheeks and reddened lips, he couldn't take his eyes off her. Her lashes seemed darker and longer, lending a sultry look.

She'd gone to a lot of trouble to meet a bunch of girlfriends.

Charles processed the evidence the way any observant cop would, and came to the only logical conclusion. "You're not meeting your girlfriends, are you?"

She held up her hands in the *busted* gesture. "No, I'm not."

"You're meeting a man." He heard the jealousy in his own voice, but he didn't care. She gave him that secret smile he'd seen so often in the past couple weeks, and now he understood it. He'd been so dense! "Anyone I know?"

In answer, she slid into the booth next to him. Charles felt a fleeting anxiety for Michelle Barratt and what she would think to find another woman sitting here, then he forgot about her, in the pain and pleasure of seeing Micki, so beautiful, here to meet some guy.

Micki took the menu he hadn't realized he was still holding and laid it down on the table. She took a deep breath, and Charles braced himself instinctively.

"Charles," she said, "I'm here to see you."

"Huh?" Oh, yeah, very articulate. But with her breasts

showcased in that slinky dress he could barely string two thoughts together, let alone produce words.

"I'm Michelle Barratt."

He waited for that to make sense, for the pieces of the story to fall into place, the way they did sometimes during an investigation if you just let all the evidence float through your mind.

Nope, not happening. "You mean, you *know* Michelle?"

"I *am* Michelle. I'm the one you've been emailing the past week. I wrote an answer to your ad. It meant I had to lie to you, and I'm sorry."

Michelle Barratt. Micki Barton. Charles's thoughts churned. Why would she do this? Some kind of prank? A joke that she and Kyle were playing on him? No, Micki loved a joke, but she wasn't mean.

"Charles, please say something." Her eyes clouded with worry. She twisted the amethyst bracelet on her arm.

"Why would you do that?" he said. "Maybe my brain's not as quick as it used to be, but—"

"Aargh!" Her cry of frustration shut him up, and startled several neighboring diners into looking at them. Her fists clenched on the table. "Charles Everson, you are the smartest, liveliest, handsomest man I know and I—"

She clapped a hand to her mouth.

*He* was the smartest…the handsomest? Elation bubbled inside Charles…tempered by incredulity. Maybe he'd misunderstood. "And you…?" He prompted her to finish her sentence.

"And I like you." Her voice dropped almost to whisper. "I really like you."

His heart threatened to jump out of his chest. He wanted to leap across the table, haul her into his arms. Yet still, a part of him figured he must have misunderstood.

"You did all this—emailed me as Michelle Barratt, hitched a ride into town with me on some phony excuse, made yourself look like *this*—for me?"

She nodded, her eyes brilliant, her smile tremulous.

No doubt about it, he wanted to kiss her senseless. He didn't recall ever kissing anyone senseless before and the strength of the longing took him by surprise.

But he was Charles Everson, fifty-nine years old, elder of St. Thomas's Episcopalian Church and a grandfather.

There could be no hauling, no kissing.

He weighed his words, a ton of regret in each one. "Micki, I am so honored."

"Don't you dare say *but*," she warned. "And don't you dare remind me you're twenty-two years older than I am."

He winced. Was it that much?

"And before you point out how weird this will look back in Pinyon Ridge, how everyone will be talking behind our backs—"

Heck, he hadn't even gotten that far. But she was right— much as he loved the town, gossip was a besetting plague.

"Just answer me one question," she said. "Do you like me the way I like you?"

"That's not the most important question," he began.

"The hell it's not!" Her flare of anger pinned Charles back in his seat. "I've told you I like you, Charles. But the truth is, I— I'm crazy about you."

His heart leaped.

"If you don't like me back, well, I guess I've made a fool of myself and I'll have to live with that," she said. "We'll go home to Pinyon Ridge and we'll never mention it again, and I'll try not to feel like an ass every morning when I serve your breakfast."

She leaned forward, her eyes narrowed. "But if you do feel something for me, then I want to know exactly what it is and what you're going to do about it."

For once, he was bereft of words.

"Well?" she demanded, her voice shaky, twin spots of color bright in her cheeks.

She was the most beautiful woman in the world to him.

Charles abandoned reason and voiced the words of his heart. "I can't sleep at night for wanting you in my arms. When I close my eyes, I see your face. I come to that darned café every day, eat a bucket-load of cholesterol, drink enough coffee to poison myself and can't bear to leave. I'm as jealous as heck at the thought of you being here to meet some man, and I wanted to kill my own son with my bare hands when I caught you kissing him." He stopped. "Does that answer your question?"

Micki thudded back in her seat. "Yes. Thank you."

It seemed he'd taken the wind out of her sails. They sat, looking at each other, both breathing heavily.

"So what now?" Charles ventured. No point throwing up a slew of objections that she wasn't about to accept. And since Micki had known exactly what would happen tonight—he still couldn't believe she liked *him*—she must have done some thinking about the next step.

"Now," Micki said, and her voice quivered, "we get to know each other."

"I feel like I know you better than I've ever known anyone."

She reached across the table and covered his hand with her own. Like last time, her touch set him on fire. But this time, he gripped her fingers and reveled in the squeeze of reassurance she gave him.

"Me, too," she said. "But you've still got a ways to go in thinking of me as girlfriend material."

He snorted. "You're not girlfriend material for me, there's no doubt about that."

"Yes, I am," she said firmly. "But we'll keep it simple tonight. We'll have dinner, we'll talk and then you'll drive me home."

"We can do that," he said, relieved that the plan demanded so little. He signaled to the waitress, who came over immediately. Then he realized neither of them had looked at the menu—Charles ordered the first thing he saw, the T-bone steak, and Micki went for the rack of lamb. They ordered a glass of wine each—Charles wasn't about to crack open a bottle when he'd had that whiskey earlier.

Then the waitress left, and it was just the two of them, sharing a table, the way they did most mornings. Only now it was completely different. New situation, new rules.

Charles cleared his throat. "Okay. So what shall we talk about?"

"The same things we always do, I guess," Micki said.

He cast around, but his mind was a blank. She wasn't producing any sparkling conversation, either. He couldn't recall it ever being like this before—neither of them having a word to say.

He eyed her with a consternation that matched hers.

Then Micki started to laugh, and he caught the bug and joined in.

"After all that hard work," she gasped, "I can't think of a thing to say."

"You can start," Charles said sternly, "by telling me what that kiss with Kyle was about."

JANE LICKED THE LAST of her crème brûlée off the spoon. She noted the way Kyle focused on her mouth. He'd polished off his apple tart a few minutes ago.

"Do you realize," she said, "tomorrow is the last day of the four weeks we agreed I'd stay?"

He jolted back in his seat. "But you're not leaving yet, right?"

His certainty cloaked her like a blanket, made her feel warm and…wanted. But she knew better than to jump to conclusions.

"It would be unsettling for Daisy if I left tomorrow when we haven't discussed it recently," she agreed.

"*I'm* not ready for you to go," he said.

Still, she didn't jump. They'd been in limbo for the past week, neither moving forward nor slipping backward in their relationship with each other. The sizzling sensual tension still fizzed at every casual touch, but neither of them had acted on it.

To move on from here would require a decision Jane wasn't sure she was brave enough to make. What was Kyle's excuse?

"So what would you say is going on between us?" she asked.

To his credit, he didn't flinch from the question. When she set down her dessert spoon, he reached for her hand. He turned it over; his thumb traced a slow circle on her palm.

"Okay," he said, "let's talk about what's going on. There are a hell of a lot of things I like about you. Starting with your pj's and your gorgeous legs."

She laughed.

"Then," he said, "moving swiftly on to your incredible figure, your luscious mouth. I can't stop thinking about your mouth, by the way."

"I noticed you staring." The obvious hunger in his eyes set up a fluttering in her stomach, dried her throat.

He grinned. "I like the feel of you in my arms. I'd like to feel that again."

She nodded her agreement with the sentiment.

Silence fell.

After a moment, she said, "Getting back to my original question, what's going on?"

"I'm still figuring that out," he said with an honesty she appreciated. Sort of.

"So…you wouldn't say we're dating?"

"I'd say this is a date," he said. "I like you, Jane. A lot."

She listened for subtext, any hint *like* was an understatement. Nope, none.

"And I want you," he said. "A lot."

Her traitorous body responded instantly, heat pooling within.

"Why don't you stay a couple more weeks, give us a chance to explore things?" he suggested, his voice deepening in a way that suggested exploring would include physical intimacy.

"If I stayed," she said, "while we're figuring out if we have anything serious, I'd also need to be preparing Daisy for my departure, just in case we don't."

He frowned. "I agree it's not straightforward. But I think it's worth a try."

He still had her hand in his. Now he brought it to his lips, kissed her knuckles. Totally innocuous...yet that flame in her belly leaped.

"Okay," she said. "Two more weeks. To explore."

THEY LEFT THE RESTAURANT SOON after that. Kyle drove them home. He parked in the driveway, then came around to open Jane's door.

When they reached the porch, he stopped. "I had a great evening," he said, then chuckled.

"What's so funny?"

"That trite old line. What every teenage guy says to give himself time to figure out how and where he's going to kiss the girl."

Jane smiled, conscious of a pang of regret. "My dates didn't tend to end like that." Boys who'd asked her out had been quite open about the fact they were after a piece of *Slutter,* as they'd so wittily bastardized her surname.

"Really?" He took a step closer, so she was forced to tip her head back. It drew his attention to her mouth yet again. "You mean you didn't have that will-he, won't-he pause on the front porch?"

She shook her head, half laughing, half sad. "Nope." It had been more, how soon would she need to fight them off, and would this be a night when she resorted to a kick in the crotch.

"That was always the most nerve-racking moment of the whole night," he claimed.

"I can't imagine you were ever nervous about your dates," she said drily.

"Of course I was." He took a step closer, and the movement seemed to suck up all the oxygen in the vicinity. His fingers wrapped around her upper arms, his touch light but firm. "There were so many things that could go wrong."

"Such as," Jane said shortly, "your date might not welcome your advances." She had trouble making that sound convincing when she couldn't help swaying toward him.

"That wasn't an issue," he said, and she wasn't sure if it was arrogance or a taunt. But with the comforting strength of his grip on her arms and the faint fan of his breath, bearing traces of coffee and wine, on her face, she was more susceptible than she'd been in years.

"So what could go wrong?" she asked.

"Bumping teeth," he said. "Big problem."

"Reeking, as it does, of ineptitude," she agreed.

"Ouch. I don't think I was that bad."

"Hold that thought," she said kindly.

He grinned, and she caught a flash of his white teeth in the porch light. "The problem was," he said, "I always knew the authorities—her parents, my dad the police chief—could open that front door or pull up in the street at any time, and put an end to that moment I'd been waiting for all night. Right now, Dad's in Frisco, but any moment, my brother could take it into his head to open the door and break the mood."

She raised an eyebrow. "There's a mood?"

He swiped her derriere, and somehow his hand stayed there. "Yes, there's a mood."

She grinned. "So back to the History of Teen Dating 101. In those days, you had to move fast?"

"But not too fast," he pointed out, "for fear of being

clumsy. So right now, I could kiss you until you're putty in my hands...."

"Your very capable hands," she suggested, and he grinned.

"Yeah, that." His eyes glazed over for a moment, as if he was already a few steps ahead.

"So I'd be putty in your hands...." she prompted, and just saying the words made her insides flutter.

He shook his head, as if to clear it. "Then I'd whisk you inside and make it plain to Gabe that we're on a mission."

"You'd tell your pastor brother that we're going to have sex?" Aargh, she hadn't planned to be the first to say it. Jane clamped a hand over her mouth.

Kyle grinned like he'd hit the jackpot. "Maybe you're right. Without ever saying anything condemnatory, Gabe has a way of making you feel guilty." He rubbed his chin. "We'll tell him you have food poisoning and I need to help you upstairs."

"*Lying* to your pastor brother," she said. "So much better."

"Glad you approve." His hands cupped her face. "Okay, time for the putty-in-my-hands part."

"I'm ready," she promised.

Except it turned out she wasn't ready. Not for the tender, passionate onslaught of his mouth, or for the fevered exploration of his tongue. This was new, wonderful, terrifying.

Yet how could she do anything but reward him with her very best effort? Her arms went around his neck, she matched him kiss for kiss, taste for taste.

As the kiss grew hotter, an insistent voice in her head raised a question. *If we're going to get intimate, do I need to tell him about Charles and Micki, for the sake of honesty?*

For a moment, she was torn.

Then his hands glided over her curves, caressing, cupping.

Jane mustered a shred of logic and reminded herself Kyle hadn't made any emotional commitment to her. That list of things he *liked* about her had been a bunch of physical attributes.

*He doesn't need to know about Micki and Charles yet,* she told herself. And not just because there was virtually no chance Charles would have the gumption to put aside years of conservative family values to date a woman young enough to be his daughter.

Micki was Jane's friend, who'd made their friendship a priority. She'd earned Jane's confidence. Kyle was…a guy who liked her legs and her lips. A lot, obviously, but that's all it was.

When it came to where Jane's loyalty lay, it was a no-brainer. She was free to do whatever came next with a clear conscience.

She abandoned herself entirely to his mouth, his hands, and the heat turned combustible.

"Putty?" he murmured against her ear.

"Putty-ish," she confessed on a gasp.

His quiet laugh was exultant; his hands hiked the silk skirt of her dress higher.

Next second, the front door was wrenched open, and Gabe stood there, the halo of light from the entryway turning him into an angel in jeans and T-shirt.

His expression was harried.

"I thought I heard you," he said. "Thank God you're back."

He seemed rattled, his words a genuine prayer. Kyle released Jane instantly. "Is it Daisy? What's wrong?"

Through her preoccupation with trying to smooth her dress down to decent levels, Jane heard the fear in his voice. Kyle's love for his daughter was real and strong.

"Daisy's fine." Gabe cast an agitated glance over his shoulder. "Jane, you have a visitor."

## CHAPTER FIFTEEN

MICKI WOULD REMEMBER the long drive back to Pinyon Ridge forever. Not because anything had happened, but for the sheer pleasure of sitting next to Charles knowing how he felt about her. The contentment that filled the cab of his truck, threaded with an undercurrent of sexual desire, would always be a treasured memory.

They'd gotten past that moment of awkwardness in the restaurant and once they started, they'd talked nonstop, words falling over themselves to be said and heard. They'd been the last to leave the restaurant, more or less thrown out by bored staff. Micki had never felt more wide-awake. But also entirely at peace.

It was nearly eleven when they pulled up outside the Eating Post. The streets were deserted, save for a couple of parked cars.

Charles turned the engine off and they sat there, neither wanting to break the companionable silence. The simmering tension grew. Micki wondered if it was all on her side. Or was Charles wondering, as she was, if he would kiss her good-night?

"I had a wonderful night," she said. Teenage and trite.

He twisted in his seat to face her. "I can't remember when I last had such a great time. Certainly not since…" He trailed off.

"Not since Patti died," Micki said.

Charles nodded, and she saw in his eyes the lingering pain of his wife's death. "What would she think," he said, "to see me here with you?"

"Charles, you and Patti had a great marriage. Everyone knew that. I'm not asking you to deny the love you had for her." Had she gone too far, presuming she could ever matter that much to him?

He smiled, took her hands in his, and everything was all right again. "You're right, I loved her," he said. "So much, I wondered if I could survive her dying. But I did, though for a long time it wasn't much of a survival. Getting out to this place—" he indicated the café "—was a big help." He lifted Micki's hand to his lips, and after a moment's hesitation, planted a series of tiny kisses along her knuckles with a tenderness that melted her bones. "Patti would understand what I'm feeling tonight."

"What are you feeling?" Micki whispered.

His thumb caressed the corner of her mouth. "I want to live."

She leaned into him, and his mouth claimed hers. Gently at first, drawing comfort and succor. Then something shifted, and his arms went around her, his lips grew more demanding. Micki's good intentions of giving Charles time to get used to the idea of a relationship evaporated in the rising heat inside the truck, and she parted her lips beneath his. Charles hesitated for the barest second, then he took what she offered, exploring her mouth with the thoroughness of a man who'd wandered too long in a desert and now planned to savor every drop of life-giving water.

She ran her hands over his back, pressed herself closer to him and yielded. She had no idea how many minutes had passed when, with a shuddery sigh, Charles drew away from her. "We need to stop, sweetheart."

Micki wrapped her arms around herself to ward off the sudden chill that accompanied the deprivation of his embrace. Comforted herself with the "sweetheart."

"So what happens next?" she asked. When he'd asked that question earlier, she'd only got them as far as this point.

He caressed her cheek. "I think we should hold off telling folk around here what's going on. I need some time to get used to this...and to get to know you in a different way."

"Agreed," she said.

"Sit with me in church tomorrow." He broke into a boyish, mischievous grin.

It was so unexpected, Micki said, "Huh?"

"Kyle will probably bring Daisy. You sit on the end of the row next to them, and I'll join you when I'm done with greeting duty."

How had he gone from that incredible kiss to church in the morning? "I guess no one will think that's unusual," she said.

"I want you beside me," he said. "I want to share a hymnbook with you, have your voice mingle with mine. I want to bend my head next to yours as we follow the reading, have my leg touching yours through the sermon."

Micki laughed, and Charles looked sheepish. "Does that sound stupid?"

She kissed him. "You've just made church sound more exciting than I've ever known it."

"Micki!" he scolded.

"And I can't wait." She opened her door. "If we can't tell anyone about us, sitting together in church will be the next best thing."

"I'll have to tell Kyle and Gabe, of course," he said.

She stopped, one leg out of the car. "Uh, Charles...I don't think we should tell them yet, either."

"Not tell my boys?" he said, surprised.

She grabbed his hand, lacing her fingers through his. "They won't be happy at you taking up with a woman twenty-some years younger—with one of their friends. I'd like time to...to cement this, before they try talking you out of it."

He shook his head. "They couldn't talk me out of it. But okay, point taken. We'll bed this thing down—metaphorically speaking," he said regretfully. "Then we'll tell the boys."

"Thank you." She leaned across and pressed a swift kiss to his lips. "I know you hate the thought of lying to them."

"It won't be for long." His clipped tone told her it was a bigger deal than he was letting on.

Charles Everson, the man who wielded the truth like a sword, was willing to set it aside to protect her.

She pressed a finger to the crinkle of concern in his forehead. "Not for long," she promised.

THE WOMAN WAITING in the living room of Lissa's cottage had hair that had obviously been dyed black. She wore two studs in her nose, a skin-tight sweater and a micro-skirt that barely covered her butt.

When she saw Jane, she lifted her chin and hooked her thumbs in the waistband of the barely there skirt. "Hey, Janelle, long time no see."

"Cat." That was all Jane could muster from the swirl of conflicting emotions. The first, selfishly, was dismay at the interruption to her plans for the night with Kyle. Then irritation at her sister's skimpy attire, which made her look like a two-bit hooker—which there was every chance she was.

Then came dread, as Jane wondered why Cat was here, and annoyingly, beneath all that, a tug of familial care. This was her sister. For better or for worse.

Cat stepped forward, her hands lifting slightly, as if she were planning a hug. Jane tensed; her family didn't do that kind of thing. Which is why she'd loved it when, throughout her teenage years, she and Lissa had hugged constantly. And the occasional hug or shoulder pat from Barb had been a source of comfort. But within her family…she couldn't remember any physical affection.

"Where did you come from?" Jane asked sharply.

Cat's hands dropped to her sides. "Vegas. I've been there the past couple of years."

"What brings you here?" From the corner of her eye, Jane

glimpsed Gabe's concern at her coldness. He wouldn't be so worried if he knew the real question she should be asking Cat: *How much do you want?*

Cat's chin jutted. "Maybe I wanted to surprise my big sister." Then she darted a mischievous grin at Gabe that made her look about sixteen years old. "And my high school boyfriend."

Gabe shifted from one foot to the other. "Cut it out, Cat."

Jane had never seen him anything less than composed. Now, he looked distinctly uncomfortable. He'd taken Jane to the senior prom…had Gabe been seeing her sophomore sister at the same time? That would explain his discomfort. Then again, who cared if they'd dated back in high school?

Kyle closed the gap between him and Jane. "I don't think we've met." He stuck out a hand. "I'm Kyle Everson."

"I figured," Cat said. "You have that air about you." As she shook hands, she gave him a sultry look from beneath preposterously long, presumably fake, eyelashes, and said a husky, "It's nice to meet you." Her scarlet fingernails rested on his wrist.

Kyle's withdrawal of his hand was polite enough, but he didn't look pleased to have Jane's sister show up out of the blue.

Any chance of intimacy between Jane and Kyle tonight had gone so far south it might as well have migrated for winter.

"I assume it's no coincidence that you rolled up in Pinyon Ridge while I'm here," Jane said to Cat. "How did you know?" She didn't ask why again—she didn't want Kyle and Gabe to hear her sister's demand for cash. Although maybe Cat had already hit up Gabe, which would explain his relief to see Jane.

"Dad told me you were back," Cat said.

Kyle gave Jane a sharp glance—she hadn't told him she'd visited her father. In fact, she'd told him she wasn't in touch with him.

"I'm only here for a few weeks," Jane said. "And since I'm staying with Kyle, I don't have anywhere to put you up. How about I call you when I'm back in Denver?"

"You're going to throw me out on the street?" Cat asked. She managed to sound vulnerable and very young.

Both Kyle and Gabe were looking at Jane as if she were a monster.

"Of course not."

"You could stay here tonight," Kyle offered, surprising Jane. "Then figure out what's next in the morning. It'll have to be the sofa, but if you don't mind that…"

Of all the times to develop an improved tolerance of Slaters, this wasn't a good one. Next thing, Cat would be hitting Kyle up for money.

"Too kind," Cat drawled. "The sofa sounds perfect." She tossed her small, tattered backpack onto it. "Is it my imagination, or is it warm in here?" She tugged her thin sweater over her head.

Beneath it, she wore a tight-fitting tank with a very deep scooped neck that showed a considerable amount of cleavage. She was much better endowed than Jane.

Gabe's dismay was palpable.

Did she plan to get undressed right now?

"I have a better idea. You can sleep in my room with me," Jane said. Who knew what Daisy might walk in on in the morning?

Cat shrugged. "Whatever you say."

"I should get going," Gabe said. "I have an early start tomorrow."

"Do you still like to run in the mornings?" Cat asked. "I might go with you." She did *not* look like someone dedicated to the wholesome pursuit of exercise.

"I have church," Gabe said.

"*You* go to church?" Cat said, incredulous.

Jane realized Gabe hadn't told her sister he was the pastor. How long ago had Cat arrived?

"I'm the pastor," Gabe explained, flushed beneath his tan.

Cat laughed—then stopped when it was clear no one else thought it a joke. "No way."

"I'm not the guy you knew back in school, Cat."

"No? That's a shame," she said, so suggestively that Gabe's color deepened. "Maybe I'll come to church tomorrow. Is that okay?"

"Of course," Gabe said, and he seemed to mean it. "You'd be most welcome. Jane can bring you." He winked at Jane—he'd been trying to coax her into going to church for a few weeks. "You can pay forward my babysitting services, Jane." He sounded more like his usual, relaxed self.

"Not likely," Jane said. "Cat, time we went to bed," More than anything, she wanted to get Cat out of here. Away from Kyle, away from Daisy. Jane had a sense of impending trouble that she imagined was something like what the rest of Pinyon Ridge felt when they encountered a Slater.

She hated feeling like that.

*Deal with it.* It wasn't like she didn't know her family's hot button. She would find out how much money her sister wanted, hand it over and Cat would be gone by lunchtime tomorrow.

UPSTAIRS IN THE GUEST ROOM, Jane closed the door. Cat dumped her backpack in the middle of the floor.

"What do you want?" Jane demanded.

"Like I said, to see you. *Not* to see Gabe, like I also said. Dad told me you were here."

Jane groaned. "What's his cut in this?"

Cat rolled her eyes. "There's no *this,* no cut. I visited Dad yesterday. When he said you were here, I thought I should take the opportunity to see you."

"You just *happened* to visit Dad right after I did," Jane said sarcastically.

"*You* just happened to show up right before my monthly visit," Cat said.

Jane scoffed. "You come from Vegas to Bentwood every month?"

"Pretty much." Cat eyed the area of carpet next to the bed. "Should I sleep down here?"

Jane wanted to say yes. "You can bunk in with me. No kicking." The warning slipped out, the same one she'd given Cat when they were kids, when they'd shared a bed much smaller than this for a couple of years. Cat grinned, and for half a second Jane was taken back to the time, when she used to help her sister with her English homework.

Next moment, Cat peeled off her tank to reveal a red lace bra a size too small for her generous boobs.

"I hope you have pajamas," Jane said.

Cat unhooked the bra, pulled a T-shirt from her backpack and slipped into it. Its threadbare state made it marginal for decency, but at least it covered her. "Good enough?"

Jane nodded. "You probably heard from Gabe that I'm helping out with Daisy, Lissa's daughter. You'll need to keep your words clean around her."

"No problem, not these days," Cat said. "And before you mention it, I do have a longer skirt. I find this thing—" she patted her butt-skimming mini "—more effective when I'm hitchhiking." She slipped the skirt off and stuffed it in the top of her backpack.

"You hitchhiked from Vegas?" Jane's mind filled with gruesome scenarios.

"It takes two or three days," Cat admitted, as if that was the only problem. "But the truck drivers like to look at some thigh as they drive and you can trust them. Mostly." The last word came out with an air of regretful reminiscence Jane didn't want to investigate right now.

Jane undid the tie of her wrap dress. Kyle had liked the way it showed glimpses of her legs. "Since when have you been a regular visitor to Dad?"

"I made a few changes over the past year," Cat said. "I wanted a life more…normal, I guess. And normal people keep in touch with family."

"Surely that depends on the family," Jane said.

"Dad might not be much of a father," Cat said, "but thanks to the Colorado Corrections Department you always know where he is, which is more than I can say for the rest of you."

"You know I'm based in Denver," Jane said skeptically, stepping out of her dress. "You could find my number on the internet anytime you wanted."

"Dad needed the connection more," Cat said. "I'm also trying to be more generous in the way I live."

Jane recognized a leading remark when she heard it. She crossed to the closet and hung up her dress. "How much do you need?" Not that she could afford *much*—she never had been able to.

Cat didn't pretend not to understand. "I'm not here for money. I'm talking about emotional generosity. I'm here to mend fences. With you."

Jane snorted.

"You have reason to disbelieve that," Cat agreed. "But here's the thing. Last September, I hit rock-bottom and it wasn't pretty. I met a couple—the Boyds, Dee and Andy— who let me stay with them, helped me get back on my feet. Watching how they lived—setting goals and then achieving them through hard work, putting each other first, thinking about the greater good of their church and community—it affected me."

She wrinkled her nose. "I guess it's like the experience you had with Lissa's family, which I never understood back then."

Jane nodded. "What was this couple's motive?" she asked. "Were they trying to convert you?"

"No, but I did start to think they might be on to something with their church stuff. They—" Cat shrugged "—they had a lot of peace and contentment. I realized life's more enjoyable when you're not always moving around to avoid the people you've conned."

"I could have told you that," Jane said. "I *did* tell you that."

Cat spread her hands in apology. "Would it help if I said that now that I've seen the light, I want to get closer to you?"

Jane stiffened. She didn't trust anyone in her family—she'd learned that from bitter experience. "No, thanks, I'd rather not hand over any money to someone who'll spend it on booze and setting up elaborate cons," she said. "Such as your imminent religious conversion."

"That's not a con, Jane. If it happens it'll be for real. And I'm not here for money." Cat lifted the duvet and climbed into bed.

"Other side," Jane ordered. She hated that something about Cat's story tugged at her heartstrings. She hated how much she wanted to believe it. *I should know better. I* do *know better.*

Cat obediently moved across the bed.

"You'll need to leave in the morning," Jane said. "I'll buy you a bus ticket back to Vegas, but that's the only money you're getting."

## *CHAPTER SIXTEEN*

WHEN CAT WAS GONE from the bed on Sunday morning, and her backpack nowhere in sight, Jane hoped her sister had gotten the message and left town. It would be worth finding her wallet cleared out just to be free of the potential trouble Cat could cause.

Jane needed to resume the conversation with Kyle that her sister's arrival had interrupted. It seemed they'd agreed Jane would stay in Pinyon Ridge a couple more weeks. But that wasn't a heck of a lot of time to figure out where she might fit in Daisy's life…and Kyle's, too. If there were any chance of a relationship, she needed to make like Micki—do whatever she could to show Kyle that it could work. Starting now. Without her sister around to mess things up.

Unfortunately, she hadn't taken into account Cat's considerable powers of persuasion.

Turned out her sister had risen early to talk Kyle into letting her stay a little longer. When he'd heard she had experience as a laborer on a construction site, he'd hired her to help with the finishing of his new house.

Jane heard all this when she went to the house to pick up Daisy, who'd been to church with Kyle in the morning.

"You gave Cat a job?" she asked, aghast.

"I thought you'd be pleased." Kyle set down the paintbrush he'd been using to stain the decking. "You're the one who said no one in Pinyon Ridge would give you a chance at a job because you were a Slater."

"Yeah, but *I* wouldn't give Cat a job." Jane was aware of the irony of that, but the fact was, Cat couldn't be trusted, and Jane didn't need her sister screwing up her best chance to be a part of Daisy's life. She glanced around. "Where is she, anyway?"

"I sent her to the store for more undercoat—she's painting Daisy's room."

"You gave her money? And a car? For Pete's sake, Kyle, you might as well phone 9-1-1 right now."

Kyle ran a hand through his hair. "Okay, you didn't say anything last night to make me think you didn't trust her."

"I didn't want to say it in public in front of her—surely you noticed I was cool toward her."

He grinned. "I thought that was because she'd stymied our plans for—"

"It wasn't," she said quickly. "Cat only ever shows up when she needs money."

"All the more reason to give her a job. Cat told me she's turned over a new leaf. My first reaction was doubt, but I decided that was the kind of narrow-mindedness you've called my family on before." Kyle walked to the edge of the deck and inspected the sky where gray clouds were rolling in. "I might have to call it a day out here. Look, I watched Cat for half an hour this morning before I left for church—she's not built like a typical construction worker, but she's strong and she knows what she's doing."

"When are you expecting her back?" Jane would talk to Cat herself, see if she could convince her to leave.

He checked his watch. "Nearly an hour ago," he said, surprised.

Jane groaned. "I hope you weren't too attached to that truck, because—"

Before she could finish her sentence, the truck pulled into the driveway, Cat at the wheel. She made no effort to park, just stopped in the middle of the pavement. She sprang down from the cab, slamming the door behind her. Having hoisted two large paint cans from the truck bed, she stomped up the steps.

At the sound of another car pulling into the driveway, she stopped.

"It's Gabe," Kyle said, when he saw the red Ford Focus. "Why is he here?"

"Because he has no freakin' sense of humor," Cat snapped. She tossed the truck keys to Kyle, then planted her hands on her hips and waited for Gabe to get out of his car.

"Don't start," she yelled, before he took so much as a step in their direction.

"You think I should let you get away with what you just did?" Unlike Cat, Gabe didn't sound mad…more a controlled kind of angry.

"I didn't say anything she didn't deserve," Cat called.

Jane traded glances with Kyle. What the heck had Cat done?

"You don't think it was unacceptable, calling my secretary an old prune?" Gabe demanded.

"If you knew what I really wanted to call her," Cat snapped, "you'd admire my restraint."

"I don't give a f— A hoot." *Now* Gabe looked mad. At himself.

"He hasn't even come close to cursing in years," Kyle murmured to Jane.

Gabe continued more calmly, "I know Alicia isn't the easiest woman to get along with…."

"She asked if I've changed my thieving ways or if she should lock up the collection plate!"

Jane snorted, earning a glare from her sister.

"We don't even have a collection plate, it was a joke. Her sense of humor can be inappropriate." Gabe sounded more himself. "That's got her into trouble before, as anyone in town can tell you. I gave her a job as part of a plan to improve her people skills."

"It's not working!" Cat stormed. "You shouldn't hire someone out of pity if they're not up to the job."

"Kyle hired you," Gabe said.

Jane sucked in a breath, and was pretty sure Kyle did the same. Cat turned scarlet. She opened her mouth, ready to vaporize Gabe.

"Cat's good at her job," Kyle said. "The fact that she's a pity case is secondary."

Amazingly, though Cat glared, she didn't explode. "I'm going to get that undercoat on those walls," she muttered, then disappeared into the house.

Gabe watched her go with an enigmatic look on his face.

"Is it true you used to date Cat?" Jane asked.

He jolted. "Uh, yeah. In senior year."

"You took *me* to the prom. Were you two-timing me with my own sister?"

Kyle took a step toward his brother, as if he might be prepared to land a punch if Gabe had been that much of a jerk. A warm, cozy feeling spread through Jane's chest. *He'd do that for me. Just like he hired my con-artist sister for me.*

"Of course not." Gabe didn't look entirely comfortable. "You and I didn't date after the prom—"

"Because I wouldn't sleep with you."

He winced. "A few weeks later, Cat and I…got together." The dull red beneath his tan told her exactly what "got together" meant.

"She was a sophomore!" Jane said.

"We were both underage," Gabe admitted. "What we did was wrong, but Jane, it's not for you to judge. I've put my past sins behind me." He met her gaze steadily, his meaning clear: she, of all people, should be willing to do the same. "Now, I have a few more words to say to your stubborn sister."

Well, huh. Despite that unspoken homily to Jane, he looked anything but forgiving as he walked after Cat.

"Did he make you feel guilty or was it just me?" Kyle asked.

Jane turned to him in relief. "How does he do that without saying anything?"

"I don't know. All I know is, we sinners need to stick together." He took her into his arms.

Jane turned her face up to his.

The kiss was different from last night's. Slower, more tender, exploratory. It put a curious ache in her chest.

The purr of a powerful engine broke them apart.

Kyle swore. "What is this, Grand Central Station?"

Charles Everson had just arrived. And seen them in the clinch, going by the frown on his face.

*Just let him say something,* Jane thought. Micki had given her a blow-by-blow account this morning of their night out in Frisco, so he was hardly one to comment on whether or not she was a suitable recipient of Kyle's kisses.

"What do you want, Dad?" Kyle asked shortly.

Charles barely seemed to notice his son's bordering-on-rude manner. "I thought— I don't know, just a chat. But you're busy." He glanced from Kyle to Jane.

Cat marched back out onto the deck.

"Tell your brother to stop harassing me or I'll quit," she told Kyle.

"Or you could just quit anyway," Jane suggested.

Cat narrowed her eyes.

"Dad, this is Jane's sister, Cat." Kyle performed the introduction.

"Hello, Cat," Charles said, his greeting neither warm nor cold. An improvement on the welcome he'd extended to Jane a month ago. "Short for Catherine, if I remember rightly?"

"Short for hellcat," Cat corrected him.

Charles pursed his mouth, but didn't say anything.

Jane's eyes met Kyle's…and found him stifling a laugh, just as she was.

"Families," he murmured. "Can't live with them…"

"And they won't let you live without them," she finished.

He grinned, that open, unstinting smile he was getting good at, the one that had such a powerful effect on her heart.

*I could fall in love with this man.*

What the heck? Jane froze. No, she could *not* fall in love with Kyle Everson. Not without an ironclad guarantee that he would never hurt her, and that wasn't going to happen. She could love Daisy—or rather, she couldn't *not* love Daisy—but when it came to Kyle, she had a choice.

She could like him, flirt with him, kiss him, maybe even sleep with him. She didn't have to fall in love with him. She *wouldn't.*

"DID YOU RESOLVE your spat with Gabe?" Jane asked as Cat helped unload the dishwasher that evening. Kyle had eaten dinner with them and set Daisy up at the coffee table in the living room with her crayons and coloring book before going back to work at the new house. He'd refused Cat's offer of assistance.

Jane was glad to see him go. She didn't want to think about the feelings he'd stirred up today. She also wanted to establish some kind of truce with Cat, one that would involve Cat promising not to make trouble, in exchange for being allowed to stay a bit longer.

"My spat was with that old prune in his office," Cat said.

Jane rolled her eyes. "What were you doing visiting Gabe, anyway?"

Silence.

"Cat?"

"Thought I'd catch up for old times' sake," Cat mumbled as she hung two mugs on hooks in the cupboard. "Figured he'd be there on a Sunday, and he was."

"You don't…still like him, do you?" Jane asked with trepidation. Because the complications between the Slaters and Eversons were already manifold. They really didn't need any more.

"I still think he's hot," Cat said. "It was a bit of a shock to discover he's a pastor."

"I gather he's good at it," Jane said as she finished sorting the silverware into its drawer.

"Gabe's good at everything he does." Cat's expression turned faraway.

Jane snapped her fingers in front of her sister's face. "I hope that doesn't mean what I think it means. I haven't seen Gabe so riled about anything as he was with you today. Do you think he still likes you?"

Cat's mouth flattened. "*Like* never came into it on his side. He wanted an easy girl, and I wanted him. I *liked* him. We did it every which way till Sunday, but he never once took me out on a date."

Jane felt a surge of indignation for her sister. "That's awful."

"To be fair, he offered to take me to a movie the first time we went out," Cat admitted. "I said no, because I knew it would cause a fuss and his parents would hear about it and he'd likely be forbidden to see me. After that, he assumed I was happy just to hook up for sex."

"Man, he really was a jerk."

"I wanted him badly enough to agree," Cat said. "And I didn't have any self-respect to get in the way. But, yeah, he should have known better. I think I'm a reminder of a time he's ashamed of."

"What about that forgiveness thing he preaches? Shouldn't he have gotten over the past?"

"We might be forgiven, but it's human to have regrets," Cat said knowledgably.

"What are you, a Baptist?"

Cat grinned. "Thinking about it." She laughed at Jane's shocked expression. "I told you, I got kind of interested in church stuff in Vegas."

"I thought you were making it up."

"Nope, I'm just not sure if I want to give up my bad habits and go all the way."

"Gabe could advise you, I suppose," Jane said dubiously.

Cat wrinkled her nose. "I wouldn't want to give him the satisfaction of converting me."

Jane laughed.

"So what's going on between you and Kyle?" Cat asked.

"Nothing." She said it too fast. "I mean, we're cooperating, for Daisy's sake. We might even be friends." Mention of Daisy reminded her to check on the little girl. Jane glanced through the dining room to where she could see Daisy, busy with her coloring.

"And those hot and heavy glances you keep exchanging?"

"I don't know what you're talking about." Jane straightened the glasses in their cupboard.

Cat might be her sister, but Jane wasn't in the habit of sharing confidences, especially when she didn't entirely trust Cat. Heck, she didn't trust anyone in her own family.

*I trust Kyle.*

Cat's eyes on her were all too knowing.

"We both want to do our best for Daisy." Jane deliberately transferred her gaze to the little girl, intent on her coloring in the other room.

Cat came to stand beside Jane. "Cute kid," she said. "There's something about her face…."

"Yeah, she really is adorable." Jane heard the emotion in her own voice, and winced. "Poor girl. She misses Lissa horribly."

In the living room, Daisy screwed up her face in concentration, and the tip of her tongue came out the left side of her mouth.

Cat's hand clamped over Jane's forearm, the nails digging in.

"Ow!" Jane yelped.

"I just figured it out." Cat shook her arm. "I can't believe you didn't tell me. This is unreal."

"What are you talking about?"

Cat hauled Jane to the other side of the kitchen. "That thing Daisy's doing," she hissed. "The tongue and the screwed-up face. Who does that remind you of?"

*Oh, hell.* "I'm sure lots of kids do that."

"I *said* there was something about her face—it's the shape of her chin." Cat smacked her forehead. "I can't believe I didn't see it before, it's so freakin' obvious." Her eyes were bright with excitement.

"Calm down," Jane ordered. "Cat, whatever you think you know, you mustn't—"

"I'm not blind, Janelle. It's obvious Darren's been sowing his wild oats too close to home."

Busy cudgeling her brain for alternative explanations her sister might believe, it took a moment for Jane to hear what she'd said. She frowned. "Darren—what do you mean?"

"That kid's a Slater, it stands out a mile off." Cat's eyes narrowed. "Which means your friend Lissa must have done the deed with one of our brothers. Or our father, which is too creepy, even for him. Johnno would have been in Australia by the time Daisy came along, so I'm picking Darren as the father."

"That's insane," Jane snapped.

"I wonder if Kyle knows," Cat mused. She broke into a sly smile. "Even better, I wonder if Gabe knows."

"Don't you dare say a word," Jane warned. "You have no idea what you're talking about."

Cat folded her arms across her chest. "But *you* know. I can see it in your eyes, Janelle Slater, you were never any good at lying. And if I want to give Mr. Self-Righteous Let's-Pretend-We-Never-Had-Illicit-Sex a kick in the teeth, I will." She was growing louder as she spoke.

"Shut up," Jane said. With a glare at Cat, she walked to the doorway. "Daisy, sweetie, it's time to go upstairs. Brush your teeth, I'll come see you in a minute."

Daisy obeyed without comment. But the heavy silence didn't escape the little girl; she gave Jane a worried look. Jane blew her a kiss. She'd been doing that lately. Not physically kissing Daisy, which might seem like staking a claim, but just this casual, keeping-her-distance kiss.

When Daisy was gone, Jane pointed to the kitchen table. "Sit," she told Cat. "I'm going to tell you the truth, because I don't want you spreading wild rumors about Lissa and Darren. But I need you to promise you won't tell anyone."

"Sure," Cat said, too glib, as she pulled out a chair.

"I mean it," Jane snapped. "This isn't about you taking Gabe down a notch or two, this is about destroying the world of an innocent child."

"Whatever." Cat rested her chin on her hands, elbows on the table. "Okay, okay, I won't say a word, I promise."

Jane had little choice but to believe her. She could always offer Cat a loan—or a gift—to encourage her silence. "Darren's not Daisy's father," she said. "I'm Daisy's mother."

Saying those words for the first time to someone other than Kyle, so baldly, had the most bizarre effect. Her stomach lurched; tears welled in her eyes.

Cat swore. "This is insane, Janelle. Tell me what happened. Now."

So Jane did. "You can't tell anyone," she reminded Cat at the end. "No one else has noticed any resemblance between me and Daisy."

"Because no one else shared a bed with you while you did your homework into the night with your tongue sticking out."

"You won't tell," Jane said. She deliberately made it a statement, not a question.

"I won't tell," Cat agreed.

CHARLES SET HIS KNIFE AND FORK down on the turned-leg dining table in Micki's apartment, his plate of chicken Marengo untouched. "This is driving me crazy."

"My chicken Marengo?" Micki smiled at him, and his chest clenched.

Blast that candle she'd lit, which stopped him from leaning across and kissing her.

"Your cooking is incredible, and you know it." He took an appreciative sniff of the warm air still wafting off his plate.

Micki smirked.

"It's driving me crazy that I have to sneak in here every evening," he said. "Tonight I had to pretend I was reading realty listings until the Grays walked on by. And you know Betty Gray, it'll be all over town tomorrow that I'm looking for a new house."

"You wouldn't have to sneak in," she said, "if we told people we're dating."

And have it all over town that Charles Everson was making a fool of himself over some young thing?

Correctly reading his expression, Micki flicked her napkin at him. "It's time. We've had dinner together every night, breakfast every morning."

And nothing in between dinner and breakfast, but that was how it would stay, no matter how much he wanted to make love with her. He'd always believed sex should be sanctified by marriage.

"It'll be a sensation at first, I admit," she said. "But people will get over it."

"I don't know," he said, unused to being indecisive...and not liking it much.

She reached for his hand across the table. "At the very

least, maybe I was wrong to say you couldn't tell Kyle and Gabe. What if they figure it out, or someone else does and tells them? They'll be hurt."

Charles frowned. "They're big boys, they're not that sensitive." He'd been worried at the thought of keeping the truth from his sons at first, but now he liked that they couldn't subject him to an inquisition about his feelings and his plans. The kind of inquisition he never hesitated to put them through.

"But they'd be…surprised you're dating someone my age. More specifically, me. A friend of theirs."

Charles began to eat. He preferred not to share every thought, liked to reach a conclusion before he spoke. He loved that Micki knew that, that she let him work through his meal.

When he was done, he set his cutlery to the side of his plate and wiped his mouth on his napkin. "This might be a shock for the boys—that chicken was incredible, by the way—but they'll get over it. They want me to be happy."

"So we should tell them now. Let's just tell everyone."

He hesitated.

"Are you worried about your reputation?" she asked. "Do you think people will think we're doing something wrong?"

Hell, yes. But that wasn't the main issue. "I'm not worried about what anyone else in town thinks. Not enough to stop me."

"Then what's the problem?"

He swirled the last of the red wine in his glass. Good for the heart, Micki had said when she poured it. *She* was good for his heart. "I guess I'm scared," he blurted.

He could hardly believe he was saying this, but that was the thing about Micki, he could tell her anything, *wanted* to tell her everything. "Scared you can't go on feeling the way you do about me." He rushed the words out. "Any minute now, you'll realize I'm too old, too boring, and that'll be the end of it. If that happens *after* everyone knows we're seeing each other, it's going to be difficult for both of us."

"Sounds to me like you want to make it easier for us to break up."

He backed down from her ominous tone. "*I* don't want us to break up. Absolutely not."

"But you don't trust me to know what I want?"

Somehow, Charles seemed to be making this worse. He kept trying. "Sweetheart, people break up all the time. They get tired of what they had and want something new."

"But that won't happen to you, right? You won't get tired of me?"

"Certainly not," he said with total conviction.

"But it might happen to me?"

Uh-oh, minefield alert.

"Ah, I didn't say that," Charles reminded her.

"Because I'm too young, at nearly forty, to know my own mind?"

"No, that's not it. And you're not nearly forty, you're barely mid-thirties."

She rolled her eyes. "Tell me how you know you won't change *your* mind."

He was as brave as any cop when it came to walking into a homicide scene. He'd been shocked to discover he was a total wimp when it came to affairs of the heart. "I don't have to tell you that." He poured some more red wine, not planning to drink it.

"Yes, you do."

"Don't." He took a slug of the wine and set the glass down.

"Do." Micki whipped his glass away. "If you can't tell me what gives you such incredible prescience and makes me such a flake, it's time you left. Good night."

"Micki, you're being—"

"Childish?" She raised her eyebrows. "That's because I'm twenty-two years younger than you. I'm not always going to react the same way as you or show your impeccable maturity, but you know what? It doesn't matter a damn!"

"You're one of the most mature women I know." He had no idea if that was the right thing to say.

"Most men your age would revel in having a younger woman and want to shout it from the rooftops, but not Charles Everson," she said.

Evidently it hadn't been the right thing.

"No," she continued, "for you it's a dark secret." She drew breath, presumably to tell him just what she thought of that. But maybe she caught sight of his stricken expression, because she softened. "But for some dumb reason, I don't want any of those guys. I had to fall for the most ornery old coot—"

"I love you," Charles said.

## CHAPTER SEVENTEEN

THE WAY MICKI CAME to a screaming halt was almost laughable. "*What* did you say?"

Charles reached across the table, slid the candle aside, then took her hands in his. "This ornery old coot loves you. I love you so much, that's how I know I'm not going to change my mind. I've seen you every morning and every night for the past two weeks, and with every moment I love you more. But—"

"I knew there'd be a *but*," she said fiercely.

He loved that she was so fierce. He shook her hands. "*But* a part of me is scared. Scared that one day you'll wake up to just how ornery and old I am—I have arthritis in my left knee, did you know that?—and you'll want something else."

"I love you back," she said, and his heart quickened. "Believe it or not, Charles, what I feel for you is more than lust for your gorgeous body—including your arthritic left knee."

"Micki…" He was pretty sure he was blushing; her laugh confirmed it.

She moved around the table and sat on his knee. His mouth found hers and for a few minutes there was silence, save for tender murmurs and needy noises.

"You're right," Charles said when he surfaced. "We have to tell the boys. Tell everyone. I want to walk down the street holding your hand. I want to lean across my table at the Eating Post and kiss you in front of the whole world."

From Micki's arrested expression, he guessed the full consequences had just sunk in. She looked as if she couldn't imagine that happening in a million years. "Maybe you're right—there's no rush," she said.

Charles chuckled. "Cold feet, huh? You know what we need, sweetheart? We should go away for a few days. Camping. Somewhere private, where we can be together all day, doing all the kissing and hand-holding we like, just to get ourselves used to it. Then we'll come back and give this place something to talk about."

Micki's face lit up so wonderfully, he couldn't doubt the strength of her feelings.

"I can't think of anything I'd like better," she said. "I'd have to ask Margaret to run the café…and maybe I could ask Jane to help—I've been giving her barista lessons."

"Jane Slater?" Charles thought he did a pretty good job of keeping disapproval out of his voice, but Micki sent him a sharp look.

"Jane's been a wonderful support to me while I've been angsting over my feelings for you."

"She *knows?*" he said, appalled.

Micki rapped his knuckles with her dessert spoon. "If I hadn't had her to talk to these past few weeks, I'd have gone crazy."

"If Jane knows, maybe I do need to tell Kyle," Charles said. "Who knows how much those two share?"

"Can we have our break together first?" Micki asked. "Jane's overnighting in Denver tonight, catching up with clients, but I'll talk to her about helping out in the café when she arrives back tomorrow. If we can get away this weekend, it might be best not to tell Kyle until after that. To keep it simple for now, to what it's really about. Which is you and me."

With those wide eyes pleading, resistance was futile. "Just you and me," he agreed. "For now."

JANE'S CELL PHONE rang at five-thirty Saturday morning. She fumbled on the nightstand, thumbed the right button more through good luck than design. "Hello?"

"Jane, it's Margaret."

Huh? Oh, yeah, Micki's assistant.

"What's up?" Jane wasn't due at the café until seven-thirty—the Eating Post opened at eight on the weekend.

"I've been up and down since one o'clock this morning, with food poisoning." Margaret groaned. "I went to my niece's wedding yesterday—I *knew* there was something strange about that shrimp."

Jane's brain started to resume normal service. "You want me to open the café. No problem."

Margaret groaned again. "Thank you. From the bottom of my heart."

"What time do you think you'll get there?" Jane pushed her covers aside and got out of bed. "Sounds like you need at least a couple of hours' sleep."

Silence. Then Margaret said, "Jane, I can't go near the Eating Post. Health regulations forbid anyone with food poisoning cooking or serving in a food premises."

"But…I can't do it on my own," Jane protested.

"I'm really sorry, but you have to," Margaret said. "Micki always leaves a list of instructions a mile long, so you'll have no trouble getting the hang of it. And I know she assembled the muffin mixes before she left yesterday afternoon. Her cell is switched off, but I left a message—with any luck, she can come back by lunchtime."

Jane knew Micki's phone was out of range—she'd warned Jane she and Charles would be unreachable.

Not that Jane would want to break into their time together.

"Don't worry," she told Margaret. "I'll handle it."

Margaret couldn't get off the line fast enough.

Around the same time as Jane realized there was no way she could handle the breakfast rush at the Eating Post, she realized she was alone in her bed. For the past week, Cat had occupied the space next to her.

Where was her sister when Jane needed her?

And who else could she call on at this hour? There was only one answer to that question.

She padded down the hallway and tapped on Kyle's door. Quietly, so as not to wake Daisy.

No reply, so after a moment's hesitation she went in. Kyle lay sprawled across the bed. Topless. In the gray dawn light that filtered through the gap in the curtains, Jane discerned a muscular chest with just the right amount of hair that tapered as her gaze moved lower....

*Get a grip.*

She advanced to the bed and touched his shoulder. "Kyle?" His skin was warm, like raw silk.

He didn't stir.

She shook his shoulder. "Kyle?" she said louder.

His eyes opened. "Ducks," he said with a lazy smile.

Of course, she was wearing *those* pj's.

Before she could tell him she had more important things on her mind, his arm snaked out and wrapped around her waist, tugging her down.

"Oof." She landed on him, on his unyielding frame. "Kyle..."

"Mmm, so you said." He hooked a finger into the neckline of her pj top. "I was just dreaming about this."

She slapped his hand away. "We don't have time—I need your help at the Eating Post."

"Whoa." His voice sharpened; his eyes opened fully. "What?"

She told him about Margaret. "So I'm wondering if you can help out?"

"Sure." He pushed the covers aside, giving her a moment of thrilled alarm. Only to discover he was wearing boxers.

"Maybe you could get Daisy up and take her to Gabe's place," Jane said, trying not to look at the boxer region, "then get to the café as soon as you can...."

"I'll be right behind you." His gaze traveled over her, more leisurely than it should, given the emergency. "Especially if you keep wearing those pajamas."

"I'll go change," she assured him.

Downstairs, she found a note from Cat on the dining table.

Running an errand in Frisco, hitching a ride on the milk truck, back by lunchtime.

No use to Jane at all. She scribbled a note of her own at the bottom of the page, asking Cat to come to the café as soon as she arrived back in town.

A pot of yogurt later, Jane headed out into the fog-wisped street and walked the five hundred yards to the Eating Post.

She just hoped Micki's instructions would prove as comprehensive as Margaret promised.

She let herself into the café with the key Micki had given her and disarmed the alarm.

A flick of the light switch revealed the immaculate café. On the counter sat two sets of two stainless-steel bowls. One set was labeled blueberry and pear muffins, the other cheese and onion. According to the neatly typed instructions on the counter, all Jane had to do was combine the wet mix and the dry mix for each variety. Pour into greased pans, stick the pans in the oven and voilà.

"Easy," she said, startling herself in the quiet.

Once she figured out how big a spoonful was needed to fill the muffin pans three-quarters full, preparing them took just a few minutes.

Jane opened the oven door, ready to cook.

"Damn!" No welcoming heat or helpful light. She'd forgotten Micki's first instruction, handwritten at the top of the page and underlined in red: before you start, turn the oven on to four hundred.

Jane turned the dials now, and the light came on and the reassuring whir of the fan started. But what about her muffins? Micki's notes said it was essential the wet and dry mixes weren't combined until just before the muffins went in the oven. So Jane wouldn't be able to allow the oven twenty minutes to heat, as per the instructions. Fearful that even as she dithered, the uncooked muffins were in some way spoiling, she slid the pans inside and shut the door. She'd give them a few minutes' extra cooking time, to allow for the cold oven. Not ideal, but she didn't have much choice.

Having done that, Jane read down the list of instructions. *Take toast bread out of freezer. Precook sausages. Make scrambled egg and omelet mixes, using recipes on the counter.* All three tasks were quickly accomplished, giving her confidence a boost.

*Make sandwiches.*

No problem. The rolls and paninis had been delivered by the Frisco bakery and just needed bringing in from outside the back door. Jane pulled butter from the fridge, along with Micki's neatly labeled canisters of fillings. Turkey and cranberry, smoked chicken salad, ham and mustard, egg salad. She set to buttering and filling the sandwiches.

By the time she was done, it was six-forty-five. An hour and a quarter until opening. That sounded reasonable. Jane read down her list.

*Chocolate cake out of freezer.* Oops, she probably should have done that earlier. Still the cake was easily found, and it wouldn't take long to thaw on its cake stand, now that the oven was heating up and transmitting some of its warmth to the kitchen.

Blast! The muffins were still in the oven. Jane grabbed a mitt and pulled the door open. They weren't burned—the oven must have taken a while to heat up. On the other hand, nor were they the beautifully risen creations Micki produced every day.

Jane set the trays on the cooling rack for a couple of minutes while she turned on the coffee machine and filled the filter. She put out cream and skim milk for the coffees she'd make later and filled carafes of water. Then she twisted the muffins out of their tins, thankfully without difficulty. At least they would be ready for opening time. Which was more than she could say of the quiche.

Micki had left two empty quiche shells in the fridge, along with instructions on how to prepare the filling. Jane decided one quiche would be enough for now. She could fill another later in the day, during a quiet moment.

She smirked in self-satisfaction as she remembered to turn the oven down to three-twenty-five. Then she caught sight of the clock—ten minutes until opening! Where the heck was Kyle?

She worked like a maniac, beating eggs, adding milk, chopped onion, mushrooms and ham. She poured the filling into the crust and got it in the oven just as the big hand moved to the twelve and a knock sounded at the door of the café.

Who the hell turned up at 8:00 a.m. on a Saturday?

Jane forced herself to smile as she opened the door. Kyle. Phew. She dropped the fake smile as she turned the sign to Open. "About time."

"Sorry." He headed to the counter. "I had no idea how hard it is to get Daisy up and ready in a hurry."

"Welcome to my world."

He snickered. "Tell me what you need from me."

*A promise you'll never hurt me. A few more kisses wouldn't go amiss, either.* "You know a lot more about this place than I do," she said. "If you can see anything I've missed, just do it."

He rolled up the sleeves of his plaid shirt, baring tanned wrists. "I'll put out a stack of cups, like Micki does. It'll save time when we're busy. And I'll crank the dishwasher up."

"Sounds good," she said, distracted. That chocolate cake must be thawed by now, the kitchen was sweltering. Jane found a batch of frosting in the fridge, and set to icing the cake. *There, that didn't look too bad.* Micki had said it should be cut into a dozen slices. Jane selected a broad-bladed knife, chose her starting point and sliced into the cake.

The cake resisted.

"Something wrong?" Kyle asked, watching.

She shook her head, gritted her teeth and pushed the knife down harder. This time, it sank half an inch into the dense chocolate surface before it stopped.

Kyle edged forward to observe. "Maybe you should—"

"I've got it." She lifted the knife, clamped her other hand around it, too, so she was holding it more like an axe, and whacked it down on to the cake.

The rock-hard cake shot off the tray and over the side of the counter, landing with a thud on the floor.

Jane swore.

She went around the other side of the counter and picked up the cake, which was still in one solid piece—she wasn't sure if that was cause for gratitude or not.

Behind her, the door from the street opened. "Morning," called Wayne Tully.

"Damn." Jane shoved the cake into Kyle's hands before wiping up a smudge of frosting from the floor. "Hi, Wayne, take a seat and I'll be right over."

She gathered up a pen and notepad, and headed for the table by the window where Wayne was pouring salt from the shaker on to his fingers and licking them. "What can I get you, Wayne?"

He looked at her doubtfully. "You got eggs?"

"Sure do." *Fried, or donor?*

"I'll take eggs, sausage and hash brown."

"Coming right up."

Back at the counter, she found Kyle looking decidedly stealthy, hunched over something she couldn't see.

"What are you doing?" she asked.

"I'm dusting off the cake and reapplying some frosting as needed. Thankfully Micki keeps a pretty clean floor."

"We can't serve cake that's been on the floor!"

He raised an eyebrow. "Three-second rule. It didn't do me any harm when I was growing up. More important, you can't *not* serve Micki's chocolate cake. There are people who drive out from Denver on Saturday just for a slice."

Jane had quoted the three-second rule to Daisy a couple of days ago. It would be hypocritical to reverse her position now. "Fine," she said. "But I don't want a speck of dust left on that thing."

The door opened and two men came in for coffee. Simple filter coffees, thankfully. Jane poured two cups, then got to work on Tully's breakfast. She hadn't asked him how he wanted his eggs for a very good reason. Sunny-side up was the fastest, easiest way of doing them, so that's all she was offering today. She hoped Micki wouldn't mind.

Jane got the sausage and hash browns into the pan just as the oven timer dinged. The quiche was ready.

Uh, no, it wasn't. While the crust was the perfect golden color, the filling was still semi-liquid. When Jane set the tray down, an eggy wave splashed over the side onto the stove top.

"What's that?" Kyle abandoned his Herculean attempt to slice through the frozen chocolate cake to inspect Jane's handiwork.

"Quiche soup," she said.

He inspected the quiche. "You must have put too much milk in. This is supposed to have set."

"If only I'd asked your advice earlier."

He grinned. "My mother always said not everyone can make quiche—there's a knack to it."

"This is so interesting…and I have so much time to discuss it."

"A knack," he continued, "that I happen to possess."

It took her a moment to process that. *"You?"*

He nodded.

She couldn't resist. "Real men don't make quiche."

"Are you doubting that I can make quiche or that I'm a real man?"

She pressed her lips together, teasing him with her eyes.

"I'm happy to demonstrate either," he said.

"I'm gonna have to choose the quiche," she said regretfully. She waved at the refrigerator. "Eggs are in there."

She delivered Wayne Tully's breakfast to him. He'd been joined by two other men—his campaign workers, going by the gist of the conversation.

"Anyone with half a brain can see our plans for the town will bring prosperity that will make Everson's scheme look like small change," Tully was saying. He glanced at Jane. "And you can quote me on that, little lady."

"I would, if I was remotely interested," she assured him.

"That's the other thing," he told his colleagues. "The other towns around here have had low voter turnout in their recent elections. Like this little lady here—" he thumbed at Jane "—a lot of younger people don't take an interest. The people who do vote will be the older folk, who remember the good times the town enjoyed when I was mayor. Folk who don't believe in global warming and aren't going to vote based on greenie issues. We're offering those people a repeat experience—did you get that, Jason?" he asked the younger of his two colleagues, who was scribbling in a notebook.

Jason nodded.

"Put the comment about Everson's scheme being small change in your press release, too," Tully told him. "Just how I said it, don't mess with it." He glanced at Jane. "You still here?"

She returned to the counter to greet fresh arrivals. Who would have believed so many people in Pinyon Ridge could want feeding all at once? Several people canceled their food orders and settled for toast when they saw how much trouble she and Kyle were having. But others didn't see why they should back down simply for her convenience. One man ordered a cheese and onion muffin, and stared at the offering Jane presented.

"Did it shrink?" he asked, with apparently genuine bewilderment.

Kyle stepped in. "These are our new mini-muffins, Ed. Half the price of the regular ones, but bigger than half the size."

Ed brightened. "I'll take three. And one of them berry ones, too."

Great! Now Jane would have to make another batch of muffins from scratch. And she was probably losing money on every single one.

"Is it normally this busy in here?" she demanded of Kyle, once ten o'clock came and went and the rush still showed no signs of thinning.

He eyed her with concern. "You need to sit down for a minute. Just until someone else wants to place an order."

Jane looked at the mess on the counter, the dishes piling in the sink. "I can't."

"You can." He pushed her into a seat at the table where she'd sat that first morning with Micki. Kyle grabbed a cup of coffee off the counter and set it in front of her.

"That's Dave Clark's coffee."

"I'll pour him another one."

She let out a little sigh as she wrapped her hands around the cup. "Before I forget, Tully's telling his staff he'll win the election because not enough younger people will get out and vote. You might want to do something about that."

"Noted. Though I'd very surprised if Tully knew anything at all."

Jane sniffed the air. "Is something burning?"

"The quiche!" Kyle practically vaulted the counter in his rush to the oven. Too late. The quiche had set all right, its blackened surface was positively crispy. He scraped it into the trash in disgust.

"What did I tell you?" Jane demanded, triumphant. "Real men don't make quiche."

He threw back his head and laughed, the sound rich and warm.

Somehow, they survived the next couple of hours. Jane was even able to make two more batches of muffins, which came out the right size. Plus the chocolate cake finally thawed enough to cut.

At ten to twelve, Kyle stuck a handmade sign on the door—Back in 10 minutes—and they collapsed into a booth, one each side.

"Lunch won't be so bad," Kyle said. "I read through Micki's instructions. Other than preparing more sandwiches, everything's already made. Chicken salad is in the fridge. The chili is heating on the stove, and so is the soup—it's tomato and onion."

A knock on the café door had her groaning. "Can't people read? Tell the schmuck to go away."

Kyle stuck his head around the booth to look. "The schmuck is my brother. With Daisy."

"We'll take Daisy, send Gabe away."

Kyle went to open the door.

As it turned out, Gabe was here just to pick up a sandwich for Daisy.

"I didn't have so much as a loaf of bread in the house," he said. "I'd have asked Dad to feed her, but he's at that retired cop convention."

That was the excuse Charles had fabricated to explain his absence. The fact that Jane knew where Charles was and who he was with pricked her conscience.

*Micki's my friend,* she reminded herself.

"I'll get you some food," Kyle said. He was just returning with an egg salad sandwich and a chicken wrap when there was another knock on the door.

This time, it was Cat.

Jane let her in. "About time—" she began. Then stopped. "What happened to you?"

Her sister's left eye and cheek were swollen and red, the eye half shut. Another few hours and it would be black.

"The guy I hitched a ride with back to Pinyon Ridge braked suddenly," Cat said. "I was thrown forward into the dash."

"You weren't wearing a seat belt?" Jane demanded at the same time as Kyle said, "You were hitchhiking?"

"No to Jane, yes to Kyle," Cat said. "No big deal, folks, I just won't be winning beauty contests for a week or two."

"We need to get you to a doctor," Kyle said. "You could have a concussion.

Cat grimaced. "I do have a killer headache."

"I can't leave here," Jane said. "Kyle, could you—"

"I'll take her," Gabe offered.

Cat glared at him. "It's okay, I can wait until Jane's ready."

Gabe rolled his eyes. "Don't disobey a man of the cloth. And do plan on wearing a seat belt in my car."

"I didn't know you cared," she taunted.

"Daisy will be with us, so behave yourself."

Jane winced on her sister's behalf. Weird how Cat could bring out the worst in Gabe.

He fished his keys from his pocket. "Are you steady on your feet, or do you want take my arm?"

"I'm steady," Cat said through gritted teeth.

He gestured toward the door. "After you. Come on, Daisy."

"Bye, Daisy," Kyle said. "Love you."

She glanced back over her shoulder at him, but didn't reply. Kyle had been making an effort to say it every so often— Jane just hoped he didn't get discouraged by Daisy's lack of response.

"Do you think Gabe likes Cat?" she asked to distract him.

"Are you crazy?" Kyle said. "It's obvious he can't stand her."

"You men are such simple creatures," she said.

He rolled his eyes. "I'll concede they have some unfinished history, which might make things a bit more complicated."

She wondered if that was how he saw her and him, too.

"Cat isn't typical pastor's girlfriend material," Kyle said.

"That's for sure. Your dad would have kittens."

"He'd have something to say," Kyle agreed. "The trick with Dad is to listen to what he has to say, which always comes out of his love for us, then make up your own mind."

Jane supposed Charles's interference might be tolerable, maybe even welcome, if the recipient knew it was grounded in love.

"Plus, Dad is always honest," Kyle said. "You can trust what he says, no hidden agenda."

She should tell him about Micki and his dad. If—when—Kyle learned the truth, he'd be hopping mad to discover Jane had known all along and not told him.

"About your father," she said.

"We'd better take that sign off the door," Kyle said. "It's gone twelve, the hordes will be here any second."

She checked her watch. "It's just—"

"Don't look so worried," he said. "Lunch will be a lot easier than breakfast, I swear."

"You've been a huge help," she said. "I couldn't have done it without you."

"That cuts both ways," he said. "We make a pretty good team."

"I— Yes. We do." She flipped the sign on the door. Through the glass she saw diners converging. "You may be wrong about lunch versus breakfast. Those people look hungry."

"No problem," he said. "We'll get through. I'll be here with you."

*I'll be here with you.* Five simple words that combined to form a powerful promise.

*He means for lunch,* Jane reminded herself. *That's all.*

But what if that promise could be more than lunch? A whole lot more? A lifetime's worth?

In a moment of startling clarity, Jane realized that was what she wanted.

*I love him.*

She loved Kyle, wanted him to be with her for always.

"Jane?" Kyle called. "I'll sell chili and sandwiches, if you'll make the coffee."

"Good idea." On autopilot, she pulled cups down from the top of the machine and started setting up for coffee. *I love Kyle.*

What was she supposed to do with that?

A brief attempt to convince herself he wasn't worth loving failed entirely.

Kyle Everson was a man of honor, a determined and devoted dad. He cared about the people around him and had a big-picture view of life's possibilities. He was loyal, generous and made Jane laugh. Why *wouldn't* she love him?

The tougher question was, could he love her?

JANE HALF EXPECTED Micki and Charles to drive into town in convoy on Sunday evening, and tell the world they were an item. Instead, they returned as they'd left, completely separate, an hour apart.

Jane knew this because Micki called and invited her over for a debrief.

"So how did it go?" Jane asked, kicking her shoes off and curling her legs beneath her on the couch. Since the moment she'd realized she was in love with Kyle, she'd thought of nothing else. She needed a distraction.

Micki beamed. "I just had the best weekend of my life."

"Nice campsite, huh?" Jane teased.

"That, too." Micki's smile turned cat-got-the-cream. "You're talking to a woman who's officially in love."

"Wow." It was logical, given the length and strength of

her attraction to Charles, but still Jane struggled to get her head around it.

"Charles feels the same," Micki said smugly.

"That's fantastic." Jane got up to hug her. "So you'll tell Kyle now? And Gabe?"

"Soon," Micki said. "We need a few more days to settle into this. Now, tell me how things have been here. Any excitement? Did people love your breakfasts?"

"Let's just say no one died," Jane said. And hopefully, no hearts were set to be broken.


"HOW WAS THE CONVENTION?" Kyle asked his dad on Monday. Charles had stopped by to view the latest progress on the house, of which there'd been quite a bit. Cat had turned out to be very handy. Right now, she was installing shelves in the linen closet.

Charles rubbed the back of his neck. "Fine. Good."

"So what do retired cops do for entertainment?" Kyle asked. To his surprise, his father colored. "Dad, what did you get up to at that conference?"

"Nothing to concern you," Charles said quellingly.

"Which is not the same as nothing at all," Kyle pointed out.

Cat came in to borrow the electric drill. She had a real shiner on that eye, but she'd insisted on coming in to work.

"Did you meet someone?" Kyle asked his father. "A retired lady cop?"

Charles sputtered; Cat glanced curiously in their direction.

Kyle's cell phone buzzed. He didn't recognize the number on the display. His thumb pressed to open the message.

I know the truth about Daisy's mother

## CHAPTER EIGHTEEN

WHAT THE HELL? Instinct had Kyle deleting the message, which he realized right away was a mistake. He felt the weight of his father's scrutiny as he stared down at the phone in shock.

Maybe the message didn't mean what he thought it meant. Maybe someone knew something else about Lissa. Which wasn't good, obviously, but so long as they didn't know the real truth...

His phone buzzed again. He didn't want to look. He looked anyway.

If you don't want the world to know Jane Slater is Daisy's mother, I'll need $5,000

Blackmail?

"I need to go pick up some...stuff," Kyle said, the words staccato and completely unnatural. "I'll see you later."

"See you, son." His dad looked relieved—it took a few seconds for Kyle to remember he'd been about to interrogate Charles about his love life. Hell, the last thing he cared about right now was his dad flirting with some old lady cop.

"You okay to carry on here?" he asked Cat.

"Sure. Unless you need some help with your errand?" She was looking at him with concern; he needed to get out of here before everyone realized he had a major problem.

"I'm fine." He rammed the phone into the back pocket of his jeans.

He drove a little way down the road and stopped. He pulled out his phone and called the number back.

No answer—no surprise. The phone clicked through to a generic voice-mail system, no personal message recorded. Kyle waited for the beep.

"Forget it," he said into the phone. "You're not getting a penny." He hung up.

Had he done the right thing? Would the rumors be flying by dinner time?

He needed to talk to Jane. Right now.

"BLACKMAIL?" JANE STARED AT the screen of Kyle's phone. He hadn't deleted the second message. "But who on earth would know—" She stopped. Frowned. Shook her head. "Who would know what Lissa and I did?"

He took the phone from her and set it down on the console between them. Jane had been in the supermarket when he called her; he'd asked her to meet him in his car in the parking lot. "Maybe Lissa told someone. A supposed friend who, now that she's gone, is happy to use the information for gain."

"Blackmail's a serious crime," Jane said. "No one would do it lightly." She meant proper blackmail, of course, not the kind she'd used on him. "You need to tell the police."

"Yeah. Maybe."

"You are going to tell them, right?"

Kyle raked a hand through his hair. "I know I should— Dad always had zero patience for people who thought they could deal with this kind of thing themselves."

"Quite right."

"But my father's the retired police chief," Kyle reminded her. "If I involve the cops, there's simply no way Dad won't find out. Besides, this person might have no real intention of blabbing."

"I know what's at stake if the whole world finds out," Jane said. "Barb and Hal would be hurt, someone might be cruel enough to tell Daisy...."

"Don't forget the election," he said. "Another mess-up in

my personal life, plus a connection with the Slaters—it'll be the end of my campaign."

She tried not to take that last remark personally. "Whereas if you tell the police, they might catch the guy. In which case the worst thing that'll happen is your dad will find out. Is that so bad?"

"It'll change everything," he said. "I don't want Daisy to feel like a second-class citizen with him."

"Surely, he wouldn't…"

"How does he make you feel?" Kyle demanded.

"Like a second-class citizen," she admitted.

"Exactly."

"So what's next?" she asked.

"I left a message refusing to pay." He grimaced at her gasp. "Yeah, I know it was hasty. But if this guy's serious, he'll come back to me."

"Or she," Jane said. "If it's a friend of Lissa's, it's more likely to be a woman. Do you know who Lissa's confidantes were?"

"I think so." He named several women she'd never heard of. Jane didn't feel the expected twist of jealousy that Lissa had replaced her with these people.

She tilted her chair back onto two legs. "Any of those women could have told a boyfriend or another friend. And maybe it wasn't a friend. Maybe someone who worked at the clinic…" It was possible, but unlikely after all this time. "There's also a chance," she said slowly, "that this person is just guessing."

"Even if that were true, once the word got out, I'd have to prove it wrong, which I can't," Kyle said. "Besides, how would anyone guess something so outlandish?"

"Everyone knows Lissa had fertility problems." Jane puffed out an anxious breath. "Maybe someone noticed a resemblance between me and her."

"I worried about that at first," he admitted. "But in reality, I don't think the resemblance is so great that just anyone would pick up on it."

"Cat noticed."

His head snapped up. "You told her?"

Jane bristled at the accusation. "She saw the resemblance and jumped to the conclusion that Lissa had slept with Darren, our brother. I had to tell her the truth to set the record straight."

"She's the blackmailer," he said on a note of revelation.

Jane's chair clattered back onto all four legs. "It's not Cat. I admit, she's the first person I thought of when you told me, but it's not her. It can't be."

"Of course it is," he said. "Come on, Jane, it makes sense. Your sister has a history of con artistry, according to Gabe. You said yourself she only shows up when she needs money. And it's not like anyone in your family is a stranger to blackmail."

It was as if he'd knifed her in the ribs. Pain, sharp and deep, radiated through her chest.

"Cat's turned her life around," Jane said. "You said yourself what a hard worker she is. She's not perfect, but she's earning an honest dollar, and she wouldn't do something like this. Not now." She drew a breath. "Besides, didn't you say she was in the room with you when the first text message arrived?"

He nodded. "I believe it's possible to schedule text messages in advance."

She snorted. Kyle pinched the bridge of his nose.

"It's easy," he said, "for people to fall back into their old ways when the going gets tough." He reached across the table for Jane's hand.

She batted him away. "You mean once a Slater, always a Slater." She opened her door. "Isn't this exactly what I said would happen? Something goes wrong and you want to blame the Slater DNA."

"I'm not blaming you," he said. "Not at all. I'm saying Cat—"

"You have no evidence. Do you realize how much it'll hurt her to be accused of this?"

"I'm sorry," he said with flat finality.

"You're not sorry," Jane proclaimed. "You've been looking for an excuse not to feel anything serious for me and now you have it."

He flinched, but didn't deny it.

"I thought you were honorable and decent. I thought you *respected* me. But you're just like all those people who think the Slaters are trash."

"This isn't about you," he insisted. "I do respect you, and if you'd just think logically about this…"

"If you care about me at all," she said, "you'll drop this accusation against Cat."

"Next you'll be saying I should go ahead and pay her the five thousand," he snapped.

"I'm asking you to believe," she said. "Believe in the power of people to change. I'm asking you to set aside the past."

He had to know she wasn't just talking about Cat.

For what seemed a long time, he stared at the cell phone containing that vile threat, but obviously not focusing on it.

He lifted his eyes to Jane. "I'm sorry, Jane."

He didn't believe. He never would, which meant she could never risk giving him her heart.

*Too late.*

Jane blinked rapidly. "I—uh—it's time to collect Daisy from school," she said hoarsely.

She was up and out of there, heading for her own car, before he could protest. Not that he tried.

CHARLES ACCEPTED THE BOTTLE of Sonoma cabernet that Kyle had brought to dinner.

"Looks good," he said. He was of the I-don't-know-much-about-it-but-I-know-what-I-like school when it came to wine, but this label looked familiar.

He opened the drawer in the sideboard that sat along the wall between the kitchen and living room, and fumbled for a corkscrew. He was nervous as heck. "Shall I open it now? Where's Jane?"

"She's not coming," Kyle said. The flatness in his voice told Charles not to ask questions.

He and Jane must have had a fight. Charles felt ashamed of himself for hoping it might be the end of their relationship, but there it was. He turned the corkscrew until it was firmly embedded, then eased the cork out.

"How's that sister of hers doing at your place?" Charles asked.

Kyle hesitated. "Not sure."

The doorbell rang.

"Who's that?" Kyle asked.

Charles practically ran for the door. Micki stood on the porch, beautiful in a coral-colored top that was loose-fitting but semitransparent, and gray slacks.

"You look lovely." He kept his voice low.

"So do you." She went up on tiptoe and kissed him. It took all of one second for the kiss to turn serious.

He pulled back quickly. "Wow."

"Just making sure you don't get cold feet." She grinned as she slipped past him into the hallway.

"Believe me, nothing's cold right now," he muttered.

In the kitchen, Kyle looked surprised to see her. "Hey, Micki. You dropping off some coffee?" Like a lot of people in town, Charles bought his coffee from her—she ground the beans to order and delivered them.

Micki darted Charles a reproachful glance for not having said she was coming.

"Kyle just got here," Charles said. "I invited Micki for dinner," he told his son.

Kyle's barely concealed eye-roll confused him. Then he realized: Kyle thought Charles was trying to fix up Micki with him or Gabe.

Just the thought made his gut churn. And reminded him he was way too old for her.

An awkward silence fell.

"Would you like a wine, Micki?" Charles showed her the bottle.

"Sure. I'll check on dinner." She headed for the oven and Charles couldn't take his eyes off her rear in those snug pants.

He felt like a pervert. The kind of guy he would have had zero respect for when he was a cop. Would have told himself he knew what a sicko he was, and he'd be keeping an eye on him.

"You came to dinner and you have to cook?" Kyle asked.

Micki peeled the foil off the casserole dish in the oven. "I brought this over earlier. It's nothing fancy."

Gabe arrived ten minutes later. Charles relaxed a little. This was all falling into place.

"Dinner's ready," Micki announced a few minutes after that.

Call him old-fashioned, but Charles loved seeing her in his kitchen. He helped her serve up, and his heart almost burst at the pleasure of sharing a simple task with the woman he loved. His hand brushed hers as he served the mashed potato, just a glancing touch, but Gabe's sharp eyes caught it.

His son said nothing, but Charles turned clumsy. By the time they carried their plates to the table, the tension in the air seemed tangible. Or maybe that was just him.

Charles said grace and they started to eat in near silence. They all seemed preoccupied. This wasn't how Charles wanted to share his and Micki's news. He'd envisaged them all laughing and bantering, and him slipping in a casual mention that he and Micki were seeing each other.

Micki read his thoughts; she gave a rueful smile and a slight shrug, as if to say, "What can you do?"

Charles knew what he couldn't do. He couldn't wait a minute longer to come clean. He set down his knife and fork, wiped his mouth with his napkin. Micki's lovely eyes widened.

"Micki and I are dating," he announced.

Well, that got everyone's attention. Both Kyle and Gabe jerked their heads up. Kyle's knife and fork were suspended halfway between plate and mouth.

It would be nice if someone said something.

"It's been going on for nearly two weeks, though we've both been interested for much longer," he said. "I would have told you sooner, but we wanted to be sure we were serious before we went public." *Before we risked public disapproval or ridicule.*

Still, no one spoke.

"I didn't go to a cop convention last weekend," he said. "Micki and I went camping. I'm sorry I lied to you."

"Are you nuts?" Kyle's question exploded into the silence. "She's half your age!"

Gabe opened his mouth, and closed it again. The math might not be right, but he obviously couldn't disagree with Kyle's gist.

"I'm twenty-two years younger," Micki corrected him. "We're well aware of the age gap, Kyle. Why else do you think we haven't said anything before now?"

"What exactly does *dating* mean?" Kyle asked.

Charles felt heat around the back of his neck. "I'm sure you're not asking for details of my personal relationship."

"As a matter of fact, I am."

"Me, too," Gabe said. He didn't look quite as unhappy as Kyle, but he wasn't thrilled.

"This wouldn't be happening if I didn't care about Micki a great deal," Charles said.

"And the feeling's mutual," she added.

"Dad, you're an elder of the church," Kyle said.

"There's no prescribed age gap for couples in the Bible," Charles said. "I haven't done anything that's at odds with the conduct required of an elder, and I don't plan to. If people object for their own reasons, they can vote me out at the annual meeting."

Gabe spoke up. "Don't take this personally. But if you weren't my father and you—" he glanced at Micki "—weren't my friend...if you were a couple in my church I was counseling, I'd ask if you've talked about what happens twenty years down the track, if Dad gets sick or gets Alzheimer's."

"I could get run over by a bus tomorrow," Micki said.

"Not in Pinyon Ridge," Gabe pointed out. The town didn't have a bus service at this time of year. "Sure, anything can happen, but the most likely scenario is that at some stage, Dad will be relatively infirm, and you'll still be a young woman."

Charles grunted. "We've talked about this." Admittedly with rose-tinted spectacles on...but it was only natural to focus on the fact they were both healthy and strong.

"If I was counseling you, I'd suggest you likely have two separate groups of friends and ask how comfortable each of you will be socializing in the other group," Gabe said. "I'd also ask if Micki wants to have children—"

"I don't," she said.

"—and I'd point out that people change their minds on that score, so even if you think you don't want them now, what happens if you want them in a couple of years' time?"

"You're talking marriage?" Kyle said, aghast.

"We haven't talked about marriage," Micki said. "We've been dating two weeks."

"But if it gets that far, I don't mind if we have kids," Charles said. Right away, he realized he'd said that wrong.

"The idea is you're supposed to both want the same thing," Gabe said.

"All relationships require compromise," Micki said.

"And kids shouldn't be one of them," Kyle interjected. "Believe me, I know. You two have no right to be so irresponsible."

"Shut it, Kyle," Charles growled.

Kyle jerked back in this seat. His dad *never* spoke to his kids like that. Now he was dating a young woman and turning into a stranger.

"I can't believe it," Kyle said. "For years you've lectured me and Gabe not to start any relationship that doesn't fit with our values and principles, and now you're chasing after a bit of skirt—"

Charles shot to his feet; the table rattled. "Don't you dare talk about Micki like that."

His face was red; Kyle guessed his words had hit home.

Micki looked furious.

Good. "Come off it, Dad, you're nearly sixty. If you had a kid in a couple of years, you'd be eighty when it graduated high school. You know you always laugh at those old men on TV who are on their second wives. Dotage dads, you call them."

Kyle couldn't believe this was happening. He'd come here tonight planning to confide in his father and Gabe, though he hadn't quite figured out what he was going to say. Something about...*I like Jane Slater a lot...but I'm not sure we can get over the past.* But now Dad was embroiled in something equally unsuitable, and apparently not giving the issues a second thought.

Kyle suspected the strength of his own reaction was in part because he'd screwed up with Jane and was feeling like a jerk. But how was he supposed to be the good guy when he really did believe her sister was the blackmailer?

He'd had another text from her on his way here. You have 48 hours. Confirm you will pay and I will give instructions. He was almost considering paying, if it would get Cat out of town and give him time to figure out how to deal with this whole mess.

"Kyle, you need to lighten up," Micki said.

"Are you speaking as my friend or as my future step-mother?" he demanded.

There was an arrested pause as that ludicrous image filled the imaginations around the table.

His dad looked hurt.

"We're only dating at this stage," Micki reiterated. She came around the table to stand behind Charles. She put her hands on his shoulders. Charles softened and straightened at the same time. When he looked up at Micki, his face filled with tenderness.

"We know this won't be easy," she said. "But it's what we want. We would appreciate your and Gabe's support, but the lack of it won't stop us."

No way, Kyle thought. This was a disaster waiting to happen.

"If the Episcopalians throw you out, you can always come to Pinyon Ridge Community," Gabe joked. "You might find us more accepting."

"Not funny," Micki snapped. Like the rest of them, she knew how much Charles loved St. Thomas's.

Charles looked stricken. "We haven't done anything wrong."

"You're making a fool of yourself," Kyle told his father.

Charles had always basked in the good opinion of others; it was important to him. Now, his father shook his head, his mouth set in a mutinous line. But Kyle discerned a flicker of doubt.

He did his best to fan it into a flame. "I'm sure when you're together it all seems very romantic. But the minute you step out in public, you'll be nothing more than a joke."

His father flinched.

Micki shot Kyle a look filled with dislike. "I think you're wrong. Jane didn't laugh."

It took a second for her meaning to sink in, helped by Gabe's indrawn breath.

"*Jane* knows about this?" Kyle demanded.

Micki nodded. "I asked her not to tell anyone, so don't go blaming—"

"When?" he barked. "When did you tell her?"

"A few weeks ago. She's been very supportive."

What? All this time, while he and Jane had been growing closer, sharing the delight of Daisy's progress, she'd known his dad and Micki were dating?

"Did she know you went camping?" He didn't know why he bothered asking. Of course she did.

Micki's little nod confirmed it.

Jane had let him help her in the café, working side by side in a way that had felt...*special*. And all the time she'd known Micki and his dad were off making out in the woods?

Kyle dumped his napkin on the table and pushed back his chair.

"We haven't finished our conversation," his father said.

"Later," Kyle snapped.

## CHAPTER NINETEEN

"I DON'T THINK the color's quite right," Jane said as Daisy steered the electric beater around the bowl of frosting they were mixing for the cupcakes they'd just baked.

The cupcake craze was sweeping kindergarten and "all" of Daisy's friends were making them with their moms....

Daisy had asked Jane to make them with her.

Not as a mother, of course, but still...

After the argument she and Kyle had had this afternoon, this might be the last opportunity Jane got to do something special with Daisy.

She'd wanted to prolong it, so they'd made the cupcakes from scratch. In the end they'd produced ten perfect cupcakes and two somewhat misshapen ones.

It had been hard to be upbeat with Daisy when all the while Jane was seething about Kyle's comments this morning. He'd written Cat off without a shred of evidence, and more or less said outright he and Jane had no future. A combination of hurt and anger burned a hole in her chest, but somehow she kept smiling for Daisy.

Jane added a couple more drops of red food coloring to the bowl—the aim was princess-pink frosting—and Daisy chased them with her beaters. When her little arm tired, she offered the mixer to Jane. Jane gave it a few more seconds, then lifted the beaters out. "What do you think?"

"Just right." Daisy beamed. She was still a child of few words, but very different from the girl she'd been six weeks ago.

They heard the front door open. Was Kyle back from dinner already?

Seconds later, he appeared in the kitchen doorway. Tension radiated from him, and his eyes glittered dangerously. What did he have to look mad about? *She* was the one whose sister had been unjustly accused. Jane glared at him.

He glared back, positively ferocious. Then he turned to Daisy and the glitter left his eyes. He smiled, one of those forced grins Jane hadn't seen in a while. "Hi, sweetie."

"Hi, Daddy," Daisy said.

"I need to talk to Jane privately," he said. "Can you go upstairs?"

"Why can't I talk, too?"

Wow, Daisy had just answered back.

"We need to let this frosting firm up a little," Jane said. "How about you go upstairs and play with your Lego?"

"I'll play with my princess doll," Daisy decided.

Her willingness to state a preference, even when it went against Kyle's or Jane's suggestion, was a wonderful new development.

There was a long, tense silence as they listened to Daisy walking up the stairs, then the click of her bedroom door closing.

Jane jumped in. "I hope you're here to apologize."

"For what?" he demanded. "My stupidity in trusting you?"

"You *don't* trust me," she said. "Or my sister. This morning you threw away the—the bond that's grown between us, all that hard work, because you're totally hung up on my Slater-ness."

"You're the one who threw it away," he roared, taking her by surprise. "You *knew,* and you didn't tell me."

"Knew what? I'm telling you, my sister is *not*—"

"Micki!" he snapped. "And my father."

Oh. That. Help.

"You *knew* my dad was seeing Micki and you didn't tell

me. You let me help you run the Eating Post, and the whole time you were deceiving me. You knew there was no way I'd have lent my support to their relationship."

Jane winced. "Micki asked me not to say anything…."

"You didn't have to agree!" He prowled the kitchen like a tiger staking out its next meal. "You could have decided that you and I owed each other the truth. That what we had depended on honesty and trust to survive."

"What we had?" she demanded, incredulous. "We *had* nothing, not if you could accuse my sister of a crime without a shred of evidence. And when I asked you what was between us, all you could come up with was that you like my damn pajamas!" She flung out a hand in disgust, and almost sent the frosting flying. She pushed the bowl to the back of the counter. "You couldn't commit to any more than wanting to sleep with me."

"I was working on it," he shouted. "And all the while, you were working on keeping a secret. Another damn secret, Jane."

His voice cracked; he stopped.

Jane drew in a sharp breath. "This is *nothing* like what happened with Lissa. What Charles and Micki do is none of your—"

"It's exactly like Lissa," he said. "Only back then, you didn't owe me anything, I accept that. But now…"

"I owe you the same level of respect and admiration you've given me," she said. "Which is zilch." He opened his mouth to protest, and Jane held up a hand. "Oh, yes, there have been moments. Moments when it seemed we could put our differences aside. View each other without the lens of history in the way. But when it comes down to it, we're not going anywhere because you're worried you can't win the election with me in your life. And you can't trust me."

"I have every reason not to trust you," he yelled. "You just hid from me that my dad is crazy—and I do mean crazy—for Micki."

"They genuinely care for each other, it's not just—"

"That's not the point. The point is, I *did* trust you. I spent the afternoon feeling like crap for accusing your sister of blackmail. For hurting you like that. And all along…"

He stopped, sounding defeated. But only for a moment.

"Hearing that you knew about Dad and Micki just reinforced that I was right not to trust you," he finished.

"Your father and Micki are good for each other. They deserved a chance."

"And you know this because you're an expert on functional relationships?"

She sucked in a breath. "That was uncalled for."

"What was *called for* was honesty."

A sound in the doorway had them both turning. Daisy.

Kyle raked a hand through his hair, tried to think of something innocuous to say. Thought about faking one of those smiles.

"Honey," Jane said, "I thought you were upstairs."

"Are you and Daddy upset?" Daisy asked.

"Just discussing stuff a bit too loudly."

Kyle crouched down at her level. "What do you want, sweetie?"

"Sarah in my class said you're not going to be the mayor anymore," Daisy said. "Is that why you're upset?"

The concern in her eyes went straight to his heart. "No, sweetie. I hope I am going to be the mayor, but even if I'm not, I won't be upset." Not true, but the last thing Daisy needed was to worry about him. He kissed her forehead. "Love you."

"Love you," Daisy said, and Kyle toppled backward on his heels.

Did she just say…? A glance at Jane told him yes, she did. Jane's eyes brimmed with tears, a tremulous smile hovered on her lips. For a heady moment, he was thrilled beyond measure to have shared this milestone with her—before he remembered he was so damn mad at her.

Then Daisy started giggling at his clumsiness, and he made a production of needing her massive strength to help right himself, and the most tender moment of his life was gone, just like that.

He would never forget it.

He snuck in a kiss on the top of Daisy's head as he sent her upstairs with a promise to come say good-night.

Then it was just him and Jane in the kitchen once more.

Them and everything that stood between them.

"You and Daisy," she said, her voice damp. "That was wonderful."

He nodded, not sure he could trust himself to speak.

"It's time I moved out," she said. "Those extra two weeks were up on Sunday. I need to get back to Denver. To my work."

He found his voice. "There's no rush—you could have a few days down in Denver with clients, then come back." Because, angry though he was, he wasn't ready to say goodbye.

"What's the point?" she asked. "You don't trust me, and I don't appreciate your attitude." She paused, but he didn't fill the gap. Her shoulders slumped. "I'll go stay with Micki tomorrow, if she'll have me."

The mention of his father's girlfriend was enough to rile him up again. "Fine. Go."

"I'll start weaning Daisy off my company," Jane continued, "and plan to leave Pinyon Ridge next week."

Part of Kyle wanted to protest, to demand that she stay. But she was right. He didn't trust her. He couldn't be the man she needed.

He nodded stiffly and followed his daughter upstairs.

"ARE YOU GOING to tell me why we had to leave that nice cottage and squish into a tiny apartment?" Cat asked.

"I'm too mad to talk about it." Jane pushed her suitcase under the bed. Micki had been generous to offer both her and Cat a bed. But the apartment above the Eating Post was petite—the room she and Cat were sharing was about half the size of the one in Kyle's cottage with no storage. They'd be living out of their bags for the next week.

"So you and Kyle *did* have an argument. Thought so." Cat smirked. "What was it about?"

"I don't want to discuss it." Jane hadn't seen Kyle this morning, thankfully. She'd packed up her stuff and Cat's, then after school, she'd dropped Daisy at Kyle's new place. Daisy had been positively chatty in the car, and hadn't seemed to mind the news that Jane was moving out. Which was the way it should be.

Once she was used to the fact Jane wasn't living with her and Kyle, it would be easier for her to accept Jane's return to Denver.

Also as it should be. Oh, yes, everything was hunky-dory.

The fact that Jane felt as if her heart had been torn from her chest and skewered on a blunt stick was neither here nor there.

Micki stuck her head around the door. "I made coffee. And there were *friands* left over in the café." She wrinkled her nose. "The fancy stuff never sells well outside of peak season."

"We're coming," Jane said.

Micki never seemed to tire of coffee; she sipped a cup of her favorite brew and gave a little aah of satisfaction as Jane and Cat joined her.

"So are you going to tell me about your bust-up with Kyle?" Micki asked.

"No." Jane bit into an apple *friand*. "This is wonderful."

"As his potential future stepmother, I need to know what's going on," Micki deadpanned.

Jane rolled her eyes.

"And as a thorn in his brother's side, I deserve to know,

too," Cat said. "We're on the same team. If Kyle hurt you, I'm happy to make both Everson brothers' lives a living hell." She pressed her fingers to her lips. "Oops, Gabe doesn't like me using that word."

"So much for being on my team," Jane said drily. But she was touched by Cat's offer. Her sister had been moody and withdrawn the past few days, which Jane had attributed to her ongoing feud with Gabe. And Micki's genuine concern was a balm to her wounded heart. Ironic that as her time in Pinyon Ridge came to an end, she was starting to feel as if she would miss the place.

"Give us a hint," Micki pleaded. "We'll make up the rest."

Jane rolled her eyes. "Okay, how's this? Kyle's a narrow-minded, judgmental, conclusion-jumping jerk. And he probably learned it all from his dad," she warned.

"Probably," her friend said mildly. "I like Charles's stiff-necked ways. I think they're cute, but he also doesn't mind when I call him on them."

"I'm still creeped out by you dating that old guy," Cat said with a shiver.

"Butt out," Jane and Micki said simultaneously.

Cat made a rude sign with one finger.

"Classy," Micki said.

Jane yawned. "I don't know why, but I'm exhausted."

"You can go to bed as soon as you've told us what your bust-up with Kyle was about," Cat said.

Micki nodded. "Consider it your rent."

Their inquisitive expressions told Jane they weren't going to let it drop. She sighed. "Okay, if you must know, Kyle accused Cat of blackmailing him."

"No way," Cat said, outraged.

"What kind of blackmail?" Micki's voice rose. "What about?"

"I can't tell you," Jane said. "A...a family secret. You'll

just have to trust me that none of the Eversons have done anything wrong."

"But why would Kyle blame Cat?" Micki asked, mystified.

"Because she's a Slater. Like me." Jane pressed some *friand* crumbs from the plate into her finger and transferred them to her mouth. "I'm amazed he didn't accuse me, as well. I accused him of not trusting me, and he admitted it. End of relationship."

"What a creep," Cat said fiercely. "I'm used to people thinking the worst of *me,* but he knows you."

"Kyle really screwed up," Micki said. "No wonder you're mad."

"It's not all his fault," Jane admitted. "He was mad at me because I didn't tell him about you and Charles."

Micki groaned. "I'm sorry. If I'd realized how serious you and Kyle were…"

"We weren't serious." Jane leaned back on the couch. "We have too many differences for it ever to have worked out. Kyle's never going to trust me—and nor is his dad. Which is a big deal, with a close family like the Eversons."

Micki snorted. "Charles isn't infallible. If he's rude to you, I'll smack him upside the head."

Jane smiled. "Thank you. But I just need to go, leave Pinyon Ridge."

"Maybe I'll come with you to the city," Cat said.

Jane sat back. "Really?"

"Just for a while." Cat stretched her arms behind her head. "I'm not expecting you to support me, by the way. I'll ask Kyle for a reference, find a job. Even if he thinks I'm a blackmailer, he might give me a reference to get me out of town."

Jane found she liked the idea of Cat coming to Denver. Really liked it. "That'd be great. Unless you think you should stay here and get some closure with Gabe. Or whatever it is you're trying to do with him."

Cat shook her head. "Not going to happen. Gabe knows an

awful lot about forgiving other people, but he can't forgive himself. The poor guy's too tormented to have me around."

"You're saying you're leaving for his benefit?"

Cat wrinkled her nose. "Mine, too. There's something about those Everson men. They're hard to get out of your system."

"Don't say that," Jane said, depressed.

CHARLES HESITATED OUTSIDE the door to Micki's apartment. This was it, they were going public with their relationship today. Not that they were going to make a big announcement. But from today on, they would act in public the way they did in private. Without the making out, of course.

Her door opened, startling him.

"I saw you from the window," she said.

She looked charming in a peach-colored blouse and black pants, with little strappy sandals. She went up on tiptoe and kissed him before he realized what she planned. He reared back.

"I thought we were out in the open now." She sounded hurt.

"We are," he said. "Of course we are. Sorry, sweetheart, it might take me some getting used to."

"We can keep quiet a bit longer, if that's what you want." Disappointment underpinned the offer, so although he was tempted, he couldn't accept it.

"I want people to know how I feel about you," he said. Besides, the deception had gone on long enough, and he wasn't comfortable with even a lie of omission. So he'd warned Reverend Thackeray about his new relationship—the reverend had been surprised, but not disapproving—and now he was ready to widen that out to the population of Pinyon Ridge. At Reverend Thackeray's suggestion, Charles had emailed the other elders last night. They were a good bunch; he could rely on their support. Once they got used to the idea.

He took Micki's hand. "Let's go."

They walked hand-in-hand the two hundred yards to St. Thomas's.

On the church steps, Sheila Marshall, a friend of Patti's, was on door duty, greeting folk and handing out the weekly newsletter. When she saw Charles and Micki, she stopped midway through her conversation with the reverend's wife and stared.

Huh, it seemed that the contents of Charles's email to the elders hadn't made its way through the church directory yet.

"Morning, Sheila," Charles said.

Her gaze was stuck on his and Micki's linked hands. "Chief," she managed to respond, then added a strangled, "Hello, Micki."

"Hi, Sheila." Micki sounded shy.

"Just to make it clear," Charles said, "Micki and I are dating."

"So I see." She was still looking at their hands.

Inside the church, Kyle and Daisy sat on the end of a full pew, with no room for Charles and Micki. Charles wondered if that was deliberate.

So they sat three rows from the front, which would give an excellent view to all those who wanted to speculate.

Charles wasn't comfortable holding hands in church, never had been, but when the congregation stood for the first hymn, he and Micki stood close enough to each other that he could feel the heat of her arm against his.

During the offering, Bert Munro, another elder, gave Charles a wink.

"This isn't so bad," Micki murmured, as they sat down after the offering prayer.

But after the service, where usually he would have been in the thick of any action, no one approached him with questions about the agenda for the next elders' meeting or suggestions for how the working bee should be structured.

"Let's get coffee," Micki suggested. Usually she spurned

the less-than-excellent brew the ladies on the coffee roster produced.

Charles procured two cups and carried them back to Micki. They stood to one side of the foyer. Plenty of people gave them sidelong glances, but no one came to talk.

"I wish Jane was here," Micki said.

"I don't." Charles gave her an incredulous look.

"She knows all about how to handle being the butt of speculation and disapproval," Micki said. "You and I could take a lesson from her."

He certainly knew nothing public disapproval. "There's speculation," he said, "but I don't think it's disapproval. Folk aren't sure what to say. They'll think about it this week—" and talk about it over Sunday lunch "—and next Sunday it'll all be fine."

Then he heard it. Quite clearly, the tail end of a sentence spoken by a woman he'd thought he was friendly with. "...he's just a dirty old man."

Micki heard it, too. She wheeled around.

Charles grabbed her arm. "Don't."

"They can't talk about you like that."

"There's no law against it." Heck, he'd think the same thing if, say, Bert Munro took up with a girl twenty-some years his junior. Charles shifted his stance, putting distance between himself and Micki.

"You're pulling away," she said sharply.

"Maybe, since it's our first day out, we should be a little more discreet."

"More discreet than drinking a cup of coffee together? Like, maybe we should be in different buildings?"

Her voice had risen slightly; Charles glanced around. "I just think we don't need to rub it in."

Her cheeks were pink, her eyes bright with moisture. "The first day is the hardest," she said, her voice shaky.

"I'm sure you're right." He wasn't sure at all. There would definitely be gossip. Backbiting, as the Bible put it.

Micki would be lacerated. He wasn't too keen on having his own reputation cut to shreds, either. He didn't want to be the subject of public disapproval. Or worse, ridicule. He didn't want his status as former police chief, pillar of society and all-round good guy undermined by what people would only see as a weakness.

"Charles," Micki said sharply. "I said, shall we leave now?"

He nodded. Micki took both their cups to the serving hatch. She brushed the palms of her hands down her pants.

"Ready?" she asked with forced brightness.

He cleared his throat. "Yep." He knew from that hand-wiping that she was expecting him to take her hand. He couldn't do it.

He turned and led the way through the crowd, hoping she thought he was just clearing a path. Hoping she was following. He muttered a hello to a couple of subdued greetings that came his way, but mostly, he avoided the stares of the curious.

When he made it outside, it felt like he'd come up for air after being trapped underwater. His lungs were bursting.

Micki was breathing heavily, too; he saw the rise and fall of her chest beneath that peach-colored blouse.

"We made it," he said.

"Do you realize what you did in there?" she demanded.

Uh-oh, he had a feeling she was about to tell him.

"You acted as if you have something to be ashamed of. And that something is your feelings for me."

"I didn't— I just felt awkward…."

"Charles, that was about the least hostile environment we're going to get—your friends and mine, in an environment conducive to gracious behavior. Instead, you made *me* feel guilty."

"I'm sorry…."

"I don't want to hear it," she said. "Either you're with me and you're proud of it, or you're not with me at all."

"I just need a little more time," he began.

"No problem," she said, and he grabbed her hand in relief. She disentangled her fingers from his. "Take all the time you like, Charles Everson, but don't come back to me until you're proud to be my man, proud to have me as your woman."

Before he could assure Micki that he was plenty *proud* already, and that was in fact the problem, she stomped down the road. Without him.

JANE HAD THOUGHT she'd feel relieved to be leaving Pinyon Ridge. Instead, her heart was a deadweight in her chest, and she had the dumbest urge to cry.

"I'll have to take you to Sally Sue's BBQ," she told Cat in Micki's apartment Wednesday at lunchtime, trying to muster some enthusiasm for their departure. "The food's great, and a real bargain."

"Sounds good." Listlessly, Cat inspected the cheese sandwich she'd made a few minutes ago when she'd arrived back from her work on Kyle's new place. There was almost nothing left to do there now.

Jane wondered if Cat would miss the work—maybe that explained why she'd been glum for days now. Or maybe...

"Have you talked to Gabe?" Jane pressed Send on the email she'd been typing to a client and closed the lid of her laptop. "What if he wants you to stay? I'd love to have you in Denver, but if Gabe makes you—" She stopped. She'd been going to say *happy*. But although there were sparks aplenty between Cat and Gabe, neither of them looked happy together.

*I was happy with Kyle and Daisy.* She hadn't realized just how precious those times had been until they'd ended. She blinked away tears.

Cat shook her head. "Things are way too complicated for that ever to be a possibility. It would take a miracle."

"Presumably he believes in miracles," Jane pointed out.

Cat wrinkled her nose. "Besides, you're the one who's walking away from what could be a good thing. I thought you liked Kyle."

"*Like* him?" Jane said, her voice hollow.

"Uh-oh," Cat said. "You're telling me it's more than that?"

Jane had never told anyone something that personal, not even Lissa. The exception was the confidences she'd shared with Kyle.

So now, she just nodded.

"You *love* him?" Cat supplied the words. "As in, the whole nine freakin' yards?"

Jane nodded again. "Dumb, huh?"

"Not if he loves you back." But Cat sounded doubtful.

"He doesn't."

"Did he tell you that? Or is it you being all prickly and defensive and putting up fences again?"

Jane's gaze flew to her. "I don't do that."

Cat snorted. "Seriously, you should tell him you love him."

"What's the point? I don't want a man who thinks my family is to blame for everything that goes wrong around here. I don't want him looking sideways at me every time twenty bucks disappears from his wallet."

"He wouldn't do that," Cat said. "He's not that bad. As bosses go, he's one of the better ones I've had."

"Why are you trying to sell him to me?" Jane demanded. "He called you a blackmailer, Cat. I told him it wasn't you and he flat-out refused to believe me."

"Okay, so he's not perfect. Neither are you."

"I'm well aware. But I'm not going into a relationship as a second-class citizen, scared he'll dump me at the next hurdle." To her horror, she burst into tears.

"Jane, don't." Cat hesitated a moment, a victim of the Slater lack of relationship skills. Then she wrapped her arms awkwardly around Jane.

"I'm sorry," Jane blubbered. "I love him and I love Daisy and I don't want to leave him, but he doesn't give a damn about me, all he cares about is his precious family and their reputation, and he's so freakin' judgmental...."

"I did it," Cat said.

Jane lifted her face from her sister's shoulder and took a long, wet sniff. "Did what?"

"Kyle's right," Cat said. "I'm the blackmailer."

## CHAPTER TWENTY

JANE WRENCHED HERSELF from Cat's hold. "Is this a joke?"

"I texted a demand for five thousand dollars to Kyle," Cat said. "I used a prepaid SIM card that I swapped into my phone when I sent the messages."

"But you were with him when the first one came through." Jane's heart pounded, blood rushing in her ears.

"I used a scheduled SMS."

"How many messages?" Jane demanded.

"Three. Two on the first day, one a week later." Cat hooked her thumbs in her jeans, defiant. "What, you don't believe me? Grow up, Jane."

"I thought *you'd* grown up," Jane said, dazed. "I thought you'd changed."

"Yeah, well, it's not as easy to leave your past behind as you may think."

"What the *hell* does that mean?" Jane demanded, getting angry now. She'd *defended* Cat to Kyle, sworn she was innocent.

"I needed the money," Cat said baldly.

"I knew it." Bitterness clogged Jane's throat. "The only reason you ever visit is when you need cash. And you have the nerve to say you wouldn't expect me to support you in Denver—is that because you'll be living off the proceeds of your extortion?"

"Don't be dumb," Cat said. "If I'd known you loved Kyle I'd never have pulled that stunt."

"Too kind."

"Shut up," Cat said fiercely. "I told the truth about why I

came to Pinyon Ridge—to connect with you, not for money. But a guy tracked me down after I got here…someone I'd helped with a couple of scams in Vegas. He wanted me to start up the same thing in Colorado with him, and when I said no, he said I owed him five grand, and I'd regret it if I didn't pay up. I went into Frisco to meet him, hoping to talk some sense into him—"

"Your black eye!" Jane said, appalled.

"He punched me," Cat said. "Told me it was a down payment on the beating he'd deal me if I didn't find the money."

"You should have come to me," Jane said, feeling sick.

"You already thought I was after you for your money." Somehow, Cat managed to sound humorous. "When you told me about Daisy, it seemed an easy way to make money off a guy who could afford it and who was a bit of a jerk anyway."

"He's not," Jane said quickly.

Cat rolled her eyes.

"Did you consider going to the police?" Jane asked.

"Pete—the guy who hit me—threatened to give the cops an anonymous tip-off about my past crimes." Cat shivered. "I've stayed mostly within the law, but not entirely. I have a record. But I've never been to jail, and I don't want to start."

Jane could see that.

"Anyway, even if I could talk the cops into going easy on me, word would get back to Charles Everson in two minutes. Which wouldn't help you and Kyle any."

Jane scrubbed her face with her hands. "What a mess."

"It doesn't have to be," Cat said. "I'm giving up the blackmail. I'll text Kyle and tell him."

"What about the guy, the one who punched you?"

"I can stay one step ahead of him."

"Don't be stupid," Jane said. "There must be something else we can do. Between us, we can come up with an idea."

"Right." Cat sounded unconvinced.

"But first," Jane said, "I owe Kyle an apology."

JANE FOUND KYLE in his office at city hall.

"Jane!" He stood with such alacrity, for a moment she thought he was as pleased to see her as she was him. That he might walk around his desk and plant a kiss on her.

Barely two days since she'd last seen him, and already she missed him so much it hurt.

But his alacrity wore off fast—she almost saw the "Hang on a minute, this is the woman who keeps secrets from me" flash across his face.

"What can I do for you?" he asked formally.

"It's what I can do for you—namely, apologize." She barged ahead, before she had time to chicken out. "Cat is the blackmailer. Or she was. She's calling it quits. But you were right."

His jaw dropped. "She told you this?"

Jane nodded. She squared her shoulders, waiting for his "I told you so," his entirely justified anti-Slater diatribe.

He came around the desk. "Jane, I'm so sorry."

She took a step backward. "Excuse me?"

He took her hands in his, and she wanted to hold on and never let go. "You had such faith in your sister—admirable. If misguided," he added wryly. "You must have been so disappointed. I really am sorry."

His sympathy was almost more than she could bear. "She was being threatened," Jane said, not wanting him to think the worst of Cat. "That black eye—a guy hit her."

Kyle tensed, his jaw jutted. "Who is he? Did you call the police?" He seemed ready to charge out and find the guy himself.

*He's a natural protector.*

"He's not here," Jane assured him. "He's some lowlife who came after her from Vegas. Anyway, Cat thought if she could buy him off, she could get back to going straight...." Jane realized how absurd that sounded and trailed off.

Kyle smiled faintly. "So why did she tell you? An attack of conscience?"

*I told her I'm in love with you, and she wanted to help.* "I guess so," Jane said. She knuckled her eyes, a combination of fatigue and emotion fogging her vision. "I thought you'd be...I don't know, smug. Pleased that you're right."

"I shouldn't have said those things about your family in the first place. I'm sorry."

"You were mostly right."

He shook his head. But it was hard to deny the truth.

The silence grew awkward.

"I'd better go," Jane said. "I have a few things to do before I leave town—I'm heading back to Denver Friday night." If he had a sudden blinding realization that he wanted her to stay, now was the time to say it.

"Okay," he said. "See you around."

CHARLES HAD NEVER FELT SO miserable in his life. Since the after-church fiasco, Micki had barely spoken to him—she'd told him to sort out his priorities and let her know where she fit.

She was number one, blast it! He dug his spade into the lettuce bed on Thursday morning, narrowly avoiding a decapitation. She should know that. She knew how hard it had been for him to give in to the attraction between them....

Not to mention to kiss her. And to spend evening after evening with her over a delicious meal, with warm, heartfelt conversation... Yeah, who was he trying to kid? Nothing in his life had felt so right, not since he'd married Patti.

But in exposing their relationship to the glare of public scrutiny, they'd cast it in a light that seemed misguided at best. Tawdry and foolish at worst.

Everywhere he'd been this past week, people had stopped talking when they saw him, or exchanged amused glances with each other. One or two had even muttered criticisms.

Sweat ran down Charles's forehead; he brushed it away from his eyes.

He still loved her—yes, it was love. But to make it work, he would have to forget his reputation, forget the esteem people held him in, and accept that though plenty of people would get over it, there would always be some who thought he was an old fool, and Micki some kind of gold digger. There would always be those who'd derive pleasure from speculating about whether he could satisfy a fit, young woman, and who'd wonder what she saw in him.

The thought of being the brunt of mockery turned his stomach. Charles took a break from his labor, resting on his spade, breathing heavily. Micki could do all that work without breaking a sweat, he suspected. He'd been crazy, thinking the age gap might not matter.

"Good morning, Charles."

The greeting startled him. He turned to find Janelle Slater—Jane—and her sister on his front walk. He hadn't even noticed their arrival.

"Ladies," he said.

Jane half smiled. "Spoken without irony—well done."

It was clearly a joke, but he wasn't in the mood.

"What can I do for you?" he said sharply.

"Told you this was a dumb idea," the younger one, Cat, said.

He pulled out his handkerchief and mopped his forehead. "It's like a furnace out here. How about we go inside?"

Jane seemed to wait for Cat to decide. After a moment, Cat nodded.

"There's tea in the fridge," he said, gesturing to the kitchen. "I'll go wash up and join you in a minute."

In the en suite bathroom, off the room he'd been hoping to share with Micki one day, he looked at himself in the mirror. He wasn't bad for his age. But he'd never compare with a younger man.

Yet Micki hadn't wanted Kyle. Or Gabe. She'd wanted Charles. And he'd hurt her. *What a mess.*

The girls were sitting at his table, glasses of tea in front of them, and a third glass poured for him. Charles downed half of it before he sat.

"Okay," he said brusquely. "What is it?" Was one of them pregnant to one of his sons? Hell, he hoped not. He didn't want a Slater grandkid, that was for sure.

"We need your advice on a police-related matter," Jane said.

That got his attention. Charles listened as they told him about some crook who wanted Cat to scam people right here in Charles's town, on his patch, and how this man had hit her.

"Why are you telling me this?" Charles asked at the end.

"I want to know what my options are," Cat said. "I seriously have gone straight, I'm trying to work things out with God—" Charles jolted in shock, and immediately felt ashamed "—and I want to put my past behind me once and for all."

"If we can work this out, I'm happy to have Cat live with me in Denver," Jane said.

"What if this guy finds her there?" Charles asked. "You've worked hard to get away from that kind of trouble, Jane."

She blinked at the acknowledgment.

"Face it," Charles said to Cat. "This guy's going to track you down again. Maybe not right away, but next time he's drunk and reminiscing and decides you're the meal ticket he shouldn't have let get away."

"I realize that, and I won't go to Jane's if there's any chance of that." Cat spread her fingers on the dining table. "How do I stop him without going to jail myself?"

A part of him wanted to say, "You do the crime, you do the time." Words he'd uttered to many lowlifes over the years. But then Jane put her hand over her sister's on the table and the two exchanged a look of loving concern that made him bite his tongue.

"Give me a minute," he said. He found himself enjoying the respite from his thoughts about Micki, the chance to think like a cop again.

"Do you have much on this guy?" he asked Cat.

"More than he has on me." She fiddled with her necklace, a cheap thing of leather and beads. "His ex-girlfriend took out a restraining order against him."

Charles perked up. "And then he hit *you?* Did you go to the hospital?" Where there would be a detailed record of her injuries.

Cat nodded.

"Good girl." Charles pulled the notepad that sat by the phone toward him and grabbed a pen from the holder. "Tell me his name, and every conviction you think he's had."

That took about fifteen minutes and left Charles with several pages of notes to work with. He assured them he'd start making some inquiries today.

"I'll call you when I know something. Don't leave town," he joked.

Both girls smiled, probably humoring him. Jane pushed her chair back and stood; Cat followed suit.

Charles saw them to the door, watched them walk out to the street. They had the same distinctive walk, though they didn't resemble each other in any other way. Unusual girls. They were, he supposed, forming a family unit in their own way.

And family mattered most. He'd lived by that creed and it had served him well. So he should be able to forget Micki, get back to being a dad to his sons, a grandfather to Daisy.

*Micki's my family.*

The thought grabbed him out of nowhere.

It wasn't true.

But it could be true. If, say, she was his wife.

Charles's heart thudded. He loved Micki, and it was the

kind of love a man felt for the woman he wanted to live with and die with—with the dying part coming a long way down the road. If he married Micki, they wouldn't be the most conventional couple—and so far, his only experience of marriage had been entirely conventional. But he was certain they'd be happy. Look at Cat and Jane—they weren't a conventional family by anyone's definition, but they'd committed to making it work.

*I love Micki. I want to marry her. I need to get over my hang-ups. Then I need to convince her to take a chance on an old coot who nearly ruined everything.*

# *CHAPTER TWENTY-ONE*

KYLE FOUND HIS FATHER sitting in his den—unusual for him on a sunny Thursday afternoon—and staring into the empty fireplace.

"Dad, are you okay?" *Contemplative* wasn't a word regularly applied to his father.

"I will be," Charles said grimly.

Kyle dropped into the armchair at right angles to his dad's. "Are you still seeing Micki?"

He'd heard conflicting reports from people around town about the state of that relationship.

"I will be," Charles said again. He ran a hand down his face. "Kyle, I'm sorry we didn't tell you sooner, but it wasn't an easy situation."

"That's why I'm here," Kyle said. "There's something I haven't told you, and over the past few days I've realized that the more secret something is, the greater power it has to hurt."

"Sounds like New Age hogwash to me," Charles observed.

Kyle chuckled. Then he launched straight into what he'd come to say. The secret whose power he aimed to destroy.

"Dad, when Lissa had the IVF treatment that produced Daisy, she went to Denver without me." He'd never admitted that to his father, never wanted his dad to know how flawed his marriage had been.

Charles frowned. "How does that work?"

"Frozen sperm," Kyle said. "Mine. But the egg wasn't frozen…Lissa used an egg donor. I didn't know until recently."

Charles straightened in his armchair. "Are you saying Lissa isn't Daisy's mother?"

"Legally, and in every other way, other than the biology, she is," Kyle said. "But biologically...Jane is Daisy's mother."

"Jane *Slater?*"

"Jane Slater," Kyle confirmed.

Charles paled. "Daisy's a Slater?"

"She's an Everson and a Peters and a Slater." Kyle wasn't expecting miracles today—this would take some getting used to. But he wanted to sow the seeds of future acceptance.

"Thank the Lord they'll be gone soon," Charles said, obviously clutching at straws. "Jane and Cat. They won't have any influence on Daisy. And I don't imagine Mike Slater would ever come back."

Kyle held up a hand. "Dad, I know Jane's a Slater, and that brings a whole lot of baggage—"

"Such as a father in jail," Charles said. "And a brother. That's more than baggage. Come to think of it, what happens when Darren gets out? Where's he going to go?" He punched his fist into the palm of his other hand. "Those Slaters, they're the most—"

"Jane gave us a gift," Kyle said, talking over the top of his father. "She did something brave and wonderful. I owe her— this *family* owes her—and I won't have you insulting her."

"I—" Charles sputtered. Then, catching something in Kyle's eyes, he said, "You're right. Of course. Not her. Not Jane. She's better than the rest of them."

It was a start, Kyle supposed.

"I don't know at this stage," Kyle said, "how Jane will fit into Daisy's life. But she's...kind of family, and I won't have her made to feel like a second-class citizen. Same goes for Daisy, now that you know the truth."

"There are no second-class citizens in this family," Charles growled. "Slater or not."

"That's great," Kyle said, surprised. "Thanks, Dad."

Charles sank back into thought, breathing heavily. Then he said, "That Jane Slater could do with learning some respect for her elders, but she has guts. And she's no fool."

"Dad, are you sure you're okay?"

Charles huffed a laugh, which reassured Kyle. "If you'd get out of here and let me do what I need to do, I'd be a whole lot better."

Kyle didn't need telling twice.

MICKI WAS WIPING DOWN the coffee machine ten minutes before closing on Friday when Reverend Thackeray came in. He wasn't a regular. Micki wondered if he was here to see why she hadn't been in church on Sunday.

"Anything I can help you with, Reverend?" she asked.

"A coffee, please, Micki. Could you make it a latte?"

She must have given a little raise of her eyebrows at the unexpectedly fancy order from a man who usually took his coffee filtered and black. Cheaper.

"Charles Everson said to order what I like and put it on his tab," the minister explained.

"Oh. Okay." The mention of Charles's name startled her; the cups she was putting away rattled. Presumably Charles planned to join the reverend here...she hadn't seen him in days, and her heart leaped at the prospect.

The door opened again to admit Alan and Betty Gray. Micki couldn't remember the last time they'd come in here.

"Two coffees," Alan called, even before he reached the counter. "On Charles's tab, please, Micki."

Charles must be running a church meeting here. How odd. And presumptuous, starting a meeting right at closing.

"Coming up," she said.

She wasn't surprised when, a minute later, two of the Sunday school teachers came in. Ten minutes after that, so many members of St Thomas's filled the café, she had no chance of making coffee for all of them in good time. Not even when

Jane and Cat heard the noise from upstairs and came down to help.

Still, no one seemed impatient about the wait for their drinks. They chatted quietly, sending occasional looks her way.

Micki started to feel harassed. What was Charles up to? She would give him a piece of her—

"Hi, Micki." Somehow, Charles had sneaked through the crowd without her noticing and now he stood right in front of her. He wore a blazer over jeans and a plaid shirt, and he looked strong and rugged and delicious.

"Charles, what's going on?" She didn't manage to sound as belligerent as she'd intended, due to her weakening knees and racing heart. In fact, she sounded positively sappy.

"If I could have everyone's attention, please." Charles addressed the crowd in his cop voice, creating an immediate hush.

"First, I must apologize for this abuse of the church prayer chain—inviting you all here to have coffee on me."

He did that? Micki stifled a laugh.

"Next," he said, "if you have a second or two to pray, I could really use all the help I can get in the next couple of minutes."

A few people bowed their heads, but most were too interested in the proceedings.

"Third, the reason I called you here is because you all know that Micki and I have been dating, and at least half of you think I'm a fool or she's after my money."

Some genuine laughs and some guilty chuckles. Micki stepped closer to him, and the look he slanted down at her was ablaze with love. She caught her breath.

"You may be right—about me being a fool, I mean. But I want you to hear this straight from me. My son Kyle told me today that the more secret something is, the greater the power for hurt. So there'll be no secrets between me and you, my friends, about what's going on here."

He put an arm around Micki's shoulders. "I didn't expect to fall in love with a woman twenty-two years younger than I am. I didn't want to. But I did, and I believe this love, and the fact that Micki feels the same, is a blessing, one I don't deserve. It won't always be an easy blessing—I can think of a dozen reasons why it's a dumb idea to say what I'm about to say. But the one good reason I can think of trumps them all."

To Micki's shock, Charles went down on one knee in front of her. "Micki, I love you—I'm asking you to marry me and make me happier than I ever dreamed I could be again. And I promise to do my darnedest to make you happy, too."

A ragged cheer broke out, but it stopped abruptly when Micki burst into tears.

Murmurs of consternation swirled through the crowd.

Charles clasped Micki's hand. "Micki, sweetheart? Tell me what's wrong."

"Nothing's wrong," she sobbed. "I love you. I want to marry you. Right now. Or next week. As soon as we can."

The emotional barometer in the room swung the other way to cheers and clapping as she bent to kiss Charles on the lips.

It was their sweetest kiss yet, and all the sweeter because there would be so many more.

When she drew back, Charles said ruefully, "I hate to say this, sweetheart, but you might have to help me up."

"Always," she said, half laughing and half crying as she pulled him to his feet. "We'll help each other always."

KYLE SHOULD BE ECSTATIC. He had one more day's work to do on the new house. He'd told his father the truth about Daisy, and they were going to be okay. And now he sat in his office with three members of the development committee who'd requested this appointment so they could assure him of their full support for his plan for the town. Though each of them had only one vote in the mayoral election, they had significant influence in the community. With their support, he might just be able to swing the numbers in his favor.

But.

The house might be nearly done, yet somewhere along the way, he'd confused house and home. To make his house a home he needed Daisy…but not just Daisy.

He'd put things right with his dad, his family…but had left things horribly wrong with Jane.

He'd hopefully secured the right future for Pinyon Ridge… but he no longer had any certainty that was *his* future.

The words of the three councilors flowed over him. Vision…prosperity…heritage…sustainable…and all he could think was *I love her. I love Jane Slater.*

How could he not have realized it sooner? *I'm an idiot, that's how.* Thank God, though, he'd realized in time to stop her from leaving.

Now, he needed to get out of here so he could tell her. So he could make her believe it. She had every reason to have zero faith in him, after the way he'd messed up. He groaned.

"Excuse me?" Councilor Penny Robbins said.

"Sorry," he said. "Penny, Carl, Mac, I'm thrilled to hear what you have to say. This is going to make all the difference to our town. But right now, I have an emergency." He was already halfway out of his chair. "Could you excuse me?" he said over his shoulder as he almost ran out the door.

He wasn't dumb enough to think he could do this on his own. So he drove to Pinyon Ridge Elementary, ran straight to Daisy's classroom and told a grumpy Mrs. Mason he was taking his daughter with him.

"Family emergency," he assured her. On the way out to the car, he told Daisy what they were going to do. It made her day.

He just hoped it would make Jane's day, too.

## CHAPTER TWENTY-TWO

JANE HAD SENT Charles and Micki upstairs for some reconciliation and maybe a spot of wedding planning. She'd promised to restore order to the Eating Post, now that the last of the stragglers had left.

She was putting away the final batch of cups when Kyle burst through the door.

"Jane!" He sounded slightly wild as he glanced around the café.

"Kyle, I'm sorry, you're too late," she said.

His face whitened. He took a halting step toward her. "Don't say that. I know I've been an idiot…."

"He'll forgive you," she said. "So will Micki."

He frowned. "What are you talking about?"

"The marriage proposal. You missed it." She picked up a sponge and began wiping the counter.

"Whose proposal?" He sounded thoroughly confused.

"Your father's, of course." Yikes, hadn't he heard? How would he feel when he did? "Your father emailed the church prayer chain to invite everyone here for coffee. I guess you didn't see the notice?"

He shook his head. "I've been in meetings, I haven't checked emails in a couple of hours. I came here to—" He stopped. "Dad *proposed*? To Micki?"

"On bended knee." She couldn't contain her grin. "Kyle, I know you might be upset, but it was glorious. They looked so happy."

"From which I gather Micki accepted," he said.

"Of course. She's crazy about your father. Totally devoted

to him." She watched the struggle that played across his hand-some face.

At last, he said, "Fine. Whatever."

"Really?"

He laughed, and he looked warm and relaxed and irresist-ible. "Why are you so excited about my father's romance?"

"Like I said before, they're great together. And I think it's wonderful you don't mind having a stepmother only two years—" She stopped, as realization dawned on his face. "Oops. Cancel that."

"Luckily I have bigger fish to fry," he said drily. Then he added, "Don't go."

She stopped, sponge in hand, aware of the tattoo of her heart. "Excuse me?"

"I was wrong. One hundred percent, couldn't have been more wrong if you paid me."

"Uh, about what?"

He barked a short laugh. "Pretty much everything. Trust, loyalty, family—the things that matter to me and how they really work." He raked a hand through his hair. "Damn, I've been an idiot. When I think of that stupid list I gave you of what I liked about you…"

Warmth spread through Jane, starting in her heart, seep-ing through her blood. "You *are* a bit of an idiot."

"Don't get me wrong, I still love your legs and your pj's," he said. "But I want to give you a new list. Starting with, I love that you are loyal. I accused you of lying to me, when you didn't owe me anything. You were being loyal to Lissa and to Micki. You're strong. You've overcome so much, and not let it get you down. You're smart and so talented in your work."

Now her cheeks were hot. "Okay," she said. "Thank you."

"You're kind and brave, willing to have faith in people who don't deserve it. People like me, I hope."

"Uh," she said.

"You have integrity," he said. "You don't give up. When you know something's right you'll fight to make it happen."

Her palms were damp. "Kyle." She tried to keep her voice from trembling. "I should point out that I'm also a wimp. Some of my loyalty to Lissa was because I was afraid of losing her friendship. And—" she took a deep breath "—I'm afraid right now. Afraid—terrified—this might not be what it sounds like."

"If it sounds like I'm saying I love you," he said, "that's exactly what it is. And if it sounds like I'm saying this is for always, that's what it is, too."

"That…is pretty much what it sounds like," she admitted, still disbelieving.

He tugged her into his arms. "I love you, Jane. I want to marry you."

"*Marry?* Kyle, are you crazy?"

"Crazy in love." He skimmed a kiss across her lips and left her wanting so much more. "Any chance you feel the same about me?"

"Some," she said, breathless.

He grinned. "You have to say the words. So the other person doesn't have to worry about how you feel." That was what she'd advised him about Daisy.

She drew a deep breath. "I love you, Kyle."

His whoop of triumph must surely have been heard upstairs. The next moment he was kissing her with a startling, deeply satisfying ferocity.

When they resurfaced, she was laughing. "What on earth do we do now?"

"Plan a wedding. Notify our flower girl about our plans."

Jane clapped a hand to her mouth. "What's Daisy going to think?"

"Ask her yourself." He pulled out his cell, dialed a number. "Roger, can you send Daisy over?" He strode to the door, opened it. "I had her wait in Roger Hurst's office."

It took Daisy less than a minute to arrive from the lawyer's office, her eyes bright with excitement.

"Shouldn't you be in school?" Jane asked.

"I pulled her out of class." Kyle grimaced. "You're right, Mrs. Mason is a battle-ax. Tell Jane what you told me," he prompted Daisy.

"I want you to marry Daddy," Daisy said. "We can all live together for always. Daddy says we can stay here or we can go somewhere else."

Jane swung to face him. "Kyle, you can't leave Pinyon Ridge. You're the mayor. You love this place. And your beautiful new house."

"I love all those things," he agreed. "But I love you more. If you can't stay in Pinyon Ridge, we'll make our home elsewhere, and Daisy can come visit her grandparents in the summer."

"Please?" Daisy beseeched her.

"This is blackmail," Jane said.

"Figured I'd take a leaf out of the Slater book."

"Kyle, maybe we shouldn't rush into this. I love you, but you and I are very different people…."

"Jane," he said, "you can argue all you like. But wherever we live, whatever we do, we're going to do it together as husband and wife. And daughter. And whatever kids might follow."

"More kids?" The prospect had never even been on Jane's radar. Suddenly, she wanted them. As soon as possible. She met Kyle's eyes. And saw in them that he wasn't as confident as he sounded. She wrapped her arms around his neck. "Oh, all right."

He squeezed her so hard she could hardly breathe. Daisy wrapped her little arms around them both as best she could, and they hauled her between them.

"One more thing for that list," Kyle murmured against Jane's ear. "You're a wonderful mother."

"Oh." It came out on a sob.

He stroked her hair, comforting her, cherishing her. "Daisy, honey, how about you go upstairs to Micki's place to visit with her and Grandpa."

"Okay." Daisy skipped toward the stairs. "Can I tell them you and Jane are getting married?"

"Yes," Jane said, which earned her a kiss from Kyle.

"And when you tell them," Kyle said, "make sure you call Micki Grandma. Ouch!" Jane had just smacked his head.

Then Daisy was gone, and it was just the two of them.

"Is it safe to be this happy?" Jane asked. "It doesn't feel safe."

Kyle tightened his arms around her. "It's not without risks, I have to warn you. I can be a pain."

"So can I."

"There'll be times when I say things about your family, and you'll be upset or mad."

"I'll do the same about your father," she promised.

He laughed. "Plus I might go overboard at times in my efforts to protect you and our kids."

"I'm looking forward to that."

"I should also warn you I'm desperate to make love to you—I'm going to want sex often."

She slid her hands inside his T-shirt and enjoyed his sharp intake of breath. "Looking forward to that, too."

"And did I mention this is forever? I'm going to be the best damn husband you could have. The best damn dad for our kids."

"I don't doubt it."

He grinned down at her, that full-blown smile she liked to think had started with her. Would finish with her.

"Those are the biggies," he said. "If you can live with those, we're all good."

"We're all good," she agreed. And kissed him.

# *EPILOGUE*

*Two years later*

THE GOVERNOR OF COLORADO stepped up to the Plexiglas lectern at the front of Pinyon Ridge Community Church, the largest auditorium in town.

He gave a charming speech—not too short, not too long—about the wonderful vision that had gone into the development and refining of the plan for Pinyon Ridge. About sustainability and heritage and getting the most important things right. The TV crew that had followed him out from Denver filmed the governor and his wife, the mayor and his wife, and the entire crowd.

"The best things take time," the governor concluded. "The citizens of Pinyon Ridge can be confident that this town's development will be a model for the rest of our state. Indeed, for our nation."

Naturally, that got a lot of applause. When the clapping died away, the governor said, "On behalf of the U.S.A. Living Foundation, it gives me great pleasure to present the Best Small Town in America award to Pinyon Ridge, Colorado. Mr. Mayor, would you please join me here on stage."

The crowd went wild.

The mayor started to make his way forward, but people kept stopping him to clap him on the shoulder or shake his hand.

Seated in the second row, Jane murmured to Kyle, "Don't you wish you were still mayor? All this glory could be yours."

"Nope." His arm tightened around her shoulders. "I don't have time for glory. I'm too busy keeping my wife happy."

"Very happy," she agreed. "You weren't kidding when you said you'd want lots of sex."

As he kissed her, his free hand moved to the swell of her belly. "We must be doing something right. We're churning these things out pretty fast."

The baby, due in eight weeks' time, kicked against his hand. "Definitely a girl," he said.

"That's what you said last time." Their son, Matthew Charles Everson, age sixteen months, was spending the evening with his nana, Barb. Hal, his poppa, was doing much better these days, walking with the aid of a stick, and mostly able to be understood. One person who always understood him was Daisy, who'd been invited to tonight's ceremony but had opted out since she didn't like to let her little brother out of her sight. Jane figured those minding skills would come in handy when they were busy with the new baby.

Kyle's hand traveled higher. His thumb caressed the underside of her right breast through the silk of her dress.

"Mmm." Jane closed her eyes in a moment of pleasure.

"When do you think we can go home?" he asked.

"Not until after the mayor's speech."

He groaned. "You know how longwinded that guy is."

"We can sleep in tomorrow," she promised. "It's Micki's day at the Eating Post."

Jane had joined Micki as a partner in the café a year ago when she'd decided that, yes, Pinyon Ridge felt like home. She still did some consulting under the First Impressions brand, but mostly she let Amy run the business in Denver. The café connected her to the community the way nothing else could, and she loved it.

Kyle was back running his own landscape architecture practice and doing very nicely. Deciding to pull out of the election two years ago was the smartest thing he'd ever done, he often said. Even if he could have overcome the prejudice against him marrying a Slater, he hadn't wanted Jane subjected to public disapproval from even a few fools. As it turned out, not only had it been easier to lobby for his development plan without the other responsibilities of mayor to contend with, but he also had more time for Jane, for Daisy, for Matthew. And soon for Junior.

At last, the mayor reached the stage.

"Ladies and gentlemen," the governor said, "please welcome your mayor, Charles Everson, and his lovely wife, Micki."

The applause grew. There was even some foot-stomping.

"Good grief, he'll think he's a rock star," Kyle said.

"I'm not sure whether it was becoming mayor or marrying Micki that gave him a new lease on life," Jane said.

"Both," Kyle said.

She nodded. "I love that he's enjoying it to the fullest. They both are."

Charles had stepped up in the ballot when Kyle dropped out of the race, and he hadn't looked back since. This was what he did best, serving his town. Second best, actually, to being Micki's husband. He was passionate about that. Jane didn't think she'd ever seen a happier couple, other than her and Kyle.

As Charles started to speak, a piercing wolf whistle came from the seat directly behind Jane. Kyle groaned; Jane snickered. Cat had arrived back in town two days ago. She'd been a regular visitor over the past couple of years as she straightened out her life. Now, she was back for good. Well, she said she was back for a year to work as a project manager for Kyle. But Jane had seen the way Gabe looked at her sister, red-haired again, as she'd been when they were teenagers. Jane suspected that if Gabe had anything to say about it, Cat would be here a very long time.

Jane listened to Charles's speech with half an ear as she silently gave thanks for her large and growing family.

Then there was more applause as Charles stepped off the stage. Before he'd reached his seat, Kyle was on his feet, tugging Jane's hand.

"We can't leave now," she protested.

"You said after the mayor's speech," he reminded her. "Excuse me," he said to the lady on the other side of Jane, "we need to leave. My wife…" His hand indicated her bump.

People immediately made way for them, assuming a childbirth emergency.

Jane was laughing by the time they made it to the door nearest their seat in the hexagonal auditorium, then out into the lobby. "Ex-Mayor Everson, your behavior is disgraceful."

He hauled her into his arms, covered her mouth in a hungry kiss that had her pressing closer to him, then closer again.

"Stick with me, Mrs. Everson," he murmured, "and I'll show you what disgraceful is."

Now there was an offer Jane couldn't refuse.

\* \* \* \* \*

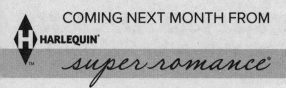